KING'S FAREWELL

Christine Marion Fraser began her life in the tenements of the Govan district of Glasgow just after the war. At the age of ten she contracted a rare muscular disease, and has been in a wheelchair ever since. She now lives with her husband in Argyllshire.

A keen reader and storyteller, Christine started writing at the age of five and got the idea for her first novel, *Rhanna*, while on holiday in the Hebrides. *Rhanna* has since been followed by six more bestselling novels about the little Hebridean island.

King's Farewell is the fifth volume in the enchanting *King's* series, which follows the fortunes of the Grant family and is set in rural Aberdeenshire and in Glasgow.

Christine Marion Fraser has also published three volumes of autobiography, *Blue Above the Chimneys*, *Roses Round the Door* and *Green Are My Mountains*.

The *King's* Series:

King's Croft
King's Acre
King's Exile
King's Close
King's Farewell

CHRISTINE MARION FRASER

King's Farewell

This edition published by Grafton Books, 1999

Grafton Books is an Imprint of
HarperCollins*Publishers*
77–85 Fulham Palace Road,
Hammersmith, London W6 8JB

First published as Paperback Original 1994
1 3 5 7 9 8 6 4 2

First published in Great Britain by
HarperCollins*Publishers* 1993

Copyright © Christine Marion Fraser 1993

The author asserts the moral right to
be identified as the author of this work

ISBN 0-26-167350-5

Set in Linotron Sabon by
Rowland Phototypesetting Ltd
Bury St Edmunds, Suffolk

Printed in Great Britain by
Caledonian International Book Manufacturing Ltd, Glasgow

For Frank Gallagher,
Friend, guru, kindred spirit, fellow Arian.
Music, stories, laughter, we have known them all.

PART ONE

Winter 1930

Chapter One

It was strange having Murn back in Scotland again. Quietly, Evelyn studied the sister who had left the family home all those years ago. How long was it? Ten years? Or was it nearer fifteen? Time had passed so quickly, so much had happened since the King's Croft days.

Evelyn drew in her breath, her green eyes softened. Poor, discontented Murn, never happy, never quite finding what she was seeking. She must be over forty now but there was no character in her round face. She still had the small button nose and the lovely grey eyes of her girlhood but the Australian sun had effectively robbed her of her fresh, rosy complexion. Her skin was dry and prematurely lined though she had retained that sweet sadness of expression that had always made her seem younger than her years.

'Help yourself to more cake, Evie.' Murn's own fingers fluttered over the plate of rich Dundee cake and she helped herself to a large slice.

Pudgy, thought Evelyn, decidedly pudgy. All that good Australian living had wreaked havoc with Murn's once slender figure, her well-corsetted body was matronly in the extreme, even her hands were plump, the rings on her fingers had almost disappeared into rolls of fat.

Evelyn nibbled her cake, Murn finished hers in no time and with a little shiver she got up to hold her hands to the fire that was blazing up the chimney.

'It's so cold,' she complained, 'I'd forgotten how raw and damp Scotland can be.'

There was no trace of the north-east dialect in her voice. It was well modulated and each word was pronounced carefully, as if she was afraid of making a slip. Even so she couldn't hide the faint trace of an Australian accent which became more pronounced when she was annoyed or excited.

Evelyn laughed and eyed her sister's expensive silk blouse. 'It's back to woolly vests and porridge now, Murn. Surely you haven't forgotten the sort of clothes you used to wear? I mind fine how you happed yourself in two layers of warm underwear one freezing winter at King's Croft.'

Murn was not amused at the recollection. She glowered at her young sister.

'You know, Evie, I see a great change in you, you've become very like Mary who always made capital out of the misfortunes of others.'

'No one could call you unfortunate,' Evelyn pointed out. 'You married a man wi' plenty o' money. He might be a widower wi' a ready-made family but he's been canny wi' his siller and gives you anything you want – it must be lovely to have that kind of security,' she added, unable to keep a wistful note from her voice.

Her heart twisted. How wonderful to be so financially secure, never to have to worry about where the next meal was coming from, never to lie in bed at night fretting over the problem of raising a family of four children without the support of a husband.

Oh, how she missed her darling Davie! Since his death she had been very low in spirits, sometimes she wanted just to curl up like a small child and allow someone to take care of her for a change . . . but what man would want to take on the responsibility of feeding and clothing someone else's children . . . ?

At Evelyn's words, Murn couldn't hide a small smile of triumph. She had made quite a catch when she had married Tom Simpson just six months ago. He was a widower whose wife had died some years before, leaving him to bring up the two daughters she had had by a previous marriage.

Tom was extremely fond of his stepdaughters and their

welfare was of great importance to him. He had stressed this to Murn before marrying her and had voiced the hope that she would be a good mother to them. At that time she had been only too anxious to promise anything to please him but had soon discovered that she just wasn't suited to motherhood. If the girls had been her own flesh and blood things might have been different, but somehow she just couldn't take to Tom's stepdaughters and she was only too well aware that the feeling was mutual.

Even so, that didn't stop her from enjoying her new-found status as Mrs Simpson. She liked the financial security it had brought her and experienced a great sense of satisfaction at being able to look down her nose at those people who had been so surprised when she had cast aside her spinsterhood in favour of the marriage bed ... She paused in her musings and shuddered ... That was the one terrible drawback of an otherwise good arrangement. The pawings, the strivings, the gruntings and the groanings. How dreadful men were when their animal instincts were aroused. But he was only thirty-four, several years younger than herself. She had to keep him satisfied somehow even though she loathed his sweating body on top of hers. And he was big, in every way *big*. His violation of her body was practically rape and made her feel as if she was being torn apart ...

A small, raw thrill shot through the pudgy loins of Mrs Tom Simpson. Trying her best to ignore it, she squeezed her fat thighs together and concentrated hard on her dislike of certain aspects of marriage. Poor Tom. Thank heaven he was a merchant seaman and spent the greater part of his time away from home ... though God alone knew what he got up to when the ship was in port ... She straightened; what did it matter? He was a good saver. He gave her more than enough to keep her comfortable and that was all that really counted in the end.

She had humoured this whim of his regarding a Scottish education for his two young stepdaughters, and was glad they were being packed off to boarding school after Christmas. Once they were settled she and Tom could return to Australia and resume their pleasant, easy life in the sun.

'I told Tom it would be a mistake coming back here but he wouldn't listen. He had a terrible yearning to see his father again and to introduce the girls to his home,' she continued, eyeing Evelyn critically.

God! What a beauty the girl was! She had expected a careworn drudge, a being without hope due to years of living in a state of abject poverty; someone old and done from birthing and rearing bairns, not to mention struggling to bring them up on her own since the death of her husband a year ago.

Instead here was a young woman with a fighting spark in her eyes and a tumble of glorious red hair about her neat, proud head. Ay, she was Maggie Grant's daughter all right. That sort never went under, no matter how many times they came near to drowning . . .

Murn gave herself a mental shake and frowned. She hoped that this very poor family of hers wouldn't look upon her as some sort of benevolent angel who had come to lift them out of the mire. She and Tom might be comfortably off but they were by no means rich and needed every penny of their money to survive – especially as his first wife had spent money like water while she was alive and those two stepdaughters of his would twist him round their fingers at every turn . . .

'He insists on the girls furthering their education in Scotland – as if it will make any difference to them, just a waste of good money in my opinion. Bessie has the brains of a flea and all Barbara wants is to be admired by boys – and her only just turned fourteen too.'

'Why don't you take them in hand yourself?' Evelyn simply couldn't help saying. 'You were a good enough teacher in your day and think o' all the money you would save.'

While she was speaking she was wondering what her

eldest sister, Nellie, would have to say about Murn when the two of them eventually met up . . . *if* that day ever came. After all, Nellie's marriage to Kenneth Mor was the reason Murn had left home in the first place. She had been besotted by him since girlhood and when he had chosen Nellie as his second wife Murn had almost gone mad with jealousy and grief . . . Even so . . . Evelyn smiled a little. Blood was thicker than water, surely Murn had gotten over her youthful fantasies and Nellie would be Nellie no matter what. With her nippy tongue and scathing opinions on life it would be very interesting indeed to hear what she had to say about Murn's meanness.

'Evelyn, how could you suggest such a thing!' Murn was horrified. 'I was an infant teacher in case you've forgotten and Tom's girls were born old! Little Miss Barbara could teach me a thing or two and as for Bessie, no teaching on earth could knock sense into that empty head of hers. Also . . .' she drew herself up and thrust out her silk-clad bosom, 'Tom would never hear of such a thing. My job now is to look after him and his home – although . . .'

At this juncture she gazed around her in some dismay . . . 'I did think he could have found somewhere nicer than this dismal flat. Still . . .' she braced her shoulders and smiled bravely. 'It won't be for long. Once Tom has gotten his father out of his system and the girls are settled into boarding school we will be free to go back home to Australia. I consider it home now, Evie, I could never live in Scotland again, the weather is so cheerless and the living conditions are so dreadfully inadequate.'

Evelyn would gladly have brained her sister there and then. Tom had returned from sea only a few days ago and in that short space of time he had managed to rent this lovely flat for his wife and daughters. Situated near the Park, in a select area of Govan, it was spacious and bright with beautiful cornices round the ceilings. An efficient little maid saw to it that the rooms were kept well fired and that meals were never late on the table.

Evelyn felt herself seething with anger and she was about to tell Murn just what she thought of her when the door opened to admit Tom and his daughters.

Evelyn had only met him once but she was aware of the immediate attraction that had sprung between them when he had taken her hand and had held onto it just a bit longer than necessary. He was a well-built man with keen blue eyes and a strong jawline which was made doubly attractive by the deep cleft in his firm chin. His eyes had looked straight into hers, his hands had been warm and somehow sensual. She had coloured but couldn't bring herself to relinquish his stroking, suggestive fingers.

Later, when they were alone for a moment, he had unhesitatingly taken her into his arms to crush her mouth to his in a kiss of unbridled passion.

And she had allowed him to do it! Davie had been dead for over a year now. She had never looked at another man but sometimes, in the loneliness of night, she ached to have a man hold her close and make her feel like a desirable woman instead of just the mother figure that the children saw every day and took for granted.

'You're beautiful,' he had told her when finally he had let her go. 'A woman of passion and warmth. Not like your cold-arsed sister who's only concession to sex is to remove her corsets in bed.'

For some reason Evelyn hadn't been dismayed by his crudeness. His eyes had twinkled all the time he had been speaking and when he had reached out to expertly fondle her taut nipples she had been too stunned by the ferocity of her feelings to ever want him to stop.

Now the glance he threw at her across the room intimately embraced her senses. He was reminding her of the secret they shared. She flushed and felt the heat of longing coursing through her body.

Barbara appeared to understand the situation and glanced curiously first at her stepfather then at Evelyn. The girl showed every indication of growing into a beauty. Her

14

breasts were already round and ripe, her deep set eyes were a stunning blue, her long, golden hair reached to her waist, her large, sensual mouth showed pearly teeth and she had an oddly disturbing habit of flicking her tongue between her lips whilst tilting her head back to survey the world through narrowed eyes.

Instinctively Evelyn didn't like or trust her and much preferred timid little Bessie whose plainness was countered by a curtain of silken brown hair that flowed around her in all its shining glory.

The opening of the door had caused a draught to sneak in. Murn went immediately back to the fire to lean over it as if she could devour it.

A mocking smile quirked one corner of Barbara's mouth. She didn't like her new stepmother one bit and took few pains to hide the fact.

'Mother, dear,' she drawled silkily, 'don't forget you're taking Bessie and me to buy new shoes this afternoon. The store closes in an hour so you'd better get your skates on.'

'Bother!' Murn turned round to glare at Barbara, 'I'd forgotten all about it, and it's so cold outside too. And please, Barbara, I've told you before, when you're speaking to me do not use such common slang. My skates on indeed! It's as well you're going away to school, it's high time some of the nonsense was knocked out of you.'

She swung her attention round to unfortunate little Bessie. 'Just look at the girl!' cried Murn, 'You've simply got no pride in your appearance at all – unlike your sister who's far too vain for her own good. Go and wash, clean your teeth, brush your hair. I shouldn't have to tell all this to a big girl like you, the repetition gets so boring.'

Bessie scampered away to the bathroom and Murn emitted a heavy sigh. 'Really, Tom, I wish you would talk to the girl, she's a disgrace to the family. I'm not looking forward at all to taking them to the shoe shop. They argue with one another all the time and it really is so cold outside.'

Tom's jaw tightened. 'A woman's touch, Murn, you said yourself that was what they needed.'

'That was *before* I married you, Tom. I couldn't know then what a handful they'd be. Oh dear, I really do so hate going shopping with them.' She turned hopefully to Evelyn. 'I don't suppose you would . . . ?'

'Sorry, Murn,' Evelyn's tone was firm, 'I told Mam I would be back by teatime – and it's almost five now.'

Murn flounced away to get ready, Evelyn pulled on her gloves, watched by Barbara who appeared to be fascinated by everything her step-auntie did.

'I like the way you do your hair,' the girl's blue eyes fixed themselves on Evelyn's shining mop. 'I wonder if you could put mine up like that.'

'Och, Babs, you're a bit young for that yet. Wait a year or two before you do all these grown up things. One day you'll wish you could go back to childhood and all it meant.'

'It means nothing to me.' The girl's voice was hard, there was a strangeness in her eyes. 'I can't wait to grow up, then I won't have to do anything silly old Murn asks me to do.'

Evelyn laughed. 'Oh, Murn's not as bad as all that, surely. I haven't seen her for years and naturally she's changed a bit . . .'

'Changed a bit!' hooted Barbara derisively, 'She's a fat old snob who eats and talks too much and doesn't in the least deserve someone as good as my stepfather. Too bad he didn't meet you first. I've seen the way he looks at you, as if there's a fire gnawing at his belly – *and* I've seen you looking at him in the same way . . .'

Murn appeared, fussing with her buttons, tugging at the scowling Bessie's hair ribbon. 'Come along, Barbara, don't keep us all waiting!'

Barbara unwillingly obeyed the command, the door shut and Evelyn stood rooted to the spot, her cheeks burning. Tom came through from the bedroom and went to pour two measures of whisky, handing one to Evelyn with an apologetic smile.

'Babs been getting at you? Don't mind her too much, she's at that awkward age for a girl.'

He was standing very close to Evelyn. Her face burned hotter than ever and she threw her drink back in one gulp just as the maid opened the door to announce that she was finished for the night and please could she go.

'Ay, run along, Sarah, you've done a grand job here today.'

He hadn't lost his Scottish accent. Evelyn liked the softness of his voice but she was in no state then fully to appreciate it. She had gulped down the whisky too quickly, her throat was on fire and try as she would she couldn't stop herself choking and spluttering.

'Here, let me.' Tom was full of charm and concern, his hand was on her back, rubbing it while he made soothing noises in her ear. He was much too close for comfort, his keen eyes very blue in his suntanned face. He looked every inch the seaman with a tattoo emblazoned on the bronzed skin of his right arm. In her heightened state of awareness she imagined that he smelt of fresh wind and tangy sea and it really seemed as if she could hear the waves breaking on the shore . . . But it wasn't the waves. It was her own heart pounding in her ears because Tom Simpson had taken her in his arms to nuzzle her mouth and then her neck. Shivers of delight raced through her body. He was back to her mouth again and this time he pushed apart her lips to kiss her fiercely while his hand pressing into the small of her back made very certain that she wasn't going to get away.

But she didn't want to escape. It had been so long since a man had held her like this she was beyond the boundaries of reason and never wanted him to stop.

She forgot that this was her sister's husband, she forgot Davie, she forgot everything and everybody, so immersed was she in her own desires and longings. And Tom wasn't just any man. She had been attracted to him from the start, he was magnetic and sensual, passionate, powerful, and totally, overwhelmingly masculine.

His hands were inside her coat, his fingers confidently massaging the swollen tips of her nipples. She gave a little groan and made no protest when he swept her into his arms and carried her straight into the bedroom to throw her on the bed. In minutes he was naked beside her, helping her to tear off her clothes, cursing with impatience at buttons and other fastenings. She had borne five children but even so her figure was superb. He gasped with admiration when the last piece of clothing was dispensed with and her firm, full breasts sprang out from the restraining cloth.

Pressing his hard body against the softness of hers he did things to her that made her burn and ache with longing. His body was covered in golden hairs that were so thick on his broad chest they had formed tiny curls below his nipples. She shivered in delight and ran her hands over every inch of him, loving his male hardness, excited by the bigness of his arousal.

'Evie.' He could wait no longer, his knees pushed her legs apart, his mouth travelled over her breasts to her belly and lower, ever lower.

'Oh, Evie,' he groaned, 'You're a real woman. That sister of yours would never let me do this. It takes me all my time to get her to open her legs.'

He should never have mentioned his wife because his words brought Evelyn swiftly and suddenly to her senses and she stiffened beneath him.

This man wasn't hers. He belonged to her sister though God alone knew how a restrained being like Murn managed to cope with such a crudely spoken, lustful creature. She knew his rough tongue owed itself to the heat of the moment and she wouldn't hold that against him since he was every inch the gentleman in the normal way of things. But he *was* Murn's man, and she was Davie Grainger's widow of just a year – also – there was Gillan. It seemed odd that, to consider a man she had only seen twice since leaving Rothiedrum thirteen years ago. But he had been and always would be someone she couldn't forget. She and he had spent so many of their young years together. He had been the youthful heir to the Rothiedrum estate, she had been a mere crofter's daughter, but their different social standings hadn't stood in the way of the warm and wonderful friendship that had sprung up between them. Later she had discovered that they were cousins and their bonds had become stronger than ever. He had always been in love with her but her heart had belonged to Davie, though deep down inside, she knew that part of it was reserved for Gillan for all time.

Tom was awash with excitement and was so immersed in extracting as much pleasure as possible from Evelyn's body he didn't notice her lack of response nor did he hear the sudden, imperative knocking at the front door.

But Evelyn most certainly did and rising up in panic she began throwing on her clothes as speedily as she could.

'Get dressed,' she ordered him as he tried to pull her back into bed, 'Someone's at the door. It might easily be Murn.'

It *was* Murn, highly indignant because she'd been kept waiting for so long.

'Where on earth is that Sarah?' she demanded, 'I forgot to take my key. That girl will have to go. All she ever wants is to get home to fritter her time away in some dark iniquitous den or other. Man mad of course . . .' She broke off to peer suspiciously at her sister.

'I thought you said you were going home? At least half an hour ago.'

'Oh, Tom and I got talking.' Evelyn, having had no time to do her hair or fasten some of her buttons, was very conscious of her untidy state. Her face flared at Murn's words and in an effort to gain some time she enquired after the girls.

'Oh, Barbara wanted to go to the pictures. I took them both to the Lyceum, paid for the seats, and left them to it. They're quite capable of looking after themselves and I wasn't going to sit in some flea-ridden cinema watching some boring film I've seen before.'

Tom had come scuttling out of the bedroom to go straight over to the drinks table where he poured himself a stiff whisky which he downed in one gulp.

Murn glanced at him briefly before bringing her attention quickly back to Evelyn. 'You know, Evie,' she said slowly, 'I think you've been alone for too long. You're an attractive woman but the only people you ever see are your own children and our mother and father.'

'Ach, Murn!' Evelyn was regaining some of her equilibrium, 'I have lots o' people in my life, the neighbours are a friendly lot, Grace isn't so far away, looking after Fanny Jean Gillespie takes up a lot of my time . . .'

'You need a man, Evie.' Murn came bluntly to the point, her eyes narrowed, she glanced again at Tom. He was very red about the ears and was pretending to search for a book in the bureau. 'It's a year now since Davie died,' Murn went on firmly, 'you're young still, the children need a father and you could be doing with a good wage coming into the house.'

'I think that's my business,' Evelyn said through tight lips. How *dare* frumpy Murn with her old-maidish ways advise anyone to take on another husband. Evelyn shrugged herself into her coat and pulled on her gloves for the second time that afternoon. 'I'm very late, Mam will be wondering what's happened to me.'

'Yes,' Murn stared at her young sister, 'she isn't the only one, is she, Evie? I too would like to know what happened while I was out. Normally you're very neat and particular about your appearance but just look at you now. Your hair hanging about your face! Your blouse undone.'

Evelyn turned away to hide her crimson face. At the door she called goodbye to Tom and was about to leave when Murn stayed her with an imperious command.

'Wait, Evie, I've been thinking a lot about you since I came home. I know how tight money is and I was wondering if you would care to come and do some cleaning for me. Sarah is capable up to a point but is quite useless when it comes to real efficiency. I know that Miss Gillespie lives quite near here so you would be killing two birds with one stone if you were to pop along here after you had seen to her. What do you think, dear?'

Evelyn was afraid to say what she thought for fear she would never stop. She also longed to take Murn by her thoughtless, fat shoulders and shake the life out of her. How dare this overfed sister of hers treat her as if she was no more than a serf! Mary had been bad enough with her airs and graces and self indulgences but Mary had eventually learned a very sharp lesson and the sooner Murn followed suit the better.

Evelyn's nostrils flared only ever so slightly when she gave Murn her answer. Eyeing the older woman's rotund figure she said with calculated calm, 'Murn, you really ought to lose some weight. Exercise, that's what you need, so why don't you do your own cleaning and get rid of the fat along wi' the dust. Two birds wi' one stone, dear Murn. Save money *and* slim down, losing and gaining pounds, if you see what I mean.'

The door closed on her, Murn turned an aghast face to her husband. '*That's* gratitude for you! And here was me, only trying to be helpful.'

'You asked for it,' he said unsympathetically. 'What a bloody cheek! Treating your own sister as if she was a servant.'

'I wasn't! I only wanted to help. She's always been too much of a madam for her own good.' She threw him a sidelong glance. 'Evie always loved men, right from the time she was just a child at King's Croft. First it was Johnny

Burns, then when he died in some terrible drowning accident, she turned to Gillan Forbes of Rothiedrum House though I do believe she kept him on a string all the time she was carrying on with Johnny. When Gillan had to go away she met a young soldier, Davie Grainger. That was quite an affair, red hot from all accounts. She nearly broke my mother's heart with her flirting and fleering and staying out till all hours.

'Inevitably she conceived out of wedlock and ended up with an illegitimate child – Alex – her eldest boy. Oh, Davie came back from war and they got married in the end but now Davie's dead and I can tell she's needing a man again. Evie could never do without a man for long. I have a feeling she thinks that Gillan Forbes will come back into her life and rescue her from her drudgery. Meanwhile she'll make do with what she can get, possibly another woman's husband, possibly even her very own sister's husband if need be.'

'Oh, for heaven's sake, Murn!' Tom said irritably, 'Nothing happened! No one, far less Evie, is going to take me away from you if that's what's bothering you.'

But Murn wasn't listening, her eyes were suddenly shining in her plump face.

'Your father, Tom, the very man.'

'The very man for what?'

'For Evie. Oh, I admit I've only met him twice but he seems strong and reliable *and* he has a steady job which is not to be sneezed at in these uncertain times.'

Tom's handsome face was suddenly stern. 'Don't be a fool, Murn. Dad is far too old to even consider marrying again! And you don't know him, he's more than strong – he's tough – he would chew Evie up and spit her out in little pieces. He's been married before, his wife – my mother – died in an asylum after bearing him *six* children. Oh, it wasn't entirely his fault, she was a weak woman who never learned how to stand up to him. In the end she simply went under. I'm fond of the old man and I'm aware that he looks upon me as his favourite son. But I know his weaknesses, he has a liking for the bottle and he also loves women. He was quite a lad in his day and could still do a lot of damage.'

'Oh, I knew he was a widower of course,' said Murn sweetly, 'That kind of state seems to run in your particular family. Nevertheless, despite what you say I think he's a good, solid, dependable man and fifty-five isn't really old especially when he looks at least ten years younger. It would do no harm for Evie to meet him.'

A muscle moved in Tom Simpson's firm jaw. 'If you think you're going to get her out of your hair by foisting her onto my father then you've another think coming. She's proud is that one, with a strong mind of her own – full of spirit and fire . . . '

By God! She was fiery all right. He remembered the sweetness of her mouth, the hard, burning tips of her nipples . . . heat pulsed in the pit of his stomach . . . his penis stiffened in his trousers. He looked at his wife.

A poor substitute for Evie but female flesh just the same, and the way he was feeling he could poke a lemon and come back later for a second helping . . .

Without ado he reached out to pull her onto his knee and clamped his hand on one of her large breasts. She gave a little shriek, he could feel the stiffening of her fat thighs, closing off that dark and difficult passageway between her legs. 'The girls,' she gasped, 'they'll be home any minute.'

His eyes gleamed, 'All the more exciting, eh? Come on, Murn, unfurl your drawers just this once! Christ woman, you don't know what you're missing! I could give you a marvellous time if you'd let me.'

So saying he jumped to his feet, took her hand and rushed her into the bedroom where he threw her roughly onto the bed. For the second time that day he removed his clothing in a frenzy of lust while Murn lay rigid on the bed, hardly moving a muscle, hardly daring to breathe.

Tom's weight bore down upon her, he began tearing at

her clothes, cursing at the layers he had to remove before he got down to the essentials. He was writhing and sweating and moving against her . . . dazedly she stared at his contorted face . . . and suddenly he wasn't Tom Simpson anymore, he was a brown-skinned, black-eyed gypsy lad of no more than twenty and she was lying in his tent, drinking raw whisky while she allowed him to kiss and bite her body before he penetrated it with brutish passion.

He was like an animal, tearing into her, gyrating above her like some hellish phantom of the darkest night . . . And all she wanted was Kenneth Mor . . . all she had ever wanted was that big beautiful Highlander with his golden haired body, his fine physique and his wonderful loyalties to those that he loved . . . But his love hadn't extended to her. In his lonely days of grief for his beloved Jeannie he had turned to Nellie and, in the end, it was she he had wed. Nellie who had always hated men, Nellie with her vinegary tongue and spinsterish ways. A cold eyed bitch like that had won a warm, marvellous man like Kenneth.

She was wet and sore and sick, she came back to earth with a start. Tom was inside her, tight and hard and huge, he was groaning and moaning and blowing into her ear.

'Let yourself go, girl,' he panted as one big hand fondled and pulled at her breasts while the other was busy between her legs. Something primitive stirred in her belly, a sharp imperative pulsing that beat into her womb. She gave a small gasp and shut her eyes. She had never experienced this with him before and she had no intention of letting him see that he was arousing her. She didn't want it, it was sinful and weak to feel like this at her age . . . She had never wanted it with any man that wasn't Kenneth Mor – not even with the man who was her husband . . .

But she was powerless to fight Tom's hand between her legs, unable to resist the thrilling sensation of his penis throbbing away inside her. He stiffened and gave a cry, he had reached his peak and was making animal-like grunts that were unbearably exciting. A feeling of weakness invaded her loins, followed by an exquisite flooding of burning heat. She stuffed her hand against her mouth to stop herself from crying out. His body slackened and he rolled away from her.

'You bitch,' he gasped, 'I've tried everything I know to rouse you but there you lie, like a hibernating frog with ice in your veins, a cold-arsed fish who doesn't know how to respond to anything or anybody that's warm and alive and human. But one day, Murn, one day you'll beg me for it and you'll keep coming back for more. There's a fire smouldering somewhere in all that fat and if I poke hard enough and often enough I'll get it to burst into flames.'

Murn turned away from him. She didn't want him to see that he had already found the fire. Her instincts told her that he was relishing the challenge of bringing out the woman in her. It was better like this, to keep him hungry and searching for that ultimate triumph.

He continued his tirade. How crudely he spoke; the years at sea were responsible for that yet, dreadful creature that she was, she actually enjoyed his boorishness in the bedroom.

She wondered suddenly when she would see Nellie again – no – she didn't care if she never saw that sharp-tongued shrew of a sister. It was Kenneth Mor that she longed to see. He would have changed – after all these years everybody had changed. She herself had grown stouter though he probably still thought of her as the slender, innocent young girl who had worn her heart on her sleeve for him.

That much hadn't changed but he would like her better now, men like him enjoyed big breasts and a rounded body. What he had ever seen in that stringy Nellie was beyond her . . .

Murn sighed. She had always loved Kenneth and always would – even so – she had to be practical. She'd had to be hard-headed during all these years of survival in Australia. Nowadays being practical meant being the sort of wife that Tom liked to come home to. In the end those foreign tarts didn't matter. He was married to her, she had him where she wanted him. An unwilling woman was something new to him, he would most certainly enjoy the novelty of trying to poke her into responsiveness.

It was women like Evie who had to be watched, she was too near home for comfort and the sooner she was sorted out the better.

Oh yes, it was time Evie had a man of her own and John Simpson would keep her in her place all right . . .

Meantime Tom had to be kept amused, the girls wouldn't be home for a while yet . . . and he was after all a very attractive man, those blue eyes, that cleft in his chin, those golden hairs all over his body – that huge member of his – now lying flaccid between his fine, straight legs. Quite a man . . . She allowed one large, creamy breast to spill out of her blouse. 'Tom . . .' she propped herself up on one elbow and leaned over him. 'Tom, I'm sorry I wasn't able to respond that time. You'll have to be patient with me, I've been alone so long I've forgotten what it's like to be loved. Would you like to try again?'

Her breast hung tantalisingly above his face; he grabbed it and stuffed the tip into his mouth, she looked down at his genitals and was gratified to see the swiftness of his arousal.

'By all means, Murn,' he said with a politeness that was soon forgotten in the strivings and strainings of the next half hour.

Chapter Two

John Simpson was a fine figure of a man. Almost against her will Evelyn had to admit that fact to herself. He was tall and straight with a good firm jawline and striking blue eyes. She saw a good deal of Tom in him and perhaps because of that her heart warmed to John despite her annoyance when Murn had arrived with him unexpectedly.

Murn had also brought Barbara and Bessie, the latter soon melting unobtrusively into the background as was her habit when faced with strangers. Not so her sister who was quick to size up everything and soon assumed an air of disdain at the sight of the shabby room with its worn furniture and other signs of poverty.

'How quaint,' she exclaimed when she saw the two double beds set into wall recesses. 'But surely you don't really *sleep* in those boxes! You would suffocate.'

Murn wriggled uncomfortably and wished she hadn't laced her stays quite so tightly. It was this chair, lumpy and hard, forcing one's stomach into unnatural contours. But it was more than tight corsets that had brought a faint blush to Murn's cheeks. Her own sentiments about poor Evelyn's living conditions had just been voiced by Barbara and even Murn for all her insensitivity couldn't stem her embarrassment at the girl's rudeness.

Murn wished Tom could have accompanied her, but he had absolutely refused to come, telling her he wouldn't assist in her subterfuge against her very own sister and that she should be ashamed of herself for trying to manipulate other people's lives for them.

But Murn was not ashamed. In spite of the lumpy seat and the stewed tea she was thoroughly enjoying herself.

27

She had seen at once that Evelyn was attracted to John and he to her. He was the epitome of good manners and consideration and had been polite to Jamie and Maggie. But feeling perhaps that they were in the way they had soon taken themselves off to The Room, taking the children with them.

Murn was mighty glad of that. Children of any sort made her feel uncomfortable and she was just the weeniest bit ashamed of her own parents. Jamie had had a good drink in him and had slurred his words while Maggie had not concealed that proud look of hers that had always made Murn's blood boil. It went back to the King's Croft days and even as a girl Murn had asked herself what right a crofter's wife had to be so high and mighty.

It had something to do with the Forbes of Rothiedrum, the high bred gentry of that airt. Evelyn had certainly mixed with them from an early age and had been great friends with young Gillan, while Maggie and Lady Marjorie had become very close and had been sorry to part with one another when the Grants had broken their ties with the lands of Rothiedrum . . .

Murn came out of her reverie and looked at the threadbare rug in front of the fire. Maggie was very far removed from these distant days yet still she remained haughty and aloof as if she felt herself to be better than anybody else. She knew that her mother would never lose her airs and graces and a small spark of grudging admiration flared in her breast only to be quenched almost instantly as Murn remembered the cool welcome home she had received from a mother who had never fully understood her and never would . . .

John Simpson's fingers lingered on Evelyn's as she handed him a glass of sherry. His eyes admired her rich red hair before travelling down to her mouth.

'You're a fine young woman, Evie,' he murmured. 'I

hope we'll get to know one another better. If you'll let me, I'll come on my own next time.'

Next time! Evelyn frowned. She was just getting used to having him here now and already he was talking about the future.

'We'll see,' was all she said and went quickly into the scullery to hide her flushed cheeks.

He had followed her; she hadn't heard a sound but knew he was there at her back, standing very close but not touching her. Something strange and frightening happened to Evelyn Grainger in those moments. Her heart pounded in her throat, beating so fast she felt it reverberating along the length of her spine. And it didn't stop there but went pounding on down till it reached her belly and invaded every aching space before branching off to her womb, her loins, throbbing between her legs with such force it felt as if flames had suddenly erupted to lick at her flesh with merciless heat.

'Please . . .' she turned . . . too suddenly; her foot caught on the worn linoleum and she would have fallen had not John Simpson's arm shot out to save her. She glimpsed his eyes; a wild beast seemed to lurk there . . . But she had no time to think about it; his arms were around her, pulling her in close to his hard, demanding, exciting body. His mouth was rough, his tongue penetrating, but in those heated moments it was what she wanted, what she had to have, and her kisses matched his for passion and desire before she tore her lips shakily away from his.

'Evie,' His voice was rough, his breath fast, 'Let me come tomorrow.'

She was afraid that they had delayed too long in the scullery and that someone might hear what was going on.

She didn't bargain for Alex arriving on the scene, his young face astounded at the sight of his mother in the arms of a total stranger.

Inwardly Evelyn groaned. Not Alex! Her eldest son, only twelve years old but so mature for his age in many ways.

He had been a great comfort to her since Davie's death, as, with great flair and initiative, he had earned valuable coppers which he handed over willingly to help in the running of the household.

And though, in his younger years, he had resented his mother for leaving him with Nellie when he was a baby, they now had a special sort of relationship that was very precious to her.

He still adored Nellie and had always wanted to live and work with her and Kenneth on their croft in Kenneray. But the early death of his father had changed his ideas; he had resigned himself to looking after his mother and now considered himself to be the man of the house.

He was, therefore, anything but happy at this unexpected turn of events and throwing John Simpson a venomous look he went smartly back to the kitchen to hurl himself into a chair and stare into the fire with brooding eyes.

Barbara Simpson looked at Alex Grainger and was fascinated by what she saw: a tall straight boy, broad shouldered and handsome, the flushed bloom of youth lying sweet and pure on his golden skinned face. His straight hair was fine and fair and curled ever so slightly at the nape of his neck.

Barbara shivered with delight, and whispered something in his ear. He got up and went readily enough with her out onto the landing. She sat down on the top step and patted the space beside her. But he chose to keep some distance between them – just enough to keep her hungry. Barbara Simpson didn't know it but she was dealing with a boy who had been sexually familiar with girls since he was eleven years old and who was, furthermore, something of an expert at keeping them dangling on a string.

She started off by asking his age and when he told her she gaped in surprise. 'I thought you were at least sixteen!'

Disappointment flattened her tones, she frowned and

stared almost disbelievingly at his well developed body. Once more she studied his face and this time she noted his eyes — the strangest she had ever seen — one green, the other brown. Fascination continued to grip her, though she was at great pains to try and hide it.

'Instead of that you're just a baby,' she taunted, 'and probably think and act like one as well.' She tilted her golden head, her eyes had narrowed to twin blue slits, and her tongue travelled slowly over her lips. 'I'm fourteen, I'm used to boys who know what they're doing with a girl. In Australia . . . '

She got no further, Alex grabbed hold of her to roughly kiss her. He probed her mouth insistently with his tongue then let her go as suddenly as he had claimed her.

Surprised as she was she was soon in control of herself again and was only too ready to further pursue the adventure. But Alex was having no more of it. With an enigmatic little smile he moved away from her and she reddened in anger.

'Just as I thought, a baby!' she taunted, 'I bet you can't do it with a girl, I bet you can't even get it to go up . . . '

A vision of his mother in the arms of John Simpson floated into Alex's mind. Anger twisted in him like a venomous snake. Reaching out he grabbed one of Barbara's full young breasts to massage it so thoroughly and viciously she gave a little scream. Then, before she had recovered from the onslaught, he unbuttoned his trousers and forced her hand inside. She was left in no doubt over the issue of his development; he was big and hard and burning. Her eyes were like huge blue lamps in her pink face, again her tongue swept moistly over her lips and her hand was soon busy inside his trousers . . .

A door in the landing opened and Mrs Conkey, alias Creeping Jesus, came out of her house wearing the apologetic air she assumed if she thought she was being a nuisance.

Alex groaned but was in sufficient control of himself to

knock Barbara's hand away, do up his buttons, and stand up to give Mrs Conkey a polite greeting before moving aside to allow her access to the stairs.

Barbara stared. What sort of boy was this Alex Grainger? Cool when he was hot, controlled in the midst of unbearable excitement, mannerly towards a neighbour when anybody else would have been irritable and snappy.

Barbara herself could gladly have killed Mrs Conkey for appearing when she did but Alex seemed to overflow with the milk of human kindness. In his younger days he had given this particular neighbour a terrible time of it with his rough and unsavoury ways. Nowadays he contented himself by occasionally rapping her letter box or shouting rude things through it. He also got a great kick out of tying her doorknob to that of Mrs Leckie in the middle flat but in general he was a likeable youngster and for some reason Mrs Conkey had lately placed a lot of trust in him which had the effect of making him strangely protective towards her.

The Conkey's had always been the butt of much unkind gossip from all quarters, mainly because of their secretive lifestyle and rather creepy habits. Albert Conkey, otherwise known as Lantern Jaws, had once been the head keeper at the local park where he had spent much of his time chasing off the cheeky urchins of the district. Now he was a chronic asthmatic who hadn't worked in years and, with his physical condition, would, most likely, never work again. With his seamed, yellow face, his jutting lower jaw and brown, mouldering teeth, he was an unbelievably ugly man. Always coughing and spitting and gasping for breath, he showed scant inclination to move very far from his own doorstep. Very little of him was seen from one week to the next, and for quite some time now he hadn't been sighted at all, with the result that speculation and exaggeration as to his welfare was, without question, the most enjoyable topic of the moment.

'She'll have killed him wi' her cooking,' was the opinion

of Mrs Alice Boyle, front close, first door on the right. 'It's always the frying pan and old grease too. The reek o' it filters down to my house and fair makes me squeamish.'

'It'll be the meths.' Isa Boag's lumpy, squashed face wore a very decided expression. 'I've seen the bottles for myself, in the midden, that's why she aye creeps down to empty her rubbish after dark.'

'And how would *you* know that?' Big Aggie had demanded. 'Unless, of course, you yourself go rakin' about in the bins at night.'

'But he has the asthma,' put in Angelina McTavish, before Isa could retaliate in her usual boisterous manner. 'He is never well and should be in hospital to be looked after.'

'Maybe he's already dead,' said Mrs Leckie thoughtfully, 'and she can't bury him because his life's no' insured. That could be what you're smelling, Alice, his grisly remains, locked away in a cupboard.'

Theresa Leckie was a thin, wiry little woman of Italian descent. As fearless as she was tough she had been known to physically eject drunks and other unsavoury characters from her chip shop situated just one street away at the corner of Camloan Road.

Everybody, including strong men and Isa Boag, who was a fearsome being in her own right, respected tiny Theresa Leckie and they were all careful, on the face of it, to agree with her opinions, even though behind her back they might say otherwise.

But not even Isa Boag could bring herself to believe that timid Mrs Conkey could have had 'the gumption' to kill her own husband and so the subject was dropped in favour of other and safer topics.

As for Mrs Conkey, she was well aware of all the gossip that went on about her behind her back and lately she had tried very hard to make herself more unobtrusive than ever.

It was, therefore, all the more surprising that she paused

halfway down the stairs to look back at Alex and say in an oddly urgent voice: 'I heard ye on the landing, Alex, that's why I came out, even though I didny want to disturb you.' The old apologetic nuance had crept back into her voice but she was sufficiently concerned about something to go on to ask him if he would mind coming with her into her house as she was 'badly needin' help to shift a heavy object.'

'Ay, I'll be glad to help, Mrs Conkey,' Alex agreed obligingly.

'I'll come with you.' Barbara made to follow Alex but Mrs Conkey was having none of that. Throwing the girl a look that could only be described as cold dislike, she said briefly, 'We can manage fine, Alex and me, you'd best go and play. A draughty stairhead landing is a place not fit for a dog, never mind a young lass.'

Thus dismissed, a furious Barbara flounced downstairs to the close, there to extract a piece of chalk from her pocket and with it to draw on the wall in large white letters: MRS CONKEY'S CONKERS. AND SO SAY ALL OF US.

At that precise moment, Mrs Boyle entered the close, her arms piled high with fish suppers. Mrs Boyle took a great pride in her close. Every week, when it was her turn to do the cleaning, she was down on her hands and knees scrubbing for all she was worth. As if that wasn't enough she decorated the edges of the close with elaborate pipeclay whorls and scrolls and was altogether a most diligent 'keeper of the close'.

So, she was not at all pleased when she beheld Barbara's handiwork, and without ado she grabbed the girl by the scruff of her collars and bundled her upstairs. In the process she dropped one of her precious fish suppers and, more incensed than ever, her grip on Barbara tightened and she fairly bulldozed the girl up to the second landing.

*

34

The first thing that struck Alex was the damp chilly atmosphere in Mrs Conkey's house.

The next thing to strike him was the heavy smell of candle grease. It clung to his clothes and lingered in his nostrils until he felt as if he could taste it on his tongue. The house itself was drab and cheerless with not even a colourful square of carpet to relieve the monotony of the worn lino.

Alex's own house was anything but sumptuous but in many ways it was comfortable: his grannie Maggie stuffed cushions with discarded bits of cloth to soften the unyielding contours of the hard wooden chairs; the beds were made bright with crocheted woollen bedspreads fashioned by both his mother and his grannie; the ever-burning range ensured that the kitchen was always warm; savoury smells were part of life – the soup pot was seldom off the stove; the steamy aroma of doughballs made Tuesdays special and took away the sting of staid Sunday afternoons; regular baking of bread and scones added its own delicious fragrance to everything else so that he knew he would remember the smells of his childhood home for the rest of his life.

Alex felt very sorry for Mrs Conkey living in such soulless conditions. He also felt sorry for Albert Conkey when it became apparent that the poor, asthmatic creature was the 'heavy object' that Mrs Conkey hadn't been able to lift on her own.

He lay huddled on the bare floor, his yellow face clammily cold, his blue-tinged mouth opening and shutting like a fish out of water while the most alarming wheezes issued from his gaping throat.

'He just fell down,' Mrs Conkey's voice was strangely devoid of emotion, 'I couldny get him up on my own – so I had to leave him here till I could fetch somebody – I was that glad when I heard your voice, Alex, I don't think I would have asked anybody else.'

The boy looked at her and saw at once that she was in

a state of shock. Without ado he bade her put a pillow under her husband's head and cover him with a blanket.

'I'll be back in a minute,' he promised and snatching a key hanging beside the lobby door he rushed out of the house to take the stairs three at a time. No one was around and vaguely he wondered about Barbara, but he had neither the time nor the inclination to dwell on his step-cousin.

Without ado he inserted Mrs Conkey's key into the lock of the stairhead lavatory and going inside he soon found what he was looking for. Jamie, his grandfather, had many liquor caches both in and out of the house but the toilet cistern was his favourite. In the peace and privacy of the cludge enclosure he could drink to his heart's content without watchful eyes noting his every move.

Alex was the one great thorn in his side. From an early age the boy had poked and pryed into his life. He had teased and tormented unmercifully and had driven Jamie to distraction with his sly hints and innuendoes.

Nowadays Jamie's senses were too well soaked in alcohol for him to care very much about anything, far less worry about the safest places to keep his drink. If Alex found it, too buggering bad, the boy might start drinking himself and give them all peace from his biting tongue.

Alex smiled a little when he found the bottle attached to a slimy piece of string. Fishing it out of the water he uncorked it, muttered 'Here's to you, Grandpa,' and swigged down a good mouthful. He coughed a little and cursed his grandfather. It wasn't whisky this time; it was bitter and burning and tasted like cat's piss. But at least it got the blood going and was so strong it might easily rouse a corpse out of its grave – so there was no telling what it would do to that poor old bugger upstairs. He was so far gone anything was worth a try and if he gave Mrs Conkey a swig as well she just might recover enough to give him a few coppers for his kindness.

With a sly little smile he put the cork back into the bottle and jumped down from the toilet seat.

John Simpson was taking his leave. Murn had opted to stay on a little longer as she was simply longing to hear what Evelyn had to say about Tom's father. She glanced at her sister and saw that her face was flushed and that her eyes were shining. Murn felt a small glow of satisfaction. She knew that look, she had seen it often enough at King's Croft when this young sister of hers had run wild and free with Johnny Burns of Cragbogie . . .

A memory came to Murn. She saw again the heather braes of her homeland. In her mind she saw King's Croft, the smoke blowing from its chimneys as it sat peaceful and quiet among its sheltering trees. The little house was cooried into them and made everything seem snug and warm and safe . . . and up there in the end rigs of the stubble fields ran Evie and Johnny, hand in hand, young and carefree and alive – so beautifully, youthfully alive.

Evelyn, with her flashing green eyes and her mane of rich red hair, blessed with beauty and brains, had been born to drive men mad with her wiles and her smiles . . .

And Johnny. A little shiver ran through Murn. Handsome, fair haired Johnny, big and strong yet sensitive and kind, so deep in love with Evelyn he had died in a tragic drowning accident after a jealous fight with Gillan Forbes of Rothiedrum.

All at once Murn felt a rush of unaccountable sadness sweeping over her as she thought about King's Croft and about the old days and the old ways. At the time she hadn't wanted any of it but looking back it hadn't been all that bad . . . she glanced again at Evelyn and was suddenly beset by a strange feeling of guilt. Life hadn't been easy for this little sister of hers, she had lost first Johnny and then her beloved Davie, she had struggled to bring up a family in the face of grinding poverty yet she was still beautiful, still buoyant of nature, able to be just and fair in her judgements of other people.

Murn looked at John Simpson, she thought he was rather arrogant looking with his hawk-like nose and his piercing, assessing eyes. He was immaculate, from his shining watch chain to his well-polished shoes. He was charming, polite, mannerly – yet there was something about him that Murn neither trusted or liked – and here she was trying to foist him off on Evelyn, as if the girl didn't have troubles enough in her life.

She recalled Tom's words, 'Dad isn't just strong, he's tough. He loves women and he's been around a lot . . . '

Murn gave herself a mental shake. What was she worrying about? Evie might be a romantic but she wasn't the sort to throw herself at the first man who came along. Or was she? That scene with her and Tom for instance. She hadn't imagined their guilty looks or their ruffled clothing.

No doubt about it, Evelyn was ready for another man in her life, if only to provide the children with a father and bring a much needed pay packet into the home . . .

A minute or so later there was a vigorous rap on the door. John Simpson was in the lobby with Evelyn bidding her a lingering and fond farewell.

'Damn!' The oath slipped easily from his tongue. Wrenching open the door he beheld Alice Boyle with Barbara held in front of her like a trophy.

Alice wasted no time in the telling of her tale of woe. John Simpson appeared to listen sympathetically, he nodded and agreed with everything that the lady said.

When she came to a somewhat breathless halt he said in his smoothest tones. 'I can well see how you would be annoyed at the girl. But she's a stranger to this country, she hasn't yet learned our wee ways. Leave her to me, I'll see that she never makes a mess of your close again.'

Alice Boyle had fully intended to make Barbara pay for

her crime with a bucket of soap and water and lots of elbow grease, but John Simpson's eyes were on her, mesmerising her, making her forget half of the things she had meant to say.

All the steam went out of her. She smiled at him and with a little half nod she went off downstairs clutching her rapidly cooling fish suppers.

John looked at Barbara. She was more angry than upset; her blue eyes were snapping in her pale face, her mouth was a thin line. With an affected gesture she tossed back a strand of shining fair hair.

John's eyes lingered on the girl's ripe young bosom, he licked his lips. This was only his second meeting with Barbara, his granddaughter through Tom's marriage to his first wife. The connection meant nothing to John, there was no blood line, nothing at all to make him feel that he was related to the girl.

Her eyes were on him, bold and beckoning. John Simpson's heart beat a little faster but the coolness of his expression gave nothing away.

Evelyn stood behind him in the lobby, reeling from the kiss he had snatched from her when they had been briefly alone. Her lips were still tingling, she felt breathless and strange and somehow not in control of herself anymore. She had seen how adept he had been in dealing with Alice Boyle and he had stood there on the threshold boldly and easily, as if he was already master of the house.

'Evie, can I talk to you?' Murn laid her hand on Evie's arm and tried to pull her back into the kitchen. But Evelyn shook her off; the last thing she wanted just then was Murn's voice droning in her eardrums.

Maggie, Jamie and the children came through from The Room. All at once the lobby was overflowing with people. Evelyn thought of how it had been just a few minutes ago, her and John locked together, forgetting everyone in their desire to be alone . . .

A vision of Gillan came swimming into her mind but she

pushed it away. He was out of her life now, far away and forgotten, John Simpson was real and he was available.

Alex held the bottle of spirits against Albert Conkey's blue lips. The man coughed worse than ever for a few moments before his eyes dazedly opened.

'Come on, see if you can get up.' Alex grabbed Mr Conkey under the armpits and heaved. He was no more than a rickle of bones, so undernourished he seemed almost weightless to strapping young Alex Grainger with his fine physique and well developed muscles.

In no time at all he had practically carried the man through to his dingy bedroom where he and Mrs Conkey between them got him undressed and under a depressing array of old coats and threadbare blankets.

'You'd best get the doctor to him,' Alex said with a nod. 'By rights he should be in hospital where he'll be warm and fed.'

Mrs Conkey was horrified at the suggestion. Grabbing hold of the boy's arm she looked beseechingly into his eyes and said urgently, 'Na, na, son, no' the hospital. Albert would die if I did that to him.'

Alex looked at her husband. His face was grey and deeply etched with lines of suffering. If he was breathing he didn't show it and privately Alex thought he was as good as dead already.

Mrs Conkey was hurting his arm, so grimly did she cling to him and plead with him to hold his counsel.

'Don't tell anybody about this, son,' she begged. 'I trust you, you're the only one I trust in this close. All the others laugh at Albert and me and say terrible things behind our backs.'

Her face crumpled. 'We've always been very private people. We don't like anybody to know our business and because o' that the gossips make up things about us.'

'I won't tell,' Alex promised gruffly, his previous notion

of making a copper or two out of the incident fading from his mind.

'You're a good lad, Alex,' Mrs Conkey said with a sniff. 'Oh, I know you used to do terrible things to us when you were younger but I aye sensed your heart was in the right place . . . and I want to give you something. Come over here a minute.'

Leading him over to the heavy mahogany wardrobe she opened it. Strong odours of damp wood and ancient mothballs came reeling out. Alex wrinkled his nose and stepped back a pace. Mrs Conkey put her hand into the pocket of a suit that was grey with mould, she withdrew something and pressed it into Alex's hand.

'Take this, son,' she whispered. 'When Albert was head park keeper this watch was his pride and joy. He used to polish it and keep it in perfect time. Now he hardly knows one day from the next, no' even Sundays.'

Alex gazed in awe at the gold and silver pocket watch in his hand. 'You should pawn it,' he advised in wide-eyed wonder. 'You could buy mountains of coal and light a fire and enough food to last ages and ages.'

'Pawn!' Mrs Conkey drew herself up. 'No, Alex, I'd rather die than have anybody see me in a pawnshop. You take the watch. I know you'll look after it. Albert has no more use o' it, it's just lying in his pocket gathering dust and dampness.'

Alex tried hard to hide his delight. He would be a man with a watch like this. No one need know that he had it; he would hide it and just look at it now and again . . .

'Thanks, Mrs Conkey,' He hid his feelings in gruffness. 'I'll take good care o' it, I'll polish it and keep it in good time.'

'Alex,' Mrs Conkey sounded hesitant, 'it's no' my place to interfere but – that girl – the one on the stairs. She'll never be any good to you, son. You mind how you go wi' her.'

Alex nodded in complete understanding. 'I know that

fine well, Mrs Conkey, and don't worry, I'll watch what I'm doing.'

They had reached the lobby, Alex opened the door. At almost the same moment the door opposite opened. John Simpson stood framed in the aperture. Boy and man looked at one another. Resentment leapt into Alex's eyes and his face grew cold and still with fear.

John Simpson tilted his iron-hard jaw; his fists curled; he looked at Alex for a long time then in a slow, deliberate voice he said over his shoulder, 'I'll be back, Evelyn, and next time I hope it will be for longer.'

Alex took a deep breath. At that moment he knew his life was never going to be the same again.

Chapter Three

'Married!' Grace stared at Evelyn as if her younger sister had just taken leave of her senses. 'To John Simpson! But you canna do that, Evie. You just canna do that!'

Grace was the most placid and sweet-tempered of all the five Grant sisters. Although she was now thirty-eight she seemed hardly to have aged since her girlhood. Her smooth skin was like alabaster, her shining chestnut hair waved naturally round her neat head, her haunting black eyes looked serenely enough at the world but tragedy dwelt there in the fathomless depths.

She was a war widow. Her surgeon husband, Gordon Chisholm, had died in a field hospital in France but his young wife of only a few months had never accepted his death.

'He'll come back to me,' she told her family with a philosophy that was frightening in its simplicity, 'we loved one another too much for it to end as easily as that.'

Murn had openly scoffed at what she called 'silly fancies'; Nellie, able to accept only what was tangible in life, kept her opinions to herself because never, never would she say or do anything that would hurt this darling sister of hers; easy going Mary had always been tolerant where Grace was concerned and went along with her ideas about Gordon, while Evelyn, born with the second sight, occasionally experienced strange and unexplained phenomena in Grace's company.

Grace's tiny, single-end apartment was cosy and tastefully decorated. On the mantelpiece was an array of family photographs. Prominently placed was a picture of Gordon

43

Chisholm, a great strong bear of a man with snapping eyes and a mop of unruly black hair.

One evening, while Grace had been in the scullery making tea, Evelyn had had a very disquieting experience. Sitting at the fire, staring dreamily into it, she jumped out of her skin when the photo of Gordon came fluttering down to land face up in her lap so that the keen eyes were gazing directly into hers.

An innocent enough happening and one easily explained, so Evelyn thought, replacing the picture on the mantelpiece.

But no sooner had she seated herself than the same thing happened. When it was repeated for a third time, dropping into her lap with the force of a heavy book, she knew that this was no natural occurrence. Her flesh had crawled, she had shivered and trembled. Grace, imagining that she was going down with a cold had made her drink a hot toddy and had sent her home to bed.

After that night, whenever Evelyn was alone in the room, the 'Phenomenon of the Photograph' as she had come to call it, occasionally manifested itself. Then the pattern of events changed, the photo began to fall into Grace's lap. Evelyn confided her previous experiences, and both sisters knew that something extraordinary had taken place. Unseen forces were trying to tell them something, and as far as Grace was concerned she knew exactly what it was. Gordon was alive, somewhere her husband was alive and well and someday he would come back to her.

Evelyn believed the opposite. She felt that the message had come from beyond the grave, a silent appeal from Gordon to let go of the past and to let him rest in peace.

Evelyn kept this opinion strictly to herself. She adored Grace and wished with all her heart that she would meet someone that she could happily spend the rest of her life with.

But Grace never gave any man a second look. She was waiting for Gordon, she said, and she was perfectly content

44

to live on her own till the one man who had meant the world to her came back into her life.

Evelyn knew that she could never be like Grace. She needed warmth and companionship in her life. She had loved and lost Davie and there would never be another like him, but she was lonely and afraid of a future on her own.

John Simpson had come into her life at a most opportune time: the children needed a father, she was tired struggling to bring them up single handed; her own father was past caring about anything beyond where his next drink was coming from and her mother wasn't getting any younger. Lately Evelyn had noticed a little stoop to those proud shoulders and she convinced herself that John Simpson was the answer to all their prayers. They were all very lucky he was so keen to take on the burden of a new wife and a ready made family.

Grace had met John Simpson only once but it was enough to make her dislike him and mistrust him with all the might of her gentle heart. She didn't want someone like him for the little sister who had always meant so much to her and for once she put forth her views on the matter, aggressively and forcefully.

'You canna marry him, Evie,' she stressed once more. 'What do you know o' him beyond the fact that he's Tom Simpson's father? Where does he come from? Where has he been? Who has he been with before he met you? He's the sort o' man who — likes women.'

Grace paused, remembering his hand on her arm when she was in the scullery making sandwiches, a hand that rested only lightly on her flesh but a burning hand, that was the only word to describe it, burning and wanting and nakedly desiring — desiring female flesh of any kind, old, young, middle-aged.

Evelyn was irritated by Grace's attitude; she hadn't expected this sort of opposition from the one sister who was more inclined to the love of fellow man than anyone she knew.

Evelyn's chin went up; 'I know that he has a good, steady job as a welder in John Brown's shipyard. Nowadays it's hard to find a man with any sort o' job and if you must know, Grace, I crave security in my life as much as I crave a bit of love and affection.'

'Och, of course you do.' Grace's lovely face softened; 'We all need love in our lives, but what you're really saying, Evie, is that you need a man's love. That's natural and right but dinna go marrying John Simpson for all the wrong reasons. He's already had six o' a family so why is he so willing to take on your four?'

Evelyn's chin set into even more stubborn lines, because Grace was asking all the questions she had asked herself. Murn had supplied some of the answers but not nearly enough.

'Tom's father is by no means a rich man,' Murn had said with a somewhat superior sniff, 'as a matter of fact he's been rather much on his uppers since the war. He came home from that to nothing, like most of the men who came back. The Depression was the beginning and the end. He drank, he slid, he came to his senses and crawled back. Tom says he's got fighting spirit – whatever that means. I'm new to this family myself, Evie, I'm still finding things out.'

She had closed up then and Evelyn had suspected that she could have revealed more if she had really wanted to. But Murn was Murn, with all her devious and evasive ways. She wouldn't give anything away if she thought it might be detrimental to herself, even if what she had to say might be crucial to her own sister's future happiness.

Tom was no better than his wife; he was frustrated in Evelyn's company. Her smooth, enticing body had been there in his grasp but, because of Murn, the joys of her flesh had been lost to him and looked like staying that way for keeps, though not for the want of trying on his part.

Tom was, therefore, in no mood to talk about his father beyond making a half-hearted attempt to dissuade her from the drastic step of marriage.

'Dad isn't for you, Evie,' was his opinion, 'He's been around, he's quite a man. One family – one *large* family – is enough for any man to raise. Look for somebody younger; Dad's happy enough on his own, you'll only make waves for everybody if you take him on.'

All this had infuriated Evelyn. Tom made her sound like a man-eater, Murn made her feel like a gold digger, and now here was Grace with all her depressing objections, the one person she had thought would be happy to hear her news.

'He's old enough to be your father, Evie,' Grace said softly, her dark eyes regarding her sister kindly. 'I ken fine how strong and reassuring he must seem to you now but in ten years time, when you're in your early forties, he'll be going on for seventy . . .'

'He'll be sixty-five, Grace,' Evelyn said firmly, 'and his age is the last thing to worry me right now. I've had to learn to live each day as it comes. John Simpson is a good, kind man, and he loves me for what I am, not for what he can get from me . . .'

As she spoke she was remembering his strength, his insistent demands on her body whenever they were alone together. Sometimes his overwhelming desires made her shaky and slightly apprehensive but she had never wholly succumbed to his pleas.

'Don't make me wait, Evie,' he had moaned against her breasts, 'it's unbearable, I dream about you till I could go mad, I can't wait, I can't.'

'You'll have to, John,' she would return, a feeling of power so strong in her she honestly believed she could do anything with him.

'The marriage bed, or nothing, is that what you're trying to tell me, girl?'

'Ay, John, that's what I'm trying to tell you.'

'Then we'll get married, before Christmas, because I swear, I can't wait any longer than that.'

At the remembrance of these exchanges a naked thrill of longing ran through her and she was ashamed that she could feel such raw desire whilst in the company of her very own sister.

Impulsively she took Grace to her breast and held her close, smelling the delicate perfume of roses, feeling the smooth, perfect cheek against her own. 'I know fine how you love me, Grace,' she whispered, 'and that you want only what's best for me, but I'm going to marry John Simpson and I hope, in time, you'll give me your blessing. I really need to have it if I'm to feel truly happy.'

Tears sprung to Grace's burning black eyes; a feeling of dread beset her. She swallowed hard and murmured, 'You have my blessing, darling Evie, and I hope and pray with all my heart that you will have a happy and fulfilled life as the wife o' John Simpson.'

Grace wasn't alone in her doubts over the impending marriage. When Jamie and Maggie learned of it they were apprehensive and afraid for their own future.

It had been bad enough when Davie was alive; he and Maggie had never got on and had argued continually over all sorts of domestic matters. Davie had tolerated Jamie fairly well even though the older man's drinking habits had not met with his approval.

But 'Better the devil you know than the one you don't'. Maggie told her husband, 'I don't like John Simpson: underneath that smooth exterior lies a tough, ruthless creature none o' us know a lot about. Tom won't say much, Murn says even less but they dinna have to. There's more to John Simpson than meets the eye and I for one am no' looking forward to finding out what it is.'

Jamie wholeheartedly agreed with every one of her sentiments. Despite his faults, Davie had been kind and

48

forbearing in his own way; he had been a young man, who fitted his role as Evelyn's husband. John Simpson was fifty-five, a widower, with a lifetime already behind him. He had six of a family, all grown and out in the world, his wife had died in an asylum ... Had John Simpson driven her to the brink of endurance while he himself emerged unscathed and ready to start all over again? ... And with Evelyn, a young woman of thirty-two with plenty of men her own age only too eager to take Davie's place?

But Evelyn had changed a lot in recent years. In order to survive she had grown less vulnerable, was less of an idealist than she had been. John Simpson had a reasonably well paid job, most of the young men of Evelyn's acquaintance didn't; it was as simple as that.

Jamie's head sunk to his chest. His princess! His darling girl! How could she, how could they all have sunk so low? They should never have left Rothiedrum; they should have stayed at King's Croft and tried to make a go of it; anything was better than this hand to mouth existence with every day the same and nothing very much to look forward to.

'If only she had married Gillan in the first place.' Maggie laid aside her darning and tried to find a comfortable spot for her aching back in the unyielding contours of her hard little chair. 'None o' this would have happened if she had.'

'Ach, that wouldna have pleased you either.' Jamie lit his pipe with a shaky hand and wondered where he had hidden his half-bottle of whisky. 'I mind fine how you reacted when Evie started seeing Gillie, you didna even like him at first.'

'It wasna him – it was all that he stood for,' Maggie said mysteriously.

Jamie sighed. 'Ay, you've told me that before but I never could understand why you should get so upset about the Forbes family.'

Maggie looked at him for a long, considerate moment. She seemed to be struggling with some inner conflict, then she said in a calm, deliberate voice, 'It's time you kent the truth, Jamie my man, I wanted to tell you a long time ago but my cousin Marjorie, the snobbish bitch, was feart to have her fine name linked wi' a mere crofter's wife.'

Jamie stared; he forgot the whisky, he listened attentively as his wife went on to tell him that her father was none other than Lord Lindsay Ogilvie, uncle of Lady Marjorie Forbes and Gillan's great uncle.

'His Lordship deserted my mother when he knew she was carrying.' Maggie had long ago lost her bitterness over Lord Lindsay's shameful behaviour towards her mother and her voice was neither hurt nor resentful as the tale of her background unfolded. 'He never contributed towards my upbringing and while my mother told me who my real father was, I never met him till the day he appeared at King's Croft offering me conscience money. He loved Evie, he said, he wanted to give her a good education . . .'

Her eyes grew misty and faraway. 'He was a fine man, no' stuck up or snobbish in any way. But he was a gentleman, noble, proud. It must have taken a lot o' courage for him to come looking for me the way he did. But I showed him the door and told him never to darken it again. To my dying day I'll regret that.'

Jamie sucked deeply on his pipe, his fuddled brain tried to make sense of everything he had heard. 'I always knew there was gentry blood in you somewhere,' he said at last, 'but I never thought it would be as grand as that.'

'Ach, havers!' Maggie said impatiently even though her chin lifted with unconscious pride.

'That means Lady Marjorie and Gillan are your cousins.' Jamie's brow was deeply furrowed as he tried to work it all out. 'They're also cousins to our girls while Lord Lindsay is their grandfather.'

'Ay, you've got it correct, Jamie, I never saw my father again but in his own way he did things, both directly and otherwise, to help our family. As for Lady Marjorie, you ken the story about her. She and me became the best o' friends and practically wept in each other's arms when I had to leave King's Croft. It was strange, the way she turned up at Dunmarnock House when we were working there – and sad that we never saw her again. Strange too, Evelyn meeting Gillan in the west end when Mary lived there. That must be nearly a year ago now. Who knows, he might just pop up again somewhere, and if he does I hope he'll be in time to prevent our lassie marrying that man.'

Maggie fell quiet, her hands busy with a pile of darning while her mind filled up with thoughts of the people who had once made up her life.

Jamie too became lost in thought. Maggie's revelations had brought the past back into his life again. He closed his eyes and tried to remember the lands of his beloved Aberdeenshire. Time had dulled a lot of his memories, the booze had done the rest.

But sometimes, on the rare occasions that his head was clear, he could recall it all plainly. In his mind's eye he saw the loamy earth falling away from the plough, he smelt its richness and knew its very texture as it curled away from the blade; he saw the great wide skies above him; he knew the wonder of the patchwork fields spread out before him; he felt the warmth of the beasts in their winter byre; he saw the peesies diving and dipping in the spring skies and he heard their haunting call far and away over the glens and the bens of Rothiedrum . . .

'I dread to think how Alex will take it.' Maggie's voice broke into Jamie's pleasurable meanderings. 'He sees himself as the little man o' the house since Davie died and he might just go berserk altogether at the idea of another man taking over, especially one who's going to be his stepfather.'

'Alex! Alex! Everybody gets so worked up about Alex! It's time he had a father's hand,' Jamie found himself saying in a most unsympathetic manner. 'The lad's getting too big for his boots and he's a buggering little thief into the bargain!'

'I take it he's been at your hiding places again,' Maggie said dryly. 'Why you bother to plank the stuff beats me. We all ken you take a bucket, there's no sense in hiding that fact any longer.'

Jamie didn't answer. Didn't the woman know it was a matter of pride? He wouldn't let every Tom, Dick and Harry look in on his private life. He had to keep some dignity, he was still a man . . . His eyes filled; impatiently he wiped the tears away with his fist.

Maggie's face softened, she laid her hand on his arm. 'We'll just have to stick together, Jamie. John Simpson willna bully us or my name isn't Margaret Innes Grant!'

Chapter Four

The Room had always been a sanctuary for the children, even when their mother had slept in it with their father in the big brass double bed.

But their father was dead now and Evelyn, who for a while had behaved as if she would like to be dead also, had changed all the sleeping arrangements.

She now slept with little James in one of the bed recesses in the kitchen; Maggie and Jamie occupied the other; eleven-year-old Margaret and nine-year-old Rachel slept in the brass bed in The Room while a disgruntled Alex had been relegated to the cupboard recess set into a box-like cavern in the wall.

'It's dark and smelly in there,' he had objected, '*And* it's got bed bugs! I can smell them at night! A horrible smell like sour old blood! Then they drop onto the bed and bite me and suck *my* blood till I come out in great big enormous festering sores running with ooze and crusted with mattery scabs. I scratch them and tear them to bits with my nails and afterwards I don't always remember to wash my hands before I set the table for breakfast.'

His brother and sisters stared at him horrified during the unfolding of the grisly tale but his grandfather just shook his head and promised he would soon rid Alex of his bed bugs.

As good as his word Jamie went ben The Room while the children were at school to paint the recess walls with paraffin.

That night Alex complained long and loudly about the fumes, coughing and spluttering for hours, keeping the others awake; marching through to the kitchen in the middle of the night for a drink of water, making plenty of noise about it; moaning and groaning and rolling about on the bed. In the morning he swore he had a headache and declared he couldn't go to school.

'Right, then,' Evelyn had had enough of her eldest son's capers. 'Just you go right back to bed and I'll come through and tuck you up nice and warm.'

'Not *that* bed!' a shocked Alex had exclaimed. 'I tell you, it stinks! I'll go into the brass bed, even though Gypsy-Wets-Her-Knickers might have left her smell behind.'

Margaret Mary, better known as Meg, was plump and lazy, but when Alex started on her like this she never failed to rise to the bait. Black eyes flashing, she would verbally attack him with a dialogue every bit as fierce and sarcastic as his own and he revelled in every tearful, nasty word.

But on this occasion she hadn't cried, but had calmly warned him that if he dared to sleep in *her* bed she would cut off his willie at the first opportunity. For good measure she had gone on to say that she would boil it and feed it to the first stray cat who chanced along.

'You'd never be able to use it again, Alex Grainger!' she had ended triumphantly. 'No' even to pee! You'd never be able to show it to the girls! It would be gone! Lost forever. Gobbled up in one gulp by a starving old cat . . . only thing is . . .' at this point her sallow face took on an uncustomary glow . . . 'the poor moggy might die o' food poisoning after eating your horrible, smelly old willie!'

The reactions to her dire threats had been electrifying and had gratified Meg completely. Jamie had stuffed his face into his hanky and had appeared to be suffering some sort of choking fit; Rachel had gaped at Meg and had wondered to herself where her sister had learned all that dirty stuff; seven year old James had put his thumb into his mouth to anxiously suck it while trying to decide if any of the toothless strays of the district could possibly eat his big brother's well developed private parts; Maggie had simply fled from the kitchen leaving her daughter to deal with the situation.

Evelyn hadn't dared let Alex see her amusement since he looked as if he could easily kill his sister in those moments.

In fact, he had felt like killing everybody that day as he was marched into The Room without ceremony to be told to undress and go back to bed.

'It's Meg who should be punished for all the dirty things she said!' he had cried, glaring defiantly at his mother.

'Alex,' she had replied as calmly as she could. 'Would you like me to personally undress you and put you to bed? I'm stronger than I look and I could aye get your grannie to help me.'

'All right!' he had wailed, rapidly swallowing his pride as the paraffin fumes hit him. 'I give in! I'll go to school! There's nothing wrong with me but there will be if I'm made to lie in this foul atmosphere all day.'

Mother and son had faced one another, Evelyn's face set in the stubborn lines Alex had come to know well in his life. He himself was possessed of the same wilful tendencies, but where she was concerned he had long ago learned that tender persuasion was by far the most effective weapon to use.

That sort of tactic was never too difficult to employ anyway, she always looked her best when she was angry; he loved the flush on her smooth cheeks, he liked the way her green eyes flashed . . .

'Mother,' he had taken one of her hands in his and had spoken in soft tones, 'You really don't want me to be ill, do you? I wouldn't be able to sell my firewood round the doors and I couldn't run errands for Keyhole Kate at the corner. Also there's poor old Dobbie to look after. He'd die if I wasn't there to feed him and you know yourself how you love horses and would hate it if anything happened to Dobs. After all, you saved his life after that terrible fire in his shed. He's special to you and he loves you with all his heart because he rolls his eyes whenever I speak about you.

'I promise I'll never complain again about the cupboard recess . . . just as long as you tell Grandpa no' to put any more paraffin on the walls. I really did feel ill last night, and more than anybody else, I know you wouldn't want your one and only eldest son to fade away into oblivion.'

At that she had burst out laughing and had easily capitulated to his persuasions. She simply couldn't help it. He was droll, this beautiful big son of hers; sometimes he seemed to have the wits of a six year old, at others he spoke with such wisdom he might be twenty instead of just twelve.

His sense of humour was sometimes subtle, sometimes crude, but no matter what, he could make her laugh and he could twist her round his little finger so easily.

Only one other person had been able to do that to her; Davie, her Davie, with his smiles and his wiles and his knack of making her forget her troubles with just a few warm, affectionate kisses.

Davie, Davie, gone from her now, like a candle flame snuffed out in the wind, leaving her in darkness and bitter despair.

Alex had been her saviour. Like a little man he had looked after her. He had held her in his young arms when all she had wanted was to die; he had berated her and encouraged her, praised her and pleaded with her, until gradually she had climbed out of the pit and back into the sunshine.

He would always be special to her and the place he held in her heart was very precious.

She told herself that never, never would she do anything that might jeopardise the trust they had placed in one another . . . but that had been in the early days after Davie's death, when she was too numb with grief to care very much about anything beyond the fact that her darling man was gone from her, never to return.

After that had come the real emptiness, the long hours of despair when she had silently acknowledged to herself how meaningless her life had become without him. She had questioned the very reasons for her own existence and had wanted only to curl up and die to have peace from her own bitter thoughts.

She had withdrawn from the world. Very alone, very afraid of an empty future, she had experienced bouts of suffocating panic seeing the years stretching ahead of her with no father for the children, no man bringing a wage into the house, no man to laugh with, talk with and – she had to face it – no warmth, no love, none of the kind of fulfilment that a woman like her needed.

Murn, the outspoken besom that she was, had hit the nail very exactly on the head when she told Evelyn she needed a man in her life again.

And, as if on cue, John Simpson had walked into her home and into her life. Before that she had been at a very low ebb; the weeks, the months, were dreary and empty and she seemed to drift through them in a daze.

She had come to dread the dawns and the days; she wanted only dusk and darkness so that she could forget herself in sleep that made no demands on her energies. Except when she dreamed of golden lands where Gillan came to her through the trees, his arms outstretched as if to carry her off into those sweet, dear places that were always just on the edge of recall, tantalising her, teasing her, tormenting her.

And then came the awakenings, bringing her back to cold reality and the beginning of another day very much like the last.

John Simpson had appeared to her like an oasis in the middle of a bleak and empty desert. He was like a rock; strong, dependable, solid. He had arrived when her spirit was at its most vulnerable and her mind was at its most receptive. She wanted, needed, desired him in her life. For the first time everything but her heart was ruling her head. The young, daft, impulsive Evie had died with Davie and had been buried forever in the past.

Evie hadn't expected the tide of opposition that had threatened to swamp her when she announced her intention to marry John Simpson. She had expected it certainly from her parents, whose tenure in the home had been precarious enough when Davie had ruled the roost. She had also anticipated Alex's reaction to the news, but never, never had she thought that Grace would be so opposed to the idea, not to mention Tom and even Murn to a certain degree – even though she was the very one who had seemed so pleased to introduce John in the beginning.

Nellie too made her disapproval only too plain when she had written.

Croft Donald,
Kenneray,
December 1930

Dear Evie,

When your letter arrived with your latest piece of news I thought at first that I wasn't seeing too clearly. So I put on my glasses (which, as you know, I only use for sewing and other close work).

Even then I thought my eyes were deceiving me and I handed the letter to Kenneth. He read it aloud and only when I heard the words spoken in his big, booming voice did the fact really sink in that you were talking about getting married again.

My dear girl, do you know what you are doing? This John Simpson is old enough to be your father. His son, Tom, is even older than you.

Murn didn't, by any chance, have a hand in the affair, did she? I know only too well what a devious besom she is and how she will go to any lengths once she gets an idea in her head. I haven't forgotten the state she got herself into when she heard that Kenneth and myself were to be wed, nor have I forgotten the shame and embarrassment she brought on herself and her family by the things she said and did. Her coming home to Scotland has brought it all so vividly back and only this very morning Kenneth was saying how he hoped she had outgrown all that silly nonsense.

I don't want to be a bossy big sister, but please, Evie, think this matter over very carefully before you make a decision that could affect your life and those of your children for many years to come.

I only wish Gillan had never gone out of your life. I had half hoped that you and he would have gotten together once you had stopped grieving so much for Davie.

However, all that's pie in the sky. I hope the bairns are well. I am enclosing a few pounds for you to buy some things for their Christmas stockings. It isn't much, but there should be some left over for things for the festive table. I know how Mam likes baking so, if you can, buy her flour and raisins, and I know Father would welcome an ounce or two of tobacco. He'll manage to get his own alcohol if I know him — so, for God's sake, don't even mention it to him — and you get yourself some warm winter stockings.

We are all well. Wee Col had a bad cold for a while but he's better now and sends his love along with all the rest of us. Kenneth David is thriving and growing into a bonny big boy.

I hope you all have a very happy Christmas.

With love and affection.

From your sister, Nellie

She had enclosed fifteen pounds. Evelyn had sat down and cried. Then she had laughed and she had loved this out-spoken eldest sister of hers with all her heart. She had then read the letter for the third time and, quite unexpectedly, cold anger had set in. How dare Nellie put forth such strong opinions! How dare any of them oppose this marriage! How dare Alex look at her with those strange resentful eyes of his and if Maggie and Jamie thought anything of her at all, they would see John Simpson's arrival into her life as timely and welcome.

Instead, they were only fretting about their own future in *her* home. Well, she'd had enough! Let them worry and fret! She had had the responsibility of them for far too long, and it was high time she had a life of her own not to mention a home where she could have some privacy and peace for a change.

As for Alex, he was only a boy after all. What did it matter if his pride was hurt for a little while? One day he would grow up and leave home; all her children would do the same, and if she didn't look to her own future now she would one day be left alone and empty with nothing to show for a lifetime of poverty, sacrifice and misery.

Alex saw the green, determined gleam in his mother's eyes and prepared himself for battle. He knew that look, he had seen it often enough before . . . in his own reflection in the mirror when he was in one of his mean, stubborn moods and wasn't going to give in to anything or anybody.

So he had called his brother and sisters together for a 'Meeting Extraordinary' as he had grandly named it.

Ever since the 'Affair of the Paraffin' to quote Maggie, he had gradually accepted the new sleeping arrangements in The Room and in time had even come to see them as being beneficial to his own status as eldest of the siblings.

'I want you all to sit cross-legged and to be quiet and attentive when I'm talking,' he ordered. 'I want to find out how you feel about our mother marrying John Simpson. I for one won't become Alex Simpson – Grainger's my name and always will be.'

Rachel and little James made haste to obey their big brother, not so Meg who scowled at him belligerently before perching herself on the bed.

'Meg,' he said heavily, 'Why are you doing this? Is it because you're afraid we'll see the holes in your knickers?

Or don't you care if our mother marries John Simpson and he becomes your stepfather?'

Meg's lower lip jutted, she tossed her black curls and her eyes narrowed. With her olive skin and dark colouring she should have been a beauty, but her face lacked sparkle; she had no zest for life, she was lazy at school and was always bringing notes home from her teacher, complaining about her careless attitude to work; she played truant all too frequently, resulting in visits from the School Board Inspector; she avoided household chores like the plague which meant that too much was piled onto the thin little shoulders of her younger sister, Rachel.

Meg had none of her big brother's initiative; she lacked her father's greedy love of life and had nothing of her mother's vivacity and sparkling enthusiasms. She took what she coveted and gave little thought to the consequences, with the result that she always seemed to be in trouble of one sort or another.

Her saving grace was her compassion for animals, be they well or sick. She saved her pennies to buy food for the back court strays, consequently bringing much ire upon herself from neighbours complaining about animal smells in the closes.

Meg didn't care. She nursed sick cats back to health; she rescued abandoned kittens and somehow found homes for them; she reported irresponsible dog owners to the police; she tended injured paws and she bandaged limbs. She had gained a reputation for herself as being the Florence Nightingale of the animal kingdom and even those adults who complained about her admired her good intentions and her undoubted prowess with four-legged creatures of all sorts.

A love of animals was the one thing that Meg and Alex had in common. He adored horses and had bought a broken down old cart horse from Fishy Alice when she had been about to send him to the knacker's yard. Dobbie Loan, who had been named after one of Glasgow's dark alleys, had been old and sick and very tired when he had

61

come into the tender loving care of young Alex Grainger.

Within a short time the old horse had lifted up his head to take an interest in life again and in summer he had become a popular attraction for the neighbourhood youngsters who didn't mind stumping up a copper or two in exchange for a ride on his broad back. In winter he was housed in a shed near the Smiddy and had recently been joined by Tinker, a sad and neglected little mare whose owner had been sent to Barlinnie jail for an indefinite period.

Tinker had received many beatings in her five years of life, with the result that she was nervous, suspicious and anxious. But Alex and Meg between them had soothed and calmed her to such a degree that she was rapidly growing to trust and love them.

Meg, a trifle condescendingly for Alex's benefit, even though she didn't really mean it, had given of her time and expounded far more of her energies in grooming the horses than she had ever given to any mundane household task. She also handed over her spare pennies to help buy winter feed while Alex was kept busy with his milk, paper, and firewood rounds and also had to devote some of his time to Dunky the Smith in return for the use of his shed.

All things considered he was a very busy young man and was in no position to refuse Meg's help. So, in this respect they tolerated one another and occasionally forgot their differences, but generally they were 'at one another's throats' as Jamie put it.

Meg certainly had no intention of ever allowing her older brother to gain the upper hand, and no way was she going to sit cross-legged at this silly meeting just because he had said so. That sort of thing was all right for the likes of Keep-The-Peace Rachel and Pee-The-Bed James but it was certainly *not* all right for Margaret Mary Grainger, eleven going on twelve, growing up fast with her sights firmly set on marrying a rich man who would keep her in all the hair ribbons and ice cream she could ever want.

'Meg! Did you hear me?' Alex boomed in the same sort of voice he had heard Kenneth Mor use when calling the horses to be harnessed for a day's work.

'I said, do you really want John Simpson to marry our mother and become your stepfather?' He glimpsed her angry, dark little face and all at once he felt sorry for this rather unpopular little sister of his. After all, she had been really good about Tinker and Dobbie; she had donated threepence from her Christmas savings to buy them carrots 'to cheer them up' *and* she had personally gone to the greengrocer's to make sure she got only the best vegetables in the shop. His face softened. 'Come on, Megsie,' he coaxed in his nicest manner, 'If you're with us, sister to sister, brother to brother, you'll come and sit beside us and give us your support.'

Meg stared at him. Brother to brother indeed! He was acting the big man as usual, trying to impress them with his knowledge and his fancy words. She was about to retaliate in her usual cheeky fashion when something silenced her tongue. She was remembering John Simpson, not so much what he had said to her but what he *hadn't* said. From the very start he had ignored her, almost as if she didn't exist. He had been sweet to Rachel, he had talked kindly to Bessie and Babs whenever they had come visiting, he had lifted James up on his shoulders and he had challenged Alex to take a drink with him one night when their mother was late getting back from Fanny Jean Gillespie's house.

Meg remembered the look in Alex's eyes, those peculiar eyes of his that expressed so clearly what was in his thoughts. Hatred had burned in their depths. He had said nothing but had stared and stared at John Simpson with that black, intense look, and in the end it was John Simpson who had turned away, muttering something about forgetting that the boy was only twelve years old and that he shouldn't have asked him to drink raw spirits.

But at least he had acknowledged the fact that Alex

existed, even if it was only to let him see that he was no longer the boss.

Meg got down from the bed and went to sit beside Rachel. 'I'm with you, Alex,' she said abruptly, 'I don't want John Simpson to be my stepfather. I don't like him and I never will.'

'Right.' Alex swiftly jotted some words onto a piece of paper before turning to Rachel. 'How about you, Rachel? Do you want that man to marry our mother?'

Rachel put her chin into her cupped hand and gazed at her big brother with troubled grey eyes. Of them all she had the most placid nature but that didn't mean she couldn't lose her temper when she wanted. She was a romantic, always seeing the finer side of life and becoming very upset when the humdrum nature of her existence often forced her to look at ugly reality. She was a staunch supporter of the underdog and didn't think twice about tackling bullies wherever and whenever they struck, even though she was so slightly built she looked as if a puff of wind might easily blow her over.

She was little Jimmy's protectress. Wherever she went he was sure to follow, even to the stairhead cludge – and this was about the only time she ever really got annoyed with him.

Since her father's death she had been extremely unhappy; everything had changed, even the sleeping arrangements. Jimmy hadn't wanted to sleep with his mother. He had cried for a week afterwards and had started wetting the bed again. He had gotten over that now but he still missed his sister and would creep to the big brass bed in The Room and crawl in beside her whenever he thought he could get away with it.

Now, with so much else happening in these last few weeks, these seemed the least of the changes Rachel would have to cope with. The appearance of her step-cousins, the Simpsons, had been one of them. She didn't mind timid little Bessie but she disliked and mistrusted Babs, who hung around Alex and made stupid eyes at him. Rachel hated the way Alex responded, sort of wobbly and soft and strange-looking with an expression in his eyes that was difficult to fathom . . .

And then there was John Simpson . . . Rachel shivered . . . She was remembering that last time he had lifted her up. He had been drinking, she could smell it on his breath. His eyes had been funny, sort of wild and reckless and leering up at her as he held her above his head. His hand had slid between her legs and he had licked his lips and whispered to her that she was 'a nice little girl.'

The incident had only lasted a moment; nobody had noticed but she had known it was wrong – wrong – for him to do that to her. She had felt dirty, as if it had been all her fault . . .

'I don't like Mr Simpson,' her voice now came out plain and clear, 'and I don't want him to be my step-father.'

'Me neither.' Little Jimmy hastened to add his voice to Rachel's, 'He hurts me when he lifts me up. He grips my arms and makes them sore.'

But that wasn't what really worried James. It was John Simpson's eyes that he was afraid of – the way they pierced right into you and made you drop things and . . . James licked his dry lips and wriggled uncomfortably . . . the way they sometimes made you wet your trousers. It was only a few drops and no one ever knew except Alex or Meg who both told him he smelled of 'piddles' and ridiculed him by saying he was too old to be doing that sort of thing now.

Alex licked his pencil and wrote James' name on the paper. 'We're all agreed,' he said triumphantly. 'I'll take this petition through to our mother. She'll *have* to read it and think about it and realise that she's making a big mistake bringing a strange man into our home and making him the head o' the house.'

But Evelyn was never to see her eldest son's brave attempt to try and alter the course of fate because, at that very moment, the matter was taken entirely out of his hands.

The door of The Room burst open and there was John Simpson, his strong face aglow with triumph. Behind him came Evelyn, bearing a tray laden with bottles, glasses and a plate piled with thick pieces of fruit cake.

'Bairns,' John filled four glasses with fruit wine and two with sherry, 'Join your mother and me in a toast to the future. We're being wed next week. Your mother's a fine woman, she's struggled against the odds to bring you all up on her own but I'm here now. She needs someone like me about the place; you weans need a father ... and I know you'll agree with me that it's high time this house had a man in it again ...' He stared at little James, he smiled warmly at Rachel, he ignored Meg. 'Don't worry, I know we'll all be friends; we'll be a proper family. You can trust me, I'll be a good father to you.'

Meg was cramming cake into her mouth, little James had a moustache of blackcurrant juice on his upper lip and Rachel was chinking her glass solemnly against her mother's and wishing her good health.

Alex scowled. Already they had forgotten the petition. Some cheap fruit wine, a slab of cake – that was all it had taken to win them over. He glanced at his mother; her eyes were sparkling. She looked young and radiant and extremely happy.

Evie tried to catch Alex's eye but he turned away and she was glad that Maggie and Jamie came through to join the company. In the confusion Alex made tracks for the door only to find John Simpson blocking the way. The man stuck out a large, steel-hard hand.

'Shake, son,' he said jovially. 'You'd better get used to having me about the place ... after all, you're about to have me as a father-figure in the home.'

Alex's lip curled. 'I'm Alex Grainger, my father died

only last year, no one will ever take his place in this house.'

He spat the words contemptuously at John Simpson and John Simpson threw back his head and laughed as if he hadn't heard anything so amusing for a long time.

Chapter Five

Murn had never been happier. She had insisted on holding Evelyn's wedding reception at her house and she had had a very busy and happy time of it, arranging, planning, bossing people about. She had caused Sarah much anguish, ordering her to do this and that, even following her around the house to make sure she cleaned all the corners. Sarah had been on the point of leaving several times, but work of any sort wasn't so easy to come by these days and so she had taken a few deep breaths and had stilled her tongue every time she felt like telling Mistress Simpson where she could put her job.

Both Barbara and Bessie had spent as much time away from the house as they dared while Tom, much to Murn's disapproval, had taken himself off to the local pubs with his father, often creeping in very late and very drunk.

This was a side of him that Murn had only previously glimpsed and she was filled with self-righteous horror at the very idea of her husband walking through the Glasgow streets drunk and incapable. She told herself that the sooner he was back at sea the better but he was on a three month leave from his ship and so had plenty of time left in which to indulge 'his weaknesses' as she put it.

But if she thought this new and disquieting side to his nature was shocking enough, it was to pale into insignificance the night he never came home at all and was found with his father sleeping off his excesses in an urban garden. Father and son had been carted off to the local police station to spend the remainder of the night in a cell and Murn would never – no, never – get over the shame of such a degrading incident.

'Och, c'mon, Murn,' Tom had pleaded a trifle wearily, 'it was only a bit of fun. Dad and I had a lot to talk about and I saw no harm in treating him to a jar or two. It won't happen again, I promise you, so get down off your high horse and come to bed. A good feel of the arse is what you're needing, you're starting to enjoy it, Murnsie, and don't go all coy on me and pretend that you hate sex the way you used to.'

In bed, his passions fiery and insatiable, he had behaved more like an animal than ever, and she had lain beneath him, loving every brutish movement even while stuffing the sheet into her mouth to stop herself from crying aloud in her excitement.

Murn hadn't told Evelyn about John Simpson's habits although on several occasions she had been on the point of doing so. But each time something had held her back, the 'something' being her very own Tom who still ogled Evelyn every time he saw her and often looked as if he could easily eat her.

Despite his weaknesses, Murn wanted to keep Tom. For the moment he served her purposes very well, and so she held her tongue about John's drinking and about several other unsavoury little titbits of gossip that had recently come her way concerning his past life. Evelyn would find out for herself soon enough – and surely he wasn't really the big bad ogre that his daughter Moira had made him out to be.

Tom had insisted that they go and visit Moira. 'It's high time you got to meet some more of my family,' he had said, taking Murn to a run down street in the Gorbals where Moira lived in a single room with her family of four children, her husband, Bob, having died three years before from gas poisoning he had received in the Great War.

Murn had been shocked to the core at the shabbiness surrounding Moira and her family. The place had smelled of cabbages and gas and though the young woman had been clean enough and the children surprisingly polite, Murn just could not get over the meanness of their surroundings.

She had refused to eat or drink anything in such a disgraceful house; one never knew what sort of germs were lurking in the motley assortment of cups with chips on the rim and tiny hair cracks round the sides. *And* there had been no saucers to put the cups on! Surely everybody could afford saucers – even if they got them from the ragwoman who came regularly to the Glasgow streets.

Yet there was something about Moira herself that was mannerly and kind. Her clothes had seen better days and a good hairdresser would have worked wonders with her hair: such beautiful hair, Murn had to admit, golden brown with just a hint of red where it shone in the gaslight, and such eyes: deep, deep blue, fringed by dark lashes that really did curl at the tips. Murn had sighed and felt rather jealous of those eyelashes as, all her life, right from young girlhood, she had wanted lashes just like them.

Then she had given herself a mental shake. How could she be envious of this poor girl with her spotty skin and her half-starved appearance? She looked as if she could be doing with a good dinner and Murn experienced a tiny inner glow of satisfaction as she visualised herself tucking a copper or two into Moira's apron pocket as she and Tom graciously took their leave.

So taken was she with her visions of philanthropy that it was quite a few minutes before she realised that Moira and Tom were discussing their father and that Moira was very shocked and concerned at the idea of him marrying again.

Turning to Murn she said urgently, 'You canny let your sister do this, Murn. My father is best off living on his own. He's already put one woman in an asylum – my mother, God rest her! He drinks, he womanises! He, he's cruel! No woman should have to put up with the likes o' him for a husband and if your sister is anything like you she'll be a lady and will never be able to cope with a man so ill-tempered and selfish.'

Murn hadn't listened to any more. Soon afterwards she and Tom had taken their leave, Murn, in her anxiety to be gone from the house, forgetting all about her former benevolent thoughts towards Moira.

But Tom was making up for her lack of charity. At the door he pressed some notes into Moira's hand and Murn wondered – unkindly – if the young woman's tears were of genuine gratitude or were simply an attempt to put on a show for the occasion.

As it was, Murn could hardly wait to get her husband home before tackling him about several questions that were running riot inside her head; the main one being just how much money he had given his sister and didn't he know that charity began at home, especially with two growing girls to feed and clothe and send to boarding school as soon after Christmas as was possible.

It was then that he had delivered his bombshell. He had decided that his daughters weren't going to boarding school. He wanted them to go to the same sort of school as other girls of their age. He wanted Murn to forget about Australia and stay on in Scotland to look after her stepdaughters. The education system in Scotland was second to none and anyway, as his first wife had squandered most of his savings, he simply couldn't afford fancy schools for the girls and that was the end of it.

A flabbergasted Murn had raged, threatened, nagged. No wonder they were poor! Drinking their money away in sickening binges that were the talk of the place! Giving all his money to people like his sister who looked quite fit enough to go out to work – any sort of work to make ends meet. How dare he expect her to stay on in this freezing country when she had been used to years of good and gracious living. How could he be so selfish as to deny her things like a decent home and a respectable quality of life. How! How! How! Why! Why! Why! She had gone on and on till in the end he had taken her by the shoulders and given her a good shaking and told her that she was a selfish bitch who thought only of herself and what she could get out of life.

'If you don't like things the way they stand, you can always leave and go back to Australia on your own!' he had warned. 'But me and the girls stay and that's final. The reason I went drinking with my father was to try and dissuade him from marrying Evie who deserves so much more than he could ever give. Not that that seems to worry you. Right from the start you've encouraged him in this matter and now, thanks to you, it's too late to change anything.

'As for my sister, she has done more work in one day than you have ever done in the whole o' your fat life! She would work her fingers to the bone – as she has done – if she could find a job. You live in a cosy little cocoon, Murn. You don't see or hear or care what's going on in the real world. But the time has come for reality, Murnsie, and you'd better learn to face it before it's too late.'

His ultimatum had deeply affected Murn. She had known a fear and an uncertainty for her future that she had never before experienced and it was a feeling that she didn't at all like.

So wrapped up was she in herself she completely forgot all about Evelyn and Moira and other poor souls like that. Her own wellbeing was at stake and that to Murn had always been far more important than anything else in the whole of the world.

She didn't want to lose Tom, she needed him very much in her life and even if his first wife had spent a good deal of his money there was plenty more where that had come from. Tom had always been a saver, he made good money in the Merchant Navy and things would improve with time.

When she had thoroughly analysed her own situation and had decided that it would be in her own interests to let Tom have his way for the time being, she turned her thoughts to Evelyn.

All things considered it was really just as well that her sister was going to marry John Simpson – who was she to stand in the way? With Tom having decided that they were all going to stay in Scotland, a footloose Evelyn would simply go on presenting a threat to Murn's security. There was no way that she was willing to cope with that – even if it meant the odd bout of unhappiness for Evelyn.

No, no, best just to leave things as they stood. Moira could talk herself blue in the face about her father for all the difference it would make to anybody. She was quite possibly exaggerating everything anyway. People like that always liked an audience and loved a bit of melodrama – it lent some excitement to their humdrum existence and made them feel much bigger than they were. All in all it was better just to ignore the likes of Moira McMaster and let events take their natural course.

It never occurred to Murn that she had interfered with the natural course of her sister's life when she had introduced John Simpson into it. She airily told herself that they would have been bound to have met up with one another sometime.

With all that off her mind she then turned it to the actual wedding itself, an excitement growing in her when she thought how suitable it would be to hold the reception here, in her own house . . . and – at this point she fairly bristled with the magnanimity of her own good intentions – she would ask Tom to pay for it . . . everything . . . He surely wasn't as insolvent as he was making out and Evelyn *was* her sister after all, as poor as a church mouse, the brave little dear, and quite unable to pay for anything herself.

'A salve to your conscience?' Tom had suggested dryly when she put all this to him, not bothering to conceal his disbelief when she made haste to assure him to the contrary.

'Of course, we'll have to be very careful who we ask,'

she hazarded, keeping her voice pleasantly conversational. 'Moira, for instance, would be a bit out of her depth . . .'

'Moira wouldn't come supposing you dragged her,' he had said dourly, glowering darkly at this maddeningly superficial wife of his. 'She hasn't spoken to my father for ten years, ever since he cut Bob open with a bottle for daring to oppose him over something trivial.'

'Cut him – open?'

'Ay, you heard, that's good old Pop for you. But back to the subject in hand. I'll pay for Evie's reception, I owe her that much. But first, hadn't you better ask her if she wants a reception at our house? She has her pride, lots of it, and she might not take too kindly to you arranging her life for her without her consent.'

'But of course she'll be pleased, Tom,' Murn had returned, genuinely surprised at the suggestion that someone in her sister's position could refuse such a generous offer.

'Ach, go ahead and accept,' Maggie had advised her youngest daughter, seeing her mouth setting into stubborn lines. 'Tom's a good man, he wouldna offer to do this unless he really wanted to. As for Murn, she's just a poor lost cratur who has never kent what she wanted from life, far less what other folks want from it. She'll enjoy arranging this party and there's no reason why you shouldn't just sit back and let her do all the hard work. After all, she foists Babs and Bessie onto you often enough and owes you a few favours.'

'Oh, Mam . . .' Evelyn, her mind in a turmoil over so many things at that point in her life, looked at her mother doubtfully. 'I'd hate having Murn cast any o' this up to me in the future. She's such a superior madam and is aye looking down her nose at what she calls "unfortunates".'

'Hmph.' Maggie made a face. 'It's herself who's been an unfortunate all her life through her own foolishness. She's never behaved like a mature woman and I doubt if she ever will. But you'd be the fool if you didna take Tom up on his offer. Just think, you'd be able to ask Nellie and Kenneth, Mary and Greg. It could be a real family reunion with all o' us meeting up together for the first time in years.'

Evelyn's green eyes were sparkling at the visions conjured up by her mother's words and she decided there and then to accept Tom's kind offer. To see Nellie and Kenneth again – and maybe Wee Col – would be worth anything that Murn might dole out in the future.

That night, when everyone was in bed, she sat at the kitchen table, pen poised above a blank page. It was hard, oh, so hard to swallow her pride and accept Murn's charity and for a long time she sat with her chin in her hands, staring at the shadows on the wall, her mind in a turmoil as it filled with thoughts of her future with John Simpson.

She had heard things, little snippets of gossip from the neighbours that made her feel uneasy every time she thought about it.

Alice Boyle was bedazzled by him and never tired of telling Evelyn how lucky she was to be getting a 'fine strong man like that.'

Theresa Leckie had no such illusions, 'The man's a lecher,' she told Evelyn bluntly. 'He's well known in the Gallowgate for his boozing and his womanising. What kind o' home does he keep, I'd like to know. Have you ever seen it, Evie, have you?'

Evelyn hadn't, and she had wondered about the same things as Theresa Leckie.

'It's only a little place,' John had told her smoothly when she had questioned him. 'A single man doesn't need more than that but you don't have to see it. I only sleep and eat there, the rest o' the time I'm working.'

Further questions were stifled when he placed his mouth on hers and she would forget everything but the excitement of being held in strong arms that made her feel safe. So safe.

It was the thought of his lips on hers that made her finally start to write an epistle that was brief and to the point:

December 1930

Dear Murn, Dear Tom,

I would be very glad to accept your kind offer to hold my wedding reception in your home. It needn't be anything grand, John and I have been wed before and he agrees with me that a quiet family affair would be best. Naturally I want all my family to be present, if possible, and hope you will discuss the guest list with me when the time comes.

Yours with gratitude,
Evie

When she had finished writing she put her pen very carefully on the table. She thought of Rothiedrum. She remembered the young Evelyn, brimming over with joy and the love of life, no worries, no cares; she remembered snow and sunlight; she thought of green parks and brown earth; she remembered Johnny and Florrie, both so young and filled with life, neither of them dreaming in those carefree days that they would lie too soon in the cold, dark earth, the moss and the ivy creeping over their gravestones gradually to erode their names.

And Gillie, darling Gillie, coming to her out of the dream that never left her, no matter what else happened, stepping out of the shadows to take her in his arms and lead her away to a wide clear path dappled with sunshine . . .

'Gillie, oh, Gillie,' she whispered into the silent room and putting her arms on the table she buried her head in them and wept.

Murn had had a wonderful time arranging everything to her satisfaction. She had started by having the decorators in to paint and paper 'the lounge' as she liked to call the large living room; she had haggled over prices with the caterers and had thoroughly enjoyed every minute of it; she had seen to the cake and the flowers and had remembered every last detail.

Tom had tried to tell her she was spending too much, but for once in her life she had thrown caution to the wind in her determination to show everyone just what she could do when she set her mind to it.

'It's a matter of principle, Tom,' she had told him severely. 'You wouldn't like a shoddy little do for my sister and your father, would you now? Better to do a thing properly if you're going to do it at all and in that way no one can cast anything up to you later or tell you that you have stinted.'

Tom was glad now that he had allowed her a free hand because he had to admit that she had made a beautiful job of everything. The buffet table was set with a mouthwatering array of cold hams, chicken, duck, turkey. Candlelight glinted on the crystal glasses and winked off the little jugs hanging from their hooks on the punch bowl. Baubles and tinsel sparkled on the enormous Christmas tree standing in a corner of the room.

On a small table stood the wedding cake, unpretentious as Evelyn had requested, decorated simply with a sprig of white heather and a spray of wax orange blossom.

Murn hadn't gone to the Registry Office with Tom, saying she wanted to be on the spot to see to the guests as they arrived. In truth she just wanted the house to herself so that she could wander about and savour the results of her labours.

She was wearing ivory silk that day. The gleaming folds of the material flattered her heavy bosom; her too-tight corsets gave emphasis to what was left of her waistline; a long dark skirt took away her stumpiness and gave the impression of a tall, well made, but elegant woman.

Her hair was swept up in dark, shining coils. She had spent hours in front of the mirror, resulting in dark-shadowed, mysterious eyes, perfect bow lips and a china doll complexion that owed itself to lashings of peach coloured make-up. This helped to disguise the age lines she had acquired in Australia – as long as she stayed out of harsh, revealing lights.

Wandering into the bedroom she sat herself down in front of the mirror to examine her reflection critically.

She liked what she saw – in fact she could hardly take her eyes off herself. Standing up she studied her figure side on. Her tightly restrained stomach looked satisfyingly flat, emphasising the soft, curvaceous swell of her silk-clad bosom; her hair was so gloriously bouffant it made her white neck seem swan-like and delicate; her eyes were big and dark with excitement, her face glowed.

She put her fingers to her lips and gave a self-satisfied chuckle. She would outshine them all, even Evelyn with her tumbling mass of rich hair and her wonderful good looks. One needed much more than mere beauty to pass muster in the eyes of the world. Poise, elegance, intelligence, a woman needed all these attributes to get on in the world and poor Evelyn had none of these graces. Little wonder she'd stayed in a rut all her life and would probably go on in the same miserable fashion for the rest of her days . . .

Murn's eyes strayed to the mirror again. She instantly forgot Evelyn and instead concentrated all her thoughts on the afternoon ahead. Mary and Greg would be here shortly, as would Nellie and Kenneth Mor . . .

Kenneth . . . Murn's heart began to beat swiftly and strangely and a tiny pulse throbbed deep in her groin.

Oh, he couldn't fail to notice her now! She had burgeoned into a ripe, desirable woman, one very far removed from the plain little slip of a girl he had once rejected in favour of that skinny, boyish Nellie with her breasts so flat they had seemed like pancakes straight off the girdle. But nothing about Nellie could be as hot as that! She had been a cold bitch — cold and stiff and unresponsive.

How a rich-blooded man like Kenneth Mor had looked the way of a born spinster like Nell Christina Grant never ceased to amaze Murn. But then Nellie had practically thrown herself at him — and poor Jeannie hardly cold in her grave. He had been too numb with shock and grief to know what he was doing at the time and Nellie had made sure she was available, in the right place at the right time.

Murn forgot how she had thrown herself at Kenneth; she forgot her drunken orgy at a tinker's camp in a field near King's Croft when she had danced naked round the fire for all the world to see. She forgot how Kenneth had berated her and had warned her never to speak ill of Nellie again . . .

'She has heart and blood and guts, that woman, and I'm honoured that she's going to be my wife!'

The voice of Kenneth Cameron Mor seemed to echo down through the years . . . 'You'll never be a fit woman for any man until you stop thinking so much of yourself! Never, ever again in your life must you bring such shame on your family as you have done this night . . .'

Murn put her hands over her ears as if, by so doing, she would shut out such memories forever. The feelings of disgrace and humiliation of that dreadful time had festered inside her for years . . .

But it didn't matter now. With a self-satisfied tilt of her head she pushed all such black thoughts to the back of her mind and concentrated instead on the future.

It was eerie, the way time had of changing everything. Soon she would see Kenneth again and they would fall in love as they ought to have done all these years ago. He had always loved her but cold and calculating Nell Grant had manipulated him into thinking otherwise.

'All things come to she who waits,' Murn whispered to her reflection in the mirror — and a voice over her shoulder

Chapter Six

Jamie was sorry now that he had worn the shirt Maggie had said was much too small for him. As usual she was right – she always had been. If he had listened, he wouldn't be feeling that he was being stifled in this too-hot room of Murn's. That little maid with the watchful eyes seemed always to be popping in to check the fire and kept heaping on the coal as if her life depended on it.

Then Jamie remembered. Murn was never done complaining about the cold. No doubt the maid had been given strict instructions not to let the fire go down even if the guests were roasted to death in the process.

Jamie ran his fingers round the inside of his collar and hoped there would be something stronger to drink than pink punch. Murn hadn't asked him what he wanted, but had abruptly and without ceremony pushed a little jug of the pink liquid into his hand and had gone sweeping on to gushingly ask someone else what they would like to drink, there was plenty to choose from.

As Jamie watched her, he came to the conclusion that he really didn't like this shallow-minded daughter of his very much. Somehow she had never fitted into the family and it wouldn't have broken his heart if she had stayed on in Australia for the rest of her days.

A defiant expression came into his eyes and he fingered the gill of whisky nestling in his pocket. He had promised Maggie he wouldn't drink too much of the hard stuff today – but to hell! One little mouthful wouldn't do any harm. He needed something to pep him up, God knows!

He considered the wedding party: Evelyn marrying John Simpson, an unknown quantity who was about to enter their lives and turn everything upside down; Alex skulking and sulking in a corner and hating his new stepfather with all his heart; that calculating little minx Babs, eyeing the boy in her sly fashion, and Murn, bloody Murn! Ready to turn on the charm for everyone but him, teetering about on shoes that were too tight – in fact, in an effort to control the rolls of fat, everything Murn had chosen was too tight.

The corners of Jamie's mouth lifted in a mischievous smile. He waited to catch her eye, then openly and deliberately he took out his bottle, uncorked it, and poured a generous amount down his throat . . . he wasn't going to waste it by adding it to the innocuous pink stuff she had doled out.

'Father!' She came immediately over to him and tried forcibly to wrest the bottle from his hand. 'You can't behave like that! Not here, in my house!'

He grabbed the bottle back and glared at her. 'Would you like a tug-o'-war, Murn lass?' he asked grimly. 'When our guests arrive we could get everybody to watch and maybe give a prize to the winner.'

'Oh, Father,' she said in exasperation but shrank back from him as if she had been bitten. She gave her hair a little affected pat and looked anxiously towards the door.

Where *was* everyone? They should all have come together, with the exception of those who had gone to the Registry Office to see the couple being married. Maggie and Jamie were to go, but Jamie had been ill for the last day or two and had said he didn't feel up to going to Glasgow and Maggie hadn't wanted to go without him.

His liver, Murn thought grimly. As for Maggie, she could have gone if she had really wanted to but she had never hidden the fact that she didn't like John Simpson one bit and was bitterly opposed to the marriage.

The doorbell went . . . Murn's heart missed a beat. In through the portal Sarah was ushering a large, well-upholstered woman with a happy red face and black hair pinned in coils round her ears. She was extremely deaf and was speaking in a loud, hearty voice that everyone could hear whilst grinning benevolently all round the room as if she was royalty personified.

In front of her she was pushing an enormous wickerwork wheelchair containing a tiny, wizened woman with a querulous voice and poor eyesight that made her peer closely at everything and everyone.

Murn groaned. Fanny Jean Gillespie with her dogsbody, big Lizzie! For quite a few years now Evelyn had worked for Miss Gillespie in her drab, grey villa in the Drumoyne area of Govan and, though the imperious little woman often drove her to distraction with her whines and her demands, she had grown attached to both her and Lizzie over the years.

But Murn hadn't imagined that the attachment had gone this far! To invite them to a wedding reception in *this* house. That dreadful wheelchair, wrinkling the carpets! Squelching and squeaking on the polished wooden floors! Lizzie's rough voice. Fanny Jean's reedy tones.

'Oh, look!' Lizzie was pointing, in a most common manner Murn thought with a shudder, to the table containing the show of wedding presents. 'There's our tablecloth! Right at the front.'

So saying, she grabbed Miss Gillespie's wheelchair in a most businesslike manner and propelled it over to the table. Both elderly ladies glowed with gratification at the prominent position of their gift. And little wonder; it was an exquisite cloth, hand embroidered by Fanny Jean herself, the luxuriant edging of frothy lace having been added by Lizzie who had painstakingly hand-sewn on every flounce.

Fanny Jean had declared she had spent the last of her eyesight executing all the close work needed on the cloth; she had complained long and loudly to Lizzie about poor lighting, thread that kept breaking, needles with eyes that were too small.

She had, in fact, put Lizzie through hell in the weeks it had taken to do the cloth. Every time Fanny Jean picked it up she had complained. She would never get it finished in time! Never! In the normal way of things, the kind of needlework she had been taught as a daughter of the manse would have taken months to execute. For this kind of work she needed time, lots of time. She simply refused to turn out a shoddy job. Shoddiness went against her principles and talking of that, wasn't it high time Lizzie polished all the brasses and cleaned the house for the festive season?

In her young days the maids had kept the manse spick and span. Weeks before Christmas the cleaning and the preparations had started. No one was allowed to be slipshod in their work, more to the point, the servants took a positive *pride* in keeping the place shining and clean.

She had always been used to proper care and attention! And though she had been taught to be self-reliant and self-sufficient there came a time in one's life when one was forced to turn to others for help. It was all so difficult. People didn't respect their betters any more and somebody with her sort of upbringing surely merited a bit of respect.

Now that she was virtually confined to a chair she needed more consideration than ever ... Oh, and would it be possible for her meals to be served in a reasonably tempting manner in future? With her delicate stomach she just could not take any more of Lizzie's rough and ready attitude to cooking and besides all that, it was a waste, just a waste of good food to simply dollop it onto a plate and expect it to be eaten. She hoped it wasn't mince for dinner again. Mince was for farmers and other menial workers, not for ladies who had been brought up to appreciate the more delicate aspects of the culinary field.

Having said that, these were difficult times. Money didn't grow on trees, one had to show an example. Thrift, that was the thing, it was respectable to be thrifty, it was vulgar to throw things away unnecessarily . . .

At the manse nothing had ever been wasted, it was all a matter of serving food properly. Her father – God rest him – had actually lowered himself once to visit the kitchen when a new cook had taken the place of her old and absolutely dedicated predecessor. There, in these lowly portals, he had demonstrated how food should be arranged on plates and dishes and other such accoutrements.

The woman was eternally grateful to him for showing her the way. Of course, that was in the days when one could help oneself from individual platters and was free to take what one's appetite dictated. Nowadays it was a case of having to make do with everything thrown willy nilly onto a plate and never mind how it looked. One was still expected to eat it. Not that she was complaining, mind you, but just a little consideration now and again would go a long way.

When she was a child, for instance . . .

At that point Lizzie had thrown a tantrum. There, in front of her employer, she had simply lost control, starting off by hurling the tray she had been carrying at the wall. It had landed with a tinny clatter; mince and mashed potatoes had slithered down onto the floor that Lizzie had polished only that morning; pink blancmange had splattered all over a painting of a Highland sunset, adding its own particular hues to those already depicted.

Lizzie had never thrown a tantrum before, that was usually Fanny Jean's department. All through her years as the little lady's companion-cum-housekeeper-cum-unofficial nurse, Lizzie's cheerily buoyant nature had enabled her to weather the storms and keep her head above water.

But Lizzie could stick up for herself, of that there was no doubt. She and Fanny Jean argued incessantly. When Fanny Jean was in one of her whining moods Lizzie could goad her to fury by pretending to be deafer than she was so that Fanny had to repeat everything and ended up yelling herself into exhausted silence.

Mostly Lizzie contented herself talking behind her employer's back, even if it was just to herself in the kitchen. If Evelyn was available the tales of woe were poured into her ears but normally Lizzie was a happy soul who was easily pleased by simple pleasures and the small enjoyments of her life.

But the matter of the tablecloth had proved the final straw. Lizzie had quite simply had enough, her over-stretched nerves could take no more. She had had a hot, busy time of it in the kitchen trying to make her mince look as tempting on the plate as was possible. Fanny Jean kept her on a strict budget. There was never enough money for the more expensive cuts of meat and with Christmas coming on the little lady had been more frugal than usual, resulting in mince being served for the third time that week.

She said, and here Fanny Jean's heart went cold with fear, that over the years, any amount of people had wanted her for their companion and she didn't know what had made her stay on in a place where she was neither wanted nor appreciated. She was going to pack her bags right now, that very minute, and she didn't care if an old, unappreciative bitch like Fanny Jean landed up in an institution for the rest of her days.

Later, when she was able to review the incident clearly and coolly, Fanny Jean maintained to herself that people like Lizzie simply didn't know how to conduct themselves in front of their more self-controlled superiors. But for now Fanny Jean, knowing that she would never get anyone else as tolerant or as capable as the good natured Lizzie, was beside herself with anxiety for her future.

The idea of an institution struck terror into her heart and so she cajoled, she begged, she wept, she wailed. But when a stony-faced Lizzie showed no sign of unbending, Fanny Jean was forced to resort to the most desperate measure of all, that of offering Lizzie a rise in wages for her services, though of course it couldn't be much since Fanny Jean was not a rich woman and could ill afford an extra burden on her already strained finances.

'A pound a month,' she had stated, not daring to look at the other woman's face because the air still boiled with heated rage.

'A week,' Lizzie said grimly.

'I could never afford –!' Fanny Jean could see only the back of Lizzie's heels as she made for the door.

'All right! All right! A pound a week! But don't blame me if we have to eat sparingly for the rest of our days.'

'You'll get mince and like it!' Lizzie had dictated triumphantly. 'You'll be served scrag-end soup, hough, rabbit – all the things I'm forced to buy wi' the pittance you dole out! If you want anything better you'll have to pay for it. If you don't, you'll get mince and tatties till they're coming out your ears and that's my final word on the subject.'

Fanny Jean had shuddered but she hadn't dared make one single protest. Lizzie had gotten her rise in pay, Fanny Jean still got her hough and her suet pudding, but the air had cleared considerably since 'The Day of the Tantrum'. The two ladies were more friendly than they had ever been. They had worked together on the tablecloth in an amicable fashion and when it was finished they had poured praise into one another's ears until they were filled to bursting with pride in themselves.

The cloth was truly a work of love. They both thought the world of Evelyn and genuinely hoped she was making a move for the better by marrying John Simpson, even though in private they thought he was much too old for her but understood that the children needed a father and she needed a man about the place again.

They had been delighted when Evelyn had issued them with an invitation to the wedding and they were out to enjoy themselves even though that odd elder sister of Evelyn's was watching them in rather a haughty fashion and making no move to welcome them to the house.

*

87

Murn's nerves were stretching tighter and tighter with every passing second. When the doorbell went again she gave a visible jump and held her breath as Sarah rushed to answer the summons.

This time it *was* the wedding party, piling inside, all talking at once. Grace, who had been matron of honour, had given Evelyn much of her time and attention that morning. Evelyn's dress of palest green complimented her auburn hair which was tied up with ribbons woven through with white roses. Her green eyes were glowing and she held onto the arm of her new husband – a fine handsome figure in a dark suit with a white buttonhole.

Grace herself, ethereal in white, was more beautiful than ever but her smile didn't quite reach her eyes and she kept them strictly averted from John Simpson even though he was being very attentive and charming. He had pawed her several times in the course of the day. No one had noticed, he was far too careful for that, and Grace felt sick every time she looked at Evelyn and wondered what sort of future was in store for her as the wife of such a lecherous creature.

Greg and Mary bore down on Murn to kiss her and exclaim and make a fuss, even though Mary and Murn had never really seen eye to eye and had barely tolerated each other when they were all children together at King's Croft.

Mary had lost a good deal of the weight she had put on when her life had been too soft and bountiful. Not so very long ago she had been a lot like Murn: spoiled, self-indulgent, conceited, but she had learned a sharp lesson when Greg had almost died from a stroke and now they were very happy living in the country just outside Edinburgh.

Greg, his dark hair liberally sprinkled with white, was walking with only one stick. One day he hoped to take up doctoring again but for now he was quite content to potter in his garden, to paint, walk his dog, catch up on all the things he had missed when he had been too busy to appreciate the simple pleasures in life.

His greeting to Murn was full of his usual warmth but she wasn't really listening to anything he said, she was staring past everyone, ignoring Tom, ignoring even Nellie whom she hadn't greeted yet. Her eyes were only for Kenneth Mor, out there in the lobby talking to Sarah in his friendly fashion. His big, hearty voice boomed out of the massive lungs of him, his laugh was rich and sweet and deep. Murn seemed to float out to him as if she was a feather, feeling strange and weightless and light-headed with exhilaration.

He turned, he saw her. 'Murn! Murn, lass! After all these years,' he cried and without ado he folded her to his great, broad chest. She lay heavily against him. She had waited years for this moment and now that it was here she wasn't going to waste a second of it. Her heart was beating a tattoo inside her breast, she felt beautiful, desirable, desired. She knew he had waited for this moment too and was savouring it as much as she.

His enfolding arms were tight and strong around her, his kiss on her cheek was filled with controlled passion. She smelled the heat and the virility of him and her legs trembled with mounting excitement.

'Kenneth, oh, Kenneth,' she whispered into his neck. 'I've waited so long for this. I can hardly believe it's here at last.'

'Ay, lass, ay.' He patted her back with a hint of awkwardness. 'But look now, I'm no' the only one waiting to welcome you. Nell's here, you and she will have a lot to talk about after all this time.'

Murn's arms tightened around his neck. His cool blue eyes took on an expression of unease. He had been taken aback at this first sight of her. His last memories had been of a thin young girl with a sweet face and a sad expression in her eyes. The bloated, harshly-made-up woman who had come rushing out to throw herself at him would take some getting used to. She was like a stranger to him and he didn't like the way she was clinging to him and saying his name in that breathy, intimate fashion.

'Come on.' He shook her off and all but pushed her away from him. At that precise moment someone snapped on the overhead light in the lobby. Murn had been very careful with the lighting that day. She had made sure that only the soft glow of pink-tinted lamps lit the rooms, and she winced as the harsh white light flooded the narrow lobby.

She no longer looked like a painted china doll. Her over-zealous welcome to Kenneth Mor had caused her carefully arranged hair to come undone so that it now hung in crinkly loops around her face; her eye shadow had smudged; the merciless electric light probed every powdered wrinkle in her skin. She looked tired and old and very fat and she was certainly in no fit state to come face to face with Nellie who appeared in the lobby just then.

It was a terrible moment for Murn. From the corner of her eye she saw Babs slink away, her face alight with satisfaction at having shown her stepmother in her true colours, so to speak.

Murn's face had gone pale with embarrassment and matters weren't helped by her first glimpse of Nellie. Of all the Grant sisters she had been the least attractive. She had been gaunt and flat chested; the high cheekbones of her face had always made her seem more mature than her years. At fifteen she had looked twenty, at twenty she had looked thirty but had stayed that way for years. Now at forty she looked ten years younger: she was still willowy but her bosom had filled out; her hips had burgeoned; her face was fuller; her beautiful eyes were like emeralds; her fair hair shone in the light; her full, sensuous mouth had tempted many a man but it was Kenneth and Kenneth alone who had her undying allegiance.

Murn's surprise was total. She bit her lip and her double chins trembled. Nellie's greeting was typically blunt and to the point. 'You've changed, Murn,' she said gruffly, 'I wouldna have kent you if I had passed you in the street.'

Murn looked as if she was going to cry. Nellie's heart softened. 'We've all changed, quine, it's grand to see you. I wondered what it would be like after all these years and I'm thinking it's good to have all my sisters around me the way it was when we were young.'

Nellie didn't like what she called 'palaver', but she unbent enough to hug her sister to her bosom and kiss her on the cheek. 'I've a surprise for you, Murn,' she said when she straightened. 'Remember Wee Col, your baby brother? Well, he's here, waiting to see you.'

She took Murn's hand and drew her into the room to Wee Col as he had always affectionately been known, the only surviving son of Maggie and Jamie Grant. He had been born mentally flawed and physically frail and there had been no place for him in the busy hustle and bustle of King's Croft. Maggie had always blamed herself for not having given her husband a healthy son and she had found it hard to reconcile herself to Col.

From the start he had adored the one person in his life who had ever been able to handle him and in the end he had gone to live with Nellie and Kenneth in their croft in Kenneray where he had been reared with patience and with love.

Now almost twenty-two, he was thin and frail and looked as if just one blow would easily break him in two. The doctors had told Nellie he wouldn't live much beyond thirty, and more and more she treasured every minute of Wee Col's life. She had always poured her love into him but now she gave him even more of her time and affection so that he seemed so overflowing with love it spilled out of him and over every one he met, with few exceptions . . .

Nellie took his hand and led him over to Murn. 'This is your sister, Murn,' Nellie explained carefully and slowly.

'She's been living far far over the sea but has come home now to be wi' her family.'

Murn didn't like this little introduction one bit. She glared at her brother and an expression of distaste crept over her bloated features.

With his head on one side, Col gazed at the very mature looking woman 'Nella' had said was his sister. His cornflower blue eyes were large and dreamy and, at that moment, strangely wise looking. His loose blubber of a mouth dripped saliva onto the knuckles of his big, awkward hands. He stared at Murn for several long moments before he stepped back, shaking his head.

'Take Murn's hand,' Nellie urged even though she would have liked to have knocked some sense into this overfed sister of hers.

Not so very long ago she had felt the same about Mary when she had behaved towards Col as Murn was behaving now. But Mary had learned her lesson, not least from Col himself when he had treated her like an immature child in front of her maid. But Nellie somehow knew that Murn was not going to learn any lessons, from Col or from anyone else.

The idea of physically touching this bony, frail lad, 'dripping with saliva' as Murn put it to herself, was enough to turn anyone's stomach and she kept both hands very firmly to herself.

Col himself took matters upon his thin shoulders. 'Not my sister,' he stuttered in his indistinct voice. 'Old, too old. Fat, too fat. Gargoyle, gargoyle, gargoyle.'

Murn was able to make out only some of this highly insulting assessment but it was enough for her to seize Col by the shoulders and shake him till his thin neck wobbled on his shoulders and his golden-red head flopped helplessly this way and that.

Mary got there even before Nellie. She wrested the terrified boy from Murn's vice-like grip and both she and Nellie led him away to sit him down on a sofa to soothe his terrors. Evelyn and Grace also came over to comfort him followed by Maggie. In minutes he was surrounded by family and love and, his courage returning, he peeped between all the feminine bosoms to Murn, standing heavily and haughtily in the middle of the room, trying to look as if she was in full control of herself. 'Gargoyle,' he repeated triumphantly. 'Fat gargoyle.'

The dimples showed in Evelyn's cheeks. 'Where did he learn *that*?' she asked Nellie.

Nellie's lips twitched. 'In a children's book o' fairy stories. I never thought he had taken much o' it in but it just goes to show – you can never tell wi' our Wee Col.'

Alex was bored with the reception. It had been wonderful to see Nellie and Kenneth again but they were too taken up with the family to pay much attention to him. He glared over at his new stepfather who had been the essence of good nature and charm ever since his arrival at fat old Murn's house.

But Alex had watched him closely and had seen the beast emerge from the thin veneer of civility he was putting on for the occasion. First it had been his hands sliding all over his new wife's body when he thought no one was looking. Evelyn had been embarrassed and had admonished him before moving away to talk to Nellie and Mary.

Babs had soon filled the gap. She had wandered over to him, wiggling her hips, her head tilted back in that provocative way of hers. John Simpson had fairly ogled her, his very own step-granddaughter! She was no blood kin of course ... even so ... the idea of a man his age eyeing a young girl was repulsive to Alex. She was a tease and a flirt, but he was old enough to know better and should have sent her packing with a few choice words.

And this was his mother's new husband! The cold reality of that hit Alex afresh and his hatred of John Simpson kindled anew. He vowed he would do everything in his power to make the man's life as unpleasant as possible. He wouldn't do anything that was asked of him; from now on he would go his own way and lead his own life and serve them all right if one day he ran away and never came back.

He glanced over at his mother. She was sparkly-eyed and beautiful. Her simple green dress looked wonderful on her and her hair was the colour of a ripe chestnut, all piled up on top of her neat little head. How different from that frumpy Murny sister of hers. Alex wished he could build up a hatred against his mother but the only emotions he could muster were resentment, sadness, and strong pangs of dread for the future that lay ahead of all of them.

Poor old Grandpa Jamie, sodden with drink and growing weaker every day; poor, big, strong Maggie, each year sapping the strength out of her till she had lost a good bit of the fight that had once shone in her.

Alex thought of his sisters and brother. Meg would get by. Although she felt bitterness towards John Simpson she would survive, by fair means or foul.

Little Rachel, sensitive, gentle and kind, would fight bravely to remain an individual. In spite of her gentleness she had her Grannie's spirit and she would keep her head above water.

But little James would go under. His nervous disposition meant that he couldn't take trouble and stress and there was going to be a lot of that in the coming years. John Simpson would try and flatten them all with his tempers and his demands.

He was basic, raw, mean. Alex had sensed all these things from the start and he was surprised that his mother hadn't sensed them also. She had strange powers, she had the second sight ... Alex sighed. John Simpson had blinded her, she was besotted by him, she hadn't been herself ever since he had come into her life and the awakening was going to be a rude one when it came — as it would in the very near future.

So, young Alex Grainger, possessed of a wisdom that often went beyond his years, summed up his family and his life. So wrapped up was he in his thoughts he didn't notice the approach of Babs till she was standing so close to him he could smell the heavy sweet perfume she was wearing.

'Alex,' her voice was deliberately husky, 'you've been avoiding me all day. Didn't you see the trick I played on my dear stepmother? When I switched on the light her poor face was a picture – one that she didn't want anyone to see.'

'It was a rotten trick to play,' Alex growled, for even though he wasn't very fond of his aunt he had felt the acuteness of her embarrassment as if it were his own.

'Never mind her,' Babs went on, her tone of voice rising slightly. 'I only did it because I was bored with all these old people gassing away about nothing.' Her eyes narrowed, she tilted her head. 'I know a place we can go, Alex, a place with a door that locks. You haven't been very nice to me ever since that day old Conkers took you into her stinking house. I've missed you, Alex, you showed such promise too . . . I never thought any boy of twelve could be so – well endowed.'

Alex looked her full in the face. She was running the glistening tip of her tongue over her top lip in a very suggestive fashion. He could see the little trail of moisture it left in its wake.

Painstakingly, because she was no seamstress, Babs had succeeded in lowering the neck of the rather drab dress that Murn had bought her for the reception. The smooth, white swell of her breasts rose up invitingly from the restraining folds of material. Alex could plainly see the hard, swelling tips of her nipples thrusting out and he knew she was feeling sexually excited.

He glanced over at John Simpson and wondered what he had said to Babs to make her react like this . . . but in the next second the boy remembered his last intimate encounter with her and he realised she needed no encouragement to behave as she was doing.

Ever since that incident he had kept well out of her way. She was a bit too hot for him to handle; there was something utterly reckless about her; she was exciting and she was dangerous. He would be playing with fire if he took her on and he wasn't yet ready for the sort of sexual adventures she had in mind.

'Alex,' she said persuasively, 'I've got to go to the bathroom. It's a nice place, there's a carpet on the floor and the door locks. But it's dark in the lobby, Stepmummy put out all the lights. I wonder if you would come with me because I'm afraid of the dark?'

She gazed at him meaningfully, her tongue sweeping slowly over her lips. He felt a stirring in his trousers, excitement mounted in him. He didn't even glance backwards as he followed her out of the room and into the lobby.

Together they slipped into the bathroom. When she turned to face him the remainder of her bodice buttons were undone and her breasts were hanging out, full, ripe, tantalising.

'They're for you, Alex,' she said and her voice had changed. It was low, breathless and imperative. She fumbled with his trouser buttons, her eyes growing as big as saucers when she saw how sexually aroused he was.

'Alex Grainger,' she said in delight, 'you're enormous! You'll kill me with that, you'll burst me wide open.'

'I won't,' he grunted. 'You needn't worry about anything like that. I know what I'm doing, you're not the first.'

They kissed in a frenzy; he pushed her to the floor. Everything about her was moist, willing, and waiting, and she was ready to give this strapping young Grainger everything she had.

John Simpson watched the youngsters slipping away. His eyes gleamed. He was remembering the way that Babs had looked at him a few minutes ago. He had openly eyed her body, she had gazed insolently back at him.

'One o' these days, my fine young lady,' he had whispered, his blue eyes snapping with excitement.

'One of these days, *Grandfather*,' she had replied, holding his gaze with her own while she took exaggerated breaths that pushed her cleavage to its limits.

John Simpson saw the future stretching before him, rosy and full. At last he would have a decent roof over his head, proper food in his belly. He would soon sort out the Graingers and the Grants, have them running to his bidding.

He thought of Babs again. 'Bloody wee hoor,' he thought, 'she's asking for it and I've got plenty to give her.'

But for now he had bigger fish to fry. That bonny bitch who was now his wife had made him wait long enough for his rewards – but tonight he would make up for it – by God and he would!

Chapter Seven

Evelyn would always remember her first night as the wife of John Simpson. There had been no tenderness or love, but he had subjected her to nightmarish hours of lust, perversion and cruelty, from which she emerged bruised, bleeding and disgusted.

He had made quite certain that they had the kitchen to themselves. There had been no question of a honeymoon, only the rich could afford such luxuries. Maggie and Jamie had been relegated to The Room to sleep with the children. Meg had moaned long and hard about having to give up her lovely big brass double bed to her grandparents but she soon quietened when John Simpson put his face close to hers and said, 'Maybe Miss High-and-Mighty would prefer to sleep on the floor? I could arrange that quite easily.'

Meg held his eyes with a look of such blackness he could feel it oozing from her every pore. His hands had balled into fists, he held them threateningly close to her face but she was not to be browbeaten. In Margaret Mary Grainger he knew he had met his match.

Alex had intervened at that point. His own fists hard and ready, he spoke warningly to his new stepfather.

'The conquering hero, eh?' John Simpson sneered, his eyes flashing in delight. 'And wi' Miss Gypsy-Wets-Her-Knickers too. Don't think I don't know about that because I do. I know everything that goes on and is ever likely to go on in this house . . . which by the way is now mine and will soon have my nameplate on the door.'

'We'll see about that,' Jamie piped up. 'The brass plate wi' the Grant name on it stays, and no question about it.'

'Ay,' Maggie said supportively. 'You're no' going to get all your own way, John Simpson, so you can just think again about whose house it is.'

He had laughed then; a soft, insidious laugh which seemed to leave his throat as a living creature to go crawling along every shivering spine in the room.

Both Maggie and Jamie shuddered and the children huddled into a tight knot.

'I have better things to do wi' my time than stand here arguing,' John Simpson sneered. 'My bonny new bride awaits and I will serve her right well, I can assure you o' that. Meanwhile, you'd best all get to bed, you've had a tiring day . . .' here he glanced meaningfully at Alex, 'and an early night won't do you any harm.'

Rachel lifted little James into her arms and Alex put his arm round Meg's shoulder. She glanced at him shyly, grateful to him for risking their stepfather's ire on her behalf.

Rachel climbed into one end of the chair bed with little James, Meg got in at the top, Alex retired to his cupboard recess and Maggie and Jamie sat at the hearth, waiting for the children to sleep so that they might get privacy to undress.

John Simpson turned down the gas mantle as if he was the warden of a home for delinquent youngsters.

In the darkness Jamie struck a match which he applied to his pipe. In the small flare of light his eyes were black, something of the old Jamie lingered in their depths. 'A big change from a model lodging house, Simpson,' he said softly. 'Oh, ay, I ken all about you. You're notorious in the Gallowgate and just lately I've been having a bit o' a chin wag wi' some drinking cronies o' mine. I found out quite a lot about you so you watch your step in this house or there'll be trouble and it will all be yours. You found yourself a soft number when you married my daughter but I warn you, lay one wrong finger on her and I will personally cut off your hand.'

'An old soak like you! Threatening the likes o' me!' John Simpson's words were sarcastic enough but his voice was uneasy in the darkness. 'Go and sook your bottle, old man, for that's about all you're good for now.'

Without another word he left The Room. Maggie smiled. 'You've got him worried, Jamie, my man. He'll aye try to browbeat us, it's in his nature to be a bully. But there's only one o' him, thank the Lord, and, as far as we're concerned, there's safety in numbers. So stick together, bairns, and you'll be safe.'

'Ay, Grannie,' came the chorus in the dark. But no one sounded very enthusiastic. It had happened. John Simpson had married their mother. They had a new father. Nothing would ever be the same again.

Alex thought of Davie, his real father. He remembered when Davie had taken his slipper to him and had thrashed him for the first time in his life. He had been humiliated and hurt beyond measure but he had needed that hiding and he had learned his lesson. The slipper had never again been taken to his backside.

A vision flashed into the boy's mind: his father smiling, his shock of curly, earth brown hair blowing in the wind, his arm reaching out to Alex to pull him in close and tell him he was a good lad. Alex felt his throat tighten. He missed that man, he missed him so much he sometimes wished he was dead himself so that he wouldn't hurt anymore.

His thoughts strayed to his mother. She had loved his father with all her heart. She had pined for him till she was worn to a shadow and had seemed neither dead nor alive. Alex had imagined that she would always grieve for her husband and never ever look at another man. How could she? How could she touch another man's body after being married to his father?

Sounds were filtering through from the kitchen. He tried to imagine what was going on in there but it was too difficult to believe that she would let John Simpson kiss her or touch her or do anything else that she had done when she was really young.

But she *had* allowed him to kiss her! He had caught them at it in the scullery that very first time John Simpson had come to visit.

He thought about her beauty, her sparkling eyes, that aura she had of earth and light and air. She wanted, she needed ... He thought of the things he had done with Babs in fat old Murn's bathroom and at this point his thinking became confused and disjointed.

A small, faint cry penetrated the night. He half sat up. She needed him. She was crying for him. He loved her more than he loved himself. It had taken him a long time to realise that but now he did and he had to protect her from everything.

But she had found another man, she had married John Simpson and he, Alexander David Grainger, was no longer the man of the house.

The cry came again. Sweat broke out on his body. His throat felt as if it was on fire. He put his head under the blankets and he wept.

Evelyn had had no idea of anything that had taken place in The Room. She had been too busy preparing herself for her new husband. She had taken her time about it, slowly, oh so slowly brushing her hair at the mirror, staring at her reflection as she did so. Her face had been pale in the glow of the paraffin lamp, her eyes big and anxious. The hard, starched material of her nightdress was certainly not meant to be sensuous, but it was white and it gave her a virginal-looking quality, especially with her hair hanging down her back like a golden-red curtain.

Sitting there she remembered her first night as the wife of David Grainger and it was as real to her as if it had happened just yesterday.

They had honeymooned at Croft Donald, a place of magical sounds and sights and smells. At night they could hear the familiar creak of the old timbers groaning and sighing as they settled down in the cool darkness.

Davie and Evelyn had lost themselves in the strength and the passion of their love. The billowy folds of the huge feather bed had enclosed them in a cloud of warmth while they immersed themselves in an ecstasy of love that seemed never ending.

Then had come the dawn and the awakening to a life that was good and sweet amongst the hills and the seas around Kenneray.

But for David and Evelyn that part of their life together was soon to be just a pleasant memory. The reality would come in the years of hardship that followed: there would be betrayals, heartbreak, grinding poverty, but somehow they would survive to emerge closer than they had been at the beginning, when all they had had was their passion to keep them together.

She had never failed her Davie; she had never been unfaithful to him; she had loved him with undying loyalty, even when she knew his allegiance to her had faltered and he had fallen.

And then he had died and the great love of her life was no more, only the grey ashes of her emptiness remained.

It had taken her a long time to realise that her life wasn't the meaningless void she had imagined it to be: Davie had given her his children, in them he still lived on, and because of that she had to give them the best start that she could.

But, in the dismal reality of the thirties, that idealistic outlook hadn't lasted long. There were no jobs, there was no money, no hope. She had become ill with worry and despair . . . and then had come John Simpson, a man who claimed he had a good steady job in the shipyards. The answer to her prayers had arrived: the children would have a father, she would have a husband who would go out to work every day, there would be no more poverty, no more pain . . . and what did it matter if she didn't love him? He would be a companion to her, he would talk with her and laugh with her, he would sleep with her and bring her comfort, and that was more than enough to keep any woman happy.

Davie, her love, was gone, Gillan was just a shadowy figure of the past, someone who came to her in dreams and what good was that in the harsh daily grind of her existence?

Even so, she remembered Gillie with love and affection. When she wasn't thinking about Davie she was thinking about Gillan Forbes of Rothiedrum, and imagining what it would have been like if he had come back into her life when she most needed him. In the impossible flights of her fancy, she would picture him marrying her and carrying her off to Rothiedrum House where they would all live happily ever after . . .

And now she was John Simpson's wife. Gone were the dreamings and the longings; the memories of Davie floated off into another sphere, the dreams of Gillie drifted off into infinity . . . She gazed into the mirror . . . and – strange, oh so strange! – she seemed to see the hazy images of both Davie and Gillie in the blotchy glass. Odd . . . her heart skipped a beat . . . Davie was the first to disappear, quite suddenly and abruptly, while Gillie remained for what seemed to be a long time before he too vanished, but slowly, like the mists she had known in the morning fields of King's Croft so long ago, so far away.

'Davie,' she whispered, 'I loved you so.' She put her hand to her eyes. She was crying. 'And Gillie,' she murmured, 'I loved you too, I always did – I still love you. I should have married you when you wanted me to.'

She started. What had made her say that? Never, ever in her life before had she even admitted it to herself. Her face was very white in the mirror. Her lips formed Gillie's name. It was out in the open now, the thoughts, the feelings she had always suppressed.

'I should have married you, Gillie.' She whispered the words into the warm darkness of the kitchen. Her whisperings seemed to bounce back at her from the shabby walls. This wasn't the place, this wasn't the time. All that was over ... over ... over. It was too late ... late ... late. The echoes of her voice were all around her. She shivered. She arose; no time now for regrets. She was John Simpson's wife – and the marriage bed awaited.

She had never imagined that any man could be so sexually insatiable. He had been like a beast of the wild, savagely claiming her body without thought to her feelings. When she had protested he had covered her mouth with smothering kisses that made her fight and gasp for breath.

'Evie, oh, Evie,' he had grunted over and over. 'You should never have made me wait so long. You've maddened me with waiting and wanting and I can't help myself tonight. You've got to do as I ask, you've – got to ...'

Behaving like a stag in rut he had made her kneel on the floor where he had penetrated her with brute force, not once but several times. In his madness he had bitten her legs, her stomach, her breasts and all the time she had been afraid to cry out because she didn't want any of her family to hear her cries of pain.

Sometime in the night, exhausted, lathered in sweat, he had fallen away from her to sink into a deep sleep and she had lain thankfully back, the swiftness of her heartbeat suffocating her, her breasts, her buttocks, aching, her mouth bruised and swollen.

With the exception of Whisky Jake, who had once tried to rape her in a house in the Aulton, she had never been afraid of any man. But, as she lay there beside her new husband in the dank, semen-smelling darkness, she knew that she was terrified of John Simpson.

Frightened to move in case she would wake him she had remained perfectly still and quiet for the remainder of the night. Only his snoring breaths broke the stillness. Outside the window the stars were shining. She watched the biggest and brightest winking in the heavens and some small measure of peace crept into her troubled breast.

Tomorrow was Christmas Eve, a day she had always loved for its air of quiet expectation and its atmosphere of tranquillity. There would be nothing very much for any of them that Christmas, nobody had any money to indulge in luxuries.

Nevertheless the children had been preparing for it. For weeks they had been making little gifts, hiding them from one another, building themselves up to make the coming event as exciting as possible.

They had made paper chains and lanterns which Alex and Jamie between them had hung around the house.

Alex had brought in a tiny fir tree, telling her he had done a deal with a street hawker. 'I gave him some o' my firewood in exchange for the tree,' Alex had explained, his eyes shining as he studied her face, waiting for her reaction.

She knew fine well that there was more to the tale than he was telling but she didn't pursue the matter further, instead she helped the children decorate the little tree. Now it stood on the dresser, its silver-paper baubles glinting in the darkness, the big star that Rachel had laboriously fashioned from scraps of shiny tinsel and cardboard also catching fragments of light from the window.

Evelyn's throat tightened. What had she done to her children? In marrying John Simpson she had exposed them to so many new experiences God alone knew what lay in the future for all of them.

Evelyn's mind strayed to the reception. It had been so good to see Mary and Greg, Nellie and Kenneth, but though Grace and Murn between them had offered to put the visitors up, not one of them would hear of it and indeed, they had all been very anxious to rush back to their homes.

So brief had been their stay the whole episode now

seemed like a dream. But Nellie's farewell words to her youngest sister had been real enough:

'You mind how you go wi' that new man o' yours,' she had warned. 'He's a tough one, like a broken bottle inside and as slippery as an eel on the outside. If the going ever gets too rough, you ken where to come for an escape. Kenneth and myself will aye be glad to welcome you to Croft Donald and dinna you forget that.'

She had taken Evelyn to her bosom and her arms had been protective and strong. On the way out she had treated her new brother-in-law to a venomous stare and the look Kenneth had thrown at him had also been distinctly lacking in affection.

Very carefully, Evelyn turned her head on the pillow to look at this man that nobody appeared to like very much. In the grey darkness everything about him was soft and blurred. His strong face looked peaceful in its repose, his arms were flung over the pillows like an innocent child, he had thrown off the blankets so that his strong, muscular chest was exposed.

Despite what he had put her through in the last hours she was unable to curb a small unwilling stab of longing in her belly. She had waited a long time to know the pleasures of John Simpson's body. If only he had behaved less brutally she knew she would have enjoyed her first night as his wife . . .

As it was . . . she shuddered. A mouse squeaked in the skirting . . . a little Christmas mouse, all alone and lonely in the sleeping house . . . just like her.

There had been mice at King's Croft, field mice seeking shelter from the winter elements. As a child she had often thrown crumbs to the tiny creatures, especially at Christmas when it seemed right and proper that every living thing should have some comforts.

Christmas had been wonderful at King's Croft, with the snow weighing down holly boughs that were already heavy with bunches of red berries. The bracken had made splashes of bronze at the edge of the woods and the fields were virgin-white except where footprints had made tracks across the great white plains.

Inside the croft all would be warm and steamy with Maggie or Nellie making clooty dumplings on the stove while mince pies and shortbread, black-bun and Christmas cake, sat cooling on the table.

She couldn't remember how many times Nellie had rapped her fingers for helping herself to a piping hot scone or a big, juicy sultana plucked from the depths of the black-bun. But Nellie's bark was often worse than her bite and to make up for her short temper she would give her sister a special little black-bun at the end of the day's baking.

The smells and the sights of those Aberdeenshire Christmases would remain with her forever. Nothing like them would come again and not even Murn, for all her fancy ideas and her big, flashy Christmas tree, could ever capture the flavour of those long ago festive seasons.

Thinking about Murn and her showy tree turned Evelyn's mind back to the reception. She remembered Murn, her behaviour with Kenneth Mor in the lobby. Poor, misguided, immature Murn. She had made a complete and utter fool of herself in front of everyone but had she learned her lesson, Evelyn wondered? Once she had tidied herself and had drunk a whisky or two she had made a good recovery and indeed, she had hung about Kenneth for the remainder of the afternoon. She had been most anxious for him and Nellie to stay the night at her house and she had gone harping on about it until it had become a point of embarrassment.

In the end Nellie had curtly told her to stop acting like a bairn while Kenneth himself had been glad to escape from his sister-in-law's clutches – but not before she had invited herself to Croft Donald for a holiday.

'Summer would be best,' she had decided, gazing into Kenneth's ice-blue eyes like a moon-struck schoolgirl. 'We can go walking together along the beaches. I always used to enjoy walking in Aberdeenshire and am quite looking forward to the bracing air of the sea. Kenneray sounds idyllic; perhaps we could picnic and sunbathe and swim and just enjoy the simple pleasures of life. Oh dear,' she had giggled girlishly, 'I am so convincing myself that the weather is going to be perfect I know I shall be *quite* devastated if it rains all the time during my stay. But never mind,' she brightened and treated Kenneth to a dazzling smile, 'I'm sure we shall find plenty to do indoors. I can help Nellie with the cooking and baking, the cleaning and the polishing. I was always a homemaker and I'm sure it will all seem quite delightful in the warm cosiness of that dear little croft-house.'

Kenneth, never one to suffer fools gladly, had stared at her during the first part of this discourse as if she was mad. Was the woman really as naive as she was making out? A farmer going on picnics! Sunbathing! Swimming! In the middle of summer! When every hour that God sent was filled with farm work!

He had lowered his brows and had looked at her. She had been brought up on a croft, Goddammit! Surely she knew she was talking rubbish and could no more expect a busy farmer to sunbathe than she could expect a newborn babe to rise up and walk.

Nellie had hidden a smile at the look on his face and had caught Evelyn's astounded eyes. Both sisters knew Murn only too well. In the blithe but busy days of their girlhood they had known what it was like to work in the fields from dawn till dusk while Murn stayed at home, her nose buried in a book, her ambitions to one day be a teacher firmly fixed in her mind.

At home she had been lazy, unwilling, unhelpful. Only under pressure had she ever dirtied her hands with menial croft work. She had never enjoyed exertion of any sort and would beg, borrow or steal a lift rather than walk anywhere. Only on sufferance did she lift a finger to help with household chores and Nellie had often been forced to take on more than her fair share of work.

Maggie had had continual rows with Murn on the subject of her laziness but Murn had gone on her way thinking only of herself until she had realised some of her goals.

But never content, never happy, she had wanted more and more from life and, in the end, had wanted that which was most out of her reach, Kenneth Cameron Mor. He had gone and married himself to Nellie which only went to prove that he had been too blinded with grief for Jeannie to rightly know what he was doing at the time.

But all that was in the past. He must have come to his senses a long time ago and had only put up with Nellie for the sake of convenience, for what else could he possibly see in her except a woman who made his meals and kept his home in reasonable order? He was just marking time, that was all, waiting for the day that his Murn would come back to him, offering the love and warmth that he had lacked all these years.

Murn had smiled at the expression on his face as she described her holiday with him at Croft Donald. She could almost feel his excitement; his eyes had been strange and glittering with anticipation, and she knew he had been visualising the two of them, strolling arm in arm along the wide, white beaches, a picnic basket in one hand, a rolled up tartan rug in the other.

And all the time he would be looking, seeking out a private, sheltered spot where they could lie together in the hot sun, his kisses searing her lips as frenziedly he released all the white hot passion he had bottled up for so long . . .

Murn's heart had missed a beat at that point, she hadn't dared let her thoughts carry her any further . . . besides . . . both Nellie and Evelyn were looking at her strangely, almost as if they could read her thoughts . . .

*

Evelyn moved her cramped limbs. The grey light of day was filtering in through the window. She forgot about Murn and concentrated instead on her aching body. She felt soiled and degraded, she knew she couldn't face any of her family until she had washed away the sights and the smells of John Simpson's excesses.

But some things could not be got rid of. After bathing her face in cold water for several minutes her mouth was just as swollen as ever and she wondered what her sharp eyed mother would have to say about it when she saw it . . . And what about her father – and Alex? They both disliked and mistrusted John Simpson. In their hatred they were united and would be only too ready to pick on anything that might help them to get back at him . . .

'Evie,' John's voice came heavy and sleepy from the bed recess. 'What are you doing up, lass? It's early, come back to bed.'

'I'll get you a cup of tea,' she said hastily. 'I'm dressed, John, the children will be through any minute.'

'Bugger them!' he said gruffly. 'They were well warned to stay away until I told them otherwise. Forget the tea and *undress*. You're my wife now and when I say a thing I mean it.'

She hadn't dressed at all but she stayed in the scullery as long as she dared, playing for time, praying that he would have gone back to sleep when she finally emerged. It was cold in the cheerless little enclosure; her feet and hands were like lumps of ice; she longed to make a cup of tea but didn't want to make any noise in case she should disturb him.

'Bed, Evie,' his voice came again, more insistently this time. Her heart as heavy as her feet she climbed back into bed to find him wide awake and ready to start again.

Without ado he gathered her into his arms, exclaiming a little at the feel of her coldness against his burning skin.

His lips nuzzled her hair. 'No wife o' mine stays cold for long,' he said with a mocking chuckle. 'Relax, girl, I'm no' going to eat you . . .' the laugh came again . . . 'Maybe just nibble you here and there till you're nice and willing.'

'Please, John,' she tried to push him away. 'I'm sore after last night, you were too rough. I can't stand any more o' that kind o' treatment.'

'Evie,' his hand slid over her breasts. 'I'll be gentle this time, I promise. I couldn't help myself last night. You made me wait too long, lass. This time you'll like it, this time you'll open your legs willingly and beg for more.'

His hands glided over her body, his finger-tips whispered over her nipples. He was tender and loving, persuasive in both his actions and his words. She could hardly believe that he was the same man of last night. She forgot her bruises and her aches, she forgot everything but his demanding mouth, his hard, exciting body. When at last his hand slipped between her legs she knew that she would always forgive him anything just as long as she got his tenderness and his love at the end of the day.

'Evie,' his lips moved against her neck. 'In time you'll grow to love everything I do to you. You'll enjoy the rough with the smooth. I'm that kind o' man, I can't help behaving like an animal . . . especially with a beautiful woman like yourself . . .'

With a strangely primitive moaning noise he mounted her and moved against her. His hands roughly tore at her breasts, his fingernails seared the skin of her belly. With a growl he drove himself into her, so roughly she felt faint with the pain. He bit her neck and her breasts, so immersed in his own pleasures he forgot everything but his desire to extract as much pleasure as possible from her body.

He was big and hard and burning inside her and he seemed to grow more enormous with every passing second. And then the curses came, filthy obscenities that she had only ever heard spoken in the meanest of the Glasgow streets.

Tears coursed down her face. Amidst her pain and her despair she concentrated hard on her memories of Gillan

Forbes of Rothiedrum and strangely ... he came to her vividly and clearly, reaching out to her to take her in his arms. It was as if he was right there in the room with her, comforting her and telling her it was all right. Telling her that one day they would find each other again and be together as they should have been when it had all begun for them – in the golden days of yesteryear when they had played and laughed as children in the woods and fields of their beloved countryside.

PART TWO

Summer 1931

Chapter Eight

Murn picked her way over the dusty pavements of Camloan Road as daintily as her girth allowed, and breathed a sigh of relief when number 198 hove into view.

Mrs Jenny Jack was sitting at her window, watching the world go by. She was a fearsome-looking woman with a jutting lower jaw, yellow-brown molars, and wiry grey hair scraped into a bun at the nape of her bulldog-like neck. One massive wrinkled arm, patched with dark brown liver marks, rested on a blue velour cushion on the window sill.

The children of the neighbourhood were extremely wary of Old Evil Eye as they had christened her. Her large unsmiling countenance was framed in the window from morning till night.

Never once had she been seen to smile, but she was wont to glare through her large round glasses at anybody who looked at her, especially children, and the only way they would dare to pass her window was as speedily as possible, staring straight ahead. Rumour had it that she had turned one of the backcourt moggies into a pillar of salt for daring to catch her eye. It didn't matter that the grown-ups said that the cat had fallen into a bucket of cement. As far as the youngsters were concerned, Old Evil Eye had cast one of her wicked spells over the unfortunate creature and no one else was going to run a similar risk.

In reality, poor old Jenny Jack was just a sick old woman with enormously swollen rheumaticky legs that kept her a prisoner in the house. Her only solace was the window and the activity of the street, since her husband, Jack Jack, a dapper man of near dwarf-like proportions, left her strictly to her own devices.

If anything, the children feared Jack Jack more than they feared his wife. His lack of size was no deterrent at all when it came to self defence, and indeed, his small stature was a distinct advantage when it came to dealing with children, since it meant he was just the right height for serving a hefty swipe with his surprisingly meaty fists. When he had first come to live at 198 Camloan Road he had been a source of ridicule amongst the youngsters, but he had soon gained a reputation as a bully among other things. Jack was a betting man. He was lucky on the horses and made enough from his winnings to enable him to indulge some of his fancies; he was also partial to refreshment in one of the 'better' pubs of the district; but his most talked of vice was his clandestine meetings with ladies of doubtful morals. He had been seen several times 'up a close', his breeks around his ankles as he 'rutted away' at some 'painted hussy'.

'But he pays good money,' Isa Boag had informed her cronies in a somewhat thoughtful tone of voice. 'Some say a fiver just for a quick poke in the back close.'

At this, Big Aggie stuck her nose in the air. 'I wouldny be seen dead wi' the wee runt, no' even if he paid me in tenners.'

Isa smirked, 'You'd be lucky. The wee man likes value for his money – so I'm told,' she added hastily.

Big Aggie was about to retaliate with venom when little Theresa Leckie intervened. 'Know the latest?' she intoned eagerly. 'Maisie Smith told Betty Wilson that Big Bella McDonald got a tenner off him for giving him a wee bit extra in a back close cludge in Younger Street.'

'Extra?' Isa Boag tried to keep her voice on an even keel.

'Ay, extra.' Theresa made them all suffer for quite a few moments before she relented. 'It would seem . . .' – here she lowered her voice to a reedy whisper – 'that she stood on the toilet pan and gave him everything she had.'

Big Aggie drew her fat brows together in puzzlement. 'She stood on the toilet pan . . . but I'm told he's that wee he canny do it in the normal way unless a hussy goes on her knees to him. How could he reach if she was standing on the toilet . . . ?'

'Aggie!' Isa spoke as if to an ignorant child. 'Use your imagination, think o' the things he could do to *her* from that angle.'

'Oh, ah see.' Big Aggie sounded none the wiser.

'Ay,' said Theresa with an impish smile. 'And when he had got her worked up good and proper she was supposed to have shouted "Geronimo!" and leapt on top o' him from the lavvy pan. Seemingly they went that wild they broke the lavvy seat and left the bum paper scattered everywhere.'

'It just goes to show.' Big Aggie shook her head and for once her dialogue was distinctly lacking in colour. She walked away, wondering if there was more to the facts of life than she already knew. The next time she came face to face with Jack Jack she stared at him with renewed interest, while in her imagination she pictured Big Bella throwing herself on top of him from a cludge seat in Younger Street.

Murn didn't know about the Jacks. In fact she knew very little about any of the residents of Camloan Road. She rarely visited her family, even though she lived just a few streets away. It was enough that *they* visited her occasionally; she was always on tenterhooks in case they should be looking for aid, financially or otherwise. In her opinion, people, whether they be family or no, should earn what they got — only down-and-outs and beggars looked for free handouts and they couldn't be expected to know any better.

But neither Maggie, Jamie or Evelyn had so far asked her for a penny piece and she did wonder about that since their circumstances were so dreadfully impoverished. Somewhere, buried at the back of her mind, was a vague memory of the Grant pride: Maggie's haughtily-tilted head, Jamie's spirited glance, Evelyn's proud shoulders.

But all that was such a long time ago and things had changed so drastically since then.

Sometimes, and here even Murn squirmed a bit at her own snobbishness, she half-wished they *would* ask for help just so that she could have the satisfaction of pointing out the benefits of self-sufficiency. Tom had told her often enough that it was easy for *her* to be self-sufficient since she wanted for nothing, and what could she do but let him know of all the little sacrifices she had to make through having his daughters continually at home.

Murn lifted her head and squared her shoulders. Yes, these girls were indeed a handful for any woman, especially that Babs, who very often stayed out till all hours and never did anything she was told. Her body seemed to grow more seductive every day and even Tom himself had been telling Murn to try and get the girl to show off less of her burgeoning breasts. As if she could! The girl was hell bent on making a career out of being a temptress, all she ever thought about was boys — and men — oh, yes, she ogled men too. Young, middle-aged, elderly, it didn't matter to Babs as long as they could show a good sized bulge in their trousers. Murn smiled to herself as she thought about these things. It was Tom's doing; he was so crude in the bedroom she hadn't been able to help picking some of it up and what harm did it do as long as she kept it strictly to herself?

Jenny Jack was in her usual place at the window. The sun had baked her fleshy arm a bright lobster red; her glasses winked in the light so that you couldn't see her eyes; one large wart on her temple had been bleeding, it looked raw and repulsive and Murn took one look and shuddered. How dreadful! How revolting! What a perfectly disgusting old woman! How could Evelyn live here? How could she pass this horrible old lady every day without vomiting?

Murn went on into the close. Jack Jack was just coming

out of his house. He was wearing a light coloured flannel suit, the wide trousers of which encased stubby little legs. His round, florid face leered out from the brim of a scone-shaped bonnet. But wide though his trousers were they couldn't conceal the fact that he was very well endowed in the luggage department.

Murn simply could not help staring. She had thought Tom to be especially well developed but this little man was an out and out winner.

'He dresses to the right!' The thought came wildly and quaintly to Murn. She couldn't help smiling, then, shocked at herself, she immediately composed her features. Jack Jack came towards her, and he pretended to fix his shoe as she drew alongside.

'It's yours for ten bob,' he mouthed, forming one corner of his mouth into a kind of pouch. 'The biggest thrill your fanny is likely to get for many a long day. A pound for a bit extra time. I've got the key o' the cludge. It's ours for as long as you'll give me.'

Murn couldn't believe her ears. Her face flared up, bright and burning.

'Don't act all coy on me,' said the little man, 'I saw you looking . . .' he bent his head downwards . . . 'at my johnny. Never seen one as big, eh? You should be paying me for the privilege of getting it.'

Murn's nostrils flared, and with an exaggerated toss of her head she made a rush for the stairs. The mocking, high-pitched laugh of little Jack Jack ringing loud and clear in her ears.

Mrs Conkey came creeping out of her house just as Murn made it to the first landing. She didn't seem at all well these days; her face was white and strained. She had a half-starved look about her; several angry red and yellow boils on her nose and cheeks looked as if they might easily burst at any minute. She was wont to slink about more than she had ever done, as if she was trying hard to disappear altogether without making too much fuss about it.

No one had seen Mr Conkey for a very long time but Alex, who in his own gruff, boyish way, was kind to these particular neighbours, was able to report that the old man was alive, though only just, and was certainly anything but well.

Maggie in her caring way, sent in bowls of soup. When Evelyn was able to afford it she sent Alex through with a sausage casserole, and while the Conkeys were grateful for the offerings they were so overcome with embarrassment that it was all the boy could do to persuade them to actually *eat* the food.

'She's saving for something,' Alex told his mother. 'I saw great piles of pennies on the table below the gas meter but she never uses them for the gas. She burns candles for light and she doesn't use the stove to cook anything. Sometimes I've seen a pan on the fire and the furniture seems to be disappearing. I think she's breaking up her kitchen chairs to keep the fire going, *when* it's going. Quite often it isn't lit at all and the house is freezing and though I've offered to give her *my* wood she won't take it.'

But it was summer now. Neither the Conkeys nor anybody else needed a fire for warmth. It was stiflingly hot in the tenement buildings. The heat melted the tar on the roads and brought out the smells of the backcourt middens. This, combined with the odours of cooking filtering from the houses, did not make for pleasant summer scents and the delights of the Younger Park, situated at the top of Camloan Road, were much sought after at the end of a sultry day.

Murn was certainly quite hot and bothered by the time she had climbed the stairs. She was in no mood to be nice to Mrs Conkey or anybody else and the sight of the woman's boil-bedecked countenance did nothing to rouse sympathy in her hard-hearted breast. Instead she experienced the same sort of revulsion she had felt on spying Jenny Jack's bleeding wart and with a curt, 'Good day,' she made haste to ring Evelyn's doorbell.

John Simpson had wasted no time changing the nameplates on the door. The one bearing the name *Grant* still remained but *D. Grainger* had gone. In its place was one inscribed *J. Simpson*, a much larger plate than Jamie's, and fixed in a very prominent position.

When Alex realised what his stepfather had done he had stayed away from home for two nights, spending them in his stables beside his beloved horses. It had been winter, freezing cold, damp and raw, but Dobbie and Tinker between them had kept him warm and when Babs had come creeping in one night the air had become positively overheated with hot breath and steamy lust.

When the pair realised how easy it was for them to be alone together they had taken full advantage of the situation and had had a high old time to themselves. Alex's absences from home were now an accepted part of life and no one became too concerned when he disappeared for nights on end. Dunky the Smith fed him in return for his labour. There were always turnips in the fields and fresh creamy milk to be taken from Dairy Joe's cart when he wasn't looking.

So, whenever there was trouble at home, Alex simply took himself off to his horses. Although Evelyn hated the idea of her eldest son sleeping rough there was little she could do about it, especially when her husband told her to 'leave the little bugger alone. He's got tink blood in him and probably prefers living out like one.'

As for Babs, she simply got Bessie to cover up for her, an easy enough matter in the circumstances since their father was away at sea again and their stepmother slept like the proverbial log.

But Bessie hated these absences of Babs' and she would

sit up half the night, her knees to her chin, her hands clasped around them while she worried and fretted and wondered what her sister was up to. That cunning young lady, with an excited gleam in her eye, had only hinted that she was seeing Alex Grainger.

'Alex,' Bessie would whisper into the darkness. 'Don't let her get you into trouble. Please don't let her get a hold of your life.'

But both Alex and Babs were too lost in their youthful ardour to care very much how they managed to see one another, just as long as they did. Every night they drowned in their fiery passions; every opportunity they got they petted and played with one another, Alex simply taking what was being offered to him on a plate, Babs only too eager to open her legs to him wherever and whenever she got the chance. She never said 'no'. Deep down Alex knew that he would have respected her more if she had. As it was he burned with wanting and desire and could never get enough of her smooth, ripe young body.

'You'll never leave me for someone else, will you, Alex?' she would plead.

'No, never,' he would reply, hardly knowing what he was saying in his excitement at holding her big, heavy breasts in his hands.

Murn experienced a small pang of guilt when she saw how pale and strained her sister was. She didn't look nearly so beautiful now, not with her hair tied back in a thick ringlet and her emerald eyes lined with tiredness.

She was six months pregnant, but thin for all that and Murn wondered if she was getting enough to eat.

Genuine concern rippled into Murn's heart and, for once, she really did want to give this little sister of hers some money for food without making it seem like a charitable gesture . . . then she remembered the Grant pride and she sat back, quite nonplussed.

The thought came unbidden to her: It's my fault, I should never have thrown John Simpson at her. Tom was right after all. She didn't know how to handle this kind of self-reproach and for several moments she couldn't bring herself to converse in her usual prattling fashion.

'I'll get some tea.' Evelyn wasn't exactly delighted to see Murn. She would be wanting something as she seldom came visiting without an ulterior motive.

'Here, let me help.' Murn was at her back, filling the kettle, spilling half of it over the stove – so concerned with wiping the splashes off her dress that Evelyn had the tea ready and poured before Murn had time to do any more damage.

Settled in a chair, a cup of tea in her pudgy hands, Murn came to the point of her visit. 'It's about the girls,' she crooned, throwing Evelyn her best smile, 'I've arranged to visit Nellie and Kenneth in Kenneray. I leave next week but can't possibly take Tom's daughters. The school holidays are still a week or two away and I don't want them to miss any lessons if I can at all help it. Bessie needs all the learning she can get and Babs just needs discipline.' She leaned forward in a very ingratiating manner. 'You're so good with children, Evie, could you take the girls off my hands? Only for a week or two, you understand . . . and of course, I would pay you generously for their keep . . . '

Maggie came through at that moment. 'Oh, it's you, Murn.' Her greeting was distinctly lacking in enthusiasm. 'I couldny help hearing you talking to Evie.' She drew up a chair and accepted a cup of tea from Evelyn. 'I'll speak straight to you, Murn, as I've aye done to all my daughters. To be blunt, I think you've a damned nerve asking Evie to take on the lassies, they're big quines now and where do you think we're going to put them, I'd like to know? We're cramped enough in this house. Babs and Bessie are used to a lot o' space . . . '

John Simpson appeared as if on cue. He stood looking down at Maggie with a hard gleam in his eye. 'The lassies *can* come, there's plenty o' room for them. They can sleep here in the kitchen, Rachel and Meg can go back to sleeping in The Room. Of course . . .' he turned to Murn and said smoothly, 'we would have to take you up on your offer for their keep. Times are hard, Murn, and we must all share what we have.'

Maggie's face turned crimson at his interference, while Evelyn just sat quiet and still by the empty grate, hearing all the talk but not quite taking any of it in. It was her only way of coping as the wife of John Simpson.

Each day she arose, bone weary and sore after another night of sexual abuse; she drifted through the hours; she cooked, cleaned and sewed; she looked after her children; she did everything that was expected of her . . . but she didn't laugh or sing any more. The spirited Evie, the fun-loving Evie had long departed, and in her place was a shadowy figure who had given up hoping for a better life.

John Simpson had lied to her about having a good job in the shipyards: 'We all hit hard times, Evie,' he had told her glibly. 'I've had a run o' bad luck but don't worry, I'll find work, I'll soon have plenty o' money to give to you and the bairns.'

But he never did. Any money he received from the employment exchange went straight to his stomach in the form of hard liquor. He would do anything for drink and didn't mind how low he had to sink in order to get it. It hadn't taken him long to discover all of Jamie's drink caches and he had soon stolen every bottle he could get his hands on.

He also found the battered old tin box that Evelyn kept hidden under her bed. In it was stored all the small treasures of her girlhood, together with her diaries recording the important happenings in her life. But John Simpson wasn't interested in any of these youthful keepsakes. He had pounced on the valuable garnet necklace that Evelyn's grandfather had given her long before she knew that he even was her grandfather. She had treasured the necklace for years, more for its sentimental value than anything, but it had always been there should her need ever become desperate.

Just a few weeks ago that rainy day had arrived. Too exhausted to remain with Fanny Jean Gillespie any longer, and with only her mother's pitifully sparse earnings as a washerwoman coming into the home, Evelyn had felt she couldn't go on and had unwillingly come to a decision to try and sell the necklace.

But John Simpson had beaten her to it. He had pawned the piece of jewellery and had frittered the money away in drink. Without apology or remorse of any sort he had handed his wife the pawn ticket and her heart had almost stopped beating with the knowledge that she would never, ever find the money to redeem the precious necklace.

After that Evelyn had sunk into a state of apathy. She ate, she slept, she went through all the motions of living, but the real Evelyn was lost somewhere in the depths of her being. Both Jamie and Maggie wept for her and wondered if they would ever be able to reach their daughter again.

Maggie often looked at her, lonely and withdrawn, and a vision of the former Evelyn would come to her, running free and wild over the fields and braes of King's Croft. Her heart would grow sore with longing for those lost days, not just for Evelyn but for them all, and in particular Jamie who never spoke about his beloved Aberdeenshire any more, though Maggie knew he pined for it every day of his life.

The advent of John Simpson into all of their lives had been a bitter pill to swallow. But Maggie was made of stern stuff – she hadn't survived all these years as a crofter's wife for nothing – and if Evelyn had temporarily lost her fighting spirit her mother was right there at her side to give her all the support she could.

John Simpson would get away with nothing without a fight and Murn would get away with even less. Fancy the cheek! Gallivanting off on country holidays with not a care in the world! Well, she would pay through the nose for her freedom and Maggie would make damned sure Evelyn and no one else but Evelyn received the money.

'Right.' Briskly she squared her shoulders. 'We'll look after the lassies but money on the nail it is, Murn, quine. Twenty pounds for the fortnight, in Evie's hand right now! And I'll be here to make sure it stays in her hand until we both go out and spend it on whatever she likes!'

Murn was so flabbergasted her mouth fell open and remained open until she had regained enough equilibrium to close it. She hated her mother at moments like this. How dare she interfere in such a rude manner! Then she looked at Evelyn again and saw the hopeless expression in eyes that had once sparkled with life.

A feeling of guilt seized her anew and suddenly she realised that *here was* the opportunity to give her sister a gift without making it seem so.

'Thirty pounds,' she said abruptly, 'I'll make it thirty pounds. I'm sure Tom won't mind and no one can have the satisfaction of calling me mean behind my back. I haven't got that amount in my purse but if you send Alex round tomorrow I'll give it to him.'

The matter was settled. Maggie ignored the venomous look John Simpson threw her and went to put her arms around Evelyn to give her a hug of pure triumph.

'We'll have a grand shopping spree, lass,' she gloated. 'We can buy some really good food for a change and get you a nice new summer smock.'

'Ay, Mam.' Evelyn didn't want a new smock. A garment like that would only serve to emphasise the fact that she was pregnant and she didn't need reminding of that. But, for her mother's sake, she smiled and tried to thank Murn for her generosity, although somehow she couldn't instill any sincerity into her voice. She didn't want her selfish sister's money. She didn't want Babs here with her flirting and sly smiles but it had all been arranged whether she liked it or no and she was too tired to make an issue out of it.

Murn was fussing, making preparations to leave. She kissed Evelyn on the cheek, she ignored her mother, she glowered at John Simpson, then tripped over the lumpy hair mat in the lobby and cursed under her breath.

'Here, let me.' She hadn't heard John Simpson at her back but he was there just the same, putting a steadying hand under her elbow, speaking in a very respectable tone. The next minute his arm was around her waist, and he was squeezing her hard before his hands came round openly to fondle her breasts.

'How *dare* you, you dirty beast!' she gasped.

He put his mouth close to her ear. 'You loved it, you hot bitch,' he mouthed. 'I watched you at my wedding, wiggling that fat fanny o' yours at that big red-headed Highlander. Asking for it you were, so just remember, I've got plenty and more to spare and if you ever feel the need, just let me know.'

'Really!' Murn wrenched open the door and made her escape, almost falling downstairs in her hurry to get away from 'that awful house' as she put it to herself.

Jessie Jack came fleering in from the backcourt, chasing a small boy who was clutching a bag of broken biscuits in one sticky hand.

Jessie was the grandniece of Jenny and Jack, an enormous maiden of seventeen, whose parents were both dead. Jessie had suffered an attack of meningitis as a baby which had resulted in her being mentally retarded for life.

Her abnormally large head sprouted a wild mop of spiky ginger hair, her nose and mouth frothed continually. She was belligerent and mean and took a great delight in terrorising the neighbourhood youngsters. If she wanted anything she just took it, she slapped and nipped babies in their prams and stole their toys. No one was safe from her and, when she was in the vicinity, the cry went up, 'Clout's about! Clout's about!' whereupon children fled and babies were whipped indoors.

It was obvious that this particular small boy had not been alert enough to escape 'Clout's' clutches.

Murn recoiled as the pair stampeded past. Mrs Boyle opened her door and looked out. 'Is that bitch Jessie at it again?' she demanded. 'I've just pipe-clayed my close and her bloody great clod-hoppers make more mess than an army o' weans.'

Murn didn't answer. Instead she hurried out of the close without a single glance at Mrs Boyle's fancy pipe-clay scrolls, or at Jenny Jack seated at her window, her palsied head nodding back and forth on her hunched shoulders like a marionette.

Murn had no desire to familiarise herself with any of the residents of 198 Camloan Road. It was enough that her family lived there and that she had to show her face to them now and then, without having to get to know their neighbours as well.

She had almost reached the top of Camloan Road before her pace slowed. Her brow was no longer creased in a frown, she was smiling. In the last hour or so two different men had made passes at her ... her smile broadened ... It all just pointed to the fact that she was very attractive to the opposite sex, men liked women with a good padding of meat on their bones. She lifted her head. If these two common runts could hardly keep their hands off her, just think how it would be with Kenneth when the opportunity arose for them to be alone together ...

Murn straightened her shoulders and took a deep breath. The scent of roses drifted to her from the park; she felt drunk with the power and the passion of her feelings and went on her way with a spring in her step.

Alex took Meg along with him when he went to collect his mother's money. He wasn't too pleased at the idea of Babs coming to live with them, even if it was only for a fortnight. He hadn't been seeing nearly so much of her lately. She had grown demanding and clingy; she wanted just to lie about with her breasts hanging out and her legs open, while he delighted in being out in the sun with his horses, grooming them, riding them, talking to them.

Babs didn't like horses, that had been the real clincher in his going off her the way he had. Sex was all right in its place but too much of it on a plate, without a challenge of any sort, had taken the edge off his appetite, and he had more to do with his time than just sweet-talk a little whore like Babs all day. For that was all she was, he had known it from the beginning and now it was plainer to him than ever. One day Babs would get herself into real trouble and he wasn't going to be the one to get her into it.

Meg was quite happy to go along with Alex. They had been getting on a lot better lately and he didn't call her names nearly so much as he used to.

When they arrived at Murn's house she boldly rang the bell while he hung back slightly, hoping that Babs wouldn't paw him in front of everyone the minute she saw him. She had been throwing caution to the winds these days and he knew it was because she was mad at him for his lack of response to what she called 'a body any man would kill for.'

It was Sarah's day off. Bess answered the door. She flushed a bright crimson when she saw Alex but had no time to speak; Babs was at her elbow, rolling her eyes, sliding her tongue over her lips.

'Come in,' she said in a suddenly husky voice. 'Step-mummy is in her room putting on her distemper. It helps to fill the cracks.'

She laughed, a high-pitched, grating sound. Meg, Alex, and Bess looked at her but none of them smiled. She was trying too hard to be smart and her words were cruel without being funny.

The visitors didn't stay long, Murn made sure of that. It was bad enough having Babs and Bess under her feet without the added burden of their cousins.

At the door Babs told Alex she would see him soon, to which he hastily replied that he was so busy with school, paper rounds, odd jobs, and his horses, that he hadn't much time for anything else these days.

'I'll help with the horses if you like.' Unexpectedly Bess spoke up, her voice low and shy. 'When I was in Australia I had my own pony and I miss him terribly. I'd love to come and see yours.'

'Oh, you *would*!' said Babs loudly. 'It would suit you to smell like a horse to cover up all your own nasty smells.'

Bess coloured to her roots and for the first time Alex really noticed her. Her silken brown hair was tied back in a big blue bow, her sweet little face was open and honest and clean and was so deliciously smooth it looked as if it might taste of peaches and cream. Her lovely grey eyes had grown shiny at her sister's words but she didn't cry, instead she just looked him straight in the eye, steadily and openly . . . and kept her head up . . . Alex liked that, he liked it very much indeed.

'Ay, Bess,' he nodded. 'You come along and help me wi' Dobbie and Tinker. You'll like them. They're great horses.'

Meg grinned, not because she was in the least interested in the ups and downs of her brother's love life – girls had chased him since he was nine and he'd had a wonderful time pretending to run away – it was the look of sheer, frustrated rage on Babs' face that tickled Meg's fancy. She had never liked this stepcousin; she had always loathed the way she fancied herself and ogled men as if she could eat them.

Yes, Meg very much enjoyed Babs' discomfiture in those

moments but at the same time she knew the girl was daring enough to try anything. Now that Alex was going off her he had better watch his step. Babs was more than capable of tripping him up and standing back to gloat when he fell flat on his face.

Chapter Nine

It was warm in the railway carriage. The June sun was beating down through the window, pouring over Murn, burning into her legs until she rose and pulled down the blind with an impatient snap.

'I do so hate rail travel,' she complained, her mouth down-turned because she really was most uncomfortably hot. Beads of perspiration had popped out on her brow, her under-arms were sticky and a trickle of moisture tickled her cleavage.

And yet, despite the heat, despite the fact that she was so far gone in pregnancy, Evelyn looked cool, calm and collected, as did Grace, sitting tranquilly in her seat, her white dress making her look as refreshing as a summer breeze.

She might have been sitting at a crystal fresh stream, so pure and sweet did she present herself to the world ... With a sigh of discontent Murn plumped herself back into her seat to stare morosely at the countryside rushing past.

Of course, if she had had her way, Grace and Evelyn wouldn't be here at all with their smiles and their chatter and their knack of making her feel plain and ungainly.

It was all their mother's doing. Everything that had happened in the last week had been all her fault. Murn had been livid when Maggie had suggested to her that she take Grace with her to Kenneray.

'The lass hasny been well since that last bout o' stomach trouble. A breath o' clean country air is just the thing she needs to put her back on her feet – and she would be company for you, Murn, the pair o' you could have a great time wi' Nellie and the bairns.'

To make matters worse, Maggie had said all this in front

of Grace, making it very difficult for Murn to object. Like everyone else she loved Grace – of all the sisters she was the one with the fewest aggressive tendencies – but Murn hadn't planned on taking anyone with her to Kenneray. She had wanted just to be on her own; she needed to have Kenneth's full attention and having Grace as chaperone would cramp her style dreadfully.

Grace herself hadn't been keen on the idea either. Although she loved Croft Donald, she didn't much fancy going there with Murn whose silly airs and graces always put a damper on any situation.

'I'll think about it.' Grace had hedged, and for a day or two the question of whether or not she accompanied Murn remained in the balance.

Then Maggie dealt another blow. 'Why no' take Evie as well? God knows she could be doing wi' a break. Some o' the money you gave her would help to pay her way. The rest can go to keep Babs and Bess with a wee bit left over for a treat or two for everyone.'

Murn groaned and receded into the background. Thanks to her mother the matter was out of her hands; the interfering old busybody had dealt a cunning hand. She had asked too much for the girls' stay in that smelly hole of a tenement, and Murn, falling for Evelyn's look of tragedy, had unwittingly paid her rail fare to Kenneray.

Thinking about all this had made Murn's heart swell with self-pity. She had thrown herself onto her bed to give herself up to a gluttony of wailing and weeping.

But her troubles were only just beginning. Not long afterwards Tom had given her even more to cry about when he had informed her he was cutting her housekeeping allowance, since the hole she had made in his savings would soon be big enough for them all to fall into.

Evelyn was over the moon about the proposed holiday to Kenneray, particularly as John Simpson hadn't objected too strongly to her going. He had also cheered her with the news that he had managed to get a part-time job in a factory. The money wasn't good but at least it would help to keep the wolf from the door until something more permanent turned up.

There were times when he could be quite charming to his wife, the way he had been when he had wooed and won her. He could also be tender and caring when it suited him and, on hearing about the plans for Kenneray, he had put his arm round her shoulders and held her close.

'You go, lass, you need a holiday,' he had said benevolently. 'I'll keep an eye on things here. One thing though – take James with you. It's near enough the summer holidays so he won't miss much schooling.'

John Simpson had developed a strange aversion to Evelyn's second son. Although the boy was barely eight, James had a way of looking at his stepfather that totally unnerved him – yet all he did was to fix his big, dark compelling eyes on him and treat him to a long, unblinking stare.

Quite simply, James had turned the tables on his stepfather. In the beginning, he had been frightened to death of the man and had hated the way his eyes had pierced right into him, as if they could see inside his head and knew that fear made him wet his trousers.

Now John Simpson was afraid of *him* and, small though he was, the boy made full use of the strange powers that he had inherited from his mother. It had gotten to the stage where the rough, tough, drinking man from the Gallowgate had begun to avoid the small boy as much as possible.

'You keep that lad away from me,' he had warned Evelyn in uneasy tones. 'There's something gey queer about him. If you ask me he's no' the full shilling . . . or else –' here he wiped his nose with the back of his hand and looked worried – 'he has the devil in him. I've seen that look before, in my first wife, before she was taken away screaming. She had that expression in her eyes: wild, mad, dangerous. James isn't like other lads o' his age, he's a loner, he's got a violent temper, he just doesn't fit in here and one o' these days I'll do something to him that I might regret. I hate the way he looks at me in that brooding way o' his so just you make sure he doesn't get under my feet too often.'

Evelyn had shivered at his words; she knew that his fear was born of ignorance. She was well aware that her little boy often perceived things that were still in the future. As a child, she had fought against the self-same abilities until old Hinney, the midwife, had told her she too had 'the powers' and had to learn to live with them.

Evelyn hadn't wanted her children to have such extra-sensory perception, in particular James who was so nervous and afraid he could hardly cope with the world as it was.

Yet he was coping well enough with his new stepfather. She had seen him at it, sitting as still as a statue, staring, just staring at John Simpson and while one part of her rejoiced in the knowledge that such a thin little scrap had won this round, she was afraid that one day the boy might push his luck too far. There was no telling what would happen then.

Grace was in raptures watching the green and blue country-side slipping past. It was vast, it was beautiful, it was heaven, and there was so much still to come; the rugged grandeur of the north west, the sea, the mountains.

Euphoria bubbled up in her. Something wonderful was going to happen to her one of these days. It might be tomorrow, or next month, even next year. Whenever it came she would be ready for it and she gave a great sigh of deep contentment . . . Then she glanced at Murn and her happiness faded a little . . . She gave a little shudder . . . A shadow seemed to have fallen over everything, yet outside the sun was still shining as brightly as ever.

*

Evelyn was quite happy just to sit back and relax. Every bone in her body was heavy with exhaustion and she concentrated on just letting herself sink into her seat, allowing each limb gradually to loosen until she could feel her tension oozing away.

It was lovely, so lovely, to be going back to Kenneray again. It was like a dream come true to see the countryside flashing past, the cows and sheep in the fields, the little white houses amongst the trees, the burns, the rivers, the heather moors stretching off into infinity. Now the fields again: crops burgeoning, green corn, ripening hay, and away up there on the lush hill slopes, the ponies, running, tails and manes blowing in the wind . . .

Suddenly she thought of Alex, how he would love to see the horses running in all those green acres. When she had left that morning he had been very attentive to her. His goodbyes had been stiff-lipped and stoic but there had been something about his eyes, a desolation that no amount of acting could quite disguise.

'Give my love to Nellie and Kenneth,' he had instructed and had turned quickly away – but not before she had caught the tell-tale glimmer of tears in his eyes. She knew he would have given anything to be going with her to Croft Donald. For years he had longed to live with his favourite aunt in the country, but he had learned to accept that it couldn't be, especially after the death of his father when he had concentrated his young strength on guiding his mother through one of the most difficult times of her life.

Oh, Alex, Evelyn thought as the train thundered along, I would give you the world if I could, my son, my darling, darling son. You're so much a part of me I feel my own heart twisting with pain when you're sad and lonely.

Long ago she had realized that Alex was very, very special to her. He had been a love child, born of the passion she had shared with Davie when their love had been fiery and insatiable.

Strange, so strange the way the passing years changed

so many things, especially the emotions of the human heart. There had been a time when Alex had deeply resented her for having left him with Nellie in Kenneray when he was just a baby.

Evelyn would never get over the uncanny side of her eldest son's nature. She had often asked herself how such a young child could possibly have been aware of her desertion but, to this day, she had no answer to her question. She could only assume that, like her, he knew things that went far beyond normal understanding and she of all people should know about that.

But all that was in the past. Heartache, sorrow, loneliness and the passage of time had brought them so closely together that very often each knew what the other was thinking without saying a word.

Alex, oh, Alex, she thought, I wish you were with me, of all my bairns you're the one . . .

Child of her heart. At times so young, like a wild spirit roaming free over the endless plains of life . . . At others . . . so responsible, so weighed down with the worries and cares of his existence . . . and so . . . grown-up.

When she married John Simpson she had thought that Alex would never forgive her for what he saw as her betrayal of his father. But he had gotten rid of his anger towards her in his own inimitable way. He had quite simply run wild, like a young horse, unbroken, unbridled, and in so doing he had managed to come to terms with the many new and unwanted aspects of his life.

But never, never would he accept John Simpson's place in the home. Evelyn knew that and understood perfectly, for he was certainly not alone in feeling the way he did. She knew she had made a terrible mistake marrying such a man and she hated herself for having brought so many trials and tribulations on her family.

She sighed; she didn't want to think about John Simpson, not now, when she was relaxed and contented for the first time in months.

She folded her hands over her stomach. Something round and hard nestled under her fingers and from her pocket she withdrew half a crown. Alex had pressed it into her hand that morning when he had kissed her cheek to say goodbye . . . 'Here, take this,' he had ordered in the deep, manly voice he had adopted to cover up his feelings. 'I saved it up from my odd jobs for Dunky. It isn't much, but it might help you to enjoy your holiday. Just – send me a postcard when you have time.'

The young boy had taken over then, and that was when she had glimpsed the tears before he had hurried away . . .

'He's a good lad, is Alex.' Grace, who had witnessed the boy's gift to his mother, squeezed Evelyn's arm. 'One day he'll grow into a fine young man, one that you'll be proud of.'

'Ay,' Evelyn had agreed. 'Davie always had faith in Alex and would say the same things you're saying now. I thought he was too wild and devilish ever to want to change but he has and I don't need to wait till he's grown up to be proud o' him.'

She returned the half crown to her pocket and settled back in her seat, wishing, wishing so many things . . . and quite unbidden the image of Gillan popped into her head and simply refused to go away . . . It was really very pleasant to sit there, the summer sun in the heavens, the green countryside rolling away . . . and thoughts of Gillie safe and secret in her own private little world of dreams.

James sat in his corner, staring out at the fields and the hills with unending fascination. He had never been to the country before, the nearest he had ever got to it was to the Younger Park at the top of Camloan Road and the furthest he had ever travelled was on tram rides to the various parks and greens surrounding Glasgow.

To him, public parks were vast places, places to hide in

and get lost in and two years ago he had done just that when Alex, Meg, and Rachel had taken him to Kelvingrove Park on an Easter picnic.

He would never forget the great cathedral of trees in Lover's Lane. It had been dank, dark and mysterious and yet he hadn't felt apprehensive or afraid. The green silken waters of the River Kelvin had swished along between the banks, kissed by lacy green fronds bowing down from the trees.

To James it was a magical spot. He wasn't in the least afraid of the secret dark corners. It felt natural and right to be in a place where wild flowers grew undisturbed and little green frogs looked safe and snug amongst the wet grasses.

So much had he enjoyed the experience of being alone with these things that he hadn't given a lot of thought to his brother and sisters but had sat himself down against the trunk of a tree to eat his picnic. He had been very careful and fair about it, consuming only his share of the food but was quite unable to resist taking a bite out of each of the little fairy cakes his Grannie had baked specially for the occasion.

When the others eventually found him they were hungry, hot, and furious. They had stood in a row in front of him, silhouetted against the fat, sticky buds of an enormous horse chestnut tree. He'd had to crane his neck to look up at the three faces and had been very relieved to see that his beloved Rachel wasn't all *that* angry looking, just a bit hot and bothered and more anxious about him than she was about the food.

It had been all right in the end. They had forgiven him for sampling all the fairy cakes. They had eaten the remainder of the food after which they had rolled their eggs down a grassy slope, then, following Alex's example, they had rolled *themselves* down. They had laughed and talked and had been good friends, and, at the end of the day, James was very reluctant to leave the delights of Kelvingrove Park for the gloomy, grey streets of the tenements.

Now, here he was, being pulled along by an L.M.S. steam locomotive, miles and miles of trees and fields rolling by, everything lit by the sun pouring down from a blue sky with little puff ball clouds sailing along above the hills.

If only Rachel had been here, everything would have been perfect. Like him she had never known what the countryside looked like and he wanted her to share all this with him. He remembered her face when she had hugged him goodbye that morning. It had been pale and thin with dark smudges under her eyes and he could plainly see the tiny scar on her nose where he had chipped the bone with a soup spoon that had been meant for Alex. James worshipped this sister of his and had been so devastated by the accident he had cried himself to sleep for a week afterwards.

He was normally a quiet and well-behaved boy but was possessed of a temper so fearsome that even those playground bullies who normally took a delight in tormenting him kept out of his way when he was upset.

His temper made him do the oddest things to the people he loved most. It had made him cut off Rachel's thick, dark lashes one night while she was asleep simply because she had refused to take him with her to her best friend's house for tea.

He didn't want her to have a best friend. He only wanted it to be him and her forever. He had told her that and she had been very quiet and sad and had cried a little with the beauty of his words. He had also told her that he wanted to marry her when he grew up and this time she hadn't cried but had laughed instead and said that brothers didn't marry their sisters.

She had had a lovely time at her best friend's house, even though Millie Richardson had buck teeth and straggly hair and always smelled of stale, home-made chips.

That very night James had taken the little pair of work

scissors from his Grannie's darning basket and had smuggled them under his pillow.

He had lain awake for hours, hot and sticky with apprehension, his heart thumping in his chest, his tongue so dry it had stuck to the roof of his mouth and he hadn't dared to get up and go to the kitchen for a drink.

Rachel usually did this for him. No matter how tired she was or how fast asleep she had been, she would make scant protest as she dragged herself out of bed and crept through to the scullery.

Thinking about this almost made him change his mind about the grim action he was about to take. Then he had remembered how she had laughed at him and without more ado he had shone his torch in her face and had quickly snipped off her long lashes before he could change his mind.

It had been a wicked thing to do. Rachel had cried for a whole day because some of the little hairs had got into her eyes and the stubble that was left on her lids made them very sore. She had known he was to blame but she had never told on him and he had been very ashamed and heartbroken because of all the suffering he had caused her.

He had vowed there and then that never again would he do anything to hurt her. That had been two years ago and, except for the occasional misdemeanour, he had never broken that vow. Now he was going away from her, far, far away, to a place he'd never been to before. Tonight he would lie in a strange bed and listen to strange noises, and Rachel wouldn't be there beside him to soothe away his fears and hold him in her arms as she had done ever since he was a baby and she was just a toddler.

The thought saddened him and he stared out of the window with hot, dry eyes. He wanted to cry for his darling sister and for all the lovely things he remembered about her, but the tears wouldn't come. Alex had told him it was cissy to cry at his age, especially in front of women and girls.

James surveyed his mother and his two aunts. His mother's eyes were closed but she was smiling a little to herself which meant that she wasn't really asleep but just pleasantly day-dreaming.

Aunt Grace's head was flopping a little on her shoulders so he knew that she was enjoying a nice cosy dozy.

James liked to make words rhyme like that. They sounded so much better than just using them in the conventional way and it was fun to make up words of your own and say them out loud to see how they sounded. One day he wanted to be a writer. He loved words, he loved writing them down and playing with them till they made poetry and verses and stories.

Yes, very decidedly, if he couldn't marry Rachel he would just stay single and write stories into jotters all day long. She might come to visit and they would have tea and eat hot pancakes while they talked about the days when they were children together and had to wait for ages sometimes to get into the stairhead lavatory.

James smiled at this. His glance fell on Aunt Murn. She was very decidedly and fatly asleep, that was how he put it to himself, in capital letters because it sounded better inside his head.

FATLY ASLEEP. Her plump, red lips were slightly parted, her pink snub nose was twitching a bit, something like that white rabbit he had seen in a cage in a pet shop in Glasgow. She had a nervous tic at the corner of one eye. It was fluttering about inside her skin and seemed to keep time to the beat and pulse of the wheels on the rails. Tickety – tick! Tickety – tick! Plumpety – plump! Plumpety – plump! Fattity – fat! Fattity – fat! Murnity – Murn! Murnity – Murn! Daftity – daft! Daftity – daft!

He clapped his hand over his mouth to stop from laughing out loud while the wheels whirled round on the rails, making all those lovely daft sounds inside his head.

A fly was buzzing around inside the carriage, a very restless sort of fly. It landed first on his mother's hair, then

142

it flitted to Grace to explore the folds of her dress. Finding nothing much of interest there it buzzed across to Aunt Murn to hover around her head.

Now, James thought, this is *much* better, lots of lovely sweat, a wide open mouth to explore, a nice juicy nose to crawl around in.

The little boy held his breath, and sure enough the fly landed, plunk in the middle of Aunt Murn's nose. She snored, she snorted. She woke herself up with her own dreadful noises.

'Beastly fly!' she complained. 'It woke me up! Oh, I do so hate this sticky heat. In the part of Australia where I lived it was so different, there was always a breeze from the Indian Ocean and of course, the railway carriages had air conditioning. Things are so primitive here, I wish . . .'

Grace opened her eyes and said patiently, 'Ach, cheer up, Murn, we'll be at Inverness in no time and it's not so far from there to Kyle o' Lochalsh.'

'Meanwhile we'll have tea.' Evelyn reached for the basket she had packed that morning.

In it were tea and scones, bread and margarine and a precious piece of cheese that Maggie had packed at the last minute.

Murn was extremely grateful for the tea but the bread and margarine didn't at all meet with her approval.

'Surely, Evie, with the . . .' She halted in mid-speech, her face flushing. She had been about to mention the money she had handed over for Babs and Bess's keep but had stopped herself only just in time.

Grace looked at Evelyn, Evelyn looked at Grace. Both the sisters knew that they were going to have to exercise a lot of self constraint if they were to survive a fortnight under the same roof as Her Regal Majesty, Murn the Mighty.

Maggie, fed up to the back teeth with Murn's complaining, had recently bestowed on her this lengthy and humorous title. The rest of the family liked it, they liked it very much, and somehow even to say it to oneself, or under one's breath, acted as a safety valve that was so often needed when in the company of such an embarrassingly overt creature as Murn the Mighty.

Chapter Ten

Kenneth Cameron Mor was dreading Murn's visit. If her behaviour towards him at Evelyn's wedding was anything to go by then he felt he was in for quite a traumatic time of it.

When she had written boldly to arrange a holiday at Croft Donald, she had set the dates and the times without so much as a by your leave from anybody.

> . . . of course I'll be coming on my own so no one need feel that they have to put themselves out for me . . .

She had written that some weeks ago. Since then it seemed as if the whole of Camloan Road had decided to come with her. Not that either Nellie or Kenneth minded. In fact they were relieved that it wouldn't just be Murn with her 'mightier than thou' attitude and her intense interest in herself and her affairs.

Nellie was well aware of her sister's feelings towards Kenneth Mor. They had both thought she had gotten over that silly schoolgirl nonsense years ago but had very forcibly been proved wrong. In her straightforward way, Nellie vowed not to stand any nonsense from Murn, but deep in her heart she felt uneasy every time she remembered that dreadfully embarrassing scene in the lobby on the day of Evelyn's marriage. Kenneth had been so upset by it he hadn't been able to get out of the house fast enough and he had warned Nellie never, never, to allow that sister of hers to come near him again.

Now she was coming to Croft Donald, arriving any time

within the next half hour, and Kenneth was so jumpy and restless he had already been rebuked several times by his wife.

Normally he was out in the fields at this time of the day, making the most of every God-sent sunny hour, but today he hadn't been able to settle.

Nellie had never known anything like it, her big, laughing, thundering Ken, reduced to a heap of nerves just because of silly, fat old Murn.

But Nellie knew her sister couldn't be dismissed as easily as that. She banged the rolling pin viciously over a round of dough while she kept one eye on the oven and the other on the window that looked out to the sea and the islands and the little rough road snaking its way over the hill and the muck.

Ay, there was always plenty of that on the track. When it was raining it was mud: grey, clingy mud that oozed out of the potholes and stuck to one's clothes if one dared to be less than careful when climbing out of the cart.

When the weather was dry it was stoor: the wheels stirring up great clouds of it, the wind from the sea blowing it about so that it clogged noses, eyes, ears.

Murn wouldn't like it, she wouldn't like it at all, Grace and Evelyn wouldn't like it either but they would thole it simply because they were sensible beings who had been to Kenneray before and knew what to expect during the ups and downs of the journey.

Nellie walloped the dough, her generous mouth curved into a rather wicked smile at the idea of Her Regal Majesty, Murn the Mighty disappearing forever in a cloud of stoor from the dusty road.

Kenneth's mother, Irene, a placid soul who had a wonderful knack for keeping the peace and for restoring it when it had fallen apart, was not at all placid that day. Quite simply, her son, Kenneth, was getting on her nerves, in fact he was getting on everybody's nerves.

Up, down, up, down he bobbed, from sofa to window, from window to sofa, back to the window again, peering out, straining his eyes as he watched for signs of life on the bumpy, pot-holed track that led off from the farm road.

Normally he would be delighted to take out the cart and go himself to collect visitors but today was not normal. Murn, a matron to be avoided if possible, and when avoidance was out of the question, to be taken in very small doses – as one would take medicinal arsenic – was coming to Croft Donald for a whole fortnight.

Kenneth didn't know how he was going to be able to suffer her for that length of time. It was true that the presence of Grace and Evelyn would help to make the situation bearable but even so, it was going to be the longest two weeks of his life and he wasn't at all pleased with things as they stood.

Calum Alasdair Cameron, Kenneth's son by his first marriage and better known as Cal, watched his father's pacings and couldn't stop fidgeting himself. He longed to be outside in the fresh air, working in the fields as he had been doing since he was old enough and able to hold a scythe.

But less than an hour ago his father had directed him to stop working as Nellie had requested they both be home, washed and changed, in time for the visitors coming.

'Och, Father, I don't need to be there,' Cal had objected. 'It's too good a day to stop work now. You go, I'll stay. I'd hate to be indoors on a day like this.'

Cal was almost twenty-three, a fine strapping lad with golden-red hair and iron-hard muscles the same as his father. His chest was deep and strong and enclosed a pair of lungs that were almost a match for Kenneth's, so heartily did his deep laugh boom out of them.

Cal had been a man since the age of fifteen. His steel-like fists had felled many an adversary when he had been silly and young and had drunk too much at village dances.

Wherever he went the girls followed: he had been engaged three times and had had the finger pointed at him on several tearful occasions. Somehow he had arrived at his present age, unscathed, unmarried, and fancy free. He was sometimes wild, sometimes quiet, sometimes thoughtful, sometimes thoughtless; whatever his mood he was very much his own man and felt himself to be in reasonable control of his own particular world.

But when Kenneth snapped his fingers Cal came running. When Kenneth gave orders Cal obeyed them, simply because he admired and loved his father, respected his fiery temper, and would never oppose him if he could at all help it. Only once had the pair ever come to blows and that had been when Cal had stayed out too late and had gone too far in a drunken brawl outside a notorious shebeen in the early hours of the morning. Cal had landed up in the police cells and Kenneth had had to bail him out. The boy had been sulky and unrepentant and had stuck up his fists at his father obstinately.

Kenneth had won that fight and Cal had never challenged him again. He was a good son and he did as he was told as far as he thought fair, but on the question of 'poncing himself up for visitors' on a beautiful day, he had quite decided ideas and none of them entertained Kenneth's viewpoint.

After another fifteen minutes of his father's pacings, Cal had had enough. Abruptly he stood up and made for the door. 'I'm going back to the fields,' he informed no one in particular. He waited a few moments, no one said anything. Nellie seemed absorbed in making a fresh batch of scones for the visitors' tea, Irene was busy with one of the babies, Kenneth was at the window, anxiously scanning the road.

Cal opened the door. A shaft of sunlight poured through the gap, making him more determined than ever to get out of the house . . .

'Oh no, you don't! You'll stay here and shake hands wi' Nell's sisters if it's the last thing you do!'

Kenneth's roar split the air asunder. Grabbing his son by the scruff of the neck he bulldozed him out of the house and onto the green sward of machair at the front of the house.

Cal tasted blood before he knew what had hit him. When he picked himself up it was to see Kenneth Mor's furious face: red hair and beard bristling, blue eyes snapping fire, fists bunched in front of him, kilt swinging and swishing round his big hairy knees as he danced around like a boxer in a ring.

He was well and truly roused and Cal felt his own temper rising fast. He raised his fists, he let swing, and that was the start of a fisticuffs between father and son the like of which Kenneray had never before seen.

Nellie came rushing from the house, wiping her floury hands on her apron, her strong face filled with amazement at the sight of her menfolk laying into one another.

'Kenneth! Cal! Stop fighting at once or – or I'll get the police to you!' In her anxiety she barely knew what she was saying and she might as well have saved her breath for all the good it did.

Irene came running, horror on her normally untroubled features. 'Mercy,' she cried loudly, 'They'll kill one another! Sure as fate they'll kill one another and that's no decent thing for a father and son to do. Och, I wish Iain was here, he'd sort them out, he might be older than any o' them but by the Lord, he's stronger as well!'

The sounds of the fight carried clearly on the crisp sea breezes. From the portals of Tigh na Beinne came stout Bella Armstrong accompanied by her man, Big Ben; female neighbours materialised from various little white croft-houses scattered over the vicinity; the menfolk in the fields laid down their implements and tried not to look too eager as they hurried to the scene of unrest.

Nellie wrung her hands and wished she could wring her

husband's neck as easily. 'I'll never live this down,' she said through tightly gritted teeth. 'Just look at that Bella's face! She's gloating, positively gloating! But I was no' a smart quine, gloating last Hogmanay when that lazy good-for-nothing man o' hers got carted away to jail at Kyle o' Lochalsh for stealing whisky from a baby's pram.'

Irene temporarily forgot the fight. 'A baby's pram?' She wrinkled her brow. 'Surely no one in their right mind would put whisky in beside an innocent bairn?'

'Hmph! Innocent bairn indeed!' returned Nellie sourly. 'The pram was full o' stolen spirits and Big Ben, in his turn, helped himself but wasna smart enough no' to get caught.'

The fight was growing fiercer. Cal was so incensed he forgot who he was fighting with – he was just glad to vent his feelings on someone. Kenneth Mor in his turn couldn't have cared less who was on the receiving end of his punches. Truth to tell he was thoroughly enjoying himself. He hadn't participated in a good set to for years and this young buck of a son of his could certainly hold his own.

His fists were just a blur; he pulled a mighty good punch. Kenneth's kilt fairly flew from side to side as he ducked and advanced, so light on his feet he might have been executing a lively and passionate Highland Fling.

'The visitors will be arriving any minute,' said Irene, 'And just look at those two! They seem to be enjoying the whole thing. Father and son, what a disgrace! It would serve them right if they knocked each other out!'

Nellie shaded her eyes and looked towards the road. 'The cart! It's coming!' she gasped.

The little knot of neighbours was thoroughly enjoying the spectacle of the Cameron menfolk bashing lumps out of one another. They were not anxious for any sort of intrusion that might put a stop to the entertainment, therefore they were most disgruntled to see the cloud of stoor on the road that denoted the arrival of Croft Donald's guests. Horse and cart halted momentarily; Iain was opening the gate and all too soon the stoorie travellers hove into view – and still Kenneth and his son were hell-bent on making mincemeat of one another.

'Bloody hell!' Iain Cameron was not amused at the scene which met his eyes. He took one look at it and, jumping down from the cart, he went straight into the fray to break it up by grabbing his son and his grandson by the roots of their hair and pulling down with all of his strength till he brought each man to his knees.

Iain Cameron didn't have the bulging muscles of his offspring, nor was he very tall or particularly well made, but he was tough and wiry from working all his life on the land and the strength of him was phenomenal. No man who knew him cared to get on his wrong side and any man who challenged him to a fight had to be a stranger, someone in a drunken stupor, or a person who wasn't exactly in full possession of his senses.

When he strode into the scene, the small gathering of spectators moved back from the 'ring' as one man, and when, with one swift movement, he felled the rock-hard Kenneth Mor and the iron-fisted young Cal, a wave of respectful admiration rippled through the ranks.

Grace and Evelyn were climbing down from the cart. This was the most unusual welcome they had ever received at Croft Donald and both sisters were highly intrigued by it all.

Little James sat still and observant for a few moments before he too got down to stand beside his mother, his thumb in his mouth, his eyes big and wondering and sparkling a bit with excitement.

Murn was not for moving. She had had a dreadful journey and the passing of the miles had not served to improve conditions. If anything they had grown worse but the crux had come when Iain had met them with the cart. Murn could hardly believe her eyes. After coming all those hot, sweaty miles a rough farm cart was to transport them the rest of the way!

To make matters worse, Grace and Evelyn had taken it all in their stride and were even able to enjoy the journey and to point with delight to, what were to them, familiar and well-loved landmarks.

True, the road had run beside the sea and the breeze had been cool and welcome, but the *potholes* and the ruts, the dust, and the smell from the horse's rear, had been almost too much for 'a lady of her breeding' to bear.

If Kenneth personally had come to collect them it might have served to make matters bearable but instead he had sent his father whose demeanour was anything but scintillating, even if he did have the same eyes and the same captivating smile as his son.

But at least – at least – and here Murn almost physically hugged herself – Kenneth would be at Croft Donald to meet them and kiss them hello and lead them into his home where no doubt everyone would fuss and smile and be quite delighted to talk to people from the civilised world outside the insular community they were used to.

In the normal way of things, Murn's concept of a Croft Donald welcome would have been perfectly accurate. Highland hospitality figured largely in that happy household and when visitors arrived they were enveloped in a happy blur of kisses and hugs, laughter and chatter, and, quite often, the skirl of the bagpipes if Kenneth was in a mood to play them. Orderly chaos of that sort could last for quite some time, depending on the popularity of the new arrivals.

Murn had heard all about that type of reception from Grace and Evelyn and she had been really looking forward to it. Therefore, when the cart finally stopped at its destination, she simply could not believe her own eyes. Here she was, every bone in her body bruised and sore, her throat parched, her head spinning, and not one person with manners enough to come and help her down from the dreadful contraption that had caused her so much anguish for the last hour . . .

Murn felt abandoned and forgotten; everyone was too taken up with everyone else to pay any heed to her.

The neighbours were beginning slowly to disperse, loath to abandon such an enjoyable diversion from the norm.

'Faith! The bairns!' Nellie threw her hands in the air and went rushing off to the house, followed closely by Irene, Evelyn, Grace and James – and Kenneth! Bloody nosed, hair and beard dishevelled and matted with spit and blood, flaps of raw skin on his torn fists. Hardly able to see where he was *going* never mind being fit enough to see who was *coming*!

And irony! Father and son were shaking hands, a bit shamefaced and sheepish looking but nevertheless patting one another on the back. The best of buddies after half-killing each other.

Murn stuck her nose in the air. Men! Children was all they were! To think she had always looked upon Kenneth with such deference, such reverence, and here he was, no better than any other common farmer . . .

'Murn.' Kenneth hadn't forgotten her, he was at her side, helping her down, his hand burning into her arm. 'No' a very good impression for a first,' he sounded stilted, uncomfortable. 'I'm sorry you had to find us like this – we don't behave like barbarians every day o' the week. Just you go along to the house, Nell will be waiting to greet you and make you some tea. I'll have to go and clean myself up.'

Murn immediately forgot her recent criticisms of this virile, red-headed, giant of a man. The touch of his hand on her flesh made her feel faint. She just stood there staring at him, her lips slightly parted, her eyes fixed on his face, as if she could eat him, blood, spit, and all.

She felt that she could stand there forever, just looking at him, and she was none too pleased when he led her quickly up to the house and deserted her with the excuse that he had to 'sort' himself.

In their anxiety over the fight, Nellie and Irene had forgotten that they had left the youngest members of the household to their own devices. Both women's hearts were in their throats when they went rushing back to the house and burst into the kitchen, expecting the worst.

But they needn't have worried. Wee Col was there, sitting amongst the cinders with the babies, crooning to them in an odd little chanting wail that appeared to hold them utterly spellbound.

It was true that the children had crawled into the most cobwebby corners in the room. They had also managed to open the coal box and smear themselves with coal dust from head to foot. One baby was smelly, the other had wet himself, but all in all they were hale and hearty and were utterly entranced by their Uncle Col's singing.

He had surprised and delighted Nellie with his knack of being able to handle young children. He would play with them, talk to them, and sing to them for hours. With the exception of his beloved Nellie, no adult could make much sense of his garbled tongue, but the babies seemed able to interpret his language without any bother and they would clap their little hands and laugh with joy whenever he went upstairs to talk to them at bedtime.

Wee Col watched over them and protected them with all the frail strength of his being and Nellie loved this unique brother of hers more than ever because of his compassion towards the young things of the earth.

Grace and Evelyn came crowding in at Nellie's back and saw their brother Col sitting on the hearth rug playing with the grimy babies. They laughed with the sheer joy of being back at Croft Donald with all its life and its love and its warm, caring atmosphere.

Wee Col didn't always remember the names of his sisters and for a few moments he stared at them, his eyes wide and blue in his thin young face, his loose blubber of a mouth wet and gaping. Then he was up on his big, clumsy feet, a screech of delight issuing from his throat as he cried 'Gwace! Evie!' before taking each of them by the hand and spinning them round and round till they were breathless and dizzy.

'Col, oh, Col,' laughed Grace, a tear in her eye for this delicate boy with his laughter-filled eyes and the ephemeral shadow that hung over him. He had recently been ill with a bout of summer 'flu that had left him weak and thinner than ever but it hadn't stopped him doing all the things he loved to do with his life.

Evelyn held onto his hands. They were just a rickle of bones with pale transparent skin through which showed fine, thread-like blue veins. 'It's good to see you, Col,' she said huskily. 'You're looking well, really well.'

He nodded eagerly. 'Good to see you,' he stuttered. 'Gwace-Evie . . . '

Murn appeared at that moment, hot and cross looking. What a start to the holiday! Kenneth hadn't even kissed her cheek! Nellie hadn't even had the manners to wait and say hello! The Irene woman had been just as lacking in hospitality, nearly as bad as her husband with his dour grunts and silent attitude.

Of course, what else could she expect, they were just coarse country people – no breeding, no manners, scant respect for their betters. She wished now she hadn't come . . . and that horrid creature they called their brother was here, as large as life and twice as repulsive. He was slavering like a dog, he looked like a bag of bones, and he was covered in coal dust, just like those dreadful babies who were crawling about in the dirt.

Really! What was Nellie thinking about? Allowing a retarded being like that to mix with normal people – even if he *was* her brother. As for the children: wet, dirty, unsavoury. The Nellie she remembered had been fussy and fastidious to a fault. She had driven the family mad with her fleering about the house with a broom, eternally down on her knees scrubbing the floors.

Marriage had certainly changed her: she had let herself go, she was careless and slovenly and sloppy. Just look at her! Her hair hanging in rat's tails around her ears, her face red and sweating as if she had been running. Kenneth must have lost interest in her a long time ago, and little wonder. Who could blame him if he strayed from the straight and narrow?

Murn straightened, she threw back her shoulders and thrust out her considerable bosom . . .

No wonder he looked at her as if he could devour her in one gulp . . . A small smile played at the corner of Murn's mouth. She would make sure that she looked her best during this holiday. She would look and taste like a flower, he wouldn't be able to resist her, not after years of Nellie with her gaunt bosom and her coldness. She probably didn't know what perfume was and most likely went to bed every night smelling like cow manure . . .

Murn lifted her chin. She was here and she would have to make the best of it. The coming days would certainly be a terrible trial for her but she would just have to grin and bear it. After all, she was here to be near Kenneth, beside that nothing else mattered, nothing . . .

Nellie was making a great fuss of the babies, picking them up, kissing their filthy faces. Evelyn was entranced. She had last seen Nell's little daughter soon after her birth and now Grace Evelyn Cameron was one and a half years old, a bonny child with dark auburn hair and enormous blue eyes.

And the little boy, Kenneth David Cameron, a fine healthy toddler with fair hair and laughing brown eyes . . .

Evelyn caught her breath . . . This was hers and Davie's son, the child they had given to Nellie's keeping when their circumstances were so impoverished it was all they could do to feed and clothe the rest of their family.

Nellie and Kenneth's first little girl, Jean Christina, had died soon after birth and both of them had given up hope of having children of their own. But Nellie being Nellie had picked herself up, dusted herself down, and had gone on with the business of looking after a family that she cherished.

But fate hadn't finished with her yet. Having dealt its harshest blow it then smiled on her and she was offered the gift of her sister's baby son whom she and Kenneth readily adopted.

Barely a year later, Grace Evelyn appeared on the scene and at long last Nellie, who had spent her life raising 'other folks' bairns', now had one of her own. Her happiness was a dazzling thing, it lit up every corner of Croft Donald. Her deep contentment transferred itself to everything she touched, and though she could still be 'Nellie-ish' and quick tempered she was mostly pleased with her lot and envied no one.

Col stared at Murn with a frown on his brow. Shambling over to stand in front of her, he shook his head and said, clearly and precisely, 'Not my sister, fat, too fat. Old, too old. Gargoyle! Gargoyle! Gargoyle!'

He had remembered her! And in such an oddly demeaning fashion. His face was flushed, his eyes sparking with something that could only be described as rage.

Nellie was flabbergasted. Wee Col, placid, loving, sweet tempered, displaying an emotion she never knew he possessed, as if he sensed something about Murn that penetrated the serenity of his existence.

Murn, of course, was shocked to the core and didn't hesitate to voice some of the opinions she harboured about 'a simpleton who shouldn't be let loose amongst decent people.'

Suddenly Nellie felt very sorry for this poor, misguided sister of hers. 'A cup o' tea for you, my lass,' she said kindly. 'You've had a long, tiring journey and we'll all feel better with a good hot cuppa inside us.'

Murn felt slightly mollified, and, glowering at Col she tottered over to a chair to sink herself into it with a groan. Kicking off her shoes, she took a deep breath and wished she could loosen her corsets and just allow everything to go its natural way.

Kenneth and Cal came clattering downstairs, washed, cleaned, and shining having submitted themselves to Grace's tender ministrations. They had obviously made up their differences and were once again the best of friends.

A thought struck Murn: the reason that Kenneth had fought with his son was because he had wanted all of his family to be present to welcome her on her first visit to Croft Donald. He had honoured her, not insulted her, by putting young Cal in his place. The boy was obviously a young smarty pants and no doubt needed a short, sharp lesson every so often.

Murn puffed out her bosom; the traumas, the insults, the discomforts of that day faded from her mind. Kenneth Mor wanted everything to be just right for her and that was because he loved her, there were no doubts in her heart now. He loved her, he wanted her, he needed her.

He was watching her now, oh, not in an obvious way but subtly – cool, beckoning, the ice in his blue eyes melting rapidly as his inner fires smouldered.

Murn hugged herself. She would show him what a real woman was like. Poor man. No doubt he had never been fully awakened in all of his life. That first wife of his had been an insipid creature.

And Nellie! Ah, yes, Nellie! Cold, unresponsive, spinsterish Nellie. How could she awaken any man when it was quite certain that her own emotions had lain dormant since birth and would most likely remain so to the grave.

Chapter Eleven

The house seemed very quiet without Evelyn and James. Maggie tried hard to concentrate on the pile of darning at her elbow but it was no use. She felt breathless and hot, even though it was cooler in The Room than in the stifling heat of the kitchen.

She wondered if Jamie would come home drunk again . . . no . . . she didn't wonder, she knew. Evelyn had given them both some money from the thirty pounds that Murn had handed over for Babs' and Bessie's bed and board.

Maggie knew that her daughter was only being kind but it would have been better to have given all the money into her keeping, that way she could have doled it out to Jamie a little at a time and there would have been no worries about him squandering it all on drink.

And it wouldn't just be for himself. Jamie had a big heart at the best of times but when he'd had one too many he became magnanimous to a fault, dishing out booze and cigarettes to all and sundry: the down and outs, the hanger's on, all the various chancers who saw him coming a mile off and clung to him like leeches until they'd bled him dry.

Maggie felt her nerves stretching with each passing moment. There was something in the air tonight, something unsavoury. She felt that things were shortly going to happen in the house that would bring nothing but unhappiness for everyone concerned.

A sense of doom filled her heart, oppression seemed to lurk in every corner, yet the June evening outside was filled with light and life. The birds weren't exactly filling the night with song – you had to go to the park for that – but the sparrows were chirping in a noisy row on the window-sill and the sounds of children at play drifted up from the street. A backcourt minstrel was singing *Danny Boy*. The notes trembled and echoed then grew louder and more vigorous. It was a terrible rendering of such a beautiful song and Maggie shuddered as she listened. It had to be Bawling Bob. Some of the street entertainers were reasonably musical. Squeezebox Sam, for instance, had a fine tenor voice and could extract any tune from his melodeon, some of the others were bearable but Bawling Bob was painful to listen to and Maggie was convinced he piled on the agony to make people throw money at him just to be rid of his noise.

Yet it was a familiar sound, and Maggie felt that she needed familiar things in her life that hot, interminable day.

'Evie,' she spoke her daughter's name aloud. The beloved ring of it comforted her. It was so right to hear it spoken, so good and right and pleasing.

But it was selfish to wish this precious youngest daughter of hers back home when she had only left for Kenneray that morning.

God knows, the lass deserved a break, she needed the bigness and the beauty of the countryside to calm her troubled soul.

If only . . . here Maggie paused in her thinking and frowned. If only – what?

Her heart seemed to stop beating for a moment as her thoughts carried her forward . . . If only Murn wasn't there to spoil it for everyone with her whines and her moans and her useless, crazy obsession with Kenneth Cameron Mor.

There! It was out!

Maggie moved restlessly in her seat and tucked away a strand of snowy hair.

Murn! Poor, sad, unfulfilled Murn. Sad? Or . . . mad?

Again Maggie shuddered. What had made her think

that? Murn might have many traits that weren't acceptable or pleasing – but mad! No, no, not that, not that . . .

Deliberately Maggie forced her thoughts away from Murn but, try as she would, the feeling of foreboding that had seized her refused to be shaken off.

It wasn't Murn! No, for the moment anyway it wasn't thoughts of Murn that had wrought this strange emotion in her. A chill gripped her. She glanced up from her darning and her eyes darted into the corners, the nooks and crannies, the dark places of The Room.

Evil! She felt its presence . . . And she, Margaret Innes Grant, who all of her days had boldly faced the daunting challenges that life had thrown at her, was afraid.

A cup of tea! She stood up. Her darning tumbled to the floor unheeded. She felt a tightness in her throat which was suddenly as dry as a bone.

Tea! Wonderful, familiar, life-saving tea!

She all but ran from The Room into the stuffy heat of the kitchen. Bawling Bob was still bellowing out his dreadful rendition of *Danny Boy*.

Maggie loved him in those moments, baggy trousers, filthy neckerchief, greasy cap and all. He was part of the scheme of things, he was harmless, he was Bawling Bob, plain and simple.

After she had put on the kettle she retrieved her purse from her apron pocket and, delving into the worn leather segments, she withdrew a few coppers. They nestled in her hot palm and she could smell the verdigris. It brought back memories of childhood days when a sticky farthing piece could buy all sorts of sweetmeats from the pokey little village store that was presided over by Mr Grogg.

Mr Grogg! She smiled at the memory of the name. When she had been seven years old she had wondered if his name had been bestowed on him to signify his state of health because he always looked seedy and in need of a good sleep. A year or two later she had decided he was called Mr Grogg because of his drinking habits but later still, when she was old enough to separate fantasy from fact, she had been most disappointed to learn that he was Mr Grogg because that was his bona fide name with no hidden meanings attached to it.

She sighed. Ah, for those far off days when the small dramas of youth could so pleasantly occupy one's mind. Nowadays she seemed always to be concerned with how best to keep body and soul together and the older she got the less easy any of it became.

Oh Danny Boy, the pipes, the pipes are ca-a-lling . . .

Bawling Bob was reaching fever pitch, his voice becoming more distorted by the second. Opening the sash wider Maggie stuck her head out of the window. The disgruntled faces of several other residents of Camloan Road also appeared in their windows. Bawling Bob acknowledged the show with a laconic half nod and a display of broken brown teeth.

'Bloody racket!' Hugh McTavish hauled his braces over his shoulders and looked smug in the belief that he had voiced the general opinion in the matter of Bawling Bob's singing. 'Clear off back to the Gorbals where ye belong and be smart about it or you'll get my toe up yer arse to help ye on yer way!'

Theresa Leckie was visiting the McTavish's. She appeared beside Hugh at the window and shouted down, 'Ay, and don't let me catch you raking through the bins like you did the last time! You left a helluva mess behind and the cats did the rest!'

Bawling Bob, conditioned to a lifetime of insults, blew his nose into the summertime dust of the backcourts, took a deep breath, and opened his mouth wide as he prepared to continue. But before he could, a hail of coppers rained down from the windows. Some of them landed where they would, others were deliberately well aimed and found a few painful marks on Bob's person.

An opportunist urchin darted from a back close to seize on a penny and was, in turn, seized upon by Bawling Bob who was not for sharing his hard-gotten gains with anyone.

Maggie watched the little drama and smiled. The urchin shook himself free and darted off with his spoils. Bob shook his fist at the child's rapidly retreating back and Maggie, taking pity on the man, threw down her own modest contribution of coppers.

Bawling Bob looked up, touched his forelock, and grinned. 'Bless ye, hen, bless ye,' he called up. 'Ye're a good woman, ay, that ye are.'

'Throwing good money away, Maggie, you and your man are tarred wi' the same brush when it comes to common sense.'

The hot breath from John Simpson's fiery lungs prickled the hairs on the back of Maggie's neck. She pulled her head hastily back into the room and almost collided with him, so close did he stand behind her, and she wondered if it was entirely accidental that he brushed his hand against her breasts as she swung round to face him.

Beside him was Jamie, smelling of drink but stone cold sober for all that. He was miserable looking, his eyes were dull and tired.

'I rescued him from himself.' John Simpson sounded smug, his blue eyes regarded Maggie mockingly. 'I found him in a pub at Govan Cross, all set to throw his money away on a crowd o' bloody layabouts. Lucky for him that Tom and I came to the rescue in the nick o' time. We let him have a dram or two then brought him home . . . good thinking, eh, Maggie lass?'

John Simpson had consumed more than his own fair share of liquor. He reeked of whisky, his face was flushed and his blue eyes were filled with fire and challenge. Self-confidence oozed from every pore; his hard, muscled body was taut yet tensile; he looked like a jungle animal ready to spring. Maggie was seized with the dreadful sense of foreboding she had experienced earlier.

The house, so quiet and brooding only minutes before, was now suddenly alive with people. Tom had come in with his father, he was rambling a bit, wondering aloud if Murn had made it safely to Kenneray, and Maggie realised that he was so drunk he could hardly stand straight.

He staggered across to a seat to throw himself down on it and grin at Maggie. 'Murn, dear old Murn,' he chanted. 'When the cat's away and all that. She hates me drinking, you know. The bitch was born to be a buggering old maid! She should never have married yet she loves it, every bloody minute o' it. Pretends to hate it but can't open her legs quick enough after you've exhausted your spunk trying to get all the layers of clothes off her!'

Alex, who with Rachel and Meg had been sent to escort Babs and Bessie back to Camloan Road, looked at Tom with scant respect and Tom, catching the boy's glance, threw back his head and roared with laughter.

'A lad after my own heart! Doesn't like anyone swearing in front o' the lassies! And quite right too, lad, but I've had one too many and don't care what I say, in front o' the ladies – or anyone else for that matter. In case you don't know, I'm going back to an empty house and a cold bed. Murn, my lady wife, saw fit to desert me; my lassies have deserted me also. A lonely man drinks, a lonely man weeps.'

'I'll come back with you, Dad, I'll look after you and keep you company.' Bessie spoke quickly, before her courage could desert her. The idea of staying in this cramped, stuffy house for more than a few minutes filled her with horror. She had dreaded coming here tonight. She disliked and feared John Simpson with an intensity that shook her. He was no more a grandfather to her and Babs than was Jamie. She had seen the way he looked at her sister. She knew that Babs was excited and fascinated by him – it was there in her eyes, those sultry, beckoning eyes that seemed to regard men of all ages as a challenge.

At her sister's words, Babs tossed back her long, fair

hair and said with a mocking laugh, 'Daddy's little girl! Afraid of the big bad wolf! Don't be such a baby, Bess, there's nothing to be afraid of here. Besides, you're just not old enough or capable enough to look after our father on your own!'

Tom treated his youngest daughter to a lop-sided grin. 'Afraid she's right, Bess, you'll be far better off here with Maggie to look after you. And don't worry your little head about me, I'll be fine, I promise. Two weeks will soon pass, you'll get used to it. Think how nice it's going to be, having your cousins to play with.'

Bess blushed to the roots of her hair. She looked as if she couldn't make up her mind whether to cry or run away, much to the amusement of Babs and the discomfiture of the other children.

Alex thrust out his chin and came forward to put a comforting arm round the girl's slender shoulders. 'Come on,' he said gruffly, 'I'll look after you. Tomorrow you can come to The Sac and help me feed and groom the horses and, of course, you can have a ride on Tinker round the field and up the lane.'

Bess gave a watery sniff; she put her hand into Alex's and he led her out of the kitchen, straight past Babs who glared at the pair with an enraged expression on her beautiful face.

Meg threw Babs a triumphant grin and addressed Rachel in a loud voice. 'Come on, let's go into The Room and play till bedtime. Alex has a fine new game to show us, it's called Dark Shadows and needs at least four people.'

The sisters swept out of the kitchen, Babs following slowly, feeling abandoned and unwanted – and no one *ever* humiliated Barbara Simpson and got off with it lightly.

'That's that then.' Tom gulped down the last mouthful of tea in his cup and got shakily to his feet. 'I'll be off. Thanks for the tea, Maggie. If nothing else it's put a few more hairs on my chest. I'll drop by from time to time to see how the lassies are faring. Bess'll soon settle down. She hasn't got Babs's brashness but deep down she's got guts and a fighting spirit though you'd never think it to look at her.'

He staggered into the lobby and let himself out of the house. Mrs Conkey's door opened a half inch, her shadow darkening the sliver of light from her hallway.

Tom hiccuped loudly and throwing back his head he roared with laughter when he saw the heavy wooden door close gently but firmly.

A sprite of mischief danced in Tom's eye and, standing in the middle of the landing, he addressed himself to Mrs Conkey's door.

'Creeping Jesus, come and play, out into the dusty day. Creeping Jesus, thin and slick, let me see what makes you tick. Are your knickers long and grey? Has your fanny lost the way? Or is there roses all a bloom, underneath your witches' broom?'

From behind the Conkey's closed portals there came a distinct scuffling sound, as if someone was scrabbling hastily away from the keyhole. Tom, tickled pink at his poetic prowess, lurched away down the stairs, repeating to himself the verses he had conjured from the wicked depths of his inebriated mind.

The dishes washed, Maggie came out of the scullery to find Jamie half asleep on the hard little chair by the grate while John Simpson was over by the recessed double bed on the chimney wall, turning down the bedspread, punching the pillows into shape.

The bed hadn't been slept in since his marriage to Evie as he had insisted that they have the kitchen to themselves at night. This decision had resulted in very little privacy for Maggie and Jamie and cramped sleeping arrangements for the children.

Meg and Rachel had had to give up their lovely comfortable brass double bed to their grandparents and hardly a night passed but Meg reminded them of the fact. Alex still slept in his cupboard recess, his sisters shared the chair bed with James, and all the while one of the roomy double beds in the kitchen lay empty because the mighty John Simpson had decreed it.

But tonight things were different. Tom had paid handsomely for his stepdaughters to be looked after in his wife's absence and John Simpson was making a good display of seeing to it that his son got his money's worth, although, to all intents and purposes, Evelyn had been the beneficiary.

But Maggie knew different. With her own ears she had heard John wheedling money out of Evelyn. He always needed drinking money and by hook or by crook he invariably managed to get it.

Maggie glanced at Jamie, crumpled and defeated-looking in his hard little chair by the empty grate, and something sore and sad stirred in her breast.

He wasn't drunk, just weary of life. It had been a long time since he was master of his own home. Davie had taken on that role when they had all come to live together in this house, and, young as he was, Alex had taken over when his father died.

Now John Simpson had beaten back both young and old contenders. He was an out and out bully who didn't care how he got his own way just as long as he got it.

In a moment of overwhelming compassion Maggie bent down to put her arms round her husband's neck. 'Bed, Jamie, my man,' she said softly, kissing him on the brow. 'You're done in by the look o' you.'

She helped him to his feet. He leaned heavily against her and looked at her and in the deep pools of his eyes she saw unhappiness, stark and painful.

She bit her lip. Oh, Jamie, her heart cried. Life for you is no longer the joyous thing it once was! You're tired o' it all. I can see it in those bonny eyes o' yours and there's no' a thing I can do to make it better.

His hand crept into hers. It was warm and soft and gentle. She felt a little better. The touch of his hand had always brought her comfort and reassurance and a feeling that she would never be alone with him at her side.

John Simpson was still making a great show with the bedclothes. Maggie wasn't in the least fooled by his display of domesticity – she knew he was deliberately avoiding her in case she might start asking how he had managed to get so much liquor into his belly in the course of the evening.

She guessed that Jamie's pockets would be empty. John Simpson had no qualms whatsoever when it came to indulging his weaknesses and he'd had the nerve to make out that he was the big man who had rescued Jamie from himself.

'It might be better for me and Jamie to sleep in here for the next week or so and let Babs and Bess have our bed,' Maggie spoke firmly and clearly. 'We canna very well let lassies o' their age bide in here wi' you, John. Far better for them to be wi' bairns o' their own age and inclinations.'

There was a long silence; twilight was casting its shadows in the room; a pair of cats wailed mournfully in the backcourt middens; faint sounds of a crying baby drifted up from one of the houses; Mrs Conkey, gliding downstairs to empty her ashcan, dropped it in the close. It made a dreadful clatter as it landed on the hard concrete and she was, no doubt, suffering agonies of apprehension as she waited to see who would be first to appear to find out what all the din was about.

'Inclinations! Inclinations!' John Simpson's words fell like portents of doom in the silence that had suddenly descended over everything. 'I'll tell you about inclinations, Maggie, if you have a mind to listen . . . though you might no' like what I have to say.' He came to stand in the middle of the floor so that Maggie was forced to crane her neck in order to look up at him.

'That young buck, Alex, has the inclinations o' a man twice his age,' John said heavily. 'I wouldn't trust him as far as I could throw him and I'm certainly no' going to trust him in that room wi' *my* granddaughters . . . '

He looked Maggie full in the eye. 'If you don't know what he's like by now you must be blind. He might just be a lad but already he's old enough and able enough to sire an army o' bairns . . . '

Jamie clenched his fists and glared at the other man belligerently. 'You leave my grandson alone, Simpson,' he warned. 'He's a decent lad when all's said and done and wouldn't harm either o' your so-called granddaughters . . . unless they were asking for it. We all ken about Babs and her fleering and flirting. She's no angel and fine you know it.'

John Simpson's eyes sparked but he managed to remain cool. 'Ay, Jamie, I'll grant you that, the girl's a wee tease – but she's only a bairn yet and means no harm. I'll feel easier if she and Bess bide in the kitchen wi' me at night. You go on into The Room, it's nice and cool in there. Keep your eye on Meg and Rachel and I'll do the same wi' Tom's two.'

Maggie saw the sense in his words, Alex *was* perhaps a shade too mature to be alone in the same room with the girls . . . especially that Babs with her pouting lips and her well-developed bosom! A young temptress if ever there was one! He and she had certainly been having a high old time to themselves lately. Playing with fire the pair of them!

But it was over now. Alex was far too busy with his horses and his dozen and one little jobs to allow himself to get too entangled with the sex-obsessed Babs. Even so, it might be wise not to put temptation in his path and Maggie had to concede that, for once, John Simpson was right in what he said.

She nodded. 'All right, I'll send the girls through as soon as I've seen them into their goonies. They can get undressed in the lobby before they come ben here. They're used to the privacy o' their own room and I just hope Bess can thole biding here for the next two weeks.'

'She'll just have to, won't she? It won't do either o' them any harm to see how the other half lives and I'll certainly do all in my power to make them feel welcome and wanted.'

There was something about his tone that didn't ring true. Maggie glanced at him and her flesh crept. A wild beast lurked in the gleaming depths of his eyes – lust leapt out, stark and naked.

He turned away from her quickly but it was too late. She had seen his thoughts, as if he had spoken them aloud for everyone to hear – and Margaret Innes Grant went to bed that night with a heavy heart and a prayer in her soul for all those who had to live and sleep under the same roof as John *the taker* Simpson – which was the name that Maggie had privately bestowed on a man who took everything and seemed to give back nothing but unhappiness to all who crossed his path.

Chapter Twelve

Murn sipped her cocoa and helped herself to a buttered bannock from the heaped plate that Nellie had set down at her elbow.

A contented glow warmed Murn's heart. When she had arrived at Croft Donald earlier she had truly believed that this much-awaited holiday was set to be a total disaster. She had received a welcome that had been lukewarm. No one had put themselves out for her, Kenneth Mor hadn't made any sort of fuss over her and Nellie had been mad at her son and husband for making a public spectacle of themselves. She had been hot and cross and more concerned about the children than anything else. To make matters worse, both Grace and Evelyn hadn't been in the least put out by the strangeness of their reception and had willingly, and with ease, entered into the affairs of the household.

Murn had felt left out and rejected. She convinced herself that nobody really wanted her in this house and that she was just an obtrusive presence who had to be catered for somehow.

But as the day wore on she had gradually relaxed. She had accompanied Grace and Evelyn on a gentle walk along the wide, white, deserted beach that was just yards from the house.

The ocean had been blue and beautiful. It had spumed and roared over the rocks and had lapped the silvery sand in the little bays. Seals had called from the reefs; cormorants had dried their wings in the sun; the bubbling song of a curlew had risen up from the dunes. She had been lulled, soothed, relaxed by the whisper of the sea.

Grace and Evelyn had been good companions. They had talked quietly and happily as they had done when they were all sisters together at King's Croft.

Something had entered Murn's breast as she listened to them speaking. A yearning for things lost, a sadness for what might have been if only . . . if only she had never left the family home to flee far, far across the ocean, to a place that was alien to her and inaccessible to a family too poor to cross even the English channel.

She had cut herself off from all her old ties and her letters home had been few and far between. Her long years of exile away from her native Scotland had nearly broken her heart though never, never, would she have admitted that to anyone – it had taken her such a long time to admit it to herself.

On their return from the beach Kenneth Mor had met them and had taken them to the byre to see a new-born calf. It had been tiny, doe-eyed and beautiful, fluffy, warm, trusting.

Grace and Evelyn had been enchanted with it and Murn knew what they were thinking, feeling . . . King's Croft in summer, young creatures being born, life, so much life in those far-off days.

Again Murn's thoughts took her back in time. Thoughts that were so evocative she had joined in her sisters' enthusiastic praises for the little calf and its patient mother.

Grace and Evelyn had looked somewhat surprised. Of them all Murn had displayed the least interest in crofting activities, indeed she had often been disdainful of her sisters who seemed happy to come from the byre with dung on their boots and bits of hay in their clothing.

But Murn affected not to notice their puzzled faces. She genuinely wanted to stroke the fragile, warm body of the tiny calf and to smile indulgently when the mother stuck her tongue out to give her baby a steamy lick.

Besides . . . Kenneth Mor was there in the background, watching, those cool, blue eyes of his warming to a smile as he too surveyed the calf and its mother . . .

Then he had turned the smile on her and her heart had almost stopped beating with the beauty and wonder of his glance. She had felt faint and had hurried outside for some fresh air, but her day had been made complete.

The rest of the day had passed pleasantly. Dinner hadn't been the noisy affair that she had imagined. The children had sat at their own little table in a corner of the kitchen and had been very quiet and well behaved.

Murn had been dreading sharing a table with Col. The idea of his loose mouth masticating food where she might possibly see and hear it had almost turned her stomach. Almost – but not quite, for Murn had an extremely healthy appetite and adored food of any sort, even though she made a great show of pretending otherwise!

She needn't have worried about Col. He was quite content to join the children at their table and was instrumental in ensuring that they all behaved themselves and that the smallest among them was properly cared for. In fact he presided over the table in quite a parental fashion, a well loved and much respected father figure. It was really rather touching to see him carefully spooning food into a small expectant mouth, his blue, blue eyes wide and intent, his tongue held suspended between his gaping lips.

He and James had taken an instant liking to one another. The little boy seemed able to understand everything his uncle tried so hard to convey and he was perfectly happy to join Col at his table and to leave the grown ups to their own devices. The entire arrangement was very much to Murn's satisfaction. Her maternal instincts were distinctly under-developed and she had little time for children of any sort, especially for little James whose anxious manner always succeeded in totally unnerving her.

Of all Evelyn's children James was the one who looked most like his father, with his brown eyes and curly dark hair. Murn had never much cared for Davie and now she didn't much care for his son. It was the way the little boy stared at her, as if she was some object in a glass case, and she had often found herself shivering and turning away from that black, intent gaze.

So she was more than a mite relieved when her repulsive brother and her equally repulsive nephew sat themselves down with the tinies, thus allowing the grown ups to eat their meal in peace.

Now it was ten o'clock and the children had had a vigorous romp with Kenneth Mor, Evelyn, and Cal. Evelyn had revelled in the opportunity to play with the child she had given to Nellie and Kenneth, but she tired easily these days. She was into her sixth month of pregnancy and though, as yet, it barely showed, she had been sick and exhausted for most of the time and had scant reserves of stamina.

Nellie had supervised bedtime proceedings. It had been a tiring day for everyone and it wasn't long before the children were bathed and packed off to bed. Grace and Col were upstairs with them now, telling them bedtime stories. Squeals of laughter filtered downstairs.

Nellie had been up since six that morning. She and Irene between them had cooked, cleaned, baked and served meals. Both women were used to dealing with the hundred and one tasks attached to being crofting wives, but along with those, there were certain little routines that Nellie alone liked to perform with her young family. So she had played with the children, she had bathed them one after the other in the zinc tub in front of the fire. Not forgetting her role as hostess she had prepared and set out a substantial supper and now, heavy with fatigue, she was sitting back in her chair with her eyes closed.

Murn couldn't help but steal a glance of admiration. She was having second thoughts about her sister's handling of her large family. Everything seemed to run like clockwork under her supervision. The children, even the smallest of them, seemed to hold her in great respect – that they loved her was obvious. They all enjoyed pleasing her and revelled in her attentions and were most unhappy if they did anything that incurred her displeasure.

But what a mess she was, poor thing! Her hair was like an abandoned bird's nest and she had a smudge of coal dust on her cheek. Her skin was certainly still fair and fine, although little lines had etched themselves deeply into the corners of her large, sensuous mouth.

And that apron! No more than a piece of sacking cloth tucked untidily into the waistband of her dreadfully serviceable dark brown skirt. Both apron and skirt bore large patches of damp where the bath water had soaked in *and* – here Murn shuddered – there was a very large hole in Nellie's sensible, thick stockings. It gaped like a crater on the moon, round, ragged, ridiculous.

Oh, poor, dear Nellie! She had simply no idea how to keep herself looking attractive for a man like Kenneth . . . such a man! Strong, virile, dangerously good looking . . . wanting . . . always wanting . . . that!

Murn knew it, she could sense the yearnings of a vigorous man like him. His sexual appetites would be insatiable – and to think he only had scrawny, stringy Nellie to vent his passions on.

He was sitting in the inglenook opposite Nellie, gazing pensively into the fire. Murn wondered what he was thinking. Perhaps – her heart accelerated – perhaps he was thinking about her, wondering how he could best approach her in such a crowded household.

She gaped at him openly. His shirt collar was open, his neck was like a great bronzed pillar, plunging down, down, to delights she could hardly begin to imagine. Acres of golden red hair covered his chest, his arms, his legs. They glinted in the firelight, like threads of spun gold. His wonderful head of hair was in shadow but his beard shone in the light in all its fiery splendour. She wondered what he wore beneath that flamboyant kilt of his – if indeed he wore anything . . .

Her spine tingled. A feeling of warm weakness flooded into her stomach . . . And just at that moment he turned his head and seemed to be looking straight at her. But she couldn't be sure. The lamps hadn't yet been lit and only the afterglow of sunset, combining with the fire's light, illuminated the room.

His face was in shadow, she couldn't see his eyes, nevertheless she was almost certain that he was staring straight at her – silently letting her know that he desired her as much as she desired him.

She took a deep breath, deliberately puffing out her chest until her breasts felt as if they were bursting out of her corset. Her cleavage became a tight channel as her bosoms rose higher in the restraining cloth of her blouse. She felt as if the plump, enticing swellings must surely touch her chin at any moment – and she was running out of lung capacity. He had to come over, he had to. Any man worth his salt wouldn't be able to resist the temptation of such large, creamy breasts . . .

Irene came into the room to light the lamps but, seeing Nellie so peacefully reposing in her chair, she lit only one and tip-toed quietly away again, her finger to her lips as she threw the other occupants of the room a conspiratorial wink.

Pop! Pop! Two of Murn's top buttons left their anchorage. Kenneth Mor inclined his head to gaze at her quizzically before he turned away to throw the sleeping Nellie a look of pure affection.

Murn breathed out in a furious hiss. How dare he? How dare he look with such love at that skinny frump with her unattractive body and her unsavoury clothes – not to mention that hole in her stockings gaping wide for all the world to see! How could any man find anything worth looking at in a woman like Nellie, let alone a man of Kenneth Mor's essential quality?

For several minutes Murn was so smitten with jealousy she felt ill with the strength of her emotion. But this would never do! She couldn't let herself fall prey to such useless feelings. Once, long ago, she had allowed jealousy to swamp her, resulting in years of exile and misery. But she had been young and foolish then, now she was a woman of great strength of character, one who was too wise in the ways of the world to allow anything to stand between her and her ambition.

Ambition! Yes, she had always had that. Right from the start she had worked towards her goals and she had achieved many things through sheer grit and determination.

Only Kenneth Mor had slipped through her fingers, only he had eluded her – but no more! All that was done with. He was now within her grasp and she meant to have him – by hook or by crook she was determined to win him over – and to hell with ugly old Nell, even if she *was* her sister.

Come to think of it, that look Kenneth had directed at Nellie had been a glance charged with pity more than anything else. Yes, Kenneth Mor was fond of his wife as one might be fond of a favourite old sheepdog. She had become a habit, one he had simply come to accept as part and parcel of his daily life – but every dog has its day and poor old Nellie had had more than a good run for her money.

Murn settled back in her chair. She helped herself to another scone, one oozing with home-made bramble jam. She bit into it, the jam dribbled down her chin, and her tongue came out expertly to mop up the sugary rivers. Delicious! Delectable! Nellie certainly knew how to bake, she had always been good at the domestic side of life. At King's Croft she had spent a lot of time over a hot stove, baking, cooking tasty meals.

Domesticated! Yes! definitely that. The sort of woman who had been born to clean and cook and sew and slave over a kitchen sink all day. Other than that, she was about as exciting as a grey umbrella on a rainy day and the wonder was how she had managed to hook a man like

Kenneth Mor when there had been so many other attractive young women in the Grant family . . .

Murn licked her fingers. She was sublimely happy sitting there by the fire, eating jammy scones and making lots of exciting little plans for her stay at Croft Donald.

It was stifling in the kitchen. The heat of the day lingered in every nook and cranny and made the double bed in the recess feel like an oven.

Bessie lay on her back with her eyes tightly shut and her hands clasped firmly over her chest. Every night she sent up a little prayer to her Maker but tonight her words were in desperate earnest, for things had happened in her world that had filled her with fear and insecurity.

Please, Lord, please, she said silently to herself, make it so I can go home soon to my father. I hate this stuffy house. I can't bear to live in it. If it wasn't for the fact that Alex lived here I'd get up out of my bed and run away this very minute . . .

She paused in her thinking. An image of Alex slipped into her mind. Tall, strong, handsome. Somehow very comforting to her in her present disturbed state.

I love Alex, Lord, I've always loved him, even though for a while he was mad about Babs. Keep him safe and free from all harm and I would be very grateful if you would let me marry him when we are both grown up.

She opened her eyes. The kitchen was black dark, but gradually, as her eyes grew used to her surroundings, the room became illuminated by pearly grey light filtering through the net curtains at the windows.

Everything was unfamiliar and unfriendly to her: the chairs looked like crouched up old men beside the fireplace; the dresser in front of the window reminded her of a big, black coffin she'd seen in a funeral parlour in Glasgow; the door of the scullery gaped like the huge entrance to some evil, primitive cave; the dresser mirror glinted in the dim light and – horrors! – the objects in the room were reflected faintly in the oval-shaped glass – it looked like a mouth gaping wide to show the objects it had swallowed.

Bessie's heartbeat accelerated. Her body broke out in a sticky sweat that made her feel itchy all over. She longed to scratch herself but was afraid she might disturb Babs who was giving every indication of being fast asleep at her side.

Bessie wouldn't have minded so much if it had been just her and Babs in the room, but she was very aware of John Simpson's presence in the other bed. Not that he was making any sort of sound – Bessie would have felt easier if he had – there was nothing to indicate that a third person lived and breathed in the same confined area as Babs and herself . . .

Then a bedspring creaked, just a faint noise in the hush of the night but to Bessie's keenly listening ears it was like the sound of a shot fired from a gun.

Her heart pounded afresh; she was awash with sweat; she lay stock still, petrified to move in case *he* should hear and get up to see why she wasn't asleep.

He had been the epitome of consideration just before bedtime. He had hovered over Babs and herself, making sure that they were fed and washed and finally tucked in for the night. A considerate, caring grandfather in every sense of the word only he *wasn't* their grandfather except in name only.

Bess never ceased to be aware of this. She never forgot that he was just a step-grandfather. Another man in that position might have made her forget the fact, but not John Simpson, he was too shallow, too insincere, too obvious.

Several minutes passed. The room breathed on, silent, hot, really quite harmless. Bessie allowed herself gradually to relax, her eyes and limbs grew heavy, her heart settled down to a steady, even beat. She was glad that sleep was about to carry her away from this uncomfortable, unfriendly room . . .

One last look, just to make sure that no Big Black Bogle Man, as James called the Spectre of Darkness, was lurking in the corners, ready to pounce . . .

Sleepily, groggily, her eyelids parted . . . and there, reflected in the mirror was an enormous grey shadow, hunched up and waiting, waiting to pounce – on her!

Again her heart bounded into her throat, every shred of sleep departed, and a strangled sob escaped her. Without ado she dived under the blankets.

Heat enclosed her, wrapped itself round her like a suffocating shroud. Terror gripped her like a living thing, for she knew that the waiting shadow in the mirror was not a vision of the Harbinger of Death but something much, much worse than that . . .

It was John Simpson who stalked and sniffed the night, like a wild animal stealthily waiting for the right moment to spring on its prey . . . Like the creatures of the steaming jungle this man-beast came naked out of the darkness, in a highly aroused and excited state, because he knew that the flesh he desired was just within his reach, ready for the taking.

Chapter Thirteen

Later in her life, if she had been asked to name her worst moment, Bessie would have had no difficulty in pinpointing it as 'the night of the living grey shadow' because that was how she would always remember it.

Yet, for several heart-stopping moments, as she lay in bed straining her eyes into the darkness, she wasn't quite sure if the shadow in the mirror was possessed of any real substance. It seemed to hover there for an eternity, a vague shape that might have been anything . . . a flaw in the glass . . . a blotch on the wall . . . a harmless vision fashioned from the active imaginings of a child . . .

Then the shadow moved and she knew beyond question that it was John Simpson, watching, waiting, stalking the night hours.

Bessie was so rigid with fear she could neither move nor cry out and, so painfully did her heart pound in her ears, she heard nothing as he crept silently towards the bed.

In seconds he had reached his goal, Bessie felt his weight causing the mattress to sag. She trembled as she lay there, sweating and waiting.

Beside her Babs stirred and sighed and murmured something. Her voice was low and husky and she raised herself up on one elbow . . . Bessie saw her body silhouetted against the window – and she was stark naked – her nipples were standing out, hard and swollen on her big bouncy breasts, and Bessie knew beyond a shadow of doubt that Babs had been lying awake, anticipating this moment, working up her sexual appetites as she lay beside her sister, feigning sleep.

Something cold and terrible gripped Bessie's heart. She

knew, of course, how fond Babs was of men and boys. She had been playing the field since the age of ten and never seemed to tire of teasing and tormenting and flaunting herself . . . but this man! Waiting to seduce him with everything she had, wantonly stripping off her nightclothes so that she would be ready for him when he came.

Then Bessie remembered the hot, sultry invitation in Babs's eyes whenever she looked at John Simpson . . . and him . . . practically licking his lips with excitement whenever she was near. No wonder he had been so anxious for Evelyn to go away to Kenneray and for his son's daughters to stay with him.

Bessie felt sick with her thoughts, she wanted to die in those moments. She was disgusted beyond measure by the whole ghastly affair and could only pray that Babs would come to her senses at the last moment and send John Simpson packing.

But Babs had no intention of doing anything of the sort. She had wanted this man for a long time. He both frightened and fascinated her. In him she sensed the animal passions that ran so raw and deep in her own veins.

John Simpson wasted no time. He crawled in between the sisters, breathing heavily. Bessie could smell his naked flesh, a musky, hot scent that emanated from him in sickening waves.

'Right – out, girl!' he mouthed in her ear. 'Into my bed. Say anything about this to anyone and you'll be sorry.'

Petrified though she was Bessie hesitated, hoping that Babs would say something in her favour, anything at all to alleviate the horror of the situation.

'Please, Babs,' Bessie pleaded, 'don't let this happen, you'll be sorry for it later – Father would die if he knew . . . '

'Go on, cry baby.' Babs's voice was mocking, tinged with impatience. 'Do as Grandpa tells you like a good little girl . . . of course, if you would rather stay and watch . . . maybe even join in . . . '

A sob caught in Bessie's throat. She leapt out of the bed and scuttled across the floor to John Simpson's bed. It was still warm where he had lain; it smelt sweaty and damp and of something else . . . that musky scent again, all mixed up with the heat of the night and the faint odour of cooking from the evening meal.

Bessie shuddered. The feeling of nausea intensified in her belly, her bladder had filled up and she knew she would have to get up to empty it. Then she remembered, the house didn't boast a bathroom. The lavatory was situated on the half landing, and she couldn't, she just couldn't face going down those creepy outside stairs at this time of night.

Rachel had told her there were chamber pots under the beds. They all had to use them some time or another and it was nothing to be ashamed of.

But Bessie rebelled against the idea. She couldn't, she wouldn't get up out of this bed to empty her bladder into a chamber pot while those two in the other bed were . . . were . . .

Her thoughts couldn't take her any further. As yet she wasn't fully versed in the facts of life and could only guess at what was happening between her sister and her grandfather.

She thought of Alex through there in The Room and all her instincts made her want to run to the safe, strong circle of his arms. She knew he would comfort her. He was still only a boy and gruff in many ways, but there was a warmth and a sympathy in his nature that lent him an extra special quality.

Then she remembered John Simpson's threats and she knew she would never tell anybody of this night while he lived and breathed and intimidated her with his very presence . . .

She stiffened. Her sister was moaning in the other bed, a primitive sound that made Bessie's toes curl and her flesh creep. It was the start of endless hours of animal-like noises that penetrated Bessie's senses and kept her from her sleep. She lay there, in John Simpson's bed, enduring her sleeplessness and her discomfort, wishing, oh, wishing that it was time for her stepmother to come back and for the family to be together again.

She neither disliked nor liked Murn, but she wasn't as bad as Babs made out and with luck she might hate the country and cut short her holiday . . .

Please, Lord, make it happen, prayed Bessie. She thought of Alex again . . . a small glow warmed her heart . . . John Simpson was groaning deep in his throat . . . Bessie pulled the sheet over her head and wept.

As soon as Bessie left the bed John Simpson pulled Babs into his arms and sought her mouth. He was rough and hard and demanding. 'You'll be my wee wife,' he said urgently. 'Tonight and every night for as long as I want you.'

Babs giggled. 'Yes, Grandpa, anything you say, Grandpa,' she said meekly. 'You know I would never dare go against your orders.'

'You'd better mean that, if you know what's good for you, and cut out the grandfather bit, I'm no more that to you than a fly in the air — even if you do mean it as a joke.'

There was a hint of menace in his voice and a shaft of fear smote Babs to the quick, but it only added to the excitement of the night with this man. He had barely touched her as yet but his kiss had been enough to send wave upon wave of thrilling sensations through her entire being.

His body was thickly covered in hairs . . . Suddenly she thought of Alex and his smooth young body and she was gripped by a terrible yearning. In the whole of her short, selfish life she had only ever loved herself — until she met Alex Grainger. It had come as quite a shock when she discovered that she genuinely liked him, and the feeling grew deeper as time went on.

But he didn't want her — not anymore. In the beginning he couldn't get enough of her and his youthful sexual appetites had satisfied her beyond measure. Now he had grown tired of her and seemed to prefer his silly old horses ... *And* he had suddenly noticed that Bessie existed and was paying her far too much attention, and her so plain and uninteresting. It wasn't Bessie herself of course, it was only because she was as fond of smelly horses as he was himself.

Jealousy twisted in her heart like a knife. She would show him! He was only a foolish little boy who needed to be taught a sharp lesson ... But let that keep for a while, she was in the arms of a *real* man and the knowledge of that fact thrilled her afresh.

John Simpson's breath was coming fast. The satin-smooth flesh beneath his roughly caressing hands was driving him crazy with desire. He hadn't had one as young as this before but there was nothing in her behaviour to betray the fact that she was little more than a child. It didn't take him long to discover that she was sexually mature and more than ready to meet his passions with hers. She was as experienced as a woman twice her age.

Her writhings and her moanings were driving him wild. Greedily he explored every willing part of her body before entering her with the brute force of a lust-crazed animal.

It was only the beginning of a night of uninhibited eroticism for the two of them. She made no objection to any of the brutish demands he made on her and he soon came to the conclusion that he had met an able match in young Barbara Simpson.

As for Babs, she loved every carnal moment of her first night with this man and she spared not one thought for the sister who lay in the other bed, shocked, unhappy, and very, very afraid.

*

Evelyn woke slowly but didn't immediately open her eyes. She knew from the brightness against her eyelids that sunlight was streaming into the room through the net curtains and a glow of pure happiness warmed her heart.

On the branches of the rowan tree outside the window, a blackbird was blithely singing and the young woman in the bed could hardly believe how enchanting the sound was, a sound that she had once, long ago, taken for granted.

Yawning and stretching luxuriously, she opened her eyes just to lie there, sleepily surveying the flower-sprigged wallpaper, watching the dappled pools of sunlight dancing on the polished red wood of the floor.

Oh, how lovely it was to be back at Croft Donald, with her darling Grace serenely asleep at her side. How good it was to hear the sounds of the countryside, to see sunshine bathing the land, to know that she could lie for as long as she liked with no demands on her time, her emotions . . . her body.

For John Simpson had never made any concessions to her pregnancy. She had been sick, exhausted, ill, and through it all she'd had to endure his nightly claims on her body that was often still sore from the previous night.

She had forgotten what it was like to be free from the bruises and other manifestations of his sexual brutality and, before her mother had suggested she come on this holiday, she had been on the point of telling him that she could no longer bear to have him in her life, far less her bed.

Later she thought of the child in her womb, a child she hadn't wanted and still didn't. When first she realised she was expecting another baby she had considered the idea of getting rid of it and had actually gone to see an old crone who lived in a seedy house in a rough part of the city.

God forgive her! She shuddered every time she remembered that awful old woman with her brown teeth, her mean little eyes and her claw-like fingers stretching out to pull her into a dingy room where one could almost hear the cries of agony and smell the blood and the death.

She couldn't get out of the house fast enough and she would never forget the string of obscenities that had followed her out of the close and down the filthy, brooding street.

Oh, poor little unborn babe! What kind of woman was she to deny such an innocent creature the right to life? She couldn't deny it its birthright and so she said nothing to John Simpson about wanting him to leave but decided instead to wait and see what sort of father he would be to his very own child.

She gave herself a mental shake. All that was in the future. Right now she wanted just to be here, in this peaceful, sunny place, Grace in the bed beside her, the scents of summer pervading the room, the snow white curtains billowing gently in the breeze, a bumble bee prodding the little vase of yellow broom on the windowsill.

But despite the brightness of the morning there remained a feeling of darkness in her breast. She couldn't be sure if it was the result of her bleak musings or if it was born of something else altogether – a feeling that had been growing stronger and culminated in this strange sense of foreboding . . .

Again she shuddered and thought, Oh, no, not that again, why can't it leave me alone? Will I ever be free of it?

But she had been born with the sixth sense and knew that nothing but death would ever make it leave her. She was glad that Grace stirred at her side and slowly opened eyes that were big and black and beautiful, even at that time of the morning when she had just emerged from sleep.

Grace had skin like alabaster and there would always be a dewy freshness to it, no matter how many years separated her from girlhood. Nellie maintained that she was a

Peter Pan who would never truly grow up. Nellie hoped she never would because there was a special quality surrounding this darling sister of hers and to be in her presence was like breathing the fresh, woodland air.

At thirty-eight she had the looks and figure of a young girl. Her haunting eyes were clear and wide, her expressions and viewpoint often innocently childlike. Yet there was great maturity and wisdom behind the high, smooth brow that manifested itself in times of trial and tragedy. She had always clung to the belief that her darling Gordon would one day come back to her. At first, those who were closest to her and who loved her most had tried to make her face the truth. Now they realised how her hopes sustained her and they couldn't hurt her by telling her how futile her naive dreams were.

So, in many ways, she was happier than any of them. Despite having had a delicate stomach from childhood, her life was comparatively free from stress and strain. She took things as they came, never expecting too much, never pining for possessions or coveting those belonging to other people. She was well adjusted to life and her surroundings and had many friends who loved her because of her beautiful, uncomplicated personality.

Evelyn was glad to be here on Kenneray with her. They had shared several wonderful holidays at Croft Donald and Grace never failed to be on hand wherever and whenever she was needed.

'Grace in the morning is like sunrise a' dawning,' Evelyn said with a laugh as she watched her sister stirring and stretching and smiling.

'You aye were a poet,' Grace said with a laugh. She looked towards the window. 'Oh, it's a beautiful day out there, let's go and visit the new calf before breakfast. Ten minutes won't matter here or there and we can both help wi' the chores later.'

Evelyn thought it was a marvellous idea and felt like a girl again as she and Grace hurried into their clothes and out into a morning that was fragrant with peat smoke and newly cut hay.

'Maybe we should have called Murn,' Grace said rather guiltily as they made their way to the byre.

'Ach, she's too much o' a lie-a-bed. Have you forgotten what she was like at King's Croft when the rest o' us had to get up to see to the beasts? The only thing that changed her was becoming a teacher when she would struggle out in all weathers . . . besides . . .' she linked her arm through Grace's, 'it's nice just you and me. Murn would only put a damper on things wi' her moans and groans and her goggling at Kenneth Mor as if she could eat him.'

But a surprise awaited them when they entered the steamy byre. Murn had beaten them to it and was helping Cal and Kenneth to fork hay into Bonny's manger.

At least, she was making a great show of helping but was in fact only getting in the way. She was hating every moment in the byre. To her they were hot, smelly places where one got one's feet covered in cow dung no matter how careful one tried to be. The novelty of the new calf had quickly worn off but it had been a good excuse to be in the byre with the menfolk.

She had been enjoying lying in bed that morning after such a harassing journey the day before. Irene had brought her a cup of tea and she had lain back contentedly and had let her thoughts wander. Thoughts of Babs and Bessie had briefly entered her mind but she had quickly pushed them aside. They were old enough to take care of themselves and Maggie would certainly make sure they were well catered for.

Tom had remained a little longer in her thoughts but only because he hadn't given her as much money as she would have liked for her vacation. Not that it mattered now. As far as she could see there was nothing that resembled a shop in this part of the world. One would have to travel miles to find a sizeable town and with all these dreadful roads to traverse it just wasn't worth all the effort.

No, it was far nicer just to lie back and elaborate on all the lovely little plans she had made for herself and Kenneth Mor.

When she had spotted Kenneth going into the byre with Cal she had willingly abandoned her bed so that she could be with the man she loved and, while her arrival hadn't seemed to greatly excite him, he *had* smiled at her in that nice crinkly way of his and had bidden her a pleasant good morning.

And now here she was, up to her ankles in dung, her corsets just about strangling her – for she certainly hadn't dressed herself for a relaxing holiday but still wore her silks and satins and had made sure to choose a blouse that exposed her cleavage to its maximum.

Not that it had appeared to impress Kenneth, he had merely glanced at her in some surprise before getting on with his work, leaving Cal to stare and stifle a snigger before his father recalled him to the task in hand.

Grace and Evelyn had come to stick their noses in now, looking fresh and comfortable in their print summer dresses with their faces all clean and shiny and their hair tied back in cute little ribbons.

Both Kenneth and Cal looked at them appreciatively and Murn was so furious she vowed there and then to find a shop where she could purchase some clothes suited to the simple country life.

Kenneth certainly had no ideas on how a *real* woman should look. He had proved that last night when he had ogled Nellie in her dreadful homespun garb . . . but – here Murn wrinkled her brow in concentration – perhaps that was how a man of his Highland blood liked to see his women: plain and simple, all the icing removed, no frills and furbelows to clutter his vision . . .

There was something so earthy and primitive in these notions that Murn grew quite excited by them. I *will* make an effort to find the nearest town, she vowed and smiled to herself. *Never* in all her imaginings had she visualised any man becoming excited at the sight of cotton underwear and flowery dresses. But then, Kenneth wasn't just any man, he was different in every way and this was just another example of his individuality . . .

Murn was standing in the shadows but even so Evelyn saw the odd little smile hovering on her lips and she wondered what her sister was thinking – until Murn turned her adoring gaze on Kenneth thus exposing every idle thought inside her head.

Evelyn felt uneasy. There was something terribly unhealthy about this obsession of Murn's. It was as if her years away from Kenneth had greatly intensified her feelings for him instead of diminishing them.

Most women would have gotten over such a girlhood passion long ago. However, Murn wasn't most women – she had been odd and intense ever since she was a child and, unlike her sisters, she had always been something of a loner, choosing to brood over her introverted thoughts instead of getting out and enjoying the many excitements life had to offer.

Murn had moved into a patch of sunlight but even as Evelyn watched, a dark shadow seemed to materialise out of nowhere to fall on her sister as she stood there, oblivious to everything but her own, useless innermost thoughts.

Evelyn's heart began to pound. She felt as if a giant hand had seized her lungs and squeezed all the air out of them. A strange and chilly wind sprung out of nowhere to swirl around the byre. She knew it came from the mists and mysteries of her mind, she had experienced its icy blast many times before but she could never accept this power that sprung from deep within her.

She was freezing cold and trembling. Dark, terrible visions bombarded her. 'It will be Murn.' The whispered words seemed to come from another being inside of Evelyn. Her face was white, her green eyes huge and afraid as she stared at Murn and uttered the words.

'What did you say?' Grace turned questioningly, but the blood froze in her veins as she witnessed the horror on her sister's face. 'What's wrong, Evie?' she said urgently. 'You look as though you've seen a ghost.'

'It will be Murn,' Evelyn answered automatically, almost as if she was repeating what someone else had said.

'Evie.' Grace put her hand on her sister's arm. 'You said something – about Murn – and you looked gey funny when you said it, all sort of spooky and sad.'

Evelyn stared at Grace. Her eyes were dazed and far-away. She remained like that for several moments before she shook her head as if to clear it.

'What was that, Grace? What did you say?'

'About Murn – you . . . '

'We'll have to keep an eye on her, Grace,' Evelyn said urgently. 'She has to be looked after.'

Grace's smooth brow furrowed. 'Ay, Evie, we'll look after Murn, we'll no' let anything harm her.'

Evelyn frowned, she felt sick and ill and afraid. Without another word she hurried out of the byre, into the sunlight, leaving Grace staring after her in a worried fashion – because Grace knew all about Evelyn's strange powers, connecting her with the past . . . and the future . . .

Chapter Fourteen

When Maggie went through to the kitchen to make breakfast it was to find John Simpson deeply asleep in his own bed and Babs and Bessie likewise in theirs, Bessie having been ordered to get back in beside her sister in the early hours of the morning.

At breakfast Maggie noticed how drawn and pale Bessie looked, with dark smudges under her eyes and a pinched look about her mouth.

Maggie liked Bessie, she liked her very much indeed. There was something very appealing about the girl's open face and honest eyes while the long, silken hair hanging to her waist added to her air of childish innocence.

'Are you all right, lassie?' Maggie asked kindly. 'You look as if you didna sleep too well last night.'

Bessie flushed a bright crimson. She opened her mouth and shut it again and she was very comforted when Alex sought her hand under the table and gave it a reassuring squeeze.

'It was too hot,' the girl answered – rather too quickly.

Maggie hadn't had five daughters of her own for nothing. She knew that Bessie was holding something back yet no one could deny the truth of her words as, even now, the kitchen retained the heat of the previous day. When Babs came yawning to the table it seemed as if she was suffering from the same complaint as her sister.

Babs was unmistakably untidy-looking. Her long, golden hair was in disarray around her shoulders and she had hurriedly thrown on her clothes, but for all that she still looked stunning with her brilliant blue eyes sparkling in her lovely face and her smooth cheeks rosily aglow.

There was an air of suppressed excitement about her. She spooned her porridge into her mouth demurely enough but every so often she glanced up from her plate to look at all the faces round the table, and an undeniably smug smile quirked one corner of her mouth. It was as if she was trying very hard not to show her exhilaration yet at the same time wanting everyone to know that she had something to hide.

At one point she stared at Alex in such an obvious manner he was unable to avoid her eyes. He tried to pretend that he hadn't noticed but she went on gazing at him until he had to meet her look, whereupon she tilted her head to one side and ran her tongue slowly and provocatively over her lips.

Everyone at the table noticed the exchanges between the two. Rachel reddened and went on eating her breakfast; a highly discomfited Bessie did likewise; Meg snorted and glared at Alex while Jamie frowned at his grandson and wondered what mischief he had been up to.

Maggie looked worried. She was only too aware of the attraction that had existed between Babs and her grandson – but she was certain he had gotten over all that and that he was more inclined these days to favour Bessie who shared his passion for horses and his interest in the countryside.

Yet – Maggie glanced at Babs – the little hussy was certainly sending the boy the sort of signals that suggested a liaison still existed between them . . .

Maggie felt uneasy as she wondered just what had been going on last night under her very nose. Alex could easily have slipped into the kitchen to bed himself down with Babs and Bessie. That would explain Bessie's pale face and her reluctance to speak and it would certainly account for Babs's rosy cheeks and secretive air. The little madam seemed to be an expert at driving boys wild and Alex had proved no exception.

Maggie vowed to herself to keep a close watch on the

pair of them and, so wrapped up was she in her thoughts, she failed to notice Babs slipping into the scullery when John Simpson went through to wash his hands before breakfast.

He had been out for his morning newspaper and, having more than satisfied his sexual appetites, all he wanted now was to assuage the pangs of hunger that were gnawing at his belly.

Even so he could no more resist the fresh young beauty of this little temptress than he could help breathing and, as soon as she appeared at his side and smiled, he pushed his hand up her skirt and played with her till she was panting.

'Hot little bitch,' he told her roughly. 'There's no satisfying you, is there? A time and a place, girl, a time and a place. Right now all I want is my breakfast so get out o' my way.'

'Right, Grandpa, anything you say, Grandpa,' she returned impudently.

His hand shot out to grip her arm. 'Don't come the smart arse wi' me if you know what's good for you, do you hear?'

'Yes – oh, yes,' she conceded with a gasp of pain.

He let her go and strode out of the scullery.

She stood where she was, holding her arm, her heart pounding with a mixture of fear and fascination. She knew where she stood with John Simpson – and he knew that she knew.

Kenneth Mor was never so shocked as when he went into the barn one drizzly wet morning to find Murn blocking his way.

She was wearing a thin, print, button-through dress. It wasn't exactly the kind of day for a dress of any sort. The weather had turned chilly and wet, but Murn had gone to a lot of trouble to get the wretched garment and was hell bent on wearing it. She had persuaded Grace to go with her into the nearest village some miles away and would have dragged Evelyn along if she had not been feeling sick.

'But you keep an eye on her, Grace,' Evelyn had urged, her unearthly experience in the byre still very vivid in her mind. 'There's something about her behaviour that I dinna like. She's strange and sad and reckless and doesn't seem to care anymore about the normal sort o' things.'

'Oh, all right, I'll watch over her as if she was a baby,' Grace promised with a sigh, the prospect of a day out with Murn not appealing to her in the least. But, being Grace, she accompanied Murn on her mission with scant complaint.

Murn was in one of her high and mighty moods. She looked down her nose at the village shopkeepers; she complained about the prices; she criticised their goods, and induced such hurt feelings in one sensitive lady she was asked to leave the premises and never return.

'What can one expect?' Murn said with a toss of her head. 'People like that don't know what it's like to be crossed. Their customers will accept anything simply because they just don't know any better with the result that people like her become complacent.'

Grace said nothing. She held onto her patience for much longer than the average person, but when Murn still had not purchased anything after an hour of humming and hawing, Grace's patience finally wore thin.

Murn had seldom, if ever, seen this lovely, placid sister of hers in a temper and for quite some minutes she could only stare in awe as Grace stamped her foot and declared that she was going home right there and then if *something* was not bought in one of these stores *at once*.

At the sight of Grace's livid face Murn was sore afraid and without ado she rushed into the nearest shop later to emerge bearing a brown paper parcel filled to overflowing with plump pork sausages, bursting at the seams with spicy home-made goodness.

The sight of her elegantly dressed sister gingerly holding

the incongruous looking parcel, was too much for Grace and she burst out laughing, a sight that so pleased Murn she allowed herself to unwind enough to join in the merriment.

With the atmosphere between them very much lighter, both sisters thoroughly enjoyed poking and prying into the variety of little shops that the village had to offer, with the result that Murn managed to get a flower-print cotton frock that 'wasn't too ghastly' and a set of cotton undergarments that she hated but which she accepted as being the sort of things that country women wore because 'they didn't know any better.'

Now she was alone with Kenneth Mor in this freezing barn, feeling strange and naked without her usual layers of corsets next to her skin . . . but – and here she shivered in anticipation – there *was* something terribly exciting about wearing thin cotton undies that gave no visible means of support to her curves. She had even omitted to wear a bra and for the first time in years she was aware of the movement of her breasts with every step she took.

She was utterly fascinated by the experience. The flimsy material of her frock revealed every contour of her body. She felt totally feminine and sensitive to everything around her. The sensations wrought in her breasts through merely brushing past a bale of hay were so utterly pleasurable that she repeated the action several times, and she had worked herself into a nice state of arousal by the time Kenneth Mor appeared in the barn.

Murn had known for a fact that he was coming, and for the last week she had made it her business to follow the moves of his daily routine. He had several little tasks to see to each morning before breakfast and one or two of them involved visits to the barn.

It was an easy enough matter for Murn to wait for him there and the idea of making love in such a basic place greatly appealed to her. On the chosen morning, Kenneth was no sooner in the door than she appeared from her hiding place to lay her hand on his arm and say huskily, 'I've been waiting for you, darling, ever since I came to Croft Donald I've been waiting. You're such a busy man, I've never had the opportunity even to speak to you properly. But even busy men have their needs and you're such a strong, vital man you must have more needs in a week than an average man has in a year.'

While she was speaking, she pulled him further into the shed, her eyes never leaving his face, as if she was trying to hypnotise him into obeying her. He was staring at her in a completely bewildered fashion. The last person he had expected to see in the barn at that early hour was Murn.

Murn hadn't repeated her first visit to the byre to see Bonnie, preferring instead to lie in bed and wait for someone to bring her a cup of tea. Irene and Isla Nell, Kenneth's grown daughter home on holiday from college, had been only too glad to oblige, quickly realising that it was no fun to have Murn under their busy feet at any time, far less when life at Croft Donald was up and demanding attention. They unwittingly kept Kenneth reasonably free of the cloying attentions of Murn.

So, as he usually felt quite safe from her during the hour before breakfast, to find her up and about on such a wet morning came as a considerable shock to his system. There she was in the shadows, waiting to pounce on him, as large as life and twice as formidable. He had never seen her looking so ungainly. She was more than fat, she was bloated; the dress she was wearing showed every roll of blubber and, to make matters worse, she had painted her face so heavily she looked like an enormous doll leering at him out of the dimness.

She was speaking to him in a manner that was oddly menacing. Her voice was husky and low and she was saying things that were meant to be enticing and inviting, but somehow she was only succeeding in sounding foolish and sad and somehow – frighteningly – insane . . .

The thought came to his mind like a bolt from the blue, yet – hadn't that same thought niggled away at the back of his mind ever since she had made those embarrassing overtures to him on the day of Evelyn's wedding . . . ?

'Murn . . .' he wrested his arm free and stepped back from her. 'I'm a busy man, I havena the time nor the inclination to stand here talking to you. It's chilly in here, you'd be better off back at the house. Nell will . . .'

'To hell with Nell.' The softness had left Murn's voice, it was as hard and as brittle as ice. 'Ay, and when I say that I mean it, for in the fires of hell is where she should have perished long ago. She took you from me, Kenneth, you preferred a cold-eyed bitch like that to a warm, loving woman like me but only because she tricked you into marrying her. Oh, my darling . . .' She moved towards him, unbuttoning her dress as she came, her breasts springing out from their flimsy covering.

'I bought this dress especially for you, Kenneth,' she murmured as she ran her tongue wetly over her brightly painted lips. 'I know how much you like simple materials like cotton. Oh, my love, just look at you, that fiery beard, that wonderful flowing hair, that beautiful muscular torso that drove me crazy from the start! You're a man of nature, Kenneth, as tall as the trees, as grand as the hills, a man of instinct and power. I can sense it in you, the restlessness, the longing to be free of the fetters that bind – a desire to be free of *her*. I can give you that freedom, my darling. I can give you a love that will provide you with everything you want from life, but for now – take me – take me, darling Kenneth, I promise you, you will want nothing more from life once you have tasted the sweetness of my body . . .'

She was tearing off her dress as she came towards him, revealing every rotund inch of her generous proportions, all wrapped up in white cotton knickers and a ribbed cotton camisole . . .

For several moments he stood where he was, rooted to the spot, horrified by this woman and her unreasoning obsession with him. Her eyes were staring, staring at him as if she could devour every inch of his flesh . . . In those moments Kenneth Mor knew for sure that his wife's sister was mad and probably had been from the beginning.

'Murn, Murn, lass, don't do this to yourself,' his whisper was a combination of revulsion and pity. Then, unable to take any more, he turned on his heel and walked out of the barn, away from the madness, into a rain that had sprung from the misty hills and was cold and sweet and wonderful on his moist, burning brow.

But, for Kenneth, the nightmare had only just begun. After his rejection, Murn spent a lonely, restless morning, never leaving the shelter of the barn, endlessly going over all that had transpired between them.

Cold and miserable, she huddled in the hayloft, thinking her illogical thoughts, trying to fathom where she had gone wrong in the handling of what had been to her, a perfect opportunity to seduce the man of her dreams. In the end, she came to the conclusion that she hadn't been brash enough – a man like Kenneth needed firm action. She had tried to impress him with words and, as a result, she had frightened him off.

Murn made a vow that next time she would be more definite in her approaches and with that resolve she at last made her way to the house where she slipped unseen up to her room to change into something more suitable for the weather.

Somehow she managed to maintain a normal front for the rest of that long day and no one suspected that her mind was in such a turmoil. Kenneth never once looked at her, and ostensibly she paid him no attention whatsoever though all the time she watched and waited in a fever of impatience.

For she had decided that she would successfully seduce him that very evening. This time he wouldn't get away, he wouldn't *want* to get away, not after he had seen what she had in store for him.

Strike while the iron's hot, she told herself firmly, and gave vent to a little high-pitched laugh. The idea of lying in the muscular arms of Kenneth Mor made her feel very good indeed and some of the turbulence left her mind. Even so, she was still nervy and jumpy and after dinner that night she went to the cupboard where the 'medicinal alcohol' was kept.

Without ado, she helped herself to a flagon of brandy, hurrying with it out to the hayloft where she raised it to her lips and gulped down a quarter of the contents as if it was lemonade.

Choking and gasping, she lay back in the prickly hay to wait, knowing fine that Kenneth always came to the barn after dinner to collect the feed for Bonnie's manger. Sometimes he sent Cal but Cal was paying a lot of attention to a very attractive summer visitor who shared his love of boats and the sea. They had been out sailing and fishing together every night that week, an arrangement that suited Murn perfectly.

She was wearing her cotton, button-through dress again but – and here she felt quite weak with anticipation – she wasn't wearing a stitch under it and she could hardly wait to see Kenneth's face when she revealed all to him.

If Evelyn hadn't been ill that day she would have known that Murn was heading for some sort of disaster. However, this sixth pregnancy of hers was taking its toll on her weary body and Nellie, always concerned with this darling youngest sister of hers, wasted no time in ordering her to spend a day in bed for a complete rest.

Nellie's bossy nature had often made Evelyn rebel but this time she was very glad to obey such a caring command.

She went to bed, to sleep, to eat, to sleep again, never knowing that the remaining shreds of Murn's reason were, at last, about to snap.

Chapter Fifteen

Nellie was singing 'Rock of Ages' as she rushed around the kitchen, trying to do a dozen jobs at once. She had never been particularly religious, nor had her voice ever been very tuneful, but to Kenneth her singing was the sweetest sound on earth, because it was a sign that she was happy, and to him Nellie's happiness was of paramount importance.

She was at the sink, up to her elbows in soapsuds, when he came up behind her and nuzzled her ear.

'Happy?' he asked softly.

The touch of his lips sent shivers of delight through her entire body for this big, wonderful, red-haired Highlander of hers never failed to excite her, no matter how many years had passed since their wedding day.

'Oh ay, I'm happy,' she conceded. 'You know fine I'm aye happy on a Friday.'

'Me too,' he said with a grin and allowed his hands to slide from her waist up to her breasts.

'Kenneth Cameron Mor!' She pretended to be aghast. 'Anybody could come in and find you ravishing me at the sink. Be off wi' you this minute or I'll – I'll hit you wi' a soapsud.'

He laughed. 'Later on I'll let you do what you will with me – even down to the soap bubbles . . .'

He paused, wondering if he should tell her about Murn's odd behaviour of the morning but he quickly decided against it. Why should he spoil her happiness just because her sister seemed determined to make a fool of herself? Besides . . . Murn had said something about having a headache and going to bed early. She had certainly seemed very subdued all of that day. Perhaps she had been thinking things over and had finally come to her senses. With any luck she might even go home sooner than she had intended and give them all a bit of peace.

His heart lifted. Somehow the very idea of Murn safely tucked up in bed brought him an enormous sense of relief.

'I'll go and give Bonnie her feed,' he said briskly. 'By rights Cal should be taking his turn but he's like a stag in rut these days. I just hope the visitor lassie will be safe wi' him. He's a young buck if ever there was one and will never be content wi' just a kiss.'

'Like father like son,' she returned impudently, whirling round to fend him off with her soapy hands when he tried to smack her bottom.

Murn's head was spinning. She had drunk almost half a flagon of brandy and felt as if a small fire was burning in her belly and everything around her was bathed in a rosy glow.

She hadn't eaten very much at dinner time with the result that the alcohol had gone to her head quicker than normal.

But she didn't mind, it was a wonderful sensation. She was experiencing a marvellous sense of euphoria. It wasn't exactly warm in the barn but the passions were leaping in her veins and she was very aware of her state of nakedness underneath her flimsy cotton dress. She could hardly wait for Kenneth to come to her so that she could show him how a *real* woman ought to look.

He was a long time in coming. She felt as if she had been waiting for hours – these long, summer days made one lose all sense of time. It must be at least eight o'clock and although there was still a fine mist of rain in the air it was very bright and the skylarks were trilling in ecstasy high above the fields.

It was an evocative sound, it brought back memories that she had thought long forgotten: King's Croft sitting serene and snug amongst the trees, the smoke from its chimneys spiralling into the evening sky; the sad, lonely sound of the peesies; the larks singing all day long; the smell of the earth and the sun and the sweet scent of gorse drifting down through the parks and houghs of Rothiedrum . . .

Murn lay back, remembering. She didn't know how long she remained there as her thoughts carried her back over the years, but when the rattling of the barn doors penetrated her senses she was instantly alert.

A shaft of light lanced the dimness . . . and the man she had been waiting for was outlined in the brightness . . . A great, red giant of a man who seemed to glow and grow in size as she gazed at him.

But she held her patience. She had to pick her moment, everything had to be just right for what she had in mind . . . So she waited until he was firmly inside the shed and over at the hay bales before she made her appearance.

Her heart was pounding in her breast, she could feel the beat of it inside her head. She was trembling from head to foot with suspense and for a moment she felt so weak with emotion it was all she could do to catch her breath.

He had his back to her, he was engrossed in what he was doing, completely unaware that he was not alone.

Then came that sense of another presence, an awareness that someone waited to surprise him as a tigress might wait in the trees to leap on its prey. He stiffened. His adrenalin pumped and every muscle in his body tensed, preparing him for flight.

He knew it was Murn who was watching him. He sensed that she was there in the cobwebby half-light beneath the hayloft. He could *smell* her particular odour, a sickly combination of scent and powder and soap, all of them mingling with the other subtle smell of a female moist with the heat of her passions.

Kenneth shuddered. He didn't want to turn round to the sight he knew awaited him and, for quite a few nauseous moments, he remained as he was, his hands on the hay bale, his knees braced to take its weight — while the hairs on the back of his neck rose up as if stimulated by an electric shock . . .

Murn had recovered her composure. She could wait no longer, and with a swift, theatrical movement she undid the last button of her dress and moved out of the shadows.

'You were a long time coming, Kenneth,' she said rather petulantly. 'But it doesn't matter, you're here now and we've got the whole wonderful evening ahead of us. I'll let you see what true passion is all about. I'll awaken you, my darling, such as that shapeless, sexless wife of yours never could . . . '

He swung round to face her. She advanced, he backed away, shocked and sickened by the unattractive picture that her nakedness presented to him. She was as white as lard, as grotesque as a Buddha, as painted as a Dresden china doll but with none of its delicacy.

To make matters worse she was drunk; the closer she came to him the more he was aware of the fumes of liquor on her breath . . . and to add to the unreality of the scene she began to dance, swaying towards him, her arms outstretched, her breasts flopping from side to side, her hips oscillating in an awkward, heavy movement.

'Oh, my God,' Kenneth murmured. 'No' again, can't you let it rest, girl, can't you?'

In a vivid flashback he remembered the young Murn of twenty years ago, dancing naked in front of a gypsy fire, a drunken madness in her because he and Nell were going to be married. She had been wild and reckless and had made such a fool of herself she had had to leave home soon afterwards, eventually landing up in Australia.

But it was all such a long time ago, she couldn't still be carrying a torch for him? It was unhealthy, unnatural . . . it was . . . madness . . .

'Enough o' this, Murn!' Kenneth spoke harshly. 'Dinna torment yourself like this! You're a married woman, Tom's a good man. You just canna go on behaving like a silly schoolgirl all your days. Go home to your man, go and live your own life and forget all about me.'

At that she threw herself at him to wrap her arms around him in a crushing embrace. 'No, Kenneth, no,' she implored and began to sob. Strong fumes of alcohol bathed his face and he felt repulsed beyond measure.

'I can't forget you, I don't *want* to forget you,' she went on. 'I never stopped loving you and I never will. Oh, my darling,' she raised her face to him, 'you and I could have a wonderful life together. Tom doesn't need me, Nellie doesn't need you. I've got money, Kenneth, more than Tom will ever know about. I've been saving, you see, saving up for you and me. That bitch, Nellie, doesn't deserve a man like you, she's just a dried up old prune who's had her day and it's time I had mine . . .'

'Enough! How dare you speak about Nell like that! She's twice the woman you'll ever be and I'll never stop loving her.'

'But – you love me, Kenneth, I know you do. I see it in your eyes every time you look at me.'

He put his face close to hers and there was fire in the ice-blue eyes of Kenneth Cameron Mor when he said, 'What you see is pity, Murn lass, pity for a woman who's wasted her life in silly hankerings that have no substance. You had plenty going for you but always you wanted more – childish fantasies that filled your head with nothing yet robbed you of your powers of reasoning . . .'

Two quick strides took him to where she had stepped out of her dress. Snatching it up he threw it at her. 'Here, make yourself decent! And dinna you dare go upsetting my Nell wi' your fads and fancies. She has enough in her life to cope with, without you complicating matters. In fact . . . it might be better if you went home . . .' His voice was softer now, his anger evaporating, and with its departure he realised that he had never felt as sorry for anyone as he felt for poor, bedraggled Murn, standing so still and quiet, clutching her frock to her heaving bosom.

'Go back to the house and pack, lassie,' he advised kindly. 'You ken fine that it would be embarrassing for you and me to face one another after this. You'll think o' some excuse and I'm sure Tom will be only too glad to have you back again.'

'No, Kenneth, no.' She was blinded by tears, choked with hurt. 'Don't leave me, please don't leave me.'

Briefly he gripped her arm and then he was gone, the door creaking shut behind him.

Murn didn't know how long she remained in the barn after Kenneth Mor had gone but she was cold and stiff by the time she finally mustered the strength to get to her feet. Her mind was numb, her legs felt weak, and it took all of her willpower to put one foot in front of the other. Several minutes elapsed before she reached the door.

Gloaming stretched over the countryside. It was very peaceful, the larks were still singing, and the bubbling song of a curlew rose up from the shore.

Croft Donald was in darkness. Even so it was cosy looking and gave the impression that it was snuggling into the purple-grey hills at its back.

A strange, sweet sadness tightened Murn's throat. She forgot her first impressions of this lonely part of Scotland, the dreadful roads, the dourness of the people. She didn't care about the roads anymore and the people were warm and friendly once they got to know you a little.

All at once she didn't want to leave Croft Donald and Kenneray. Kenneth was wrong to make her leave, he ought to know that she had to stay here to be near him. He knew how much she had loved him all these years and, in time, he would grow to love her too . . .

She raised her head and set her chin. I won't leave you, Kenneth, she vowed. When I go you will come with me, you really ought to know that as well as I do.

She let herself into the house, it was very quiet; the children would be tucked up in bed and the adults must be upstairs too as not a soul was to be seen.

She was about to open the kitchen door when Irene seemed to materialise out of nowhere. 'The door is snibbed,' she explained, raising her eyebrows a little at the sight of Murn's dishevelled state. 'This is Nellie's bath night, they're both in there. We're having our cocoa in the parlour if you would like to join us.'

Murn merely nodded. Irene went off and all was quiet again . . . except for the sound of muffled laughter in the kitchen.

Murn hesitated. She glanced furtively behind her to ascertain that she was alone . . . *'they're both in there . . .'* Those words of Irene's beat into her brain and without further ado she bent down and put her eye to the keyhole.

The first thing she saw was the blazing fire in the hearth . . . and then Nellie came into view, completely naked. Murn was taken aback at the sensual beauty of her body: she was slim, neat-waisted, her breasts were round and firm . . . She was in fact everything that Murn had always longed to be . . .

And suddenly Kenneth Mor was there beside Nellie. He had just risen from his bath, his naked body gleamed golden in the firelight and tiny drops of moisture patterned his skin like shining diamonds.

Murn had never seen such beauty in a man: his muscles rippled with every move he made, his legs were long and straight and perfect, his golden red hair was like a crown of fire on his head . . .

He was untying Nellie's hair, allowing the fine, fair strands of it to slide through his fingers as it cascaded down her back . . .

And then he was kissing her, pressing her in ever closer to the hard, hungry pillar of his penis . . .

Murn could take no more. Awash with sweat she jumped back from the door as if she had been scalded. The numbness in her head was growing stronger, she could hardly feel her fingers or her feet, and her body felt as if it didn't belong to her anymore . . . yet strange . . . a voice was filtering through the fog in her brain, telling her what had to be done . . . now that it was finished . . .

Like one in a dream she turned and went back out of the house, her footsteps taking her to the wild, lonely shores of Briosag Bay, Gaelic for Bay of the Witch.

It was a strange, forbidding place, littered with great pitted rocks that had come tumbling down from the hills millions of years before. The sea was ever restless here and surged and foamed around the reefs that rose up out of the water like glistening black fangs.

Murn had loved it from the first moment she had set eyes on it. Here there was no mercy from the elements, no place to hide from the tempest. It was dark, and primitive and dangerous and it appealed to the side of her nature that knew all of these things.

Murn laughed, she unbuttoned her dress and let it fall in a little heap on the wet sand. The rain had stopped. Grey clouds were still piling up in the sky but low down on the horizon a bright, watery light spread itself over the waves.

She shaded her eyes from the glare. Something was floating in the water – red, fiery strands that bobbed up and down, up and down . . .

Was that Kenneth Cameron Mor out there? Waiting for her? Beckoning to her as he had beckoned all through her life?

'I'm coming, Kenneth. I knew you wanted me after all. I knew you would be waiting.'

Quite calmly she walked into the sea. The salt water stung her eyes, clogged her nose, but she kept on walking till the waves lifted her and carried her swiftly towards the patches of red seaweed she had seen from the shore.

At the last minute she panicked. 'Kenneth!' she screamed. She reached out to clutch at the seaweed. It slipped away from her desperate fingers . . .

The tide was going out fast. The water billowed round the reefs, pieces of flotsam clung together and were swirled madly around and around, according to the whim of the current.

In among the debris a scrap of flower-sprigged cotton bobbed about with everything else until it snagged on a sharp piece of rock beneath the surface of the waves which held it and wouldn't let it go . . .

Cal shaded his eyes and stared landwards. The girl at his side stirred and covered her bare breasts with her hands. 'What is it, Cal?' she asked curiously, supporting herself with her elbow as she followed the direction of his gaze.

'Nothing. At least I thought I saw someone in Witch Bay. It looked like my Aunt Murn.'

'From this distance?'

'She's a big woman,' he replied with a grin.

'Are you sure it wasn't a seal lying on a rock?'

'Daftie! I know a seal when I see one. Aunt Murn is much bigger and she's white – very white – like an uncooked doughball.'

'I can't see anyone.'

Cal continued to stare back at the shore. He frowned. 'I was sure I saw something – *and* I thought I heard someone cry out . . .' He shrugged. 'Anyway, whoever it was is gone now.'

He snuggled back down beside the girl. The boat rocked gently, then a little more violently. Cal was too busy to give his Aunt Murn a second thought – or anyone else for that matter.

No one missed Murn until the next morning, and even then it was assumed that she had simply risen earlier than usual to go for a walk. When she didn't appear for dinner the alarm bells started ringing and by afternoon everyone was out looking for her.

When Cal returned later in the day he told his father about his experience of the previous night.

At Briosag Bay someone found the shredded remains of Murn's dress. The police were called to the scene, and the coastguard was alerted. Though they searched diligently for days on end they found no trace of Murn's body.

Kenneth Mor was inconsolable. He believed that her disappearance was all his fault and told Nellie everything that had happened that dreadful day in the barn.

Nellie was the rock he needed. She held him in her arms and soothed him, she convinced him that her sister had been sick in the mind for years and that nothing could have halted her downhill slide to disaster.

But even while Nellie said her comforting words she ached inside with anger against a sister who had selfishly brought such grief to a man as sensitive as her Kenneth. As for herself, Nellie experienced an odd kind of apprehension every time she thought of Murn who for most of her life had wanted to punish her elder sister for marrying the man she had desperately wanted for herself.

In the end Murn had succeeded most emphatically. At last she had wreaked her revenge as never, to the end of her days, would Nellie look from her window towards the sea without remembering how Murn had ended her sad, self-centred, selfish life.

Evelyn also tried to take away some of the guilt from her brother-in-law's mind.

'If you're to blame so too am I,' she told him. 'I kent fine something like this was about to happen but when the moment came I was too sick and ill myself to be able to do anything about it.'

So the members of Murn's family blamed themselves and tried to console one another but when Tom came to Kenneray he laid no blame at any door but instead examined all the possibilities for his wife's actions.

'Murn was unpredictable, she might have gone to the bay that evening with dozens of notions inside her head. Perhaps she went for a paddle and ventured further than she intended, she might even have tried to swim because although it was something she was never very good at she was fascinated by the water and liked to believe she was better than she really was.'

Tom walked up to the headland and stood gazing out to sea. The wind buffeted him, the water swirled round the foot of the cliffs far below. He knew the sea, he knew it and feared it and respected it. He had sailed the oceans of the world but he had always been in awe of their might and majesty.

Murn had hated the water, she had never attempted to paddle, let alone try to swim.

Someday he might be able to understand the mental sickness that had driven her to take her own life but for now he was too bewildered even to begin to try to fathom what had triggered such a tragic act.

The girls would have no mother now. Murn hadn't been up to much on that score but at least she had managed somehow to keep the family together.

It was over now, over and done with. The sea might

never give up her body and he would always wonder about that – wait, and watch, and wonder . . .

He shivered. 'Goodbye, Murn, lass,' he said simply. 'God be with you – wherever you are . . . '

It was time for Grace and Evelyn to say their goodbyes. Nellie had tears in her eyes when she gathered each of them to her breast and told them huskily, 'Take care o' one another, there aren't so many o' us left now. Poor Murn, she was aye a fool but she was our sister and we mustna ever let ourselves forget that.'

An unexpected memory came to Evelyn. 'I was just thinking, do you remember the exquisite embroidery Murn did for the gentry in the big houses around Rothiedrum? I had forgotten all about it until suddenly it all came flooding back.'

Nellie blew her nose, Grace's huge eyes were wet with sadness, James looked in disgust at the weeping womenfolk and wondered what all the fuss was about. After all, Aunt Murn hadn't been a very nice person. She had moaned all the time about nothing and had spent a lot of her time glowering at him and telling him to wash his 'disgraceful hands'.

Life had been pretty peaceful since she had gone away . . . in fact, he hoped she would stay away forever so that she could never again tell him to wipe his nose or to be 'a little man'.

James thought it was terrible to cry for someone you didn't really like when you could be crying for someone you *did* like.

He slid upstairs unnoticed. Kenneth found him ten minutes later, up in the room he had shared so happily with Col. 'I want to stay here – with you and Col and Aunt Nellie,' the little boy sobbed. 'Col needs me and I – I love him and I've still to show him some more o' my card tricks.'

Gently, Kenneth took the boy's hand and led him downstairs to present him to Nellie. 'He wants to stay, Nell lass.

He has a few things he would like Col to learn and besides that – he loves his uncle very much.'

Nellie bent down to take the boy to her bosom. 'Of course you can stay, a month or so in the country will do you the world o' good – that's if your mother agrees to let us have you.'

Evelyn looked at this sister of hers. Her capacity for loving children was enormous: they came to her as little visitors, they stayed as part of a big, happy family and absorbed the life and laughter of Croft Donald as if it was the element they had been born to.

Evelyn thought of John Simpson and his dislike of this son of hers. She recalled his threats to James and in her heart she blessed Nell Christina Cameron of Croft Donald.

James looked at her face. He knew her answer before she spoke and with a whoop of joy he ran to find Col who had been hiding in the barn crying *his* eyes out because his constant companion of the last two weeks was leaving.

Grace and Evelyn climbed into the cart. Nellie tucked a basket of eggs, butter and cheese in beside them and rushed back to the house before they could see her moist eyes.

Kenneth lifted the reins and the cart moved off. Nellie's hanky fluttered at the window, Irene's followed suit, Isla Nell stood at the door waving, Cal and Iain were at the field dyke to salute the cart as it passed by.

Grace buried her eyes in a scrap of lace. Evelyn swallowed and wondered when she would return to this dear place where peace abounded and love was all.

Neither of the sisters glanced towards the sea. Not until they were out of the vicinity of Briosag Bay did they turn their heads to look at the little islands rising up like hazy blue clouds on the horizon.

It was a beautiful day. Murn would have liked it. She would have hated the bumpy roads but she might not have voiced her complaints, because the big red-haired Highlander Kenneth Cameron Mor was at the helm and, to Murn, that was all that would have mattered in the end.

PART THREE

Autumn 1931 –
Summer 1940

Chapter Sixteen

Before the child was born Evelyn knew that it wouldn't live long. The movements in her womb had never been very strong and, as time wore on, they grew more and more feeble.

She was glad to be taken to hospital soon after the birth. Weak and ill herself she wanted only to lie back and let others look after her. Evelyn was relieved that she didn't have to see John Simpson's face when his tiny son died after just a few hours of life.

He had genuinely wanted to have a child by her. He had talked about it a lot and had become quite excited at the idea of becoming a father all over again. He had even taken an interest in the tiny garments both she and Maggie had been making.

Yes, he would be disappointed that his son hadn't lived, yet he would be kind to her, in his own way she knew that he cared for her. Lately he had been gentle with her and she had found it hard to believe he was the same man who had put her through such sexual abuse during the first few months of their marriage.

But men like him didn't change overnight. Her pregnancy over with, he wouldn't give her peace for long . . . and it would be back to the same weary drudgery all over again.

She could divorce him. It was as simple as that. But was anything ever that simple when everywhere there was so little money and so few jobs? The irony was, after months of little effort, John Simpson had suddenly shaken the dust from his heels and had found himself some decent work for a change.

He had been generous with his money: he had bought

her and the children clothes, he wasn't drinking nearly so much, he was nicer to Maggie and Jamie and all things considered he seemed to have taken a turn for the better.

Even so, Evelyn felt no sense of security. His child was dead. There would be no incentive now for him to go out to work, and lying in the white hospital bed, drained both mentally and physically, she felt that she could never again face the sort of life that had been hers for what seemed an eternity.

She wanted to run away, anywhere, just as long as she put as much distance as possible between herself and the cold reality of home – home where the heart lay . . . but her heart had never left Rothiedrum and all it stood for. One day she would go back . . . one day . . .

The hopelessness of her situation pressed like a ton weight on her chest. She closed her eyes, she slept . . . and in her dreams Gillan came to her as he had done ever since their parting . . . only this time there was more substance to him. He was as real as if he was standing right next to her.

'I'll see you soon, Gillie,' she whispered.

'What did you say, Mrs Simpson?'

Evelyn opened her eyes. A stiffly-starched staff nurse was at her bedside, briskly shaking a thermometer, a 'no nonsense' expression on her sharp, efficient features.

'Nothing – at least – I said I thought you looked silly.'

The nurse's lips folded into a thin line. 'Arm up,' she ordered coldly. The thermometer was jabbed viciously under Evelyn's arm and her wrist was gripped too tightly as the nurse took her pulse.

'I think I've wet the bed.'

Both wrist and thermometer were abandoned. The nurse positively gloated as she threw back the bedclothes and in a loud, bossy voice called for the assistance of a skinny little probationer.

'Mrs Simpson,' she said two minutes later. 'Your sheets are perfectly dry. You have *not* wet the bed, you are wasting our time with your foolish nonsense.'

'Sorry.' Evelyn wasn't in the least sorry, she was enjoying

herself. 'It must have been your hands, the touch o' them sent icy shivers up my spine.'

'Hmph.' The nurse pursed her lips even tighter and glowered at the probationer for daring to show a glimmer of a smile.

Evelyn lay back on her pillows, her heart lighter than it had been for months. Just the thought of Gillan Forbes of Rothiedrum House had made her feel so much better and something in her heart told her that one day – in the not too distant future – she would see him again.

John Simpson was drunk. For him that was nothing unusual, but this time he'd had good reason to drown his sorrows before staggering home late to his bed. His son was dead and his wife had hinted she would like him to be dead too, so listlessly had she raised her eyes to him when he had gone to visit her that afternoon.

He lay on his back, thinking about Evelyn. Sweet, so sweet, and beautiful: that wonderful hair of hers, cascading down her back, her face, perfect in its symmetry – and those eyes – big and green and looking at him all the time as if she would never fathom her reasons for marrying him.

She had breeding, he was aware of that. Breeding and brains and beauty. He had been desperate to own a woman like that ever since he could remember and, from the first moment he had set eyes on her, he had been crazy about her and couldn't keep his hands off her.

Tom had wanted her too, he had said as much when they had been out together on one of their drinking sprees. But he was already married to that fat sow, Murn, leaving the way clear for his father to win Evelyn's hand in marriage.

But she would never be his, he knew that now. No matter how often he possessed her body he could never possess her mind, her spirit . . . her heart. That belonged to someone else, someone who belonged to that past life she spoke about so fondly when she was with Maggie and Jamie.

These last few months he hadn't even been able to make love to her as freely as before. She had been ill and had pleaded with him to leave her alone in case he should harm his unborn child. In the end, much against his will and his desires, he had compromised by being as gentle with her as he knew how.

Fat lot of good it had done! The baby was dead. It had all been for nothing, he might as well have raped her every night instead of holding back like a bloody cissy!

He moved restlessly as the old familiar stirring in his loins took hold. Thank God for that little whore, Babs. She and Bessie had had to stay on at 198 ever since that mad sister of Evelyn's had drowned herself in the sea. Good riddance to her! Her demise had created a few headaches for Tom over the question of his stepdaughters' welfare – until his father had very kindly offered to give them bed and board for the foreseeable future.

The very idea of Babs sleeping in the same room as himself had driven him to distraction these past months. Oh, they'd had their moments. At every available opportunity they had gone wild together: in the scullery; several times in The Room; another time in the stairhead lavatory to the tune of Creeping Jesus furtively trying the door; even in the kitchen cupboard when she had had her back to him and he had crept up behind her. In fact, everywhere and anywhere that they got the chance to be alone together.

And now, here they were, Evelyn snug in hospital, himself and Babs alone in the kitchen except for that little mouse, Bessie, and she didn't matter . . .

Excitement mounted in him. He had never known any-one as ravenous for sexual adventure as Babs. Nothing he could do to her shocked or repulsed her with the result that he was as abandoned with her as he had ever been with any woman . . . but she was still just a child . . .

He pushed that thought away, he didn't like to think

about such cold facts. 'Let nature take its course', that was his motto, and he intended to stick to it now more than ever – and let the consequences take care of themselves.

There was a churning deep in his belly, he broke out in a sweat, and he knew he couldn't wait a moment longer to go to his 'little wife'.

Babs lay listening for that footfall on the floor, that creak of a floorboard to tell her that John Simpson was coming to 'get her'.

Her straining ears crackled. He was *there*, poised, ready to spring, a wild beast that stalked the night and waited – a beast that was always in heat, always . . .

Bessie had heard him also. She didn't wait to be told to 'hop it', but wrapped herself in a crocheted wool cover and leapt from the bed to scurry past 'the Old Tom Cat' as she had privately christened him.

The musky odour of his naked flesh assailed her. She shuddered as she climbed into his bed and tried to find a patch where he hadn't lain. The sheets reeked of booze and tobacco, and something else that Babs had smelled of after a night of lust.

Bessie didn't want to think about it. She had just left a warm bed – John Simpson's bed was warm but she wanted nothing of him, smelly, sly, slinky Old Tom Cat. Keeping as far as possible from the indentation made by his body, she huddled under her woolly cover and concentrated her mind on Alex and all the lovely times they had shared that summer with the horses and with each other.

John Simpson's weight crushed Babs into the feathers. 'My wee wife,' he murmured. His alcohol-tainted breath washed over her. 'I'm ready for you tonight, girl, by God and I am.'

His hands squeezed her breasts and she had to bite her

lip to stop from crying out. They had been tender for some time now, but she had tried to ignore the signs, telling herself that everything would be all right tomorrow, the next day, the day after.

She lay beneath him and feigned excitement. When he penetrated her roughly she pretended enjoyment even while her tears wet the pillow.

Luckily for her he was too drunk to be able to make his usual relentless demands on her. When he fell away to sink into a drunken sleep she sent up a prayer of thankfulness, but was afraid to move one muscle for the rest of the night for fear she would waken him.

In the morning she was stiff, heavy, and sick, and wanted only to lie in bed all day. But that old cow Maggie had sharp eyes and a suspicious mind. She would know something was amiss and no one, *no one* must ever know about herself and John Simpson.

For the next few nights he played with her as if she was a flesh-and-blood rag doll. When she wasn't feeling too bad some of her old carnal enjoyment came to her rescue but mostly she went to bed each night to writhe and moan beneath him and pretend she was loving every minute of it while the nausea rose in her throat and the bruises between her legs grew bigger.

She didn't dare refuse his attentions. She knew he was more than capable of physically harming her if he didn't get his own way – he had told her so himself and he hadn't minced his words.

'You're a good looking lass, Babs. Keep your mouth shut if you want to stay that way and don't say you haven't been warned.'

'Help me, Bessie,' Babs pleaded with her sister, 'I don't want him any more he – he's too old for me.'

'Old? He's your grandfather in case you've forgotten.'

'That's got nothing to do with it. Don't be such a baby!'

Her tone softened. 'Please, Bessie, say you can't leave your bed tonight, say you've got a belly-ache or something – anything.'

'It's too late – and you know it,' was all Bessie said before turning her back on the sister who had cared only about herself since the day she was born.

One cold, wintry morning, just before Christmas, everyone at 198 Camloan Road woke up to the sickly smell of gas. It clogged the atmosphere, clung to the nostrils, and made it difficult for some of the older residents to breathe.

It killed Mr Conkey and almost did the same for his wife. Alex was barely awake that morning when the cold truth hit him. While the neighbours were wondering what was happening, he was at the Conkeys' door, bursting inside to find Mr Conkey dead in bed and Mrs Conkey lying on the kitchen floor near to death.

Her head was near the unlit gas cooker. The hissing gas sounded like a death knell in Alex's ears and swiftly, before he ran out of air himself, he rushed around the house, opening windows and turning off the gas taps in the room and the kitchen.

His lungs bursting, he tried to move Mrs Conkey but, thin as she was, she was a dead weight. If Jamie had not appeared to help Alex drag her out onto the landing, they might both have died.

Before the police and the gas board officials arrived to order everyone to vacate their homes, Mrs Conkey was on her way to hospital, a prompt action which undoubtedly saved her life.

But at that moment very few of the neighbours were in a good enough humour to care much about Mrs Conkey's life. It was a freezing cold morning, and there had been little opportunity for anyone to dress properly, so they huddled together in disgruntled groups, cursing the

Conkeys and, in several cases, wishing that they had stopped long enough to at least don a pair of warm knickers.

The only thing that cheered them to any degree was the sight of Jack Jack flapping about in a roomy pair of blue, striped pyjamas, trying to keep Jessie under control while he manoeuvred his lumbering wife out of the close.

Finally, the neighbours from across the street came to the rescue with blankets and hot tea and a kitchen chair for poor, bewildered Jenny Jack to sit on.

'How did it happen?' Theresa Leckie wondered. 'Surely the poor souls hadn't two farthings to rub together – never mind have enough to fill the meter to bursting.'

Alex knew what had happened. He remembered the cold house, the cheerless grate, the signs of poverty, and – oddly – the pile of coppers on a table in the lobby, sitting under the gas meter, doing . . . nothing.

That little mystery now had an explanation. Mrs Conkey had been saving her pennies for a reason which was only too apparent. When the residents of the Close had gotten over their indignation at being decanted from hearth and home on a cold and frosty morning, they soon mustered their sympathy for the Conkeys.

Because it came to light that, either through pride or ignorance or a mixture of both, they had never claimed financial assistance with the result that they had been half-starved and half-frozen for years.

'A terrible state o' affairs,' said Isa Boag with a sniff. 'If they had lived in the same close as me I would have seen the signs ages ago and would have done something about it.'

'Ach you'd have been as wise as the rest o' us,' Theresa Leckie said firmly. 'The Conkeys were a tight-lipped pair and fine you know it for you've had plenty and enough to say about them in the past.'

*

226

Alex listened to the gossip with only half an ear. The plight of the Conkeys had affected him deeply and for several days he was quiet and thoughtful and so withdrawn that Evelyn thought he must be heading for some illness.

'No, I'm fine, Mother,' he assured her, when questioned about his health. 'I just want to think, that's all. Have no fear, you aren't about to lose your beloved son to the Big Bad Bogle Man.'

She ruffled his hair affectionately. 'No, I can tell that by your impudence. Alex . . .' she made him look at her . . . 'what happened to the Conkeys wasn't your fault. You mustna feel that you have to be personally responsible for everything that they did or didn't do.'

'I know that, Mother, but somebody has to help *her*. We can't just let her sink back into the pit when she comes home.'

Evelyn felt as if she had just been given a short, sharp lesson. She was very proud of her eldest son in those moments and glad to acknowledge that Davie had been right when he had said about Alex, 'He'll go far that lad, he's got a head on his shoulders and he knows how to use it.'

If Davie had been alive today he might have added that his eldest son had a heart as well, a trait that was becoming more apparent as time passed by.

'I want you to do me a favour, Megsie.' Alex spoke urgently to his sister, 'I want you to take this and pawn it for me.'

He held up the silver pocket watch that had once belonged to Albert Conkey.

Meg looked at the watch and then at her brother's face. It was bright red, and she was about to ask him if he had been stealing but something stayed her tongue.

Alex had changed a good deal for the better these days.

He was a kinder, more likeable person altogether and only rarely did he tease her and call her rude names. Instead he called her *Megsie* which sounded special and was very acceptable after what had gone before.

He was still a boy and did the sort of horribly vulgar things that boys of his age did but, all in all, she liked him better than she had ever done – though it went against her grain to let him see it. Soft people went under, she told herself – this was the hard-headed philosophy that she had been born with – and it would never do to allow Alex to get *too* close to her.

So she continued to prevaricate and show him that she was very much her own boss, though it was difficult to resist his persuasive tongue and strange, hypnotic eyes.

'Go to the pawnshop?' she hooted indignantly. 'Why don't you go yourself? I'm not your servant.'

The flush on his face deepened. 'Old Scrooge hates me. I used to call him terrible names and he's never forgotten. He wouldn't give me a fart in exchange for a diamond.'

In truth, it hurt Alex to part with the watch. He wanted to keep it more than he had ever wanted to keep anything in his life and had treasured it from the day that Mrs Conkey had given it to him.

Somehow, he had kept it from the clutches of John Simpson and had resisted the temptation to sell it to buy winter feed for Dobbie and Tinker, even though it was becoming more and more difficult to keep the horses.

It had, therefore, cost him a good deal of soul searching before making his momentous decision, but having made it he wanted to get it over with as quickly as possible. He could not bear to go to the pawnshop in person as it would break his heart to witness the expression of greed on Old Scrooge's features when he beheld the treasure.

Privately Meg thought that no one could be too rude to repulsive Old Scrooge and, reaching out, she took the watch quite gently from her brother's sweaty palm.

'All right, I'll do it,' she conceded, smiling a little at the tragic expression on Alex's face.

'Don't just hand it over for coppers,' he instructed. 'Old Scrooge hates parting with money so you make sure you get a good deal.'

'Don't worry. You ought to know by now that I'm no daftie . . .' She hesitated . . . 'Are you selling it so's you can buy us all Christmas presents? If so I'm needing a nice new pair of ankle socks to go to the school Christmas party.'

He grinned. She would never change, still the same Meg, always wondering what was in it for her.

'I don't know what all the fuss is about,' said Babs, having observed the neighbours' concern over Mrs Conkey's welfare. She gave an affected toss of the head. 'Conkers Conkey is nothing special, she's just a disgusting old lady who nearly blew us all up with her stupidity and I for one won't lift a finger to help her.'

Babs wasn't the most popular person in the Grainger–Grant–Simpson household and, being only too well aware of this, she was jealous of anyone she thought was getting an unfair slice of attention.

She had good reason to feel sorry for herself: John Simpson had grown tired of her and hardly gave her a second glance nowadays; she was lonely, afraid, and apprehensive for her future – as well she might be at barely fifteen years old and four months pregnant.

Always inclined to be lazy, she had allowed herself to become sloppy about her appearance; she was uncooperative around the house and did nothing to help with the numerous menial chores; when she went to bed at night she simply stepped out of her garments and allowed them to remain where they had fallen.

Maggie was continually tidying up after her and was sick to the back teeth of the girl's sullen, uncooperative ways and ready tongue. If it hadn't been for Bessie she would have asked Tom to take his eldest daughter away but, knowing that Bessie would loyally follow her sister, she kept her counsel for the time being.

As to Babs's opinion about Mrs Conkey, nobody listened to it. What she had to say on the subject was of little importance and hardly worth an argument.

I'll make them sit up and take notice. One of these fine days, Babs vowed to herself, they'll look at me and *then* they'll listen – they'll have to.

She thought about John Simpson's threats; she remembered his steely eyes and his ruthless hands – and she knew she wouldn't tell anyone anything that would incriminate him.

Alone and lonely she wept and she wondered how her predicament would resolve itself. But there was only one answer to that – and she dreaded it with all her heart and soul.

Meg duly set off, taking Rachel with her for moral support. It was the best move she could have made: at ten years old Rachel was growing into a charmer who, with her calm grey eyes and caring nature, could effortlessly twist anyone round her little finger.

Last winter she had endeared herself to Old Scrooge by knitting him a pair of socks when he lost his wife and he had never forgotten the little girl's thoughtfulness.

But humming and hawing was part of his business procedure and a very enjoyable part too. He also took a delight in haggling over a deal just when a customer thought they had won the day. So, for quite a few painfully suspenseful minutes, he kept the girls waiting while he tapped the side of his large, warty nose, and regarded the item in his hand as if it was made of cardboard instead of best quality silver.

In the end however he agreed to hand over a fair price for the watch. 'It's Christmas after all, little girls,' he stated smoothly, revealing broken black teeth in an ingratiating grin.

He handed Meg the pawn ticket. Gritting her teeth, she attempted to scoop it up without actually touching his greasy palm.

Mrs Conkey came home to a blazing fire and a cupboard filled to the brim with tins and packets of food. Every neighbour in the street had contributed something, no matter how small, Isa Boag even going as far as to include a bowl of home-made stuffing for 'the parson's arse'.

'It's *nose*, Isa,' Big Aggie had insisted, 'the parson's nose.'

'Nose, arse, what's the difference,' Isa had returned dourly. 'They've both got holes in them.'

Big Aggie was not to be outdone. 'When one gets too near the other there *is* a difference, Isa, as *you* ought to know, since you're never done complaining about some smell or other.'

On Mrs Conkey's bedside table was an envelope containing a little wad of pound notes and a Christmas card bearing the simple message, *Merry Christmas, from a friend.*

Meg got her new ankle socks that Christmas, Rachel got the red ribbons she had wanted, everybody got some little thing that they had desired.

Only Babs was discontented. In a few months she was going to have a little thing that she *hadn't* desired and the thought filled every one of her waking hours with dread. It was an easy enough matter to hide her condition with loose clothing – she hadn't put on much weight, worry had seen to that – but she carried her burden alone.

Bessie got what she had very much wanted that Christmas. She and Alex took the horses out riding in the frosty fields and she knew that even if she lived to be a hundred she would never be as happy as she was now.

She was thirteen years old, it was Christmas, and she was galloping on Tinker's broad back under a blue, blue sky with not a chimney in sight . . . And best of all, she was doing it with Alexander David Grainger, the boy that she loved and would till the end of her life . . . Nothing would ever take that away from her . . . nothing and nobody.

Chapter Seventeen

Evelyn awoke with the most wonderful feeling of euphoria. Today was the day she was going to Edinburgh in the hope of seeing Gillan again. She had written to him at the address he had given her two years ago when they had met so briefly in Glasgow. At the time he had told her to contact him if ever circumstances got too much for her and, with just a few days to go before the beginning of 1932, she had decided that she couldn't face starting another year without seeing him and speaking to him and reminiscing about the old days at Rothiedrum.

There was no telling if he had ever received her letter. He could be anywhere in the world by now, but she had to do this one decisive thing before it was too late.

She had gone back to working for Fanny and Lizzie again and out of her meagre earnings she had scraped together enough money for her fare to Edinburgh.

Only Maggie and Jamie knew where she was going. As far as John Simpson was concerned it was just another working day for her – but she didn't reckon with Alex's quick eyes.

Before leaving for school he stood back to look at her and putting his head on one side he observed, 'You've got on your best coat, Mother, and you've got your green-eyed look. You're going somewhere special, aren't you?'

She laughed and put her arm around his shoulder. 'There's no fooling you, is there, Alex Grainger? But as usual you've guessed right. I am going somewhere special and I'm hoping when I get there I'll *see* someone special, someone I kent a long time ago – long before your father and me ever met.'

'Will you tell me about him someday?'

'Did I say it was a *he*?'

'You don't have to. I've seen that dreamy look in your eye before and I knew that you were thinking about the man you've always thought about – even when Father was alive.'

'Oh, Alex.' She gathered him into her arms and kissed the top of his brow. 'You ken me better than I give you credit for and, yes, some day I'll tell you about this very special man who's aye been in my life – right from the time we were bairns together in Rothiedrum.'

'I wish I could go to Rothiedrum.'

She took a deep, shuddering breath. 'So do I, Alex. Oh, so do I.'

Maggie took her daughter into her arms and held her tightly for several moments. 'Good luck, lassie,' she whispered and her voice was husky. 'I hope you see Gillan. You and he were meant for one another and should never have parted.'

'You never used to say that, Mam.'

'Things change, lassie, people and circumstances change. If I had it all over again I'd like nothing better than to see you two wed.'

'It could happen yet.' Jamie took his daughter's hand and squeezed it tightly. He adored this youngest daughter of his; from the time she was a tiny child they had understood one another and the passing years had never dimmed her loyalty to him. He only wanted what was best for her and it had cut him to the core to stand by all these years and watch her being hurt and used by one man after another.

Evelyn's trouble was that her heart had always ruled her head: first it had been young Johnny Burns of Birkiebrae and then Davie, but John Simpson had been another matter entirely. She had married him hoping for security but all she had ever known with him was financial instability, emotional havoc and the sort of sexual and physical abuse at which Jamie could only guess.

He had prayed to catch the unholy bastard at it but he had always been too fly for that. Like a filthy cockroach he only crept out at night to perpetrate his foul deeds.

Jamie had never hated anyone in the whole of his life but he hated John Simpson. But thankfully, Evelyn had thrown off the apathy that had shrouded her since Davie's death and was at last showing John Simpson some of her unique spirit and independence.

Evelyn bestowed a kiss on her father's cheek and did likewise to her mother. They were a beautiful couple: Maggie, with her pink cheeks and snow-white hair was still spry and fit at sixty-eight; Jamie was almost ten years older but even though he too was white haired, he somehow seemed forever young with his dark, gypsy skin and black eyes.

The drink had certainly taken its toll of him: his face was thin, he had purple smudges under his eyes, and he seemed to have shrunk. Even so, Evelyn could remember vividly the blithe young father who had carried her high on his shoulders on 'harvest home' nights when all the world was fragrant and happy and the great autumn moon rose soft and golden above the braes of Bennachie.

The journey to Edinburgh on the train passed as if in a dream. Evelyn sat in a corner, her brow against the window, staring at the country flashing by without really seeing it. All her thoughts and emotions were concentrated on one person, Gillan Forbes of Rothiedrum, how he would look, how he would react to seeing her again, the things he would say . . .

The flying wheels seemed to chant out a rhythm: *Gillie again, Gillie again, see him soon, see him soon, Gillie again, Gillie again* . . .

She wouldn't allow herself to think that he might not be

at the place she had suggested they meet – the idea was much too awful to contemplate. But when she alighted from the train and walked along the platform her footsteps began to slow even as her heart began to beat faster.

Please be there, Gillie, she prayed, oh, please, please be there.

And he was, outside the station as planned. A tall, dark man, hands thrust deep into the pockets of his coat, his eyes scanning the faces that streamed past him . . .

'Gillie.' His name was a mere breath on her lips . . . he sensed that she was there . . . he turned.

'Princess . . .' A few quick strides took him to her side. For a few timeless moments he just stood there looking at her, his dark eyes alight in his handsome face . . . Then she was in his arms, feeling the warmth of his body against hers, knowing the sweetness of his face against her own.

He turned his head, his mouth came down on hers, and they kissed and held each other, neither of them willing to let go, locked in their own little world of wonder and warmth and love. She did love him, there were no doubts in her mind any longer. The feeling in her heart was so strong her whole body pulsed with it. She loved Gillan, she needed him . . . she wanted him . . .

'Evie,' he took her hand and kissed it. 'Princess, I've waited so long for this moment. I knew we would meet again but when and how I had no idea – and now – here you are – real and near and so beautiful I never, ever want to let you go.'

Still lost in their world they wandered along the street, talking, talking, about Rothiedrum, what it was like now, how many of the people that Evelyn had known were still alive, how many of them had died.

He told her that his mother, Lady Marjorie, was hale and hearty and that Lord Lindsay Ogilvie, the man he called his great uncle and who was also Evelyn's grand-father, was still alive and well and living in South Africa.

After that they told one another about themselves. He was separated from his wife, they had never really been well matched. It had been a marriage on the rebound as far as he was concerned.

Always it had been Evelyn, from the start it had been her. He had carried a torch for years in the hope that they would eventually get together. His mother had finally persuaded him that he was leading an unnatural sort of life and that it was high time he forgot Evelyn and found himself an unattached woman.

He was shocked when he learned that Evelyn had married a man like John Simpson.

'Evie! Why do we go on like this? Last time we met, Davie had died, you were free but I was still tied up. Now, when I'm about to get *my* freedom you calmly stand there and tell me you married some man old enough to be your father! I don't understand you, Princess. I credited you with brains! What happened to the independent girl who never tired of turning me down because of her pride!'

'The Depression happened, that's what!' she flashed back, her eyes sparking with anger. 'I needed security, I thought he could give me that – I was wrong.'

His face darkened. 'I could have given you all the security you needed years ago! You were always too stubborn to see reason. I told you to contact me if you ever needed me. I could have helped to divert a drastic move like the one you've made. Why do you keep rejecting me, Princess?'

'Och, I'm sorry. My foolish pride, my stupidity, call it what you like, but I'm here now, darling Gillie, don't let's spoil things by arguing. I promise you, I have no pride, no resistance left as far as you're concerned . . . '

He drew in his breath and held her hand tighter. He took her to lunch in a quiet little restaurant but neither of them had any appetite for food. Their hunger was of a different sort.

All they could do was look at one another. She felt as if she could never get enough of the wonderfully aesthetic face that she had dreamed of for so long, while all he could do was toy with his food and drink in every aspect of her, his eyes coming to rest again and again on her tremulous mouth, the enticing fullness of her breasts.

She was wearing a green blouse that she had re-fashioned from an old one. She had spent nights sewing by the light of a paraffin lamp. Slowly, painfully, the garment had taken shape and only last night it had received its final embellishment of a lace collar.

But the effort had been worth it. With her rich tumble of red hair and sparkling green eyes she looked stunning and desirable and Gillan could hardly take his eyes off her.

'Evie . . .' His hand came across the table to curl into hers, his voice was low. 'Evie, I want you so much . . . I . . . I have a flat here in Edinburgh . . . perhaps . . . '

Her eyes filled with tears. 'Oh, Gillie, my Gillie,' she whispered. 'I want you too, I canna pretend any longer . . . so let's waste no more time just looking at one another – we must make the most of this precious, wonderful day together.'

It was their first time with one another and they knew it wouldn't be their last. He was tender, gentle, passionate, wild, and she gave herself to him gladly.

When it was over she wondered how she could have resisted him for so long. He was more than just a wonderful lover: he was a rock to lean on, a refuge to hide in, someone that she felt she could live with forever yet always discover in him something new and exciting.

Lying in his arms she felt fulfilled beyond measure. She had just made love to Gillan Forbes of Rothiedrum, a man whose loyalty and love for her had never faltered. All through the years of their separation he had cherished her memory. Their meetings had been few and brief but somehow, despite all the odds, they had managed to keep in touch. On that special day in Edinburgh, a day of love and heartfelt confidences, she was at last convinced that they were meant for one another and had been from the beginning.

The parting was painful. They wanted time to stand still, they clung to each other and they cried together. But the hands of the clock moved relentlessly on and the moment they had been dreading came only too soon.

Yet it had been the happiest day she could remember for a long time. And, to complete her happiness, there was a letter waiting for her when she got home. Inside was a five pound note in payment of a short story she had submitted to a popular magazine.

As a child she had set her mind on becoming a writer but circumstances had forced her to abandon her ambitions. In recent months the urge to take up her pen had been overpowering, and this precious sum of money was the result – that and the sense of achievement that glowed in her heart.

It was a start – and it was the end to what had been a perfect day. She had never felt so happy or so fulfilled. She and Gillan had arranged to meet again in a fortnight – the money from the magazine would pay for her fare, with plenty left over to give the children a treat and take Maggie and Jamie to the pictures.

With a blithe heart she went to hang her coat in the lobby before going to seek out her parents. They would be waiting to hear about Lady Marjorie and Lord Lindsay Ogilvie and all the gossip about the Rothiedrum folk . . . and they would be wanting to know about Gillie . . .

Chapter Eighteen

Babs wasn't going to lie meekly in bed and just allow herself to die – because death was what she felt like on that cold, inhospitable February morning when she was wakened by terrible cramping pains in her stomach.

She had wet the bed, and she lay there on the soaking sheet, horrified at herself, dazedly thinking she must be mistaken – until she put her hand down and traced the spreading stain of moisture.

Oh God no, she thought, it can't be, I can't have . . . She lay as still as she could, sick with disgust at herself, dreading that Bessie might wake to discover that her elder sister had actually let go in the bed.

The pains were getting worse, clawing away at her innards till she felt she would go mad. She wanted to scream, to let the world know that she, Barbara Anna Simpson, was suffering the most dreadful torture in a very stoic fashion.

She knew it couldn't be the baby. According to her calculations that wasn't due for at least another three months, so the pain had to be caused by something else just as awful – just as unwanted.

Somehow she had managed to keep that particular little secret to herself. Everyone had just assumed that she had gained a bit of weight, it hadn't occurred to any of them that she might be pregnant, especially not by her own grandfather . . . the swine.

She hated him. This feeling had grown and expanded in her breast until it was all she could do not to look at him in case it brought back memories of his hot breath on her face, his hands tearing at her flesh.

There would be no more of that. He had rejected her ... *he* had rejected *her*! How dare he? How dare that drunken lecher discard her like an old boot? She who had every man and boy in this God-forsaken place panting after her like starving dogs after a bone ...

She would get Simpson ... she would pay him back ... somehow ... sometime ... Then she remembered his steely eyes and his dark threats and she knew she would never have the courage to stand up to him. She wasn't brave enough ... he would get away with it ...

Nevertheless, somebody would have to pay, somebody would have to take the blame.

Alex would. He had dared to reject her as well. She would make him suffer for that. She would wipe the self-satisfied smile off his handsome face. She couldn't just have a real live baby and say that the stork had brought it ...

A red hot band gripped her insides. It pulled her apart, then it subsided, leaving her bathed in sweat and wishing she was dead ...

When the baby came it would be adopted of course. She was too young to be responsible for it and Alex was also much too young to be a proper father ...

She wondered how her own stepfather would react to it all when he came home from sea. He had been gone three months now and she missed him. She liked Tom, he was nice for a stepfather. He always brought presents back for her and Bessie but more than that, she knew he cared about them – he really cared. He was always making excuses for her recklessness – perhaps if he had been tougher with her she mightn't have let him down like this but he was far too soft hearted and had always let her get her own way.

Babs knew that he was a bit out of his depth with daughters and had desperately wanted a mother for them after their own mother had died. Maybe that was why he had married Murn? He *must* have been desperate to do a thing like that, but there was no accounting for taste and he

241

must have experienced some terrible misgivings after the event.

He'd had a raw deal and didn't deserve any of it and for the first time she felt dreadfully ashamed of herself. Poor Tom . . . first silly old Murnsy taking her own life . . . now his stepdaughter having a baby by his own father . . .

For the first time the enormity of the thing that she had done filled her with deep and bitter regret, and she knew that – even if it was only for her stepfather's sake – she could never tell on John Simpson – never . . .

Another pain seized her. She gritted her teeth, it subsided, leaving her weak and trembling.

She had no idea of the time. It was still pitch dark outside. A backcourt moggy was yowling somewhere in the urban wilderness, another answered the challenge. There was a spitting and a howl of rage – a well-aimed boot had found its mark. A window banged shut and the night outside was silent once more.

John Simpson was snoring. The ragged sound lapped the edges of Babs's awareness. She tried to ignore it but somehow it penetrated her pain and she knew she had to get away from it.

Pushing back the covers she levered herself up from the wet bed. Something warm and sticky was seeping out of her. Horrified, she examined her nightdress: both it and the sheet were darkly stained, the marks leapt out at her from the surrounding whiteness. She hadn't wet herself after all, she was bleeding – bleeding to death!

Her heart lurched and seemed to stop beating. She felt faint with pain and fear as, for all her boasting, she didn't know a great deal about the facts of life and she wasn't well versed on giving birth to a baby.

She had been very young when her mother had died, Tom certainly hadn't taken her aside to tell her about the birds and the bees, nor had childless old Murnsy, who had probably been as ignorant as any giggling schoolgirl when it came to the nitty gritty of procreation.

Babs's baby was arriving early and she wasn't equipped, either mentally or emotionally, to deal with that sort of trauma.

She convinced herself that it couldn't be the baby; it was far too soon for it to come; it took nine months to make a baby; the bleeding would stop any minute; the pains would go away as well; all she needed was some exercise – a walk – anything to get away from this horrible bed, this claustrophobic prison of a house.

Somehow she got up and into her clothes, pausing every now and then to grit her teeth as the agony worsened. At one point she whimpered in her distress. Biting her lip she crouched there in the darkness, a lonely, frightened, young girl, needing help more than she had ever needed it in her life but too terrified to seek it.

Nothing moved, no one stirred. She half-wished that *somebody* . . . *anybody* . . . would detach themselves from the night and come to rescue her from her nightmare.

Anybody . . . with the exception of John Simpson . . .

Bessie, perhaps Bessie, but what could she do, other than stare and wonder and waken the entire household with her babblings?

Aunt Evelyn? Yes, Aunt Evelyn would do. She would be shocked at first but then she would calm down and take over in that cool, reliable way of hers . . .

Babs waited, she wanted, she needed. The seconds passed . . . no one came. She moved out of the darkness to the lobby and let herself out of the sleeping house.

The door clicked shut; Bessie sighed in her sleep; John Simpson turned over, his snoring ceased; Evelyn's dreams about Gillan remained unshattered; the occupants of The Room heard nothing; the night slept on, undisturbed.

Bessie awoke in her usual unhurried fashion. Hers was a dreamy nature and she liked nothing better than to lie for a while, contemplating the day ahead or thinking about all that had happened yesterday, in particular about the things that she and Alex had done together.

Babs never disturbed her first thing. Babs was a lie-a-bed in the morning. In fact, she was a lie-a-bed at any time of the day if she could get away with it – especially these last few months when she had grown more and more lethargic.

Bessie tucked her hands under her head and thought about her sister. She and John Simpson had certainly gone off one another and Bessie had never been so thankful. How she had loathed those nights of banishment to *his* bed to lie awake while *they* indulged in their unholy unions.

The very thought of it made Bessie shudder. On several occasions she had been on the point of telling Alex everything but the dreadful fear of retribution, bred in her by her grandfather's threats, had always stayed her tongue.

She knew there was something dreadfully wrong with Babs and that it all owed itself to the things she had done with John Simpson. Bessie was astute for her age and she had noticed the gradual changes in her sister's body when she undressed each night for bed.

She had an idea that it wasn't *fat-fat*, just as she knew that it hadn't been normal for her sister to rush into the scullery in the mornings to retch miserably into the sink before crawling back to bed looking like death warmed up.

Bessie remembered the same sort of things happening in Australia to her best friend's married sister and a suspicion had grown in her about Babs.

But no! Babs was only fifteen, too young to have a baby – or was she? She had started puberty at ten and was well developed and mature-looking by the time she was thirteen.

Bessie often worried that she was still childishly flat chested at thirteen. She had confided her fears to Aunt Evelyn who had smiled in that nice way of hers and had told Bessie she had felt exactly the same when she was growing up and *now* look at her!

She was a beaut! Bessie knew she would never be like

that but if she even had *half* of Aunt Evelyn's looks she would be content.

It seemed dreadful that such a beautiful woman had married a man like John Simpson, when she could have gotten anybody. She had said as much to Alex and had regretted it because he had gone into one of his scowly moods and had clammed up.

A few days later he had taken her aside and, in a very manly fashion, had explained how desperate his mother had been for security after his father had died.

'She was left with four children, Bess. A fifth had to go to my Aunt Nellie in Kenneray because my parents were too poor to feed us all. After my father died *I* looked after my mother because my Grandpa was too drunk and too old to be in charge. We got poorer and poorer, my mother got more and more depressed. When she met *him* she thought he would provide for us – when all the time he's a no-gooder who drinks more than poor old Grandpa.'

Bessie had taken his hand, sensing the hurt and outrage he must have felt when his mother had married again.

'Old Tom Cat,' she had said softly.

'Old who?'

'Old Tom Cat – that's what I call *him*.'

Alex had laughed and had thrown his arms around her. 'It suits the old bugger. You're no' as quiet or as shy as you used to be – are you, little Bess?'

The kiss he had bestowed on her had been very tender, very sweet, and very young, and her heart had glowed with love for him. For all his boyish gruffness, there were times when he could be as romantic and protective as any man thrice his age.

Bessie smiled at the memory. Rolling over on her side she realised that Babs wasn't in the bed beside her. 'Babs?' she said softly, raising herself up on one elbow. That was when she saw the tell-tale marks on the bedclothes, the dark stains on the sheet . . . and not a stitch of Babs's clothes to be seen.

Bessie's blood froze in her veins, her heart beat strangely in her breast. She guessed what had happened but she didn't want to acknowledge the enormity of the event.

With the tears streaming down her face she shook her head violently from side to side on the pillow.

No! No! No! she protested silently. It can't be true. It can't be. She's too young! She can't have a baby at her age.

She stuffed her fist into her mouth and stared up at the ceiling. A spider was spinning a new web in a corner. Only last night Babs had wrecked the old web even though Bessie had warned her that it would bring bad luck.

'Luck!' Babs had said sneeringly. 'What's luck got to do with anything, I'd like to know. It all just happens, Baby Bessie, there's no magic in it, life is what you make it yourself.'

The spider had almost finished weaving. Already it had caught breakfast, a juicy bed bug, not dead but paralysed, nice and fresh and all wrapped up in a neat little parcel.

'Yes, Babs,' whispered Bessie. 'You're right, there's no magic for you.'

She got up. Putting on her slippers she padded over to the other bed and shook Evelyn awake.

'It's Babs, Aunt Evelyn,' Bessie's voice was laden with sorrow. She didn't want to be standing here telling this lovely woman the things she had to be told. 'She's having a baby. She isn't in bed and I think – I think she's run away.'

It was Dunky the Smith who discovered Babs lying in the shed that served as a stable for Tinker and Dobbie.

The horses snickered a welcome as he came inside to give them breakfast. Dunky liked coming in to feed them like this. They were always pleased to see him and pushed their velvety noses into his roomy pockets to look for carrots and other tit-bits.

Dunky sighed as he wondered how much longer Alex could hang on to his beloved horses. It was all right in summer when they could crop the grass in the field but winter came all too soon, bringing with it the usual problems of insufficient funds for winter feed.

Dunky helped all he could but business wasn't so good nowadays and the time could soon come when he might have to let young Grainger go. There just wasn't enough work for the pair of them and, though Alex was a willing worker and only asked for enough to keep his horses, it was still too much in these lean times.

'There now, there.' Dunky gave Tinker's nose a last pat, rubbed Dobbie affectionately on the rump, and turned to go.

It was then that he saw Babs, sprawled on a pile of hay in a corner. He didn't think it all that unusual to find her here, she had often waited thus for young Alex and passed her time chatting with Dunky and generally flaunting herself.

Quite a lass! Dunky grew a bit hot under the collar at the recollection of her breasts bouncing about loosely inside her frock ... And her legs! Long and shapely and bare and showing a hint of white knickers, so high did she allow her skirt to ride up ... nothing much left to the imagination there.

If she hadn't been so young, Dunky might have tried to win a bit of all that for himself but she was only a child ... tempting but risky. Best leave her to young Alex ... lucky bugger ...

Dunky had come upon them once or twice, rolling in the hay, steam practically coming out their ears so hot had been their passion.

They didn't meet nearly so much now , in fact – come to think of it – it must be nearly a year since her last visit to the stable. Nowadays it was more usually little Bessie coming to help Alex with the horses. No funny business there; just two youngsters enjoying themselves as they talked and laughed and groomed the horses . . .

Dunky frowned and turned back from the door to take a closer look at the girl. Her eyes were closed, she had fallen asleep. He was about to tip-toe away when he noticed the tiny object at her side.

He grinned to himself. A little seductress she might like to think herself but that didn't stop her playing with dolls. She was still just a child after all. Good job he'd never tried anything – she would have had it all over the place and the fingers would have pointed at him . . . never at her . . . never a child like that . . .

Red! He frowned again. Red! Something . . . strange. The doll was red.

He peered more closely. Not a doll, a newborn baby, still, and cold . . . and dead.

And the girl? White. At least – her face was pure white. The rest of her was red, like the baby. She must be dead too. No one could have lost so much blood and still be alive . . . no one . . .

He didn't wait to find out. He couldn't get out of the shed fast enough, stopping only briefly to remove his jacket and throw it over the prostrate figure in the hay . . . just in case . . .

Chapter Nineteen

John Simpson was worried, more worried than he had ever been in his life. Not because young Alex was looking at him as if he would like to kill him – he could easily deal with a squirt like that – his anxiety was about much more serious matters. He had this terrible, sick feeling that he was about to pay for past indiscretions – especially for his liaison with his step-granddaughter who, when all was said and done, was still just a silly child.

It had never occurred to him that the little slut might be pregnant. He had grown tired of her long ago. Anything as available as that presented little or no challenge and besides – he liked it here. He liked being Evelyn's husband, though she had been strange and distant since the turn of the year. He put it down to the fact that she was going through a period of the sulks because he had lost his job again.

She would come round given time. Meanwhile he had his home comforts and he wasn't going to risk losing them for somebody like Babs.

Still, he was uneasy every time he looked at her, and he had caught her watching him with eyes that smouldered with dislike.

As for Bessie, there was always the chance that she would open her mouth, and he had made up his mind to ask Tom to take both girls away as soon as possible . . . before this! Worse than anything he could ever have imagined – and in his anxiety to vindicate himself he had just accused Alex of having fathered the girl's bairn.

'Look at him!' he flung out. 'Guilt written all over him! I warned you about him and now I've been proved right.'

Jamie's eyes flashed. 'Leave the lad be,' he fumed. 'He hasn't been near that quine for months. He's no angel, I'd be the first to admit it, but that doesna mean that he has to take the blame for everything that happens in this house.'

'And how would you know?' snarled John Simpson. 'How can the likes o' you supervise every one o' *his* moves when you're so drunk half the time you can't do up your own fly buttons?'

Jamie's hand flashed out to grab the other man by the throat. 'Ever since you set foot inside this house I've wanted to kill you, Simpson!' he roared. 'Now it looks as if the day has come at last.'

His fist shot out, it caught John Simpson squarely on the jaw. With a howl of rage he grabbed Jamie and shook him as if he was no more than a sewer rat.

Alex's nostrils flared; he couldn't just stand by and watch Jamie being hurt and humiliated like this and it was also a great opportunity for him to teach his loathsome step-father a long overdue lesson.

'Leave my Grandpa be!' he yelled. 'Come and get *me*, Simpson! Give me the chance to show you how much I love you!'

'Alex! Stop it!' Evelyn tried to pull her son away but he shook her off and with a jutting jaw and a burning, challenging glare, he faced his antagonist, his fists up in front of his face, emulating the fifty-bob fighters he had seen in the boxing booths around Glasgow.

For his age he was tall, strong and well-muscled, but he was only thirteen after all and no match for the iron-fisted Gorbals man who had been in fisticuff fights for as long as he could remember. For a long time now, John Simpson had itched to give the boy a good hiding, and this was just the chance he had been waiting for . . .

Mrs Conkey, ears well cocked, was listening behind her door. Opening it slowly she applied her eye to the crack and very carefully panned the vicinity. The stairhead landing was deserted but there had been a lot of coming and going in the Grant-Simpson household and somebody had left the door open. Barely an hour had elapsed since Dunky's discovery of Babs but already everyone knew of the scandal surrounding her.

The entire street was agog but Mrs Conkey wasn't to be found in any gossiping group out with the front line of action. Far better to stay put and just watch and listen, she was in a prime position to do both, and that was what she did – unashamedly.

Mrs Conkey had changed a good deal since her traumatic experience of the previous year. After much helpful persuasion by the neighbours she had applied for and been granted Government aid.

'We all have to swallow our pride in these hard times,' Theresa Leckie had told her and if bold, fearless Theresa Leckie said so then it must be all right because no one had seemed inclined to argue with her on that point.

And so the timid 'Creeping Jesus' of old was gradually being replaced by a more robust character, one who wasn't afraid to show her face in daylight and to air her views on various topics of the moment.

Her physical appearance had also improved: gone were her boils and her anxious expression; she had put on weight; she looked fit and well; she was mixing more with her fellow creatures and once a week she took Alex to the nearby Vogue cinema, complete with a bag of home-made apple doughnuts for him to eat all by himself.

She loved him like a son and would hear no ill of him. Therefore she was only too eager to defend him against anybody who might possibly harm one hair of his head . . .

The sound of raised voices filtered out to the landing . . . and Mrs Conkey plainly heard Alex challenging his stepfather to a fight. It was enough for her. Without waiting to hear more she grabbed the nearest thing that came to hand – her late husband's sturdy navy-blue umbrella with the ridged, polished wood handle.

John Simpson never knew what hit him. Mrs Conkey went straight to the attack. Wielding the umbrella at him in a frenzy she lashed out at his head, his face, his body, in fact anywhere and everywhere and all with the greatest enjoyment.

Her sudden arrival had taken everyone completely by surprise but it wasn't long before the Grants, the young Graingers and Mrs Simpson herself, were looking on with a sort of subdued pleasure – particularly Alex who had no qualms whatsoever about displaying his grinning approval of his rescuer's energetic display with the umbrella.

John Simpson's hands were up in front of his face in an effort to shield himself from the flailing weapon but his attempts at self-preservation were useless against her rage.

'You leave the lad be!' she screamed. 'Any man or boy in this street could have fathered the girl's bairn . . . !' She glared at John Simpson's red and sweating face . . . 'For all we know it could even have been *YOU*!'

Her words had an electrifying effect. John Simpson recoiled as if he had been struck with something deadly while everyone else stared at him, Evelyn in particular.

Such a thought had never occurred to her. For all his faults she didn't believe for a minute that he could sink *that* low. She really felt that Mrs Conkey was taking matters a bit far with such an accusation.

'You're nothing but a mad, bad old bitch!' John Simpson told his neighbour in a voice trembling with emotion. 'You said yourself it could have been anybody – the girl is familiar with every pair o' trousers in this district. She's naught but trouble and the sooner she leaves this house the better for everyone. The fact remains however that she and young Alex were like a pair o' wild animals together.

Ask him . . . he knows fine well what I'm talking about.'

Bessie turned away with tears in her eyes. She couldn't speak up, not even to clear the name of the boy she loved with all her heart. John Simpson had threatened to cut her throat if she so much as breathed one word against him. She was thirteen years old – and she believed him.

It was the most bitter pill she'd ever had to swallow in the whole of her young life.

It was touch and go whether Babs lived or died. She had lost a dangerous amount of blood and was so weak she could barely lift her head from the pillow. For a time she didn't know day from night nor could she tell who came to visit her in hospital, which was as well as her visitors were few and far between.

If it hadn't been for Maggie and Evelyn she might have had no visitors with the exception of John Simpson's daughter, Moira, who, on several occasions walked the fairly long distance to the hospital because she couldn't afford the tram fare.

But, every time she came, she had somehow managed to scrape together enough coppers to buy her step-niece some small treat, an apple, an orange, or a small bunch of grapes, luxuries that her own children rarely received and things that she would never have dreamed of buying for herself.

Babs didn't know this step-aunt very well and she was inclined to look down her nose at these small offerings until one day Maggie told her how Moira had to bring up four children single-handed and was so hard up she was forced to scrub floors and stairs in order to make an honest penny.

'She would never ask her father for help,' Maggie said. 'She hasna spoken to him in years, ever since he nearly killed her husband for daring to oppose him over some small matter.'

'Oh, I didn't know that.' Babs looked at the bunch of

grapes Moira had brought. Babs had seldom cried for a fellow human being – but that day she cried for her aunt and wished she had known sooner about John Simpson's treatment of his own daughter.

It didn't take Babs long to rally – she was young, resilient, and tough. Soon she was sitting up, eating her food, growing stronger by the hour, letting everyone know how dreadful her ordeal had been: how much she had suffered; how terrified she had felt having to give birth all on her own; how frightened she had been at the sight of all that blood.

'Of course, it was all your own doing,' hazarded one unsympathetic fellow patient. 'You must have known the risks involved in letting a man near you in the first place.'

'It wasn't a man, it was a boy. I didn't ever think I could get pregnant by a thirteen-year-old boy.'

'Thirteen! The lad was hardly out his cradle! You're making it all up.'

'I tell you it was a boy, one far more developed than any man I've known.'

'So, you've known a lot o' men – and you're blaming it on a boy. What's the matter, girl, are you afraid the *real* culprit will give you a doing if you open your mouth?'

This was too near the truth for comfort. Babs lifted her chin and said coldly, 'Believe what you like, it makes no difference to me, but I tell you, Alex Grainger has a lot to answer for.'

'Alex Grainger?'

'You heard.'

Babs wasn't feeling as tough as she sounded. She was tired of it all. She didn't want to blame Alex any more, she had never really wanted to get him into trouble. From their very first meeting she had genuinely liked him and had always marvelled at his strength in never going all the way with her.

But she had been mad about that too. How could he

resist the temptations of her lovely, inviting body? How could he refuse to make *real* love to her when she was pleading for it? They had played and petted and done practically everything else but always he held back at the last moment, no matter how much she tried to entice him.

It was his mother. She was never out of his mind. He didn't want to let her down, he said, and that was really the crux of the matter.

Beautiful Aunt Evelyn, the darling of his life, the delight of his world – he wouldn't soil his soul for her as then he could never have faced her.

Lucky, lucky, Aunt Evelyn, to have a son like that . . . Babs thought about her own tiny son. He had never tasted the sweetness of life but had lain there at her side, as lifeless as a china doll in those traumatic moments after the birth.

Now that she had time to think, she remembered the fair hair, the perfect little hands and feet – the eyes that would never open to the wonder and the beauty of life.

She seemed to remember everything now and Barbara Anna Simpson buried her face into her pillow – and wept.

When news of the drama eventually reached Nellie's ears she put pen to paper and wrote to Evelyn:

Alex must come to me, of course. I don't believe he had anything to do with the girl and her poor little infant but he shouldn't have to put up with all the gossip and lies. We have always got on well together, him and me, and I know fine he has always been keen to live and work at Croft Donald and Kenneth would be only too glad of an extra pair of hands. Let me know how he feels and if the answer is yes I'll send his fare.

Young James is fit and well and thriving on the country air. He's a born little farmer and says he never wants to go back to the city. He can stay forever if he likes. Meantime, have a word with Alex about my suggestion.

Ever your loving sister,
Nellie

There was a time in his life when Alex had been desperate to live with Nellie at Croft Donald. Only last summer he had been rather envious when his mother had returned from Kenneray with the news that James was staying on at Croft Donald for 'an indefinite period'.

'He isn't strong like you, Alex,' she had told him. 'Town or country, you'll aye get by.'

At her words he had looked thoughtful. 'Ay, you're right,' he had eventually agreed. 'James was always afraid o' life in the city; if he had stayed here it would have killed him . . . if no', John Simpson would have got him, so either way he would have been a loser.'

Now here was the opportunity Alex had always longed for but ironically he knew he just couldn't take it. Circumstances had changed . . . *he* had changed. He had responsibilities to face: he wouldn't leave his mother alone with John Simpson, she needed another man in the house; Jamie was too old and too tired to fight anymore, he'd had his dog days. It was time for the fit and strong to take over . . .

Besides, there was Bess to consider. For the first time in his short life he was experiencing the wonder of young love. It was an entirely different emotion from the passion he had shared with Babs. With Bess there was tenderness, consideration, respect – and always the lovely, warm feeling that this was only the beginning, that in the days and years to come there would be more and more love, growing, expanding, filling his world with its beauty.

Over and above everything else he knew that, if he turned tail and ran, it would be a sure indication of his guilt, a silent admission to something he hadn't done. Far better to stay and hold up his head. He couldn't very well tell his mother in so many words that he had never actually been with Babs in *that* way but someday she would know the truth – someday when he could speak to her about such things without blushing.

Evelyn was very proud of her son when he told her that he was staying. He didn't say why but his set, determined chin said it all.

She hugged him, she knew he had things to say to her that were too difficult for him to put into words but one day he would tell her, one day they would talk man to woman about the things closest to their hearts. Meanwhile, it was enough that he gazed at her with eyes that were steady and honest and guilt-free.

When Babs came out of hospital she opted to go to her Aunt Moira's rather than accept Grace's offer to stay with her. Babs would much have preferred Grace's cosy, clean little home. She had been shocked at the squalor of her Aunt Moira's single-end where everything and everybody was crushed into the smallest space imaginable.

But Babs had her reasons for wanting to be there. She and Aunt Moira had one thing in common, they both hated John Simpson. He had abused one and had ignored the other. Babs had to talk to someone about the emotions closest to her heart; the hatred, the anger, the fear.

Aunt Moira was a very good listener. She was patient and kind and understanding. She came to know Babs very well in the few short weeks that she was there.

And something rather unusual happened to Babs during her time with Aunt Moira. She developed a true affection for the woman who had such bad luck in her life but who had somehow managed to keep her head up.

Babs also grew fond of the children. She dressed them in their inadequate clothes; she fed them and played with them; she took them for walks in the park. She was treated as a trustworthy individual who was able to make her own decisions and for that she was truly grateful. She responded to the love surrounding her like a flower opening to the sun.

Babs had never been truly fond of her own mother, she had barely tolerated her stepmother, but in Aunt Moira she found a soul mate, a warm, loving companion who really cared if she got her feet wet or if the chilblains on her fingers had healed up.

Aunt Moira didn't make her feel dirty or degraded for what she had done. Never once was she made to feel that her poor little baby's death had been her fault, instead they had heart to heart talks about life and death and the meaning of creation.

At last Babs seemed to have found the sort of family she had always wanted but she didn't know how long it would last. When Tom came home he would have his say about a lot of things and he would certainly be making the decisions about her and Bessie's future.

In bed at night Babs cried her lonely tears, for the infant she had lost, for the mistakes she had made.

I'll make up for it, God, she prayed, and one day I'll help my Aunt Moira the way she's helped me. Give me strength, God. I've never been steadfast like Bessie and I'll need an awful lot of support to see me through. Also give me the strength to tell on John Simpson. Aunt Moira never asks though I know she suspects, but I could never tell her that I allowed her very own father to do the things he did to me.

Evelyn's heart and mind were in turmoil. Gillan was going away to Cape Town at the end of March to help Lord Ogilvie with his business affairs and he didn't know when he would be back.

'Come with me, Princess,' Gillan had urged. 'Uncle would be delighted to see you after all these years. He never stops talking about you and always hopes that one day he'll see his granddaughter again.'

'My grandfather, Lord Lindsay Ogilvie,' Evelyn had whispered, still finding it hard to believe that she and Gillan were cousins, that Oggie was her mother's father, that they were all blood kin who had found one another by accident after a lapse of many years.

'Oh, yes, Gillie, I would love to see my grandfather again. It would be like a dream come true just as meeting you again was. But I can't very well come to Cape Town dragging my entire family with me.'

Gillan's face had taken on the dark look that she had come to know so well over the years. 'Uncle would love to see Maggie, it would be a grand chance for father and daughter to be re-united before he dies. He's an old man now and can't last all that much longer.'

'I have a father as well as a mother, Gillie,' she had reminded him. 'I also have a family and a husband to consider. I can't just up and leave them all to their own devices.'

'Who cares about John Simpson?' Gillan had growled. 'He certainly doesn't seem to care about you and I would have thought you would have jumped at the chance to be rid of him.'

'Please, Gillie, don't let's fight about it,' she had pleaded. 'Every minute alone with you is very precious to me and I don't want us to spoil it for anything. We'll talk about it later when we can both be more rational.'

But a rational moment had somehow never presented itself. When she and Gillan were alone together they forgot the world, they forgot everything except the delight of being in each other's arms.

And now this thing had happened with Babs and Evelyn couldn't seem to find one rational thought in her head to help her through the traumas that were piling on top of her.

Bessie tossed and turned. She was having the same old nightmare. There in the distance was a chanting crowd, waving torches and carrying banners from which hung the black tassels of death. The cobbled wynd rang with the clatter of a hundred pairs of boots. Sweat, tears, blood, ran from the eyes, the noses, and the ears of people who looked like spectres newly risen from their graves.

'Death to Alex Grainger! Death to Alex Grainger! Baby killer! Baby killer! Baby killer . . . !'

The venomous chant went on and on, like dozens of red hot daggers piercing into Bessie's brain until she thought she would go mad with the pain of the bleeding wounds inside her skull.

The banners drew nearer, like disembodied spooks with a life of their own.

The words on them were written in blood, *Death to Alex Grainger! Death by Hanging! Death by any means! Burn him at the stake! Draw and quarter him! Death! Death! Death! Punish! Punish! Punish!*

And there, in the midst of the jostling mob, was Alex himself. Urchins and half-wits were throwing stones at him; blood was streaming down his face; one of his eyes had closed up, the other was hanging out on his cheek; his limbs were bruised and raw, his clothes hanging in tatters . . .

Punish! Punish! Punish! Death! Death! Death!

Bessie's heart was beating so fast she knew she was going to die herself if she couldn't let her screams out.

Alex had fallen. He was down on his knees; his bowed head was covered in blood; the crowd were closing in on him, a lynching mob that would show no mercy . . .

Bessie's screams split the night asunder. Evelyn came running to her aid. Maggie and Jamie rushed through from The Room. Evelyn gathered the terrified girl into her arms and smoothed her sweat-soaked hair back from her brow.

'Please don't kill him!' Bessie sobbed. 'Don't kill Alex. It wasn't him, it was John Simpson! Babs was his little wife. He wanted two wives, Aunt Evelyn and Babs. The baby was his, the dead little baby was his! Not Alex! Not Alex! Not Alex!'

'Oh, my God, my God!' Maggie took the half-crazed girl to her bosom. The truth was out at last – Alex's name was cleared . . . and John Simpson had had his day.

John Simpson met his end one dark night in a filthy Gorbals alley. He had been drinking heavily and he lurched along, hardly seeing where he was going for the tears, the booze and the mucus, that poured out of his eyes, mouth and nose.

He was crying tears of self-pity; he had poured drink into himself in an effort to forget.

Evie, his lovely Evie . . . he would never forget her . . . Babs his step-granddaughter, the little slut! He wanted to forget *her* but he couldn't! No one would let him. He would always be reminded of the part he'd played in her life. The baby, dead, a boy. He had already lost a son – his and Evie's – then Babs' infant. The poor little bastard had never drawn life . . .

A gang of corner boys had followed Simpson from the pub. The jungle drums had been beating. Everyone knew the unsavoury details of this man's life and no man could do the things that he had done without expecting to pay for them.

He was an incestuous coward, plain and simple. The boys of the back-streets didn't take kindly to such people living in their midst – especially when an innocent baby had been an indirect victim of his filthy lust.

As Simpson staggered into an alley to vomit against a wall, the stealthy figures gathered at his back. A knife rose and fell, then another – just to make sure . . . The figures melted away into the shadows and were soon lost in the night.

*

John Simpson lay writhing in a pool of blood. It took thirty pain-filled minutes for him to die . . . and when he did it was in the ragged arms of an old wino who hoped there would be something in it for him when the poor bleeding joker drew his last breath.

The laws of the jungle had prevailed and justice had been done.

Tom returned home to some terrible revelations about his family. Not so long ago the sea had taken Murn, now, in his absence, his stepdaughter had birthed and lost a child and his father had paid for his crimes with his life.

Tom cried when he took Babs over his knee and gave her the thrashing of her life. Moira pleaded with him to stop but in a kind of frenzy he kept on beating and beating until the girl's buttocks were raw and bleeding and she was hoarse from screaming.

But she knew she deserved all she got. In some strange way she welcomed the punishment, it made her feel exonerated from sin and she never wanted the strap marks to fade from her body.

But they would always remain in her mind. Many things, many impressions, many emotions from this time would stay with her forever, not least the vision of her Aunt Moira's pale, sweet face when the moment came for them to say goodbye.

'One day I'll send the fares for you and the kids to come out to Australia,' Babs said, the tears streaming down her face. 'You'll love it there, Aunt Moira. The sun, the sea, the beaches . . . the kids will get brown and you'll get strong and well.'

'I'll miss you, lassie,' Moira said quietly. 'The bairns will cry for nights on end without you there to tell them a story. Write – I'll write – you can bet your boots on that.'

She pressed a paper bag into Babs's hands 'for the journey'. Inside was a large bunch of black grapes.

'Oh, Auntie,' Babs threw herself against her aunt's bosom, 'I love you! I'll grow up! I'll work and work to make a nice home for you all, I promise! I promise!'

Bessie had pleaded with her father to be allowed to stay at 198 Camloan Road, the place she had started off loathing but now never wanted to leave.

She would miss the friendliness, the humour, the warmth of tenement life; she would miss Tinker and Dobbie; she had grown to love Maggie and Jamie and the children, she adored her Aunt Evelyn; but most of all she couldn't bear to part from Alex.

But Tom was adamant about taking both sisters back with him to Australia. When the time for parting came, Alex and Bessie gazed at one another, she with tears in her eyes, he with a face that was pale with grief.

He looked at her; he drank her in; her freckles, her glorious curtain of silken brown hair, the frankness of her eyes, the little habit she had of tilting her head to one side to gaze at him quizzically.

Their friendship had been innocent and happy. With her he had known true joy, true companionship . . . And that other thing, that knowledge of the flower blossoming within, the flower of love, one that would one day burst forth to fill him with its fragrance and beauty.

His heart just about broke in two at the realisation she was going away – so far away – across the sea . . . across the world.

'I'll send for you one day, Bess,' he vowed. 'I'll make my fortune and then you'll come back to me and we'll be married.'

Bessie looked at his handsome, eager young face and she couldn't fail to notice that his eyes – those beautiful strange eyes of his – were moist and sad.

Chapter Twenty

Evelyn nearly fainted when she opened the door one morning and found Lady Alicia Younger standing on her doorstep. Lady Alicia was a rather horsey-looking woman in her early fifties. She had 'buck' teeth, beetling brows, lots of fair hair piled on top of her head and a tanned face full of life and character.

Lady Alicia didn't hide herself away like some of her class. She mixed well with 'odds and sods' from all walks of life; she visited schools to give lectures on every sort of subject and many a child had her to thank for awakening their interest in things that might otherwise have passed them by; she opened fetes and bazaars and organised parties and picnics for deprived youngsters; she was active in local politics and interested in the welfare of tramps, hobos and pavement artists.

In her heyday she had opened several public buildings and had launched many a ship with a bottle of champagne and a few well-chosen words.

Nowadays there weren't so many ships to launch. But Lady Younger still had her finger on the pulse of Glasgow. She was aware of the lack of jobs, the poverty, the hardship. Many a charity had been started up by her, many an individual had been helped by her personal kindness and concern.

Lady Alicia's family had made their fortune in merchant shipping and in tobacco plantations in America and they had come back to settle in Scotland where they continued to amass money by investing in every venture under the sun.

Lady Alicia's grandfather had a nose for business since an early age and he had grown up further to expand the

Younger coffers. But his family had never been mean with their money. The various branches were sprinkled with benefactors and philanthropists and Sir George Younger had been no exception. To the small township of Govan he had gifted the library, a hospital, the town hall, a public convenience, and he had also had stained glass windows installed in several places of worship.

Local councils had responded by immortalising his name on streets, seats, plaques and cairns. In the local park, which was also named after him, reposed an enormous statue of himself and his good lady wife, splendid in its magnificence, meticulous in its detail, beloved by sparrows and pigeons and the occasional down and out who found the generous stone lap of Lady Jane Younger a far better bet than a park bench.

All in all, there wasn't a man, woman, or child unfamiliar with the name of Younger and nearly all had a good word to say about its members.

Over the years, Lady Alicia had fast gained a reputation as being as great a philanthropist as her grandfather and, like him, she carried out her affairs with quiet dignity, good humour, unstinting energy, and steadfast devotion.

But of all her interests and loves, horses and their welfare were her absolute passion and she adored any occasion that involved them. She owned some of the finest thoroughbred mares in the land and, true to family tradition, she had made her personal fortune by breeding and training racehorses. She had gained herself a reputation in the horse world for being able to sniff out a promising filly that someone with a lesser instinct would pass by.

In her spare time she liked nothing better than an exhilarating gallop over the countryside, or just a sedate trot through her own estates, depending on her mood. But she also liked just 'mucking about in the stables' or doing anything that was 'horsey', right down to forking out dung and, on many occasions, assisting the vet when a mare was foaling.

To add to her interests she was active in various youth organisations and loved nothing better than to sit herself down at a smoky camp fire with a sausage on the end of a stick while she conversed with a young person.

She had a knack of making everybody feel at ease, even babies in prams, but that didn't stop Evelyn feeling overwhelmed by her unexpected presence. She simply strode into the lobby, and from there to the kitchen where she plunked herself down on one of the hard little chairs and proceeded to pull a letter from her pocket which she then waved triumphantly in the air.

Evelyn's eyes darted to a pile of ironing on the table; a mountain of mending on a chair; an untidy array of newspapers that she had been in the process of rolling into twists for the fire.

It was Christmas Eve, she and Maggie had cleaned the house from top to bottom and were pulling out all the stops to rid themselves of all the household chores so that they could have the festive season clear. Last night, Rachel, with Meg's grudging help, had polished and black-leaded the grate, hence the unlit fire this morning.

Evelyn was nine months pregnant, with the result that everything was an effort for her. She had felt heavy and lethargic as soon as she had opened her eyes that morning and was taking longer than normal to set the fire, even though Alex had chopped the sticks and fetched coal from the scullery bunker before going off on his morning milk round.

'My dear,' Lady Alicia said with a beaming smile, 'this letter is from your son, Alex. I don't know whether he has told you about it but all I can say is you have a boy of great courage and character and one whom I would like to meet when it is at all convenient.'

She passed the letter to Evelyn with a flourish. Alex had not taken long to come to the point. He explained his love of horses and how he had come to be the proud owner of

Tinker and Dobbie who would have been for the 'knacker's yard' but for his timely interference.

He went on to say that it was becoming more and more difficult to find the money to feed the horses and ended by asking her if she would be kind enough to take them and give them a good home:

A place where they would be loved and cared for to the end of their days even though it will break my heart to part with them . . .

Evelyn hid a smile. Trust her son. He had never allowed false pride to come between him and his goals with the result that he seldom went short of the things that mattered in his life.

'Nothing venture nothing gain' was his motto and he believed in carrying it out to the full.

Lady Alicia obviously appreciated his frankness. She was bubbling over with enthusiasm and with some ideas she had in mind for Alex and his horses.

Evelyn was only half listening. Ever since rising she had been having cramping pains in her stomach – now they took hold in earnest and she had to stuff her fist into her mouth to stop herself from crying out.

'My dear.' Lady Alicia was on her feet instantly, making Evelyn sit down, tucking her own coat around her as it was cold in the room without the fire.

In minutes her ladyship had organised everything. Her chauffeur-driven car, had been parked at the close, causing a great stir and into it she bundled Evelyn after leaving a note on the kitchen table to explain what had happened.

In vain Evelyn protested, saying she would much rather just send for the midwife as was usual in such cases.

Lady Alicia wouldn't hear of it. 'Nonsense,' she said briskly. 'If you'll forgive me for saying so, you look as if you could be doing with a good molly-coddling and that's just what you're going to get.'

And so Evelyn was not only driven to the hospital in style, she was also given a private room, organised by Lady Alicia who didn't believe in doing anything by half.

A son was born to Evelyn at seven o'clock on Christmas morning 1932, a beautiful boy with a cloud of dark hair and the fine, sensitive features of his father, Gillan Forbes of Rothiedrum. He was the seventh child of a seventh child on his mother's side and he had been born in a lucky snood, a fine skin bag that the delivery nurse coveted but which Evelyn wanted to keep for herself.

Lady Younger was Evelyn's first visitor. She arrived in a flurry of congratulations, bearing an enormous bunch of flowers and a basket of fruit, and she went away, beaming her approval, reassuring Evelyn that she hadn't heard the 'last of her'.

Evelyn called the boy Grant Gillan Ogilvie. Maggie and Jamie knew that he wasn't John Simpson's child. Everyone else assumed that he was since his birth date fell within the proper timespan.

Evelyn would have told the world if she could, but she had to think of the boy's future. Gillan had sailed for Cape Town last March. He hadn't known that she was pregnant by him. He might never know that he had a son because he and Evelyn had parted so unhappily and had never exchanged addresses.

But he had given her the precious gift of his son and she knew that in the days and years to come, no matter how lonely or afraid she might be, she would look at this child that had been born of hers and Gillan's love, and she would remember the treasured hours they had shared before circumstances had forced them to part once again.

*

Lady Alicia was as good as her word, and set up a charity for retired horses. She bought an old house on the outskirts of Govan with stables and paddocks and a couple of cottages. To this place came two of her own old horses to 'keep Tinker and Dobbie company,' though it wasn't long before they were joined by others.

Lady Alicia employed the services of the local vet and hired a couple of stable lads to keep things ticking over until the whole project got off the ground. When Alex left school he went to work full time in his stables, living in one of the cottages during the week, travelling home at weekends. He had never been so busy or so happy. He had achieved one big ambition, now he set out with a vengeance to fulfil a very special promise he had made to a very special girl.

Bessie came back to Scotland in the spring of 1936. Alex had been as good as his word. He had saved hard for this day and when, at last, it came, he was speechless with joy as he finally beheld the face of the girl who had haunted his dreams for the past four years.

She had blossomed into a beauty with a slender figure and a face that was still innocent and child-like yet full of life and character.

With her came Babs, a vastly changed Babs from the one who had flaunted herself so shamelessly. She had grown up too quickly, too soon. At just twenty she was mature looking, there was about her a strange aura of sadness, and the blue eyes that had once shone with hunger for life were now dark and quiet in the pale beauty of her face.

She had worked hard on her return to Australia and she too had kept her word. She had saved and saved and had eventually bought a house in Sydney. Her Aunt Moira and two of her younger cousins would be travelling back with her. But first there was her sister's wedding to look forward to.

*

Alex had practically rebuilt the old house and he had fondly christened it Puddock Hall because of the amount of frogs to be found in a nearby pond.

It had been a labour of love – most of his spare time had gone into the renovation work. He had knocked down and re-styled rooms, he had created a bathroom out of an old wash-house and had hammered in nails and screwed in screws till his hands were hacked and raw.

Everything needed to make a home had been acquired at house auction sales; Maggie and Evelyn had advised him about curtains and other soft furnishings and between them had added the finishing feminine touches. In the end it was a house fit for a princess and when Lady Alicia came to see it she gave it her seal of approval together with a wedding gift of two hundred pounds.

Alex and Bessie were both nearly eighteen. They made an attractive pair on the day of their wedding: he was tall and strong-looking beside his slender little bride who wore a red rose in her silken brown hair to match the one in his buttonhole.

Red roses for love, a love that had begun for them as children and which had blossomed into full and dazzling flower.

Evelyn felt both pain and joy as she watched her son being married. A young man, tall and straight and handsome – her firstborn, her delight and her support all through the difficult years since his father's death.

How proud Davie would have been . . . a sob caught in her throat and Grant's small, reassuring hand crept into hers. Grant, Gillan's son! Black-eyed, dark-haired, a beautiful little boy who had given her nothing but happiness since the day he was born.

She took his hand, she smiled, he smiled back. His other hand sought that of his Aunt Nellie because her eyes looked funny and wet and he didn't like to see her cry.

But Nellie wasn't able to keep back her tears that day. Alex had been a very special nephew to her. She had looked after him during the first precious weeks of his life and he had never forgotten – never.

He turned and he smiled at her. She dashed away her tears with an impatient hand, still the same Nellie, hating 'palaver and fuss' but somehow always in the midst of it just the same.

It was a day for remembering. Her thoughts took her back and, in her mind's eye, she saw how it had been when youth was all and life seemed evergreen. So many people, so many different loves in her life.

Wee Col was gone now from Croft Donald. He had died of pneumonia two years ago at the age of twenty-six. Nellie had been warned that his life would be short but even so she had been devastated to lose the brother who had so enriched her life.

The last word to leave his lips had been 'Nella'. His last impression had been of her hand on his brow and his final small ecstasy had been to feel her lips touching his in a kiss of farewell that went with him to his last, long, innocent sleep.

His life had had its first painful beginnings at King's Croft. He had passed through the years, peacefully and quietly, enhancing the lives of those who had cherished him for what he was and not for what he might have been.

He had been buried in the little kirkyard of Kenneray that overlooked the wide ocean and the endless skies.

The words at the foot of his gravestone told a simple, beautiful story:

272

Wee Col
Innocent as the snowdrop,
under the shading tree
Frail yet ever-blooming,
In the hearts of you and me.

Young James still missed his beloved Uncle Col. Nellie still expected to see him coming through the door, his mouth smiling a greeting before he even knew if there was anybody to acknowledge it – and those brilliant blue eyes of his, lighting up at the sight of his adored Nella as they had done from very early childhood . . .

Nellie blew her nose into her hanky. Evelyn took her hand and held it tightly. The wedding was over, Alex and Bessie were moving out into the sunshine. There waiting for them were Dobbie and Tinker, hitched to a cart, their manes and tails expertly plaited and dressed by Jamie who had once done the same thing for his Clydes when he had entered them for the Tillietoorie horse show.

The cart was gaily decorated with ribbons and banners with a 'Just Married' sign dangling above the rear axle.

The neighbours of Camloan Road were waiting to give the young couple a good send off. Clouds of confetti billowed like snow. Mrs Conkey rushed forward to hug both Alex and his new bride.

Alex hadn't known he was so popular. With shining eyes he turned to his mother. The kiss he bestowed on her cheek was very tender. 'I love you, Mother,' he said shyly.

Before she could answer he was up beside Bessie, taking the reins, moving away, waving, his eyes smiling at everyone but coming back again and again to her.

'I love you, Alex.' Her lips formed the words. He inclined his head. He had understood the silent message.

The cart rumbled away. Her tears fell. Alex, her eldest

son, her dour, loving, protective boy, was married — and she suddenly felt bereft of a lifetime of joy and sorrow and love.

Chapter Twenty-one

Jamie could feel death in his bones. The feeling had been there for a long time now but this morning it was more pronounced and to add to his sense of unreality there was a numbness in his head and a tingling in his hands.

The house was empty but for Rachel who had opted to stay with him when the others had announced their intention of going into Glasgow for the January sales.

Evelyn had sold another short story to a Scottish magazine and in jubilant mood she wanted to take everybody 'up the town' and buy each of them something.

When Jamie said he would rather stay home she had kissed his brow and had pressed a couple of notes into his hand. At any other time she might have hesitated, knowing that he would just drink it, but this time an oddly sad expression crept into her eyes and she said slowly, 'If this money could buy you happiness it would make *me* the happiest person in the whole world.'

She kissed him again and then hugged him for good measure, almost as if she was saying more than just a temporary goodbye.

He had looked at the notes lying in his palm. 'It will bring me happiness, lass,' he whispered huskily. 'Ay, indeed it will.'

At Christmas, just a couple of weeks ago, Alex too had given him money, laughingly saying that he wasn't to spend it all 'in the one boozer'.

But Jamie hadn't touched a penny of it. He had hoarded

every spare copper that had come his way and Evelyn's generosity had just set the final seal on his plans.

Last night he and Maggie had had a long intimate chat that had gone on well into the small hours. They hadn't talked like that for many a long day and it had been wonderful to reminisce about a time when they had had the world at their feet and it had seemed an impossibility that they would ever grow old.

Of course they spoke about their years at King's Croft. Maggie normally avoided delving back into the past because she knew it hurt him to recall those hard but happy years when he had been the master of his own home and the keeper of his few bit acres of land.

But somehow she had wanted to talk last night, and when they finally went to bed he told her that he had never loved anyone the way that he loved her and he had never taken her loyalty to him for granted, even though it might sometimes have seemed that way.

She had told him to 'stop havering' and then she had cried, and after that they had fallen asleep in each other's arms, closer than they had ever been, happy in the knowledge that, even if they shared nothing else, they always had their memories to keep them together.

He had been saying goodbye to her in the only way he knew how, because he had known that today was the day – the day he was going back to the lands of his heart, back to see Rothiedrum one last time before he died.

His good suit was all ready, brushed and neatly pressed and hanging in the wardrobe. Maggie never left anything to chance. You never knew when you might be called to a wedding or a funeral or just to an unexpected outing that demanded Sunday best.

He and Rachel ate a good substantial dinner. She was only sixteen but already she was a marvellous little cook,

276

and when he told her she would some day make some man a wonderful wife, her grey eyes shone and she stretched her hand across the table to squeeze his.

She was and always had been Jamie's favourite grandchild. He knew he wasn't supposed to have favourites but his heart didn't acknowledge that rule.

In many ways she reminded him of Evelyn: mostly she was of a calm disposition but was also possessed of a turbulent temper if she thought someone was getting a raw deal; she was staunch, true, fiercely loyal to her family, romantic, warm, and loving. She had seldom failed to take her grandfather's side and there existed between them true affection and a rare understanding of one another's needs.

She was singing as she washed the dishes in the scullery. When she emerged she was drying her hands on the kitchen towel but stopped when she saw that her grandfather had changed into his good suit with his watch chain affixed to his waistcoat.

The watch chain meant that he was going somewhere special. *He looked* very special with his snowy white hair brushed back and his big bristly white moustache newly clipped into rather stark neatness.

'Where are you going, Grandpa?' Rachel asked hesitantly.

He didn't answer and she thought he was looking strange: his eyes were too bright, there was a barely suppressed excitement about him and his hand was shaking as he wielded the clothes brush over his jacket.

Rachel darted forward. 'Here, let me do that.' She took the brush from him and whisked a few hairs from his collar. For a few moments the only sounds to be heard in the room was the swish of the clothes brush and the ticking of the clock.

Rachel sensed that something big was happening in her

grandfather's life. She also sensed danger but her voice was carefully controlled when she spoke.

'Grandpa – take me with you wherever you're going, don't shut me out. We've aye been honest with one another for as long as I can remember.'

'Rachel.' When he took her hand, his was clammy and warm. 'I'm an old man. A long, long time ago me and your grannie left our croft in Rothiedrum because it had become too much for us. It broke my heart to leave, and I kept hoping that one day we'd go back. I've told you about King's Croft. I've told you about the old days and the old ways. Now I have to go back, I have to see it one last time before I die . . . '

'Please, Grandpa,' her eyes were brimming with tears, 'take me with you. Mam has told me all about the days when you were together in Rothiedrum. I know all about the hiring fairs and I could easily get a job. I'm tired o' the town, I want to escape like you. We – we could look after one another. Mam would never let me go on my own but she would if she knew you were with me. I could leave a note. They would worry about us if I didn't and might contact the police.'

Jamie gazed into her anxious grey eyes. He nodded. 'All right, lass, but hurry. I want us to get a good start before it gets dark. We'll be travelling by train some o' the way – at other times we'll have to walk.'

Rachel's hand shook as she wrote a brief message to her mother. She propped it up against the tea caddy on the table. Rather dazedly she glanced out of the window. It was January: the nights came down quickly; it was also overcast, it would get dark faster than ever tonight . . . and it would be cold . . .

Hurriedly she stuffed some clothing into a bag. She extracted her precious savings from inside the knob of the brass bed end in The Room. Ever practical she also grabbed safety pins and a needle and thread from her grannie's work-basket, and finally, a loaf of bread from the kitchen cupboard for 'emergencies'.

She took her Grandpa's hand; the door shut behind them. He didn't look back – he was going home at last and that was all that mattered.

By nightfall they had made it as far as Stirlingshire. It was freezing cold. Grey-black clouds were piling up, heavy with snow, darkening the sky.

Rachel had a blister on one foot, Jamie's hands were purple and icy cold.

They found shelter in a barn and sank down thankfully into the dry hay. The warmth was bliss after the harshness of the icy wind. Neither of them moved or spoke for several minutes, then Jamie reached out to take Rachel's hand and his voice was hoarse when he said, 'You should never have come, lass, I should never have let you. Your grannie will be angry at me. Your mother might never talk to me again.'

'Oh, wheesht, Grandpa.' Tears sprang to Rachel's eyes; she didn't like the look of him – he was grey and very old-looking and his breath was coming fast. 'We'll be fine when we've had a rest. Later we'll eat some bread and drink some o' the milk I bought at the dairy.'

Jamie took a small bottle from his pocket. 'This will better suffice me, Rachel, quine. You take the milk, it will do you good.'

That night they slept fitfully, cuddled into one another for warmth. She kept waking up, listening to see if he was still breathing, alert for any warning sign, ready to up and run for help if need be.

'Dinna worry so much about me, lass,' he told her at one point. She wondered if he was, like her, counting the night hours, afraid of the cold and the dark and the unfamiliar sounds of the countryside.

But Jamie lay listening to them with quiet enjoyment: a mouse squeaking in the rafters, an owl hooting from the barn roof, the wind rustling the trees, the swish and gurgle of a nearby river.

Sounds he had thought never to hear again; the wonderful, beautiful, natural sounds of God's countryside. The slow tears fell from his eyes and down his cheeks. He knew that, even if he got no further than this barn in a Stirlingshire field, it was worth it just to have heard, one last time, sounds that had once been such a part of his life.

In the morning they were stiff and cold and hungry but strangely, when Rachel looked at her grandfather, she saw that his cheeks held a faint tinge of colour and that his eyes were bright with interest when he stood up to look from the skylight at the ploughed fields stretching over the land; the gulls drifting in the leaden sky; a curl of smoke rising from the chimney of a distant cottage.

'Look, Rachel,' he murmured happily, 'these are the things I used to see on winter mornings when I looked from my window at King's Croft: the brown furrows, the frosty parks, a sheepdog running along the end-rigs wi' his master. It was life, all the life I ever wanted or needed.'

He took her hand. 'It's been worth it, lassie, just to have had this. Remember that — and dinna be sad.'

Breakfast consisted of dry bread and milk and two squares of chocolate each. The wind was keening round the building which made the interior seem all the cosier. Rachel was loathe to leave, not for her own sake — she was young and supple and able to walk for miles — her worries were for her grandfather. Apart from the spot of red burning high on each cheek his face looked yellow and old in the light filtering into the barn.

But as soon as he had finished eating he got stiffly to his feet and reached out his hand to her. 'Let's go, Rachel,

lass. We have a long journey ahead o' us and the exercise
will keep us warm.'

It was starting to snow. Great billowing clouds of it swirled
around them as they made their way out of the shelter of
the barn.

Some boys were playing by the river. They were in aca-
demic uniform and obviously had decided to have a bit of
fun on their way to school.

Their cries of excitement echoed in the icy air. One of
them was on the bank, hanging onto a branch of a tree
with one hand while he fished around in the river with a
stick held in the other.

The wind had whipped his cap into the foaming water.
The river was in spate and the grassy banks were slippery. The branch broke with a crack and the boy lost his
footing and plunged into the water.

His friends were yelling instructions to him. One
grabbed another branch and held it out to him and, miracu-
lously, he managed to catch it and hold on.

But the current was taking him away. His dark head
bobbed in the frothy brown foam, it disappeared only to
resurface further down.

Peeling off his jacket, Jamie ran to the scene and, without
ado, he plunged in beside the boy to seize him under the
arms and hold on for dear life.

The bitter cold of the water robbed Jamie of breath;
a band of red hot pain gripped his chest but somehow
he managed to lift the boy up out of the thundering
spume and, with the last of his strength, heave him onto
the sodden bank.

The farmer and his dog came running to the scene and
the man snatched the boy away from the river's icy
clutches.

*

Transfixed with horror, Rachel stood rooted to the spot. The snow whirled around her, faster and faster. Through the white curtain she watched as the river carried her grandfather away ... far away ...

Something crunched under her feet. It was a pipe, the stubby Stonehaven pipe that he had so cherished because it belonged to the King's Croft days which had held so many memories for him.

She cradled it in her palm, her tears dropped onto the chubby bowl ...

'It's been worth it, lassie, just to have had this. Remember that and dinna be sad ... '

His voice, that beloved lilting voice of his, spoke soothingly in her mind. Her heart faltered in her breast, and she shivered and turned away, the snow obliterating her slender figure as she walked swiftly over the whitening fields of 'God's countryside'.

Jamie had died a hero's death, but that was scant consolation to Maggie who could only imagine the pain and the cold he must have suffered before that final oblivion. She tortured herself with her thoughts and with the poignant memories of that last night they had so lovingly shared.

And none of it made sense. If only he had achieved his ambition, if only he had reached his beloved Rothiedrum, it might all have been worthwhile. But he hadn't even made it halfway home and she could hardly bear to think about it.

Then Rachel came to her, quiet and sad and pensive. She repeated what Jamie had said shortly before he died and then she left her grannie to her thoughts.

'God's countryside.' Maggie spoke the words softly. Her Jamie, her man, *had* seen the things he had set out to see before he died. They might not have been in Rothiedrum but they would have been familiar enough to make him happy.

He had looked upon the furrowed earth; he had seen the wide, wild, skies; he had tasted the frosty air and had smelt the tang of rich, brown soil . . . and he might have heard the plaintive song of the curlew shivering down the wind . . . All around the music of the earth would have filled his ears with its glory.

'God's countryside . . . '

Maggie's heart beat quiet and strong in her breast. Her man had died a hero, he had saved the life of a child. It was as if fate had placed him in that particular spot at that particular time in order to show the world that his life – and his death – had some meaning after all.

Maggie looked at his old fiddle hanging on the wall. She remembered the stirring tunes he had once played, his nimble fingers flying over the strings, his black eyes watching her, snapping with the joy of life, shining with his love for her. He hadn't played for years but she could still hear the music in her head; romantic, stirring gypsy music that she would never forget.

The world was spinning round for Maggie. She had slipped on a patch of ice outside the gates of The Infirmary on her way to visit Grace who was very ill after an operation for stomach ulcers.

Maggie had been thinking of Jamie just before she fell. She had been very lonely since his death and had reached the stage of wondering if her life held any meaning without her man at her side. He had died trying to reach Rothiedrum and ever since then she had suffered terrible pangs of homesickness for Aberdeenshire.

It was as if he had transferred some of his longings to her because her hankerings after her roots had never been as strong as his . . . Now she found herself being so sentimental about the old days she could often spend an hour or more just sitting still while her thoughts carried her away from the reality of the tenements . . .

Rothiedrum . . . King's Croft . . . Oh to go back . . . to see again the peesies birling in the sky; to watch the moon rising pale and mysterious over the heather-cloaked shoulder of Bennachie . . .

'I think she's hurt her head. She's talking to herself . . . maybe she's delirious.'

The disembodied voice grated in Maggie's ears. She *had* hurt her head but she was certainly not delirious and she wished that someone would help get her to her feet so that she could be on her way.

Grace would be waiting and she would start worrying if her mother didn't come as promised. Grace was far too weak and ill to have to start worrying about other people.

Somebody tucked a jacket under Maggie's head. Somebody else covered her with their coat. That was one thing about the Glasgow folk, kind, they were always kind, and considerate in any situation that demanded a bit of human understanding . . .

'Let me through, I'm a doctor! Stand back please, give her air!'

Maggie was aware of a presence, somebody in close proximity to herself and she knew that the doctor, whoever he was, had got down on his knees to examine her.

The hands that probed her person were gentle but firm. That voice, that soothing, big, deep, voice was asking her questions . . .

Yes, her head hurt but only a little. Of course she could feel her feet! She hadn't fallen all that heavily and knew she wasn't paralysed . . .

And why was *he* asking her questions when all the time *she* should be asking him?

That voice – dark brown, like rich, thick velvet . . . Now who had uttered that poetic description of such a voice? Evelyn, it had to be Evelyn, that lass had been born with romance in her soul. No wonder she had wanted to be a writer almost from the moment she could convey her childish wishes.

'Doctor . . .' Maggie held onto his arm and struggled to focus on him. But everything was blurred. All she could see was a dark shape bending over her, a bulky dark shape – a great brown bear of a man with keen grey eyes and a full, aesthetic mouth – a man who had wooed and won gentle little Grace Grant of King's Croft . . .

'Gordon – Gordon Chisholm . . . I'd ken that voice anywhere.'

Maggie tried to sit up but a trolley had arrived. The doctor was giving instructions. Maggie was whisked to the Casualty Department to await an x-ray. As she was lying there her head began to clear, her eyes focused. A face swam into her vision. Not the Gordon Chisholm she remembered – this man's face had been altered by plastic surgery, the taut skin, the tight eyes told their own tale – but it was Gordon Chisholm just the same, the brave surgeon who had supposedly been blown up in a field hospital in France; the husband that Grace had always believed would come home some day – home to her and the love that had never faltered through all the years.

'Ay, Maggie, it's me. Nobody could ever fool you, could they?'

He smiled and took her hand and then he grew serious. 'Look at me, Maggie,' he urged. 'What you see now is a travesty of the man you once knew but still a damned sight better-looking than the one who emerged from the ruins of war. I was ill for years. I was ill, ugly, and sorry for myself. I knew I could never go back to my beautiful Grace. Far better for her to forget me and meet somebody else who was whole and real and well.'

'Gordon.' Maggie held his hand tighter. She gazed at him, at his mop of hair that was still incredibly dark and thick, at his steady grey eyes, features that stamped him as the Gordon Chisholm she had known,

'Listen to me,' she urged. 'Grace has never stopped believing that one day you'll come back to her. At first we all tried to tell her she was living in fairyland but her belief was unshakable. She's never looked at anyone else; she's never wanted anyone else; she hasn't needed anyone else because in her heart she kent that one day you would come back to her.'

'Oh, Maggie.' His shoulders sagged, he bowed his head. 'If only you knew. If I could only tell you how I've pined to see my bonny lass. There were times I thought I would go mad from my want and need of her but I couldn't, I just couldn't – let her see . . . '

'And I aye thought you were such a brave man,' Maggie said heavily. 'One who would never let false pride stand in the way o' the things that matter most in life. Grace is ill, Gordon. She is very weak and, at this moment in time, she needs more love and more care than she has ever needed in her life before. I was on my way to visit her when I slipped on the ice. She's upstairs, in the surgical ward. Go to her, lad, go to her now.'

His eyes were incredulous.

'Upstairs . . . here?'

'Ay . . . here,' she said softly. 'So near, laddie, so near . . . and so looking forward to a visitor.'

He bent and kissed her; there were tears in his eyes. 'Thanks, Maggie,' he said humbly and went out of the cubicle with his head high and his shoulders straight.

Maggie settled herself back on her pillows. She was smiling. Miracles did happen and life was worth living after all – and Jamie would have been the first to have agreed with her on that score. It was, after all, a day of great rejoicing, the day that Doctor Gordon Chisholm came back from the war, alive and well, to be re-united with his darling Grace.

Grace's eyes were shut. She knew that visiting hour had started some time ago and she was worried because her mother wasn't here yet. She hadn't been the same since

Jamie's death and Grace sometimes got the impression that she felt life wasn't worth living anymore.

The curtains swished open. Grace opened her eyes, 'Mam . . .' The name died on her lips.

'Grace – Grace, darling.' Gordon came forward. He took her hands in his big, strong hairy ones. 'It's me, my love, I'm here, I'll always be here now.'

Grace lifted up her head. The tears welled in her haunting black eyes.

'Gordon,' she whispered. 'Oh, my darling man, I aye knew you'd come back to me. I knew you weren't dead because in my heart you were so much alive – it was as if it was beating all these years for you – just for you . . .'

Chapter Twenty-two

Evelyn gazed at her eldest son. His embarkation leave was over. He had come to say goodbye to her before going off to fight in the war.

Both Evelyn and Bessie had pleaded with him not to join up. There were plenty of other young men who could risk being killed if they wanted to, single men with few family ties, but not Alex, with his horses and his stables and a young wife who was due to give birth to their first child soon after Christmas.

'I'll be back by then,' Alex had told her blithely. 'I'll get Christmas leave – and if no' I'll be allowed to come home to see my very own baby.'

'No you won't,' Bessie had told him, her eyes brimming with tears. 'Once they get you in their clutches they'll never let go – never.'

He had taken her in his arms then to soothe away her fears as only he could. But just the same he was adamant about joining up – his eyes had been shining – and Bessie knew that he viewed the whole thing as some great adventure that wasn't to be missed for anything.

Besides, he was as stubborn as a mule when it came to decisions about his own life, like his father before him and very much like his mother: that same determined chin, that mulish expression, that set of the mouth that no amount of persuasion would alter . . .

Evelyn, knowing that her son possessed the same obstinate streak, was the first to relinquish her arguments.

Now, here he was, tall and so handsome in his army uniform, his kilt swishing about his knees as he came towards her to embrace her.

She held him away from her and her heart jumped. She was remembering her first glimpse of a young soldier, reflected in the window of a little baker's shop in Cobbly Wynd, Aberdeen . . .

It had been autumn then too – October, a warm, mellow October day: the cobbles sprinkled with red and yellow leaves; fingers of sunlight poking through the trees; old men and women sitting on the benches under the boughs, smoking clay pipes, talking and nodding with the greatest enjoyment, happy just to be there in that quaint old street; the smells of tar and brine wafting up from the harbour, mingling with the tempting aromas drifting from the dim interior of Bert's Bakery and Tea Shoppe.

And Davie, not a will-o'-the-wisp of her imagination but a flesh and blood young man, about to go off to fight for his country . . .

She had fallen in love with him that day, her Davie. So passionate, so charismatic, so very, very persuasive. That was when it had all really started for her . . . that lovely day, those unforgettable first moments in the heady company of David Alexander Grainger.

And now, like history repeating itself, his son, a boy of twenty-one whose beauty of youth and vigour charmed everyone he met, a lad – oh, just a lad – who had so much to offer the world.

Her throat tightened, but she wouldn't cry. She wouldn't send him away to war with memories of all the women in his life crying their eyes out for him, but she couldn't help it, the tears spilled over.

'Mother,' he said huskily, taking her once more into his strong young arms and holding her close, 'don't cry for me, I'll be back before you know it, nobody's going to kill me – nobody.'

Her heart twisted. How many young men had uttered these self-same words – to mothers, wives, sweethearts?

'Of course you'll be back.' She made her voice strong. She mustn't let him see how much it was hurting, the memories of Davie intermingling with this poignant fare-well.

'Mother,' he moved back from her to look her squarely in the eye, 'when I was young I never felt close to you, I felt somehow that you never really wanted me.'

'In the beginning I didn't, Alex,' she said frankly. 'I was young and frightened. Your father was at war, I didn't know if he was alive or dead. Then he came back, only half the man he had been. It's a long, long story, some day I'll tell you about it. I only know I wasn't ready to have a baby and was only too glad to leave you with your Aunt Nellie. But then you turned the tables – you didn't want me. You were only an infant in a pram and you used to turn your little face away from me. In those days it was aye your father you wanted, never me.'

'But not anymore, Mother,' he said softly. 'You were the one who suffered for us all – women always have to bear the brunt o' it. I always admired you and then I loved you so much I wanted to keep you all to myself. It was as well Bessie came along or I might have killed John Simpson with my bare hands for making you suffer the way he did.'

'Wheesht, Alex, oh, wheesht, my darling son, that's all in the past. We've got to look forward – to the future – to the day you come back to us again.'

He stepped back from her; he smiled, he kissed Rachel and Meg and ruffled Grant's hair, he gave his grannie a bear of a hug and then he was off, striding into the lobby, opening the door . . .

On the landing he was apprehended by Mrs Conkey. 'Alex, I've been waiting.' She spoke with a slight touch of her old, hesitant manner, but it was only because she was upset at the idea of him going off to fight. She pressed something into his hand.

'Take this, laddie,' she said with tears in her eyes. 'Meg told me what you did for me the Christmas Albert died. I had some insurance money left over from his funeral and I went right down to the pawnshop and got the watch back. I've been keeping it for a time like this . . .' she gave a watery smile, 'I didn't want to run the risk o' you pawning it again.'

Alex was overwhelmed. He turned the heavy watch over in his hand, remembering how he had treasured it as a boy and how much it had cost him to part with it.

'Mrs Conkey, you're a gem. This will be my lucky charm, something I'll treasure all my days,' he told her, putting his strong arms around her thin little body to give her an almighty hug which lifted her off her feet and made her laugh.

Minutes later she was standing with Evelyn and her family at their window, watching him march away down the street, a fine young man with his kit on his shoulder, waving, waving till he could be seen no more.

'God be with you, son,' Mrs Conkey whispered.

Evelyn echoed the blessing, but silently, her heart too full to trust herself to speak.

Evelyn was very tired. At just forty-two years old she felt as if she had already lived too long. What was there to live for when only last week the news had come through that Alex had been killed in the British Army's withdrawal to Dunkirk?

The German's had invaded Belgium, Holland, France. They had left a bloody massacre in their wake.

Reported missing, believed to be dead . . . Bessie had shown her the telegram. The words would be imprinted in her mind forever, like brand burns. Poor Bessie, poor darling girl. The baby, Alex's daughter, was three months old. He would never see her, never watch her grow up . . .

The days had passed wearily since the terrible news. No one laughed anymore; it was as if all the life had gone out of the family — not that there were many of them left at home anyway. Rachel had joined the Red Cross; Meg had gone to live with Bessie at Puddock Hall to help with the horses. 'Just till Alex comes back,' she had said firmly, determined to boost Bessie with her optimism. But all the time her own heart was breaking for the brother she had once loathed but whose memory she now worshipped.

Only Maggie and Evelyn remained at home – and Gillan's son, her solace, her delight; just seven years old but already showing a maturity and understanding beyond his years. A happy little boy with a radiant smile and shining dark eyes.

But he was a determined little man. Like his father he could be dour and unyielding – but loving. A loving child whose warm young arms had always comforted her and never more than since he had heard the news about his big brother. 'He isn't dead,' he told his mother, 'he said he would come back and Alex always keeps his word so don't cry anymore, I'm here to look after you till he comes back.'

How she had blessed Gillan's son for his childish faith ... Gillie, oh, Gillie, if only he could see his son, how proud he would be ...

The opening of doors, revealing the past, the present, the future – letting her see what was behind her, what lay in front of her – images that were sometimes frightening, at other times uplifting ...

When the doorbell jangled in the silence of the kitchen that sunny day in April 1940 it was no phantom of the mind but very real, very persistent, demanding an answer, compelling her to go to the lobby to find out who could be ringing the bell with such impatience.

The door opened ... the man on the doorstep ... was it a dream? A being who belonged to the night and the dreamings for he could never come back into her life again ... it would be too good to be true ... too good.

'GILLIE!' The name was torn from her lips, disbelieving, her heart beating fast, her body trembling with every emotion she had kept bottled up for so long . . . And now Gillie came out of her dreams, out of her longings, into the present to gather her into his arms right there on the doorstep and hold her as if he would never let her go.

His mouth sought hers over and over, and she felt she was drowning in a sea of emotions – love, ecstasy, joy, all mingling together.

At last he let her go. With sparkling eyes he held aloft a necklace – the garnet necklace that John Simpson had pawned and which she had thought she would never see again.

'It led me to you,' Gillan told her with a laugh. 'I bought it in a pawnbroker's in Glasgow. The man seemed quite overwhelmed at the idea of anyone wanting to buy it as it had lain in his shop for years.'

Evelyn could hardly believe the twists of fate that had brought the necklace back to her. Originally it had been a present to Lady Marjorie from Lord Lindsay Ogilvie. She had never liked it, saying it was ugly, and had given it to Maggie who had sold it to help Jamie through a very difficult time. Lord Ogilvie had spotted the necklace in a shop in Aberdeen and had bought it back, this time as a gift for Evelyn. John Simpson had pawned it to get money for drink and Evelyn had thought she would never see it again. Now, here it was – as large as life and twice as ugly yet, to her in those moments, it was the most beautiful piece of jewellery in the world.

When Gillan was settled in the kitchen drinking tea he told Evelyn some of the things that had happened to him in the previous years. He and his wife were now divorced. They had never had children; darling old Oggie died after a fairly long illness; and Gillan himself had been ill with a lung infection and had been unable to carry out his duties as the executor of his great uncle's will.

Lord Lindsay Ogilvie had left Evelyn a fortune. He was her grandfather and he had never forgotten the fiery-haired lass who had so enchanted him with her beauty and her vivacity.

He had also left a large sum of money to Maggie, the daughter he had never known, much to his regret in the latter part of his life.

'I didn't have your address, Princess,' Gillan reached out and took Evelyn's hand. 'I searched and searched for you and then I saw the necklace. The man in the shop gave me this address — and you know the rest . . . '

A door closed, there were footsteps in the lobby, and Maggie entered the kitchen, holding young Grant by the hand. For a few seconds everyone looked at everyone else before Maggie rushed forward to pull Gillan into her arms.

She could hardly take in the fact that this was Gillie, warm, and real, and smiling. Oh, such a smile, radiant, happy, as if he had waited all his life for this moment of reunion with people he had loved and never forgotten.

He looked at the boy who was watching him with interest, a frown creased his brow. 'He can't be — Simpson's child — that — that hair — those eyes. He's a . . . '

'Forbes.' Evelyn spoke the name proudly. 'Your son, Gillie, born on Christmas day, the year you went away to Cape Town. Your son and heir, Grant Gillan Ogilvie.'

She held her breath, waiting for his reaction. Nothing happened for several timeless moments, then he gave a whoop of joy and lifted his son into his arms to dance with him round the room, round and round, carrying everyone along on a tide of infectious joy.

'Rothiedrum! Here we come!' he cried, lifting Grant up on his shoulder and holding out one hand to Maggie, the other to Evelyn.

'You're going home, Princess, at last home. You have your own personal fortune now so you can't go all proud and huffy the way you used to. We're going to be married, sweetheart, as we should have been from the beginning. We were meant for one another and we have years left to us yet, a lifetime to spend with one another.'

A few days later Bessie came steaming up the stairs of 198 Camloan Road, almost tripping up in her excitement, hardly able to contain herself as she waited for the door to be answered.

Evelyn stood there, staring, wondering what all the fuss was about. Bessie all but fell into her arms. 'He's alive,' she said in a muffled voice. 'Alex is alive . . . I can't believe it . . . it's too good to be true. Oh, God bless Mrs Conkey, she's an angel in disguise.' She was babbling, almost incoherent with happiness.

Evelyn took the letter from the girl's shaking hand. It was from Alex himself. He was alive and recovering from wounds he had received on the beach at Dunkirk. Mrs Conkey's good luck charm had saved his life. It had been in his breast pocket and had stopped a bullet entering his heart. It had been dented, that was all, but not as badly dented as himself – he wouldn't be fighting again. Soon he would be home for good and he was looking forward to seeing his baby daughter. One day he would tell his grandchildren about the watch. Meantime he asked that his love be passed on to Mrs Conkey and his thanks to her for saving his life.

Bessie and Evelyn cried in one another's arms, Maggie ran to get them tea, young Grant looked at all the weeping women and took a deep breath. He wouldn't cry, it was cissy, besides, he had a father now, he would have to start behaving like a man . . . Even so, it *was* good to know that Alex wasn't dead after all. Grant hoped he would come home soon, he was longing to see the watch. He wanted to run his fingers over the dent and imagine the whine the bullet made just before it thudded into the metal.

Chapter Twenty-three

Spring–Summer 1940

Back to Rothiedrum, back to the houghs and the parks, stretching, stretching into infinity. So many impressions, so much to wonder at and laugh about: Rothiedrum House, splendid and welcoming, the fire in the sitting room leaping up the chimney to make for a cosy atmosphere; Lady Marjorie and Maggie, meeting after all these years, cousins who had started off mistrusting one another but who now laughed and embraced and told one another that neither had 'changed a bit'; a fluffy feather bed, embracing Evelyn, enclosing her in a cloud of warmth and security.

She stretched and yawned. 'You're home, Evie,' she told herself and fell asleep like a contented child.

She wandered alone through the beloved lands of her childhood, savouring it all but keeping King's Croft to the end, like a child anticipating a long-awaited treat.

First she went to the tiny kirkyard at Loch Bree where Johnny and Florrie were buried. So long ago it seemed now, so young they had been when they had died too suddenly and too soon; one her childhood sweetheart, the other her best friend.

Their stones were mottled with yellow lichen and green moss, tendrils of ivy and the ravages of the weather had all but obliterated their names.

This peaceful spot, this lonely place . . . to her it would always be special. Her darling Johnny, so fair and tall, striding over the brae towards her, his face lighting, his blue eyes crinkling . . . She could see his hand, raised in greeting, his lips forming her name . . .

Florrie, as fair as a flower, as fragile as a cobweb. Sixteen . . . only sixteen . . . too soon for such life and beauty to die . . .

A sob escaped Evelyn. Sometimes she could barely remember the faces of those loved ones; at other times they were so real she felt that she could reach out and touch them. She knew that in some special corner of her heart the memories of them would remain evergreen.

On each grave she placed a bunch of dewy bluebells and then she walked away, her steps taking her to the well-known, well-loved places of her girlhood days . . .

At this gate her father had paused so that he could light his Stonehaven pipe before joining her for a companionable 'lean' as they gazed over the acres of land. *His* acres – the loamy furrows of newly ploughed earth; the bitter green of the young corn; the pale gold of the stubble fields . . .

Down in the hollow was King's Croft, nestling in its shelter of firs, the smoke blowing from the chimney drifting away over the parks.

It was as if nothing had changed. She felt that if she closed her eyes for a few minutes she would see her father coming out of the house; her mother standing at the door, her long white apron lifting in the breeze; Nellie hurrying to the milk-shed; Grace scattering grain for the hens; Murn setting off for school with her books tucked under her arm; Mary giggling with The Orra Loon . . . and herself, into everything that was going, playing with the animals, talking to the dogs, hurrying to the byre to see the new calf or maybe the newborn kittens, blind and helpless . . .

How near it all seemed, how much had happened since then . . .

'Father,' she whispered into the wind, 'you're here, I know you're here.'

From her pocket she took a tiny casket. Inside was a lock of Jamie's hair. It was as white, as soft as thistledown. She kissed it and held it in her palm, separating each hair before allowing the wind to snatch the precious strands away from her.

A breeze blew down from the faraway hills, bringing the scents of gorse and wild thyme with it and the perfume of the bluebells growing in the little woods above King's Croft.

'You're here, Father,' she repeated. 'I can feel your presence all around me, you've come back to Rothiedrum . . . you're home.'

The silence of empty places enfolded her. The power of the earth and the might of the hills supported her.

In the sigh of the wind she heard Jamie's voice; in the beat of the earth she heard Jamie's heart and she knew that they had both come home never to go away again . . .

Then came a sensing of other things, an awareness of a love that had always been hers – right from the start.

Turning she saw Gillie, her darling, handsome Gillie, quietly waiting for her to come to him as he had waited all through the years.

He held out his hand, she went to him. His warmth, his life, pulsed through her. This was what she had waited for – a love that never had and never would, let her go.

It was a good day for a wedding. A blackbird was singing in the rowan tree outside the little kirk on Loch Bree, the day that Gillan Forbes of Rothiedrum married Evelyn McKenzie Grant of King's Croft.

Many things had changed in the landscape of the north-east: no more did the Clydes grace the land; the scythe and the sickle lay rusting in crumbling sheds, forsaken, forgotten; the ring of horses' hooves and the rumble of cart wheels were no longer such familiar sounds on the turnpike; many of the fringe folk had faded away – the pedlars, the fishwives, the itinerant shepherds.

But some things would never change: like May sunshine; the peesies birling in the summer skies; lark song echoing sweetly above the earth; the purling of the burns flowing down from the hills to join the rivers meandering through green meadows into the sea.

Evelyn and Gillan had chosen a simple setting for their marriage, the little kirk by Loch Bree, the old stones mellow in the sunlight.

Familiar faces from Evelyn's girlhood were there to fill the pews: Betsy O'Neil, still as bold, still as brash, as full of life as ever, though she was now an old woman; The Loon, his white hair spiking over his collar; Jessie Blair, wobbling like a jelly; Charlie Lammas, bald as a coot underneath his ever-present bowler.

And the family: Lady Marjorie, a striking-looking woman in her finery; beside her Maggie, straight and proud; Nellie and Kenneth, a handsome pair, his red beard now streaked with grey but still flowing as ebulliently as ever over his sark. Grace and Gordon, so in love with one another; Mary and Greg, all their differences settled; Alex and Bessie, a glowing young couple; Meg, Rachel, James, Kenneth David; Grant Gillan Ogilvie, so proud to be wearing his kilt . . .

All the other members of the family, swelling the ranks. If only Wee Col could have been here . . . and Jamie . . . but he *was* here, his presence was everywhere.

'Do you, Evelyn, take this man . . . '

She came out of her reverie. The blackbird was still singing fit to bust in the rowan tree, the glad sound of it echoing in the old kirk.

Gillan was looking at her, admiring the fiery gleam of her hair, the flash of fire in her green eyes. His hand came

Christine Marion Fraser

NOBLE BEGINNINGS

**From the bestselling author of the *Rhanna* and
King's novels comes an enchanting new saga
full of warmth and drama, in the atmospheric
setting of an Argyllshire powdermill town.**

Young Anna McIntyre's vivacity and beauty have won her
many friends in the Argyllshire community where she lives,
especially young Peter Noble, nephew of Lord and Lady
Noble of the Big House, who falls deeply in love with
Anna. She is adored by all – except by her father,
Roderick. Under-manager of the Powdermill, Roderick is a
God-fearing Christian to his neighbours, but, in reality, he
is a pompous, brutal man, with an insatiable thirst for
women – determined to crush Anna's spirit . . .

Anna longs to escape this oppressive life and, when Lady
Pandora Noble asks Anna to be her companion, she sees
her chance . . . but so does her scheming father. Roderick
has long nurtured a passion for Lady Pandora and is prepared to do anything to ensure this passion is returned,
even to shatter Anna's dreams forever . . .

**The following pages contain
the first chapter of *Noble Beginnings*,
available in hardback in April 1994
from HarperCollins*Publishers*.**

PART ONE
1889

Chapter One

ANNA

Anna lay in bed, listening to the wind sighing and whining through the corries of the hills, before it came gusting down to moan amongst the trees on the banks of the River Cree, stripping the crackling leaves from the branches, tossing them helter-skelter against the rooftops of the mill buildings.

It was like the lamenting wail of a human voice, sad, lonely, lost, a tormented soul of the night, strong and forceful in its persistence. Eerie too, out there in the darkness . . . as if it was a flesh and blood creature who stalked the sleeping countryside . . . hiding in the trees, creeping round the house, waiting, just waiting – to pounce!

Anna's heart missed a beat, in a burst of terror she pulled the sheet over her head and lay as still as her shivering limbs would allow. Half suffocating, she strained her ears – listening – listening – for what? The wind sucked in its breath, in the stillness the mournful hoot of an owl echoed amongst the trees, far in the wooded glen another owl answered the call, then there was silence.

But still she listened – for other things that were far more frightening than anything made by nature and the elements – house sounds, creaking timbers, groaning walls, mice scampering behind the skirting, bits of plaster falling down . . . the sound of feet that went creeping and shuffling through the rooms — ghostly feet – or something else . . ?

Gasping for air she threw the sheet back from her face. An oblong of light had lanced the darkness of the room. The pale face of the September moon was shining through a cloak of purple-grey clouds. The misty shreds clung on to it for quite some time then suddenly it was riding the heavens, high and clear, a huge silvery sphere that shone like a brilliant lantern above the hills.

Seen from the girl's cold little room it was like a picture, framed by the window, and she stared and stared at it, praying for the clouds to disperse so that the shaft of light lying across her bed would remain there till she fell asleep.

A smattering of dry leaves rasped against the window pane, like the fingers of someone scrabbling to get in, and Anna snuggled deeper into her sparse blankets as the wind rushed through the sash which, summer and winter alike, lay open to the elements.

'You must learn to be tough! Bairns are pampered nowdays! When I was a lad I often had to break the ice in the tub before bathing in the cold water.' She shuddered as her father's voice broke into her thoughts like a stinging whiplash. He had preached such things so often they were imprinted into her brain, just like the cruel brand burns on the beasts who grazed the slopes of the Corran Estates.

The boom of the river rose above the sound of the rain now lashing down outside. It had been a wet September, and the frothing burns on the hills had swollen the River Cree into a spate that roared into the deep bowl of The Cauldron, a peaty brown pool that swirled restlessly twenty feet below the overhanging rocks of the riverbank.

Anna loved the river. When it was calm it brought her a sense of peace, when it was a raging torrent she made herself stand on the Overhanging Rocks so that she could look directly into the gaping black mouth of The Cauldron.

With the rocks trembling and beating beneath her feet she would feel terror and heart-sinking apprehension, but above all, the knowledge that here was power, timeless, indestructible, awe-inspiring.

And Anna liked things that had their own order in the world – her small world – so often insecure – so powerless and helpless . . .

The rain stopped, the wind abated, the even breathing of

her brothers sounded very peaceful in the sudden hush of the night.

They were huddled together in the double iron bedstead in the corner, close in the harmony of their dream-world as they never were in their waking hours.

It was a sleepy sound. Anna listened and felt her eyes closing. Her limbs were heavy with fatigue yet she knew she wouldn't rest till she heard her father come home.

He never bothered to quieten his movements for the benefit of the sleeping household. Every night it was the same. She would hear him going through his nightly preamble of roughly stirring the fire with the heavy brass poker before settling down to smoke his pipe.

Back and forth, back and forth, creak, creak, creak the rocking chair would go before there was a pause in which he would tap his pipe against the bars of the grate. It was a very fancy pipe with a hinged silver hood and a transferable mouthpiece, but nothing was too good for Roderick McIntyre, under-manager of the gunpowder mill.

Creak! Creak! Creak! Tap! Tap! Tap! The sounds would go on for perhaps half an hour before he would get up to blunder along to his room which was situated at the front of the house through connecting doors from kitchen and parlour.

If the mood took him, he never hesitated to call Anna from her bed to make him a hot supper of brose and thick tea. If he came home with Nellie Jean, supper was the last thing on his mind. Anna knew she could rest easier – except for the hoarse giggles and moans that filtered through the dividing wall of his room.

But Anna had learned to accept such things as part of the night, they had been a regular feature of her life at The Gatehouse ever since her mother had 'gone away to the asylum' when Anna was just six years old.

Anna couldn't remember things before that too clearly, she only knew that her mother had been a gentle person who had loved her dearly.

'She was a quiet woman, your mother,' people told Anna. 'She always kept herself to herself and none of us knew her very well. After your brother Adam was born, it seems she withdrew into herself even more. Some say it was a difficult birth and she was never right afterwards. At times she seemed fine, then she would start shaking and crying and no one could get her to stop. She was never violent though, and never harmed anyone, but she couldn't take care of herself, never mind look after her family. In the end the doctor decided she would be better locked away for her own and her family's good.'

That had been almost seven years ago now, though sometimes it seemed only yesterday that her gentle, bewildered mother had stood trembling at the door of the cottage, tears in her eyes while she waited for the waggon to 'take her away.'

The cruel chants of the village children echoed in Anna's mind, words that she would never forget. 'Set a trap to catch a moose! Your mammy's in the loony hoose!'

'No, no,' Anna whispered, 'please don't say these things about *her*.'

The calm, hazel eyes of her mother smiled into her thoughts and the warm, firm hands of the past seemed to reach into the present to reassure her.

'You're not mad, Mother, I know you're not!'

Over the years she had longed to see her mother again but Roderick wouldn't hear of it. 'She isn't fit to see anyone, she's become violent and would tear you to pieces as soon as look at you,' he had said firmly. 'She's got worse as the years have gone by and thinks everyone's against her. Demented, the doctor called it. A deterioration of the brain. I asked if I could bring you all to visit but he advised me against it, they don't encourage children to go to these places and that's an end to the matter.'

Anna licked the salty tears from her cheeks and buried her face into her pillow. She turned her head again, straining her ears as she listened.

Because her bedroom lay at the back of the house it was difficult to make out the comings and goings on the quiet country road at the front.

It was easy enough to hear the clatterings of horses' hooves and the rumbling of cart wheels on the stony ground but footsteps of people weren't so easy to distinguish, especially the stealthy paddings of anyone not wishing to be heard.

But all was quiet, except for the wind keening round corners and moaning down the chimneys.

The clouds were scudding along and now the sky was clear, with the stars winking in the dark reaches outwith the bright halo of the moon. A ray of brilliant light lay over the rough, woollen coverlet on Anna's bed. Extricating a hand from the blankets she touched the moonbeam with a sense of wonder. So transient a thing, so cold a light, yet so welcome in the darkness.

Objects in the room stood out from the shadows. Adam and Magnus, humped shapes under a jumble of patchworks; the sturdy outline of the mahogany tallboy; the dull glint of pewter on the scratched surface of the dresser; the bulky oblong of the crofter's kist over by the window.

Everything that the room contained was purely functional. Roderick McIntyre maintained that there was neither need nor space for anything that induced 'vulgar primping'.

His one concession to anything that could be called embellishment took the form of drab samplers that hung on the walls throughout the house. Enclosed behind oblong pieces of glass each one bore a motto of a religious nature. The one above Anna's bed spelled out a gloomy message. 'A flighty spirit may soar high but never reach heaven.' Above the boys' bed, male superiority was conveyed with the words, 'Man is all things to all people; humbler creatures be glad to serve him and allow him to further his purpose.'

From experience Anna knew only too well what the samplers meant. Women were the humble creatures, put on the earth for man's use. It was wrong for females in her position to seek life's pleasures and if she allowed herself to laugh or sing too exuberantly she would pay for it later on because her spirit would somehow miss the path to heaven.

The thought worried her a good deal. Despite the restrictions imposed on her she was prone to light-heartedness and out in the open fields she often sang aloud with the sheer joy of living. Then there were those other times, when euphoria bubbled inside of her, and there was simply no way she could stop that happening. Times like now, when the Highland moon lit the dark night with silvery beams and the wind played with the rustling autumn leaves.

As the moments passed her spirit was soaring higher. No matter how much she tried to push it down, it kept on rising till her heart bumped in her throat.

'Please, God, I'm sorry about this but I can't help it,' she whispered before reaching for her shawl at the foot of her bed. It was a beautiful garment, crocheted for her by old Grace, a widow woman who lived in tiny Moss Cottage in the Clachan of Corran.

The moonlight sparkled on the shawl's rainbow colours and lovingly Anna wrapped herself into the soft folds. Gingerly she put her feet on the cold floorboards. Despite the warmth of the shawl she shivered as the keen night air swept over her.

But the moon was beckoning, and resolutely she skipped to the window to stare with delight at the black mass of Coir an Ban etched against the sky. Coir an Ban, the fair mountain, misty green in springtime, golden in summer sunlight, tawny in fiery autumn, cold and forbidding in November when the sun disappeared behind its craggy shoulder. In winter Coir an Ban was dark and bare with mist skulking in the corries and great gleaming icicles hanging from the rocks like gigantic teeth. But winter and summer alike Anna loved it and always found solace whenever she gazed up at its glowering bulk.

Tonight she could see everything quite plainly: the sparkling gleam of a burn; the glint of the rushing river; the sturdy outlines of the stone sheds; the winding water courses, black and snakelike in the shadows; the waggon rails twisting through the mill workings; the wooden bridge leading over the river to the store buildings with their thick protective baffle walls.

Huddling into her shawl, Anna murmured softly, 'River Cree, speak to me, speak before you reach the sea.'

The river swished angrily into The Cauldron and a chuckle escaped the girl's lips. She was a thin little sprite with an oval face and deep set blue-grey eyes fringed by abundant dark lashes. Her skin was fair, with a pure milk and honey complexion of an alabastrine quality. The fairness of her was doubly enhanced by eyebrows that were almost white and a long mane of flaxen hair that hung round her shoulders like a silken mantle.

She was known to everyone as Anna Ban, the fair one, the child who had been obliged from an early age to take a woman's place in the home.

When it had become apparent that Lillian McIntyre's stay in the mental asylum was to be more than a temporary one, the villagers had waxed eloquent on the subject.

Moira O'Brady, who ran the post office, had not minced words in her opinion. 'A disgrace! A child of that age cooking and cleaning for the likes o' Roderick McIntyre! Poor, poor, Lily, no wonder she went off her head wi' a man like that to contend with!'

Janet McCrae, proprietress of the local general store, had nodded in agreement, even though she knew that Moira didn't give a hoot about Anna or her welfare. Moira O'Brady didn't like children and took no pains to hide the fact. Her attitude brought out the worst in the village youngsters who simply delighted in dreaming up deeds of mischief that never failed to incite her to fury. It was quite a common sight to see a red-faced boy or girl being decanted from her premises, helped on their way by a wildly thrashing broom or anything else that came to hand.

But more than anything, Moira hated Roderick McIntyre. Very few people liked him, but Moira's aversion to him was extreme and no one, not even the most inquisitive in the community, had managed to find out why this was the case, though it certainly wasn't for the want of trying.

Moira's solicitous words about Anna didn't fool the kindly Janet but since the postmistress had very neatly voiced her own sentiments on the subject she couldn't help but say, 'Ay, you're right there, Moira, I know fine he could well afford to get someone in to see to the house but no! He has Anna! A poor mite who looks as though a puff o' wind might blow her away at any minute.'

Anna hadn't blown away. Over the years she had developed a strength of character that more than made up for any physical frailties. She had found her own ways of escaping the harsh realities of her home environment.

'A dreamer!' her father was always saying that, making it sound like an accusation. 'One o' these fine days you'll find out there's more to life than roses and rainbows!'

Sitting at the window, bathed in the white rays of the moon, Anna was certainly not dreaming of roses and rainbows. She was preoccupied with much more immediate things, matters that were of great importance to her, though they might not mean much to anyone else.

She wasn't aware of the cold seeping through her threadbare cotton nightdress. Old Grace had offered to make her one of cosy flannelette but Roderick had sneered when Anna had mentioned it to him.

'Flannelette! Whatever next will you think of? Look to

yourself smartly, madam, or you'll go naked to bed, and that's a promise.'

Anna shivered, her breath came out in frosty puffs. Next month was her birthday and, after that, she would never be twelve again as long as she lived. The realization made her clasp her hands to her lips. The enormity of the coming occasion had the effect of making her feel still and silent inside of herself.

Being thirteen meant being grown up. It also meant she was on the brink of becoming a witch! All through her childhood her father had told her she had all the makings of a witch because she liked to braid flowers in her hair and brighten her drab clothing with little pieces of lace and simple ornaments.

But to be a real witch you had to stop being a child and become grown up. Next month, on the ancient festival of Samain, the festival of Hallowe'en, she would be thirteen and, according to her father's prophesies, she would turn into a creature that nobody liked and everybody feared.

The thought was very sobering. Time was galloping away, she had only a few weeks left to hold onto her childhood.

A muffled sob broke from her lips and her eyes filled up. The moon blobbed and wavered above the crags of Coir an Ban, the stars swam together till the whole sky looked like the glistening waters of Loch Longart on a sun-bright day.